Chinatown Days

Rita Chowdhury is an award-winning Assamese poet and writer. A former associate professor of Political Science at Cotton University, Guwahati, Rita is currently the director of National Book Trust, India. An important voice in contemporary Assamese literature, Rita has written fifteen novels that portray a vivid picture of her strife-torn state. The critically acclaimed *Chinatown Days* (*Makam*) is one of her best-known works.

'A moving saga about a terrible injustice wrought upon a group of blameless people . . . Rita Chowdhury is an energetic and empathetic storyteller'

Amitav Ghosh

'This masterful saga recounts the tragic history of the Chinese community in Assam and Bengal . . . an intense and compelling narrative that explores migration, identity, and the cruel boundaries of narrow chauvinism'

Namita Gokhale

'A fascinating portrait of migration, memory and mixed antecedents . . . wide-ranging and historically valuable'

Anjum Hasan

'Rita Chowdhury's gripping story of the Chinese community in Upper Assam gives the insider version of the events of 1962. It is a history that has rarely been told before . . . and how beautifully Rita tells it'

Easterine Kire

'An important book . . . *Chinatown Days* weaves its careful magic across borders and communities, relocating within history our humanity'

Janice Pariat

'Rita Chowdhury's *Chinatown Days* is an engaging, monumental work'

Hansda Sowendra Shekhar

'[This] epic saga does not pretend to be as soothing as those first sips of life in a tea garden. It's a tale filled with the distant sounds of a war that ended in a rout ... Rita Chowdhury reminds us that those who populate her novel are our people too. It's a powerful suggestion'

Hindu

'Tracing the history of Chinese labour in the tea gardens of Upper Assam, in *Chinatown Days*, Sahitya Akademi award winner Rita Chowdhury narrates an epic saga of almost unrelieved pain and anguish, spanning more than a century and several continents'

India Today

'Chowdhury describes the customs and traditions of the Assamese Chinese, and the lives of the so-called 'tea tribes' minutely ... This could well have been non-fiction, but Chowdhury chose to turn her research into a harrowing novel. In it, she exposes the confusion, betrayal and aggression against India that still haunt the Chinese with Assamese roots, regardless of where'

Outlook Traveller

'A story of human beings pulled apart by history, racial hatred and politics – a sad tale but one that offers deep human lessons for another generation to heed . . . The history of the mixed population of Makum and the history of tea in Assam and its Chinese origins are parallel stories that Chowdhury narrates with great sensitivity and scholarship'

Scroll.in

'A moving tale of humans torn apart from their land by hatred and selfish motives, *Chinatown Days* reflects on a horrific life that was forced on a community. Rita Chowdhury's empathetic prose, full of energy and vigour delineates the author's urge to let the story be heard. She perfectly captures the plight of a group of blameless people and paints a vivid picture of their sojourn into misfortune'

Times of India

'Racy, readable and full of little human actions, thoughts and feelings, the Chinese, explored from 360 degrees, make for a moving drama that could change our beliefs about a culture'

Week

Chinatown Days

RITA

CHOWDHURY

MACMILLAN

First published in English 2018 by Macmillan
First published in paperback 2018 by Macmillan
an imprint of Pan Macmillan Publishing India Private Limited
707, Kailash Building
26 K. G. Marg, New Delhi - 110001
www.panmacmillan.co.in

Pan Macmillan, The Smithson, 6 Briset Street, London EC1M 5NR, United Kingdom
Basingstoke and Oxford
Associated companies throughout the world
www.panmacmillan.com

ISBN 978-93-86215-51-2

First published in Assamese as *Makam* by Jyoti Prakashan, 2010

3 5 7 9 8 6 4 2

Typeset by SÜRYA and Manmohan Kumar
Printed and bound in India by
Thomson Press India Ltd.

Prologue

I am not the architect of this narrative.

I am but an inept artist, the narrator of this epic saga of a people caught in the maelstrom of history.

My name is Arunabh Bora. I am a writer.

I live in Guwahati, the capital of Assam, one of the states of India. My ancestral home is near the Dafalagarh tea estate, on the northern side of the river Brahmaputra, where my eldest maternal uncle used to work as the head clerk. I was quite young when my father passed away. My mother and I then moved to my uncle's house. Growing up there, I never faced any sort of difficulty.

Even now, in Guwahati, I lead a comfortable life with my wife and two children.

It's been a while since my uncle died, but my mother still lives with his family. My aunt does not wish to part with her and my mother does not wish to live with anyone else either. She has spent most of her life within the confines of my uncle's house. As far as I can remember, she has always been quiet and withdrawn. Even though she actively took part in all the activities of the family, her mind always seemed to be absorbed in some distant world.

This is, perhaps, the only thing about my life that makes me sad. Apart from that, there is nothing much to complain about. I have gone through half my life without any crisis, hardship or trouble. After years of living in comfort and contentment, I could hardly imagine the strange future awaiting me.

It was a fateful day when Lailin arrived on the scene; Lailin Tham, a well-known Chinese writer.

Sometimes a door will open unexpectedly. A door through which we enter an unimaginable past – a past that is enmeshed with our present.

It was Lailin who opened that door for me. Before she did it, she gestured to me, looked straight into my eyes, and asked, 'Will you dare to speak up? Will you dare to speak about us who are standing on Indian soil? Do you have the guts?'

Her tone was filled with rage, sharpened by a tinge of bitterness. It was like an arrow directed at me, a challenge thrown in my face. Lailin stood in front of me like an unwavering flame in a room devoid of air. It has been almost two years since Lailin unleashed the storm. It has left my beautifully organized life in a state of utter chaos. My home, my identity and my foundation have been shaken, perhaps irretrievably.

Part One

One

It was noon in Hong Kong. Lailin was reading. For a minute she took her eyes off the pages of a book by Assamese writer Arunabh Bora, and looked out vaguely through the window.

On the twelfth floor of an apartment in one of many skyscrapers standing close together sat middle-aged Lailin. Her straight, shiny, shoulder-length hair was tied into a ponytail. She was wearing a cotton top and pants. This was her mother's apartment. It consisted of a drawing-cum-dining room with a sofa-bed, a bedroom, a tiny kitchen and a bathroom.

A few years ago, Lailin's mother had got this flat by way of a government scheme for people with low income. A few months after her mother's relocation to the flat, Lailin had moved to Canada. Since then, her mother had been living here alone. Lailin often came to visit and every time her mother would return with her to Canada for a few months.

This time, after a long gap, Lailin had come with her entire family. While she stayed back at her mother's place, the kids had gone with their father to their grandparents' house in Kowloon. They would return tomorrow. A community festival for the Chinese Indians was going to be held, and this was where the Chinese translation of Arunabh Bora's novel was to be released. This book was about the Chinese Indian community itself. Lailin and her family had come to take part in the festival and attend the book release as well. Arunabh would arrive the next day. As soon as the book had been published, Arunabh had sent a copy to Lailin's mother. Even though her mother hadn't said a word about it, Lailin knew she had already read the book. She could clearly see the emotions playing on her mother's face.

Lailin, too, began to feel overwhelmed as she turned the pages. As if the pain and anguish that had lain heavy as a stone on their hearts all these years had converged to take the form of a book. A past lay scattered across its pages, a past that not many knew about. Amidst its ruins pulsated a present that too had gone unnoticed.

Lailin returned to the page she had been reading.

I was in Toronto to participate in a writers' meet, organized by an international forum of writers. Lailin, too, was present. She had not travelled from China; she had come from a town not far from Toronto.

On the very first day of the meet, she was shockingly discourteous. Someone – I can't recall who – introduced me to Lailin at teatime. She openly ignored my extended hand and quietly passed me by. The writers around me were surprised, as was I.

After a polite pause, some people in the group commented:

'That was really rude.'

'Why did Lailin Tham behave like that? She is normally very polite.'

'Have you two met before? Has there been any misunderstanding?' I was surrounded by a group of people and almost everyone was either irritated or baffled. Unable to explain such behaviour, I felt both humiliated and angry. It made me curious as well. There had to be some reason; why would a writer of her reputation behave in that manner? I remained distraught throughout the tea break. I should have been able to move on from a matter so petty. But I couldn't. Perhaps it was because of what I had glimpsed so fleetingly in her eyes: not only hatred and anger, but something more, something I could not understand. I was drawn to Lailin. But she remained extremely composed andimpenetrable whenever I tried to approach her.

Eventually, one afternoon, I confronted her. She was sitting alone under a red maple tree.

When I greeted her, she looked as though she had woken up from a deep slumber. For a moment she appeared calm, but soon enough her eyes once again sparked with hate.

'I want to talk to you, Lailin,' I said.

'What do you want to talk about?' she retorted.

'Have we ever met before?'

'What are you trying to say?'

'I just wanted to know if I have ever hurt you unwittingly. If not, I can't see why you wouldn't want to talk to me.'

Lailin picked up her bag and got ready to leave. Then she said, 'I don't want to talk to you and I am not obliged to give you my reasons.'

'Please don't leave,' I said. 'I don't quite understand what has happened. At least tell me what I have done to you. Since we belong to the same fraternity, I presume there exists some geniality and friendship between us.'

She smiled at me with disdain. 'Do you understand what friendship means? Do you even know what it means to be genial? You! An Indian!'

So nationality was somehow related to her hatred towards me!

'What do you mean by that?' I asked, completely at a loss now. Lailin left without responding. I grew even more determined to find out.

Two days after that, on the second floor of the Rogers Communication Centre, I met Lailin again. To my surprise, she spoke to me on her own. 'Do you want to know why I dislike you? It is because you are an Indian. I hate all Indians. Don't try to talk to me again. You will get nothing from me but insults.'

I was stupefied. Before I could respond, she turned away from me and walked off, leaving little scope for me to reach out to her ever again.

The matter should have ended there, but it didn't. Lailin's words, harsh as they were, made me even more curious. She did not hate me alone, but all Indians. How could I, an Indian, leave it at that? Determined to know the reason, I chose to confront Lailin again.

It was the final night of the conference. After the valedictory session, everyone left for their respective destinations. Adequately prepared for humiliation, I went over to Pitman Hall and knocked on Lailin's door. She was surprised to see me. And there it was again, that sudden flare of anger. But the next moment she composed herself and looked at me for a while before sighing deeply. 'Come in,' she said.

'How long will I fight with you?'

Her resistance seemed to be slowly giving way. After a long silence, she began to talk.

'I stayed away from you. That was the best thing to do. I have told you that I dislike all of you. I don't want to talk to you. And yet you are so persistent. Don't you see how I'm suffering?'

'Yes, I do. That is why I'm persistent. I can see that you are extremely hurt. Tell me what happened to you. What have us Indians ever done to you?'

She looked at me, her eyes sad and tired. 'What will you do if I tell you? Can you erase the feelings that I have been carrying in my heart?'

She flared up again. But pulling herself together, she said, 'I don't want to be rude to you anymore. Please go. Leave me alone.'

We sat in silence for a while. Then I said slowly, 'I'll go back. I have no right to disturb you. But I have a question. Can one leave without knowing why his country is hated so much by someone else? Will you please tell me?'

Tears brimmed in Lailin's eyes. She looked at me for a while and answered, 'I don't know. Because, even today, I don't know which country I actually belong to.'

'What do you mean?'

'I am sorry, I won't be able to speak about this anymore today. Give me some time. Come back tomorrow. Please.'

I could sense the surge of emotions and the degree of discomfort she was struggling with. Without saying another word, and reining in my curiosity, I left.

The next morning when I went to meet Lailin, she was waiting for me, her bags beside her. Her eyes were red; she might have cried before my arrival. We sat facing each other, silently drinking coffee. I didn't want to rush her today.

After some time, she asked, 'What comes to your mind when you look at me?'

'I'm sorry, I don't understand.'

'Where do you think I come from? Look at me, tell me my nationality.'

I was at sea. With her slanted eyes, straight jet-black hair, fair complexion, slender build, what could this woman's nationality be?

'You could be Canadian-Chinese for all I know. But you don't really look typically Chinese. But you are Chinese, though you are a Canadian citizen. You are Chinese, aren't you?' I was speaking rapidly.

After a few minutes of silence, she said, 'In places like Hong Kong, China, Canada, Australia and many other countries, there are many people who are Chinese but don't look typically Chinese. Because they –' She paused halfway and then continued, 'I don't know why I chose to speak to you. I never thought I would speak to an Indian. It is your persistence that has forced me to speak. Perhaps your love for your own country has compelled me. But I have been thinking since last night: is it really necessary to talk about these things? It has been so long. So many years!'

I looked at her face; I just could not fathom what she meant.

'I don't understand, Lailin. What will you gain by not sharing? Who knows, if you share, you might find a way out. If you can think of me as your friend and not as an Indian, it might be easier for you to talk to me.'

Lailin looked down as she sat there, twirling the coffee mug in her hands.

That day at Pitman Hall, Lailin opened the doors to a forgotten land, placing before me the first page of a lost history. Standing on the threshold of this unknown land, she uttered the name 'Makum'.

'Have you ever been to Makum?' she asked.

'Makum? Which Makum are you talking about? The one in Upper Assam?'

'Yes.'

'How do you know about Makum?'

'I'll tell you. Have you been there?'

'I can't say that I have been to Makum. While going to Doom Dooma and Margherita, I have only passed through the town a couple of times.'

'Do you know that there used to be a Chinatown in Makum?'

'Was there? I only know about Tangra, the one in Calcutta. I have never heard about the one in Makum.'

'It was not only in Assam – many cities in India had a Chinatown. They might not have been as big as the one in Calcutta but there were quite a few. Have you heard about the Chinese in Assam?'

'I do know about a few Chinese families in Assam. I have also seen a few Chinese people in Tezpur. I know about the Chinese dentists. But that's all,' I said.

'It's obvious that you don't really know. Not only you, but even for most people in Assam, the past does not exist. For me, though, that past is the sordid truth from which I can never dissociate myself. When I think about it, I feel furious and totally helpless.'

'Why did you never write about all this?'

'I thought about it many times. I wanted to write and bring everything to light. I wanted to tell the whole world, "Look at the real face of India, which speaks about democracy and Panchsheel. Look at Jawaharlal Nehru's India, which vents its frustration and anger on the innocent." But, whenever I think of writing, something stops me. What will I write? What's the use of writing? Is it really worth creating something purely out of hatred? Even if there is any meaning in it, would it make any difference? I hate India. I hate Indians. My mother always says, "Don't hate anyone. A nation and its entire people can never be bad. What happened was our misfortune." But I still hate them. I just can't help it.'

Lailin's voice choked. Her eyes were filled with tears.

'Please Lailin, tell me everything,' I said softly.

'Will you come to our house?' she asked. 'My mother is here to spend some time with me. If you meet her, she can tell you more.'

It didn't take me long to decide. Everything dissolves before the curiosity of a writer. I could never imagine, however, the surprise that was waiting for me at Lailin's house.

When we reached, it was evening. The softly lit residential area was quiet. So was Lailin's house. The aroma of incense filled the air. It was my first visit to a Chinese house.

In a corner of the sitting room was a red three-layer altar. I could see incense burning. An offering of tea and fruits had been placed there as well. On a wall alongside the altar was a picture of the Hindu god Ganesha.

Lailin's mother was sitting in another corner of the room. The moment we entered the house, she woke up as if from deep contemplation.

'This is Arunabh, Maa.'

An avalanche of surprise hit me. Numb and stupefied, I stared at Lailin.

She spoke Assamese! Perfect, fluent Assamese!

Without a glance at me, she took my bag and went inside.

'She did not talk to you in Assamese, did she?' asked Lailin's mother.

'No. She didn't.'

'She doesn't talk in Assamese with anyone except me. It's been years now. She has a lot of anger inside her. Please, don't feel bad,' she said, looking calmly at me.

'You speak such fluent Assamese, and Lailin, too. Are you from Assam? Are you Assamese?' I asked, bewildered.

There was a sad smile on her face.

'I can't tell you anymore where I belong. Though I did once belong to Assam. It was many years ago, as if in my previous birth.'

It took me some time to regain my composure. Looking at her, I tried to figure out whether she was Chinese or Assamese. She looked Chinese in her black trousers and floral top; her shining almond eyes seemed to hold so much pain. But then there are many Assamese who, people say, look Chinese.

'After forty-five long years, I have met an Assamese who lives in Assam. I wish I could tell you how happy I am. I feel as if I have met someone who belongs to my family, someone who is my very own. In the last forty-five years, no one has come looking for us. Everyone has forgotten us.'

I was looking at her face.

What is hidden in the memory of this ancient lady? What is the saga of pain which Lailin has brought me here to listen to?

That night in Lailin's house the present slowly dissolved away. Lailin's mother narrated an unthinkable story, a tragedy that had been lying hidden for ages in the hearts of so many. I was there; so was Lailin and a group of bewildered-looking people. I saw them. I experienced their reality, which no history could record. I stepped into those dark corners where humanity and civilization had lost their footing, from where even history returned, shrouded in sheer indifference.

Two

1823

A fleet of boats moved steadily up the Burhi Dihing, a tributary of the mighty Brahmaputra that flows through Assam down its eastern contour. The boats were sailing towards the Singpho kingdom, situated between Assam and Burma.

The first two boats carried the navigator, the interpreters and an army of gunners or 'barkandaz'. The third boat, somewhat more elaborately decorated, carried the leader of the group and his slave. The fourth and fifth carried articles of trade, and the last one had additional numbers of the barkandaz. Dense forests stretched along either side of the river. The cries of the wild fowl mixed with those of the woodpeckers, the chirping of birds joined the chorus of the Hoolock gibbons and the eerie whines of a million crickets, filling the air with a rich orchestra of sounds piercing through the wilderness.

In the deep waters of the Burhi Dihing, the splash of oars, punctuated by the boatmen's songs, announced the presence of human beings. The boatmen, from Mymensingh and Arakan, rowed upstream against the wind. With their sweat-soaked bodies, strong and sturdy, glistening under the sun, they looked like a fearless team of adventurers, unmindful of any danger. The person at the helm of the flotilla was Robert Bruce, erstwhile major in the Bengal Artillery of the East India Company.

His vivid face and gleaming eyes revealed the cleverness of a successful businessman and the alertness of a soldier. His attire was immaculate. His spotless white high-collared shirt was adorned by a black silk cravat. Over this he wore a long coat, caught at the waist and widening out below, with a broad collar and balloon sleeves. His black-and-white striped trousers were tucked into black shoes with square heels. Here was a man who had spent his youth in the reckless pursuit of glory. Robert Bruce carried with him a spirit of daring and adventure, without which he would not have come to do business in an unknown territory, leaving behind his kith and kin in far-flung Scotland. Despite the weekly ballroom dances, theatre, and other amusements in Calcutta's European quarters, it was this region that held a special attraction for Robert.

Europeans had come here even earlier, but they had confined their activities mainly to Lower Assam. Only a few – Robert Bruce being one of them – dared to visit Upper Assam and other regions that were infested with deadly diseases. The dense forests of the region were home to wild animals, poisonous snakes and unknown insects with venomous stings. Everything about the region suggested that the natives of the land were an unconquerable lot.

At this precise moment, Robert was reading a letter from his brother, Charles Alexander Bruce, a senior army officer with the East India Company. Although they rarely met, they stayed in close contact through letters. As Robert read, his slave Deodhan stood behind, fanning him in order to ward off the incessant mosquitoes and gadflies. It had been some time now since he had retired from the Bengal Artillery, but he was still an army man with a team of paid barkandaz under him. He carried on his military activities alongside his other businesses, which earned him a sizeable fortune over the years. In the meantime, he had also become a freewheeling arms dealer without any loyalties.

Robert Bruce came to Assam at a time when the state was still reeling in the aftermath of a mutiny by a small religious section known as the Moamorias. They rose in revolt against the Ahom rulers, who had ruled much of Assam since the thirteenth century. After defeating the Ahom king, the Moamorias occupied the throne for a short period, till the Ahoms regained the kingdom from them. By that time the population of Assam had substantially dwindled. Taking advantage of these troubled times, Robert began to slowly involve himself in the internal affairs of the countries to consolidate his business interests. Given his military acumen, financial resources and enterprise, not to mention his cordial relations with the East India Company, Robert was already a force to be reckoned with inside and beyond the boundaries of Assam.

By now, the East India Company had become a power that could no longer be ignored. It had not only staked its claim as a powerful trading company, but had become a centre of power, politically, financially, as well as militarily. Until now, the Company had not evinced much interest in the internal politics of the smaller kingdoms of this region. Though the Company followed a policy of non-interference as the ruler of Bengal, there were times when it had to meddle in the internal affairs of neighbouring Assam and Cooch Behar, even though it never considered either country as a potential political threat. Its main concern was Burma – there had been rumours that the Burmese were planning to attack India. As a keen businessman, Robert was privy to every development. He knew well enough which prince or senior officer of which country was hatching plots against whom. He professionally supported the party that wanted to invade with his team of barkandaz, considering the benefits he would get if they became rulers.

'Master.'

Robert, his mind preoccupied with strategies, looked at Deodhan.

'Master, tea?' Deodhan repeated.

Sipping hot tea from his mug, Robert looked at the captivating beauty of the forest on both banks of the river. Until now Robert had not known much about this area. His business had been confined to Assam. But now he was planning to expand to neighbouring Singpho, and onwards to Burma. Before setting out on this adventure he had collected a mass of information related to the region. It was an exciting territory with lofty mountains and dense forests, inhabited by independent tribes.

The boatmen rowing upstream were cautious. Each of the gunners held a long-barrelled musket; also near at hand were their swords, spears and other weapons.

The Burmese had invaded Assam a couple of years back. It was a long tale of in-fighting among the Ahom kings and their ministers, replete with vicious court intrigues, conspiracies and counter-conspiracies, which finally paved the way for the Burmese, under the command of Mingi Maha Bandula, to invade Assam. The country, especially the upper region, was almost deserted now. Complete anarchy and unrest prevailed in the region. The Burmese army had been raiding the villages, killing and torturing people whom they believed to be loyal to the Ahom king. Very often, the locals too took advantage of the situation, disguising themselves as Burmese and looting and plundering at will. Robert and his group had to be extremely vigilant against the reckless brutality of the Burmese soldiers. Destabilized and impoverished by the political situation, most of the people had fled to the neighbouring hills in different kingdoms. Many Assamese people had been taken away as slaves by the independent Dafla tribes from neighbouring Sadiya, as well as by the Singphos living along the eastern border of Assam. Some officers of the Ahom kingdom continued to plot attacks on the Burmese from their hideouts in the neighbouring region. As a result of this turmoil, Robert's trade had suffered and was on the decline. He usually traded in European broadcloth, pearls, spices, carpets, coral, mirrors and salt, with salt being the main commodity. But the demand for salt had come down. Normally, once he had sold his goods, Robert would take back muga silk and yarn, ivory, rhino horn and other precious merchandise from Assam. The efforts to expel the Burmese were still ongoing.

On this visit, Robert had two main objectives. The first was to meet Bisa Gaam, the Singpho king; the second was to go further upstream and meet the king of Burma. Robert had the necessary entry permissions with him and he had managed to get both an identity certificate as well as a certificate of friendship from Mingimaha Tilowa, the administrator of Assam. It was going to be a special day for Robert. He looked forward to his meeting with Bisa Gaam. Robert would not have come on this journey had he not met Maniram, the son of an officer of the Ahom king, Purandar Singha, at Goalpara. It was Maniram who had told him about the beverage that the Singphos drank. He was extremely excited when he heard that it tasted just like tea. Later, during his meeting with a Singpho chieftain in the Ahom capital, Robert had tried to find out about this beverage and the chief had consented to giving him a few saplings. But the matter did not advance further. That was why he had come to the Singpho kingdom to meet Bisa Gaam personally.

The beverage that the Singpho people drank could be tea – there was every possibility of that. And if it was indeed tea, the economy of the entire world could change. The Singpho people were friendly with the Burmese, and so was Robert. It would be easy for him to establish a cordial relationship with the former.

Hearing a loud commotion, Robert looked up in alarm. Boatloads of Burmese soldiers, crowded into a number of long vessels, were coming downstream at great speed. In an instant, Robert picked up a gun and stood up, alert. The leader of the boat in front of Robert held up a banner, given to him by Mingimaha Tilowa, proclaiming their friendship. The sight of the banner was enough to soften the stern looks of the Burmese soldiers and soon, the long row of boats passed them by with the soldiers waving merrily. Robert reciprocated and, lowering the gun, he sat down. The turbulence in the water receded, but Robert's mind did not follow suit. They were now almost at their destination. Bisa Gaam's residence could not be very far. He wondered if what Maniram had said about the Singpho people was true. Did they really drink tea? He had not heard this from anyone else. People thought that China was the only tea-growing country in the world. But surely a person like Maniram, well-read and well-travelled as he was, would be aware of the food habits of his neighbours. Should this piece of information prove correct, the harassment of European traders by the Chinese would soon be a thing of the past.

Leaving Burhi Dihing behind, the boats now turned right, onto the Tirap. It was on the banks of this river that Bisa Gaam lived. The territory was divided into many parts and each part was ruled by a Gaam or chieftain. They were all headed by Bisa Gaam, who was their chief adviser.

He was waiting at the ghat when the boats docked, he a tall and slender man with small, bright eyes and a drooping moustache. He was wearing typical Singpho clothes and a silk robe, brought from Burma. His head was wrapped in a band like a turban. Dangling from his shoulder were a typical red Singpho bag and a long sword, with its ornate hilt decorated with tiger teeth. The ghat was teeming with men, women and children. Eyes shining with curiosity, they were looking at the boats and the boatmen, especially at the strange clothes that Robert was wearing. After the introductions were over, Robert was escorted to Bisa Gaam's residence.

Before venturing out on this journey, Robert had contacted Bisa Gaam a number of times. He was aware that if he entered the Singpho kingdom without prior permission, anything could happen. The area, consisting of both hills and plains, was interspersed with dense forests. Between the forests were patches of cultivated land. Robert looked around curiously. The fields were being cultivated by people who had been brought here as slaves from Assam. Although Robert noted the people and the peculiar houses on stilts that he saw everywhere, his mind kept drifting to the tea. Tea had become a popular drink throughout Europe. As China had monopoly over tea, European traders were at the mercy of the Chinese, who kept a tight grip on the business. Foreigners were not allowed inside China. They had to conduct all their transactions from the place allotted to the foreigners in the port area, outside the walled city of Kwangchow. The European traders were at a severe disadvantage, as the Chinese were not willing to exchange tea for anything but silver. The European tea traders, therefore, had to transport large quantities of silver, braving pirates, on their long oceanic voyages. The East India Company was looking for alternatives to break out of this impasse. The Company had flooded the Chinese market with opium produced in India. Many Chinese had become addicted to opium and this allowed the British to reclaim a sizeable percentage of the silver they had paid for tea. But the Chinese emperor had imposed a ban on the import of opium, putting the East India Company in a quandary. It had become extremely important that the Company explore the possibility of cultivating tea outside China. Maniram's account of the Singpho beverage therefore filled Robert's head with impossible dreams. If the beverage turned out to be tea, not only would the Company's problem be solved, Robert would also become a rich tea trader!

Robert and his company reached the royal courtyard in the middle of the village, where a special dance to honour the guests was performed by a group of men and women in colourful costumes. Afterwards he was taken to the 'sang ghar' while the gunners remained below. Robert was seated in the front room, meant for guests. Bisa Gaam and Robert sat facing each other on the beautifully decorated wooden floor, each man accompanied by his interpreter. Standing behind Robert was his slave Deodhan.

Robert anxiously watched the Gaam. He had to be cautious and wait for an appropriate moment to ask questions or else Bisa Gaam might become suspicious of his intentions. But the chieftain looked cordial and seemed to give Robert his due respect – perhaps because of Robert's friendship with the Burmese. After the initial courtesies from both sides, a bamboo tube was handed respectfully to each person.

'What is this?' Robert asked politely, unwilling to offend but curious at the same time.

'This is "chapuk". One feels happy and physically fit after having this.'

Robert looked inside the bamboo tube. The contents had a peculiar smell; it did not look like tea at all.

Slowly, he took a small gulp.

'Oh, this is wine! Singpho wine!' Robert shook his head, while the Gaam looked at him curiously.

'We make this from rice. Don't you like it?' he asked through the interpreter.

Robert shook his head.

'No, I quite like it. What other beverages do you drink? Anything made from leaves?' he asked. It took Bisa Gaam a while to understand what Robert was saying. Then his eyes widened.

'Yes, we do drink a beverage made out of leaves. "Phalap" is what we call it. Are you asking about phalap?'

Phalap! Yes, that was the name Maniram had mentioned!

'I suppose I'll know when I drink it. Could I taste a little bit?'

'Yes, of course,' Bisa Gaam nodded happily.

Soon a young girl brought him another bamboo container, this time containing phalap.

'One feels good after drinking this. It also wards off illness.'

Robert looked into the tube of reddish liquid. He took a sip, and jumped up in excitement.

'Tea! This is tea!'

'Tea?' Bisa Gaam asked in surprise.

'Yes, tea. The drink of China! This is the most popular drink in our country, and in Europe.'

In his excitement Robert had started speaking in English. No one understood a word. Realizing his mistake, Robert smiled.

'Could you show me some phalap?' he requested the Gaam.

In a moment, a lump of dry tea leaves was brought in a bamboo tube. Shaking out a bit on his palm he felt the leaves with his fingers and brought them close to his nose. Everyone was watching him. What was there to be so excited about, they thought. Slowly, Robert's face brightened.

Yes, this was definitely tea.

Putting the phalap back, he asked, 'How do you prepare this drink?'

'We get the leaves from the jungle and pound them. We then leave them to dry on the fire in bamboo tubes. Then we boil them in water and drink it.'

With the permission of Bisa Gaam, he noted down the method of preparation.

'Do any other tribes drink phalap?'

'No one drinks apart from us, as far as I know. A few people in the neighbourhood also drink this and so do the slaves that we have brought from Assam. They boil it in earthen pots. It is a good remedy for the common cold. Why do you ask?'

'This is a familiar beverage, Gaam. We call it tea. I've brought some with me. Wait, I will show you.'

On Robert's instructions, Deodhan ran to the boat to get the tea, and also the paraphernalia for brewing it. Robert extended a sample of the tea and placed it on the chieftain's palm.

Smelling it, he said, 'This is just like our phalap. Where did you get it?'

'I brought it from China. People all over the world drink tea but it is cultivated only in China. I'll treat you to some tea and you can tell me how you like it.'

Bisa Gaam was now truly curious.

While Deodhan prepared tea, everyone looked on curiously. As they drank it with sugar, everyone seemed to be overjoyed.

'How do you like it, Gaam?' Robert asked, watching the surprised look on his face.

'It is very good,' he answered.

'Would you like to go into the business of producing tea with me?' Robert asked, slowly sipping his tea.

'Business, did you say? Of phalap?'

'Yes. That is exactly what I said. We will produce tea here and sell it far away, in the place from where I come. And you will earn a lot of silver.'

Bisa Gaam's eyes widened in surprise. Would it be wise to trade in tea with this unnaturally fair man from across the seas?

After a long period of silence, he asked, 'Will this business of tea cause any difficulty to our people?'

'No, not at all. In fact, it will bring about development; lots of development.' Robert explained the techniques involved in tea trading. He talked about Europe, Calcutta and the East India Company. The interpreter kept translating while Bisa Gaam nodded. He had heard of the East India Company from many sources. Having helped the Burmese in their wars against Assam, he had a lot of information from the Burmese people. He understood that it would be to the advantage of the Singpho people if he joined hands with this European fellow; Robert Bruce was on good terms with the Burmese general as well as with the administrator in Assam.

'What would I have to do for this tea trade?' Gaam asked.

'We will have to begin with an agreement. I will take with me some leaves and a few seedlings as well, as a sample of phalap. Then, slowly, the work will move. The responsibility will entirely be mine. You need not worry one bit. If you don't have any objection, can I have a look at some phalap trees?'

'Yes, of course you can. We have some trees here, but I'll take you to a jungle of phalap trees. But let us first have our meal.'

Robert agreed, sipping tea from the bamboo tube. He was dreaming of the future.

By the time they finished their meal, it was mid-afternoon. A lot of people had assembled outside to catch a glimpse of Bisa Gaam's foreign guest. Bisa Gaam climbed onto an elephant, as did his bodyguards. Robert sat on another, and his gunners followed suit. They weren't taking any chances.

The convoy of elephants proceeded, leaving the curious villagers behind. Entering the forest, they stopped in front of a mixed patch of small and big trees. Pointing to the largest tree, Bisa Gaam said, 'There, that's a phalap tree.'

Speechless, Robert stared.

It was a slender tree, about twenty feet tall. This was the tea of Robert's dreams, and of the entire European tea-trading community.

'My child!'

Hearing her mother's voice, Lailin looked up from Arunabh's book. It took her a long while to come back to present-day Hong Kong. Her mother had returned from her shopping with a bag in each hand. Lailin took the bags from her while her mother went to the dining table. Leaving the bags in the kitchen, Lailin came and sat down at the table. Her mind was a whirlpool of emotions. She turned to look at her mother and wondered whether she, too, mulled over her past, a past that had been buried deep in the abyss of sorrow. Her mother was aware that Arunabh was arriving tomorrow. Did she nurture any new hopes? It was difficult to understand her. Her genial smile remained etched on her tired face, as always; one could never read her impassive expressions. Catching her breath, she stood up and said, 'Wait, let me get some tea.'

Lalin pulled her mother back.

'After all this shopping, must you make tea for me?'

'It doesn't matter, I'm not tired,' her mother insisted.

Lifting her mother's slender hands, roughened by time and toil, Lailin held them in her own and said sadly, 'I know you are tired, Maa. How much more will these hands of yours do? Let go, Maa, and rest.'

'I don't work that much these days.'

'Who does all this work then? You have to do this all alone. We have told you so many times to come and live with us, but you don't listen.'

'I will. If I don't stay with you, where else will I go? Let me get older.'

'Even when you get older, I know you won't come. Your friends are all you care about,' Lailin sulked. 'Can anyone take your place, my child?' she asked, stroking Lailin's head.

'Yes, your friends can. Now go and rest. Please,' said Lailin.

Glancing at the book in her hand, Lailin's mother went into the bedroom. After a few quiet moments, Lailin stood up and went to the window. The wind was blowing hard. Down below, the sea was calm. The ships and the sailboats stood steady. A restful quiet had descended on the sea. Lailin looked down at the water. Was there a Chinese junk nestled among these ships? She didn't know much about ships. She couldn't tell the difference between a schooner and a junk. She had come to know about these names from the books she had read while researching her roots. The sailing ships – the clippers, schooners and the Chinese junks which were built in the first part of the nineteenth century to provide more speed to the sea trade – were tied up with her past. It was in one of those Chinese junks that Lailin's ancestor had sailed out of southern China, some one hundred and seventy years ago. After a while she came away from the window and returned to Arunabh's book.

... as if I was walking through an ancient and unknown city. The past of this petrified city had left me stunned, time and time again. It made me cry, again and again. I was writhing in anger and in an inexplicable pain that had no remedy. I could now understand the cause of that terrible flame of anger in Lailin's eyes. I could understand her now, as well as her society.

It took me some time, for this was not a history enshrined in written words for one to read at one's will. Different pieces of it were strewn across the globe. I had to pick out each and every word of that history from the darkness of the hearts, from the tears, from the silence of people who did not want to speak. It had taken me time to piece together that history once again.

Arunabh's book transported Lailin to a distant past – the early nineteenth century. It transported her to a poverty-stricken village in southern China, where her ancestor was born. His name was Ho Han.

Three

It was a grey and dusty village. A village struck by famine.

In a corner of this village lived Ho Han.

The entire village was quiet, devoid of any sign of habitation.

Death had become a familiar fact of life and most of the villagers had died of starvation. Those who could afford to had left the village earlier. Even now a thin trickle of skeletal evacuees could be seen leaving for Kwangchow.

Those left behind were Ho Han's family and others like them, families living in such an utter state of brutishness that it seemed as though they were still in the pre-civilized ages. Cruel, selfish and without an iota of shame.

In Ho Han's home a scene of cruelty was being enacted at that very minute.

In the courtyard of the dilapidated straw and bamboo hut sat Ho Han and his three brothers. Ho Han's elder brother was eight years old while he was six and his two younger brothers were four- and-a-half and three. Uncared for, they were all dressed in dirty clothes made from hemp. They were barefoot and their ragged, skinny bodies were covered in dust and grime. Their eyes sunk deep in their sockets, flesh and muscles shrivelled and dry, it was only their bloated stomachs that were prominent. Sitting in a corner, they were watching their father who was deep in conversation with two men.

Ho Han's father looked as famine-stricken, ragged and filthy as his children. The two men with pigtails, however, looked well-fed and there was no sign of impoverishment on their attire. One of them was dressed in fine silk. His chubby face, bright countenance and well-made clothes smacked of wealth. The other man, although dressed like an ordinary villager, wore clean cotton clothes and looked healthy. He was a broker, a middleman; he looked after the buying and selling of human beings.

The two had arrived in a horse carriage. Two gunmen and the coachman kept watch over the carriage. They feared that at any moment the starving villagers might attack them because of the two bags of rice kept in the carriage, a commodity more precious than gold and silver!

Leaning against one of the pillars of the verandah stood Ho Han's emaciated mother. She was listening to her husband's conversation with keen interest as he haggled with the two strangers in a weak voice.

'Considering their age, one silver per year is too small a price, sir,' Ho Han's father pleaded.

'The commitment was one silver per year and along with it one bag of rice. Didn't you finalize the deal?' the man in the silk robe asked the middleman in irritation.

'That was the agreement. Now if he changes his mind –'

'I have not changed my mind, sir. I am only requesting you to add two or three coppers, or some beans, soya bean, or even corn.'

'I have neither the time nor the need to haggle. There is no dearth of girls. Girls are nothing but a commodity, anyway. If you don't want to sell, say so,' the man in the silk robe said, shaking his pigtail.

'No, no, sir. I didn't say –'

'Think about how privileged you are that Sir himself has come. One silver per year is not a small amount. He has even promised you a bag of rice! Bring them over. Let Sir have a look at them and decide whether they suit his requirements or not.'

Ho Han's father looked at his wife. With weak and unsteady strides, she went inside the house. After a while, she returned with both her skeletal daughters, aged ten and eleven, and dressed in their best clothes. But they looked like scarecrows. Without any sign of emotion, the mother pushed her two daughters towards the buyer. Tottering weakly, they came and stood in the middle of the courtyard with their heads bent, indifferent to their surroundings.

The rich man surveyed the girls from head to toe. His stare seemed to pierce through their clothes, like that of a meat-buyer. The girls stood there, looking as though they might faint at any moment. They stood there showing no interest in the goings-on. It was all the same to them, whether they were sold or not. Their mother had already told them that if they remained at home, death was a certainty. If they were sold, perhaps they would get food to eat at their master's house and discarded silk dresses to wear.

These dreams were floating before their eyes like a hazy mirage.

The man's fingers crept along the girls' bodies from top to toe, not excluding their newly formed but shrivelled breast lines.

'Oh, this one is too small; can't be more than ten or eleven. It is doubtful whether she is even eight or nine. She hardly has any breasts.'

'Yes, they are ten and eleven. The boys are younger. Their age –'

With a hand raised to stop the father from speaking, he said in irritation, 'That's enough. I don't want any proof. The older one is eleven, and the younger one is nine. Twenty silvers. Just tell me whether you agree or not.'

The father looked pleadingly at the middleman, who was standing behind the rich man gesturing to the father to agree to the deal.

'If you don't agree he will leave. You will regret it later. Whether or not they will live another two days is hard to tell. If they die, what will you have to sell?'

The father looked at the mother. There was no reaction.

'Alright,' he said, shaking his head in utter disappointment.

Without betraying any signs of satisfaction, the rich man instructed the middleman to get a bag of rice from the carriage. The middleman left the scene.

The man in the silk clothes took out some silver coins from a beautiful bag and started counting them. The middleman returned in a while, followed by the coachman, who was carrying the rice in a jute bag.

The girls looked at their parents, at their house and then at their brothers sitting in the corner. There was not a trace of emotion in their tired eyes. Handing over twenty silver coins and a bag of rice, the man in the silk robe left, followed by the middleman and the coachman. Behind them, the two girls followed with mechanical steps.

When everyone had gone, Ho Han and his brothers walked unsteadily towards thc bag of rice. Their pale eyes were glowing with wild greed. With a thunderous yell the father smothered the glow, and together with his wife dragged the bag into the house. Ho Han and his brothers followed. Their starved bodies were thrilled. Today they would get to eat rice.

Asking the mother for a vessel, the father put some rice into it. He took the remaining rice from the bag, divided it into several small packets and hid them in different places. Then, having bolted all the doors and without making a sound, they ate the cooked rice. The steaming aroma from the rice wiped off the memory of the two girls who'd just been sold. Their faces lit up with hope. They would move to Kwangchow, now that they had money.

Tired after their meal, they fell asleep only to be rudely woken up by a group of starving villagers who demanded that they share their rice. 'We know that you have rice in your house. Give us rice.'

'There is no rice. Where would we get rice from?' the father cried.

'Where have your two daughters gone? We know you have sold them. Now give us some rice.'

The people with whom they'd lived for years had suddenly turned alien. Disregarding Ho Han's father, they marched in and turned the place upside down. When they left, they took away almost all the packets of rice and the silver coins that Ho Han's father had hidden. The parents cried bitterly. Ho Han and his brothers stood still, terrified out of their wits.

'Our rice! They have taken our rice!'

At the touch of her mother's hand Lailin returned from the distant past and looked up. Handing her a cup of tea, her mother walked away, smiling gently.

Overcome with the sorrows and sufferings of her ancestors, Lailin slowly sipped her tea. Then she immersed herself once again in Arunabh's book.

In the midst of all the sobbing, the night came to an end. And life went on. The two packets of rice that had remained ran out one day. After that, five more unbearable days and nights passed. On the morning of the sixth day Ho Han woke up to the pleadings of his mother.

'Keep at least one. Who will look after us in the end?'

Ho Han heard his father's words, 'They will all die. They won't live to look after us. What will you do taking them with you? How can you be sure that we will be alive?'

Ho Han and his brothers did not understand much. They were scared and had gone limp with hunger. But they were aware that something terrible was going on.

After some time, the father walked in and carried away Ho Han's elder brother. Then he came back to take Ho Han and his younger brother. As they came out they found the elder brother asleep in one of the baskets that their father used to carry loads in. His body was weak and pliable, almost like rubber. Placing Ho Han and the youngest son in the other basket, the father went in to get his last son.

All the four boys cried weakly and pleaded not to be taken away, as their mother watched from the verandah. Her face was grim and lacked any emotion except her desire to survive.

Placing four bowls and four pairs of chopsticks in the baskets, the father picked up the long bamboo pole on which the baskets were hanging, and slowly began walking.

All that remained was the mother, the home of their birth, the familiar surroundings, the temple and the public well ...

In the scorching sun, the father carried his load across the field. The children were dehydrated, while the father had to put down his load many a times, panting with exhaustion. He walked along a familiar path, now quiet and forlorn. There was no sound except for the children's whimpers, the creaking sound of the pole and the two baskets he carried, and that of his own panting.

Soon, he could hear voices coming faintly from a distance. Looking towards the sound, he saw a long line of people moving forward. They were carrying their bundled-up possessions tied on poles. These had to be people from the famine-struck villages who were walking to the city.

Soon the sun rose high in the sky. The children were wilting in the heat and crying weakly.

Suddenly Ho Han's father stopped in his tracks. Near a dried-up shrub he saw a fat dog happily devouring a baby's cadaver. His face brightened with pleasure. How could this dog have escaped human hands, in the face of such a famine? He wondered if God had specially saved this animal for him. Gently putting down his load and taking hold of the pole, he advanced stealthily towards the dog. With one heavy blow he felled the animal. After a few more blows the dog's writhing stopped. Tearing out the baby's flesh from its mouth, he lifted the dog and, panting profusely, placed it in the basket where Ho Han lay. With a feeling of satisfaction he lifted his load again. The dog would now provide the two of them enough food for at least four meals, now that the children would not return.

By late afternoon, he was in a well-guarded marketplace where traders were selling rice and pulses at exorbitant rates. There was also traditional medicine, dried fish, meat, preserved eggs and vegetables, and above all, human beings.

It was a slave market and it was full of starving people who had come to sell their own offspring. Ho Han's father went to sit beside them. Pulling out the sacks that lined the baskets, he spread them in front. He placed the children on the sacks and went out to buy food. He brought back rice, water and five preserved eggs. Forcing the children to sit up, he first fed them, then ate a meal of rice and eggs.

There was a roar from the people who had come to buy the children. They were feeling, pressing and rubbing the merchandise on display with their hands. Having finished eating, Ho Han's father waited eagerly for customers.

The first to be sold was the youngest child. He was bought by a wealthy farmer. The oldest brother was next to go, to a fish merchant. The third brother was sold to a landlord. Ho Han looked on with tear-filled eyes, as one by one all his playmates left. There was nothing to say or do.

The sun was slowly setting. The marketplace began to empty. Ho Han, now somewhat revived by the food, lay on the sack again. Glancing at his father in fear, he cajoled him, 'Take me home. I can walk back. You won't have to carry me.'

The father did not answer. He sat there, staring ahead with blank eyes.

A long time passed. His patience was wearing thin and he was contemplating going back. At that moment a man with a frightening face appeared before him. Clad in dirty silk clothes and wearing a shabby pigtail, the man touched Ho Han with a rough hand. Taking out a pouch from his pocket, he enquired in a harsh tone,

'How many silvers?'

With a deep sigh Lailin raised her head from Arunabh's book. The lovely smell of her mother's cooking came wafting out of the kitchen. She knew that tonight there would be Assamese food on the table. It would most likely be daal, rice, greens and a sour curry cooked with fish and tomatoes. Whether she liked it or not, she would have to eat it or else her mother would be upset. She hated hurting her mother in any way. Her mother sometimes cooked Assamese food, trying to remember recipes from her past. Lailin had no idea, whether or not it was authentic, but her mother would insist, 'This is our own food. Our very own style of cooking. We must never forget our traditions.'

Lailin had heard her mother talk like this ever since she could remember. In the beginning it didn't mean anything to her. But now it did. She could hardly bear it. It triggered an explosion in her head. As she gradually learnt about her past, she protested against such talk. She would lose her temper and shout at her mother, 'This is not our food. I won't eat this. Why do you try to make me Assamese? I don't consider myself Assamese. I am Chinese. And these are not our traditions. After all that has happened, how can you love that country and its people? What kind of a person are you, Maa?'

'An Assamese person,' her mother would say with a smile. Looking at her mother's gentle face, she would break down.

Shaking off her emotions, Lailin returned to the pages.

Ho Han was sold off.

It was an ordinary incident. The ownership right had been transferred to another man with ease. No tears were shed. Ho Han left the market as the slave of a meat dealer.

Those were the days of slave trade during the reign of the Manchu rulers of the Qing dynasty. Ho Han's master had his shop in a marketplace adjacent to the Thirteen Factory area near the docks outside the walled city of Kwangchow. Foreign traders were allowed to trade here. The meat dealer lived in a corner of the city. It was there that he stocked his pigs and chickens and this was where Ho Han was now taken.

The story could have ended there. What could be special in a slave's life, other than hard labour and death? Other than tears and sighs? Other than captivity and brutality?

Ho Han's life could have been just that, but it wasn't, for he had brought with him a unique destiny. It was not his destiny alone but that of thousands of people of China and India. That was the time when a strong public opinion was building up in Europe and America against the slave trade. Organized movements, protesting against the inhuman treatment meted out to millions of unfortunate men and women, had begun. Slavery was banned in England, America and many other countries. But the vast Chinese world, with a history spread over six thousand years, remained untouched by these winds of change.

Meanwhile, far from southern China, in the upper reaches of Assam, the seed of Ho Han's future had just begun to sprout.

The political scene was changing. The East India Company had started to repulse the Burmese soldiers. Unable to take on the army of the East India Company, the Burmese army was withdrawing. The British army had set up camp at Kundil ghat in Sadiya near Upper Assam. The responsibility of the administration was now in the hands of David Scott, a representative of the Governor General for the entire eastern frontier.

The post at Sadiya had been set up with a view to keeping the Dafala and Singpho people under control as well as to protect the eastern border of Assam. The East India Company appointed Charles Alexander Bruce, the brother of Robert Bruce, as the leader of a flotilla of gunboats to monitor the natural waterways of this riverine state. Travelling upstream on the Brahmaputra, Charles had arrived at Sadiya. Kundil ghat was the last port on this river. The journey, via Shirajgunj between Calcutta and Kundil ghat, took eighty days. As soon as Charles arrived, he got involved in a strategic political formulation.

While the war was going on, the Singphos started their raids on Sadiya, as well as in the region between Dibrugarh and Rangpur. In 1826, an infantry division headed by Captain Neufville arrived to fight them.

Eventually the Singphos accepted defeat and pledged their loyalty to the British. The slaves that were brought from Assam by the Singphos were released by Captain Neufville. The other neighbouring tribes also offered their loyalty to the East India Company and decided to felicitate the British army in Sadiya. The process of organizing the meeting was going on.

Charles was excited and anxious. His heart was filled with emotion. He kept thinking of his younger brother Robert. Just three years ago his brother had written to him from the Singpho kingdom about tea being grown in Assam, and about the Singpho beverage called phalap. He had also told him about his arrangement with the Singpho chief. Robert had been consumed by his dream of becoming a famous tea trader with Bisa Gaam's help. But before he could fulfil this dream, he died.

Charles, however, was determined to keep his brother's dream alive. He had preserved his brother's letter about the discovery of tea in Assam with utmost care. He decided to meet Bisa Gaam. If they could grow tea in Assam, the entire tea trade would be transformed. Alexander and Robert Bruce would become immortal names in the history of tea.

Maniram Dutta Baruah was an important person for the East India Company now. When David Scott came to Assam to expel the Burmese, Maniram came with him to show him the way. He was also present during the treaty between Scott and the Singpho chief. He was supposed to be present at today's meeting too. Maniram had told Charles about his friendship with Robert. And Charles had heard Maniram talking to Beddingsfield, an officer of the East India Company, about phalap.

The previous year the English Society of Arts had announced a fifty-guinea prize and a gold medal to anyone in India, West Indies or any other British colony, who could produce twenty pounds of excellent-quality tea. After this announcement many people began to take an interest in the cultivation of tea. Charles was very excited when he was asked to come to Sadiya from Calcutta. After much thought he had brought Robert's letter with him.

Charles was waiting with this letter in his pocket. Tense, uncertain.

Four

It was a day history was about to change its course.

Ho Han groaned under the weight of the two heavy baskets balanced across his shoulders on a pole. He walked through the fields of a village situated near Kwangchow. He was a young man now, and was clad in traditional Chinese clothes. On his feet he wore sandals made of straw. It was extremely hot. His sturdy body was soaked in sweat. Ho Yen, a fellow slave who was following him, was also in a similar state. Both of them had a square-shaped scar, a mark that had been burnt onto their foreheads. Anyone could identify them now; the scar symbolized their identities as slaves.

The wounds no longer hurt. They had healed a long time ago. Ho Han couldn't remember the number of years that had gone by since the meat seller had bought him. He had lost the happy memories of his childhood. All that he remembered were the days of the famine. During some lonely moments, the faces of his sisters who were sold, and of his mother waiting in the verandah, came to his mind. He also remembered that long, hot day in the basket. To this day, he woke up sometimes at night soaked in sweat. He had no affection for his parents, or even respect. But somewhere in his heart he felt a pure affection for his brothers and sisters. Or perhaps it was just a reflection of the affection he had for himself.

He was now used to the life of a slave. Till very recently, along with a few other slaves, he had followed their master, carrying baskets on his shoulders. But now the master did not come with them. His financial status had improved enormously. He was on very good terms with the brokers near the Thirteen Factory area. The members of the Association of Brokers were very important in the foreign trade market and they handled all the business on behalf of the Chinese emperor.

Now the master's business was not limited to meat alone. He had two tea houses along with some other business in Kwangchow. But his main business was opium. Everything else had become secondary.

The Chinese government had enforced strict laws prohibiting the supply of opium. For that reason, it was being smuggled in, with help from a few corrupt officials and abetted by some members of the Brokers' Association. The Chinese emperor had been trying very hard to end the opium trade. With prohibition becoming stricter, the price of opium had also soared sky-high.

In the beginning, opium-trading was not a problem. It was easy to bribe the officials, and the boats could openly dock at the port. No one was particularly bothered when the supply of opium was unloaded. But now the situation had changed and the governor of Canton had not only ordered the arrest of the smugglers but also punished them severely. He had ordered all the ships to be searched. If opium was found on a ship, the entire cargo was confiscated and the ship was debarred from trading activities.

As a result of this, the smugglers started coming to Lintin Island at the mouth of the Pearl river. This was a British base where ships not sail-worthy on the high seas were docked. The big ships that carried opium unloaded their cargo onto these stationary boats and went back to India for replenishment. From this spot, the smugglers secretly took their quota of opium to Kwangchow and other places in small boats. Being caught meant sure death, but Ho Han and the others were used to playing with death. From Lintin they carried the opium to their master's secret godowns, where the retailers bought it.

Ho Han's master had become an opium addict himself. Heating lumps of the narcotic over the flame of a lamp, he would inhale the smoke through a thin pipe and wander into a dream world of his own. He did not go out much these days. Handing over all the hard work to his old slave Ho Han, he drowned himself in intoxication. His involvement in opium smuggling had taught Ho Han quite a few things. He also learnt a lot of things from visiting the port frequently.

The colourful port life amazed him. The vastness and vibrancy of the place, packed with schooners, clippers, Chinese junks and sailing boats, with their variety of flags from different countries, thrilled him. He would often wonder about the countries these ships came from.

Ho Han had also learnt the dialect used in the ports. Ho Yen was yet to pick up on the local parlance. He had no interest either and brooded all the time, perhaps because he had become a slave at an older age. At this moment, too, he was following Ho Han gloomily. Their master used to send them to villages to collect chickens once in a while, without any supervision. He knew they wouldn't try to run away.

This vast country was a hard place to live in. There was no certainty that they would find a better life if they escaped. They might fall into the hands of another slave trader. Where would they find work in this thickly populated land?

Ho Han had accepted this life as his fate. He had neither frustrations nor any grievances. He did not dream of liberty. His experience had given him the maturity to understand the reality of his situation. That he could live safely and eat every day in a country ravaged by war, floods, drought and famine was enough for him. What would he achieve by running away? Besides, what skills did he have to survive all by himself, except rearing and slaughtering chickens and pigs? He had the aptitude to learn new things. Whatever the task, he did it sincerely. He had picked up woodwork while helping a carpenter in his master's house. But he did not think that was enough to sustain a living as an independent man.

'Let us drop in at the marketplace,' he said, looking back at Ho Yen.

Ho Yen did not answer. They took the turn leading to the market. It was peak hour at the market. In one corner, a man was narrating tales in exchange for money. Ho Han didn't stop to listen. Another spot was occupied by a fortune teller. Passing him by, Ho Han stopped at a place where chickens were being sold and started picking out the good ones. Just at that moment they heard a noise.

A rich man dressed in silk was buying expensive merchandise at random without even haggling. He was accompanied by two healthy slaves wearing bright clothes. The people nearby started looking at him curiously. Someone asked him, 'Where have you come from?'

It was as though the buyer was waiting for just that question.

'I belong to this place. My village is just four or five villages away. But now I don't live there. In fact, I now live very far away.'

'Where exactly do you live, then?'

'Prince of Wales Island.'

'And where is that? How far is it from our village?'

'Not from your village. Ask me how far it is from our country. Prince of Wales Island is not in China. One has to go there by ship. I live there in a place called George Town. In the beginning, I used to work at a tin mine. Now I have my own business and my own ship.'

'Own ship!' They gaped at the stranger in amazement. Meanwhile, more people had gathered near him. They jostled with each other to get closer to the man. Ho Han came and stood at the back of the crowd and craned his neck to see what was happening. Ho Yen stood behind him indifferently, as if he was waiting for an order from his master. For him, Ho Han was his master now.

The man was speaking in a loud voice, as though he was delivering a lecture. The gathering looked at him in awe and kept nodding. The man wore chains of gold and pearls round his neck. He carried a pouch full of silver in his hand. His healthy appearance reflected his prosperity.

'What is not there in that country? You can say gold is lying on the streets and with just a little toil one can live there like a king. What do we have in this country? Do we even have enough to eat after toiling day in and day out? Can we live in happiness? No, we cannot. Today if it's the floods, tomorrow it will be the drought. As soon as the crops are almost ready for harvesting, there is a locust attack. We are all dying of hunger. We all know what famine means,' he said exasperatedly. He paused for a moment and then said, 'There is suffering in this land. Lots of suffering! We still live here because we love this country. We tolerate our suffering. But if we had the option of going to a country which is beautiful in every way, what would we do? Think. Think for yourself.' The man stopped.

'What would I do? What indeed?' Ho Han thought.

The man resumed, 'We would go away to that land, surely we would. I left this country after getting such an opportunity. My father was a farmer and I worked with him. Having two square meals a day was a big thing for me. But one day I met a saviour.'

He paused abruptly; the people surrounding him had started to whisper amongst themselves. After the rumbling ceased, the man started once again.

'At the time, there were a few friends with me,' he continued. 'The messiah told us that he lived abroad and had come to his old village for a few days. He wanted to show his village folk how to be rich. I asked him where he lived and that's when he told me about Prince of Wales Island. There were very few people, but plenty of jobs. A day's earning there is what we earn in six months here! His life had completely changed after going there. Thereafter, he took his brothers. After working for some time, his brothers had returned with enough money to last a lifetime. With nothing to do for himself, he came back to take a few of his poor countrymen, so that they too could live the good life. We asked him what we had to do in order to go there. He told us that we had to sign an agreement to work there for seven years. After which we would have the option either to return, or to start our own business there. Even if we returned home, we would have earned so much money that we could spend the rest of our lives without lifting a finger.'

The people were awestruck. They gasped as they listened, as though they were being told a fairy tale.

'I was lucky that I believed him. Two of my friends also believed him, the others did not. I thought if I continued to live in this place, there would be no change in my life. What was the harm in going there once? If I could earn good money, I could keep my family in comfort. So I went with him. What happened after that is for you to see. I've taken my entire family there. One of my friends came back and is living here like a wealthy landlord. Someday, if you wish, I can take you to meet him. My messiah told me, "Just as I've helped you, you too must do the same."'

Pushing his way through the crowd, Ho Han stood before the man.

'If we want to go, what do we have to do?' someone in the crowd asked.

'You have to sign a seven-year agreement. The rest of the responsibility will be mine. Your food and travel expenses will be borne by me. An amount in the form of an advance will be paid to you. You can give that to your family, or spend it on yourself – that is entirely up to you. When you become rich, you can pay me back if you wish.'

The rumbling slowly became an uproar. Some called the man a cheat, others believed him and the rest were simply confused. Slowly the crowd dispersed. A few men stayed back. Amongst them were Ho Han and Ho Yen.

Leaving the crowd behind, the man now stood in the shade of a tree. Taking a bundle from one of his slaves, he took out a handful of chocolates. Putting one of them in his mouth, he distributed the rest amongst the crowd.

They had never tasted chocolate before; it was like ambrosia, melting in their mouths. By the time it was late afternoon, eleven of them had signed the papers.

Five

There was still some time left before dawn.

Neither Ho Han nor Ho Yen could sleep a wink. Secretly putting together their clothes, rice bowls, chopsticks and a few other essentials in two small bundles, they hid them behind the chicken coops. It was imperative that the other three slaves who slept in their small, dark room should not discover their secret. They were well aware of what happened to slaves trying to flee from their masters. The death of the slave who had died vomiting blood because of the severe thrashing he'd got was still fresh in their minds. They remembered well the torture they'd faced, especially the red hot steel square stamped onto their foreheads.

Oh, that dreadful afternoon! Ho Han was squirming in unbearable pain. He was crying at the top of his voice. His young heart could not share that despair with anyone. There was no one who could feel his pain. He lay there, gagging on his tears while his master's men thrashed him soundly and left him in a closed room. No one came to see him, or to offer him any food. On that horrible day, the six-year-old boy understood what it meant to be a slave. He was made to understand how a slave should behave, what a slave ought to and ought not to do.

In the early days, it was not as if the thought of running away did not occur to him. Slogging from sunrise to sunset, he did think of escaping but what held him back was the memory of the stench of a dead dog in the same basket as him, and the blank face of his father, trying to sell his own children. What also held him back was the memory of his sisters looking back at their home and of their mother standing motionless, leaning on a pillar. Ho Han understood that the world outside may be even more cruel and horrible than what he had to endure under his master. In the course of time, he'd learnt to be a loyal slave. But now he was preparing to leave his long-time shelter and make a journey to an unknown land. The idea of the golden country that this man had spoken of mesmerized him. He wouldn't be a slave anymore. He would become a free man. In lieu of his labour, he would get enough food, necessary clothes, proper shelter and wages. The man had assured him of all this. Ho Han had always dreamt of having his own shop in the market adjacent to Thirteen Factory. But there was no way to realize his dream. A runaway slave cannot return to his country.

The man who'd promised to take them to the island was supposed to wait for them near a particular pagoda. They had to get there before dawn.

'Wake up, let's go! The cock is crowing,' Ho Han whispered, nudging Ho Yen awake.

Stealthily, the two stepped out of the house. Picking up the bundles hidden behind the chicken coop, they started running. The houses on both sides of the road were shrouded in darkness. They ran silently through the narrow, dark alleys of the ancient city. The fear of uncertainty and getting caught along with the excitement of a new adventure had quickened their blood.

They reached the pagoda some time before dawn. The man was already there, along with sixteen other youths and three horse carriages. The horse-drawn carriages sped through the fading darkness. They reached the port before daybreak.

Ho Han and his group were taken to the Thirteen Factory area.

Each of these factories had three or four storeys. The offices of the foreign traders were here. The first one or two floors of these buildings were warehouses. The third and fourth floors consisted of well-maintained, beautiful apartments. The three carriages flew past Hog Lane, lined with retail shops. Between the American and French factories was the old China Street, on which stood Ho Han's master's meat shop. The carriages rushed past this as well and at last halted in front of a warehouse on Thirteen Factory Street.

Taking Ho Han and the others to the warehouse, the man said, 'You will all have to wait here for some time. There are lots of formalities to go through before you can cross the seas. Tonight, I will come and take you away from here. Meanwhile, you must remain hidden.'

Arrangements had already been made for food and rest. Explaining what all had to be done, the man left, closing the huge door behind him. Ho Han and his group remained seated in the dark and humid warehouse dreaming of the wonderful life that awaited them. It was well after midnight when the door opened. Once again, they got into the horse carriages and were taken to the boats that would transport them to Lintin Island, where a Chinese junk, built of teakwood, with its canvas sails rolled up, awaited their arrival. The flag of the Qing dynasty displayed a dragon spewing fire. Ho Han and his group stepped on board. On the main deck of the huge vessel, built with three masts, were a few armed men. On one side of the deck stood a Chinese man in silk robes, accompanied by an European.

Looking at the man who had brought Ho Han and his companions, the European gentleman called out, 'Chin Chin ako.'

'Chin Chin,' the man grinned back.

'Long time no see. Busy?'

'Busy. My catchi one pichi wifo.' The man's grin spread from ear to ear – he was telling the European that he had got married.

The three men started whispering excitedly amongst themselves. The man who had brought Ho Han pointed a finger at the other two and shouted, 'You two pela chicken.'

'What is he saying?' Ho Yen asked Ho Han.

'He says the other two are like chickens, without guts. He is very angry.'

'Ren ren eight,' the man who had brought Ho Han said, showing four fingers of each hand.

'Eight for each man,' Ho Han translated in a quiet voice.

'No can do, no can do,' the European said shaking his head.

'You arse belong trabal,' the man who had brought Ho Han said, pointing at the other Chinese.

Lifting his palm upwards, the European asked them to stop arguing.

'Look see. No go bananas.'

The other man wanted to say something. Asking him to be quiet, he talked to the man who had brought Ho Han. He nodded and showed him six fingers.

'Okay. Ren ren six.'

'He means six per person,' Ho Han translated quietly.

'What does it mean?'

'I don't really know. Perhaps he is talking about the fare for our voyage.'

The European now nodded in agreement.

'Can do, can do.'

'Hau hau.' The man who had brought Ho Han grinned widely. Whispering something, the European gentleman announced that they were leaving the next day.

'We tomorrow maki move.'

'Bely well. Bely well.'

The European gestured and his man brought him a finely knitted handbag full of silver. The European counted some coins and handed them over to the man who had brought Ho Han who counted the coins for himself and looked satisfied. After whispering some more, the European and his companion climbed down.

'Kuai kuai, chop chop,' the Chinese companion shouted. 'Hurry up, hurry up!'

The guards on deck came forward. One of them opened the hatchway that led to the hold of the ship and ordered the men to go down.

'Something is amiss, Ho Yen,' said Ho Han.

'What do you mean?' the others asked anxiously.

'Why did the man take money for each one of us? He had said he didn't need money!'

'What's the problem? Why are you making so much noise?' the man who brought them asked, coming forward.

'Why have you taken money from that man?' Ho Han asked.

'What is wrong? Shouldn't I have taken money?'

'I can understand your language,' Ho Han said. 'Why have you taken money for us?'

'You will understand later. Now go below, I say.'

'You have to tell us before we go,' Ho Han insisted as the others too came forward. The man's face was flushed with anger. The faces of the guards hardened, too.

'I said I'll tell you later. Go down, or else –'

'Or else what?' Ho Han stared at him.

Out of nowhere a guard hit him with the butt of his gun. Ho Han fell to the floor. The man thundered at the group, 'Shut up, you! I asked you to go below. Not a word more. Go below, I said.'

Two of the guards pulled Ho Han up and pushed him and the others down the stairs. The man who had brought them there stood watching indifferently. All glow of kindness and magnanimity was gone.

Utter darkness enveloped the insides of the ship. The air was heavy with the stink of sweat, vomit and excretion. Ho Han and the others looked around. They knew immediately that there were people there with them. Their breath created strange ghostly waves. In the eerie silence, the people below looked wide-eyed at the young men who had been forced down from above, clutching their small bundles to their chests.

After a few moments of unbearable silence, a tired and agonized voice spoke from a corner of the dark hole.

'Why on earth did you all come here?'

The newcomers were in a quandary. In a trembling voice, one of them said, 'We are going to a distant place to work.'

'That man has lied to you. He is a wicked man. A cheat.'

'But we all have written agreements!'

'He has sold us all.'

'We will have to work there as slaves. For the last five days we have been imprisoned here. Not once have we been allowed out.'

The truth dawned on them suddenly. Their cries further distressed those already imprisoned, making them sob and bemoan their fate.

'They have bought us from our masters,' someone wept.

'They gagged me and brought me here forcibly, beating me all the way. Look at the wounds on my body. Look!'

'I wanted to get married, but I didn't have enough money. I thought I'd work hard and save money so that I could come back and marry. But now we will not live to come back. None of us will return alive!'

'We are poor and have no land to cultivate. I thought I'd work hard and return with loads of money. I dreamt of buying land and keeping my parents in comfort. I have a wife and children. I'll never ever get to see them again,' a man wailed.

Suddenly, Ho Yen cried out, 'I'm going back. I won't stay here.'

'Don't try to do that. They will beat you. Don't go.'

Ho Yen wouldn't listen to them. A few others followed him. They climbed up the stairs and started thumping on the iron lid, shouting, 'Open the lid. Let us out! We are suffocating without air. We will die. Let us out!'

'Call them back, there is no point in shouting. We too wanted to get out, but they wouldn't let us. Instead, they thrashed us. They will do the same to you.'

For a moment Ho Han was perplexed. Then, climbing up the stairs he tried to reason with Ho Yen. But Ho Yen was in no mood to listen.

Suddenly the hatch opened. Three men stood near the hatchway. In the weak light of a candle, they could see the gleaming steel-capped whips in their hands. They started whipping the captives. The dark abyss of the ship was now heavy with the sounds of swishing whips, the blows of the sticks, and helpless shrieks of pain. The atmosphere was made even more loathsome by the fearsome voices of the guards.

'Shut up, you! Not a word more, or else we will shoot you and dump you in the sea. Get down immediately!'

Closing the hatch over the injured men, they left. Ho Yen and the others touched their wounds gingerly and cried. Ho Han sat down, placing his head on his knees, his eyes brimming with tears.

It was pitch dark outside by then, as it was inside the ship. The hearts of the dreamers filled with absolute despair.

Six

1841

Six sturdy horses galloped furiously along a narrow road through a jungle in Matak country on the border of Upper Assam. It was a winter morning. The sun was yet to rise. Little was visible through the dense layers of fog.

The village folk living in the houses that stood on either side of the road were not fully awake, but a good many of them still came to look with sleepy eyes at the horsemen. Dew fell from the branches of the trees as the horses cut through the thick white fog; the clip-clop of their hooves resonated through the jungle. The curious villagers, blissfully unaware of what went on in the outside world, gazed at them in awe.

The riders were a familiar sight, but the villagers never ceased to be surprised at their complexion, their hair, eyes and clothes. Each time the riders went past, the rustle of curious conversation amongst the village folk lingered on long after their departure.

They had by now got an inkling of what these riders were up to. Rumours were rife that the forests around the villages were being cleared for the cultivation of tea. A few of the villagers had also been hired to do this work. The elephant mahouts and the grass-cutters brought home the news. No one knew what tea was. They just couldn't figure out how leaves used as a remedy for coughs could produce a beverage!

People kept visiting the village in search of labourers. But even though the pay was good, the villagers didn't want to step out of the village to work. They had enough to live on. Besides, most of them were lazy. Some were addicted to opium and did only what was required to get by. Some of them worked a few hours as it fetched some silver. But they could not bear to think of toiling hard, cutting big trees, and clearing the jungles, just for a little extra money.

The riders were now crossing a shallow river. They were silent, buried deep in their thoughts, in the mystical silence of the jungle. The men had come from distant countries like China and Europe to change the future of this region and its quiet way of life.

The seeds for that change had first been sown by Robert Bruce who had discovered a treasure trove of phalap trees and had dreamt of becoming a great tea trader, terminating China's monopoly in the tea trade. Bearing the dreams of his brother, Charles Alexander Bruce, now Superintendent of Tea Culture for the Assam Company – established by the East India Company especially for tea trade – was leading those riders.

A number of tea gardens had been set up in Assam, and the neighbouring Motok and Singpho regions, under Charles' guidance. It had been a few years since the tea business had begun there.

Maniram Baruah was now the Chief Officer of the Assam Tea Company. People referred to him as Maniram Dewan and with his help, the company had set up tea gardens in various parts of Upper Assam.

At the behest of the king of Assam, Purandar Singha, the East India Company went to war with Burma. The Burmese were defeated and in 1826 a treaty was signed by both countries on the shores of the Yandabu river in Burma. As a result of that treaty, Assam came under the rule of the East India Company. Keeping the administration of Lower Assam in their hands, the Company handed over the administration of all of Upper Assam, from the Dhonsiri river (barring Sadiya) to the Motok countries, to the king.

Ten years went by with Charles trying to convert his brother's dreams into reality. He was neither the owner of the tea gardens nor a trader of tea, but he nurtured the industry with his heart and soul. It was due to his dedicated efforts that the tea produced in Assam began to command a place in the world market. China's monopoly slowly came to an end. It was no simple task, and the journey was fraught with obstacles. At one point, he nearly failed because the experts in Calcutta decided that the tall phalap trees could not possibly be tea! They decided that tea gardens in Assam should be forged out of seeds and saplings from China, and with the help of Chinese experts. Charles, on the other hand, was certain that good tea could be produced from the local trees. But since he was no expert, his words fell on deaf ears.

Those were difficult days indeed. Finally in 1838, the first twelve boxes of Assam tea, manufactured from the local tea bushes, were sent to London.

It was a historic moment.

Tea had changed the socio-economic and political order of Assam and the other small countries of the region. Charles, now middle-aged, became the superintendent of these experimental tea gardens. The policies of the East India Company too had changed, and offering a pension to the Purandar Singha in 1838, the Company took over Upper Assam. Rongpur in Upper Assam became the new capital under the British, and Assam a part of the Bengal Presidency. The British now established a direct relationship with the chiefs of the Motoks and other neighbouring tribes.

Charles now worked from the headquarters at Tingrai and his entire day was spent on horseback as he visited the gardens in his own division. He was also given the additional responsibility of expanding the Naoholia tea estate. This is where Charles was now headed.

The jungle was enveloped by the smoke that rose from the fallen trees. The sounds of cutting and felling trees, the cacophony made by the elephants and their mahouts and the men shouting out instructions turned the forest into a noisy place.

Charles got off his horse along with two other Europeans, one local man and four Chinese men with pigtails.

A group of workers were planting saplings. While one lot dug holes six feet apart, another group placed the foot-high saplings in them. A fourth group was busy digging drains.

These saplings had been collected from the forest; it was more profitable to use these and to expand the number of tea gardens quickly. The garden would be ready for plucking the next year.

It was important to use only the tender new leaves of young plants for tea production; they had to collect only those leaves that grew at the very top of the bush. Charles had discovered that, by cutting down the big mature trees and setting them on fire, new plants could be grown from the stumps. He, in turn, had learnt this technique from the tribes who practised 'jhum'. It was a quick method. He was also producing saplings by sowing seeds alongside the plants. Three years later it would be accepted as the main technique used in future tea gardens.

Swathes of forest land were cleared to expand the Naoholia tea garden. Charles was more relaxed. He was watching the two Chinese tea experts instruct workers on the proper method of planting. They were picking out the plants that were a foot tall and straight, discarding the others. They then instructed the workers to put four to five plants together in the same hole. This technique was explained to the local man who would later be in charge of the plants.

The work was slow, and the workers had to rely on sign language to communicate with the Chinese experts. This sometimes annoyed Charles, but there was nothing he could do, for without the experts the local workers wouldn't know how to proceed. Besides, he had been instructed by the East India Company to treat the Chinese with utmost care so that they would not be dissatisfied in any way. At present, they were the company's most valuable assets. The heads of the East India Company, as well as the Tea Committee and the Assam Company, had not accepted the Singpho method of manufacturing tea. They wanted tea similar to the tea from China, or a version better than that. In the international market too, Chinese tea had a special place and it was clear that if the company was to compete, it would be important to follow Chinese methods of cultivation.

Under the leadership of the Chinese experts, local labourers were employed. Charles had to deal with a host of problems, of which labour was the biggest. A huge workforce was needed to clear the forests for digging, planting, weeding and plucking. The locals were unwilling to work as labourers; they found the work difficult. However, after a ban was imposed on gold washing, a large section of unemployed Kacharis were compelled to work in the tea gardens. Other tribes, including the Nagas, joined as well.

With the help of the Chinese tea makers, Charles was training several locals, but with the number of tea gardens increasing rapidly, there was a growing demand for more labour. The Company, meanwhile, was trying to recruit Chinese coolies, tea makers and skilled workers. In 1839, fifteen Chinese men from Calcutta were sent to work in the gardens. This was followed by more men from the Chinese neighbourhoods of Calcutta. The tea committee had also made arrangements to recruit Chinese labourers from Malaya, Singapore and Penang, as well as from the infamous coolie depots of Macao.

The Chinese did not know any other language and so the Company employed Lum Kwa, an expert in Chinese medicine from Calcutta, as an interpreter. When Lum Kwa arrived in June 1840, he brought eighteen Chinese workers with him.

Lum Kwa was not in Assam now. He had returned to Calcutta to receive more Chinese coolies who were supposed to arrive from outside India.

It was almost noon. Four Chinese men were eating rice with chopsticks and drinking tea under a shack. The locals stared at them. The deft movement of their chopsticks and the quick manoeuvring of the rice from their bowls to their mouths held people spellbound. Charles was eating porridge and fruits, and sipping hot tea under the shade of a tree. Soon he would leave for Keheng, with the two Chinese tea makers, while the tea experts would stay on in Naoholia. Tea factories had been constructed in Keheng and Tingrai, where the tea makers produced tea using leaves collected from different gardens. But because of the distance, the tea leaves tended to rot. Charles was sure he would be able to sort out this problem as soon as more tea makers were brought in and the local men properly trained.

By the time Charles and the tea makers reached Keheng, the labourers had got everything ready. The large clay ovens were already fired up. In the leaf house, the labourers were clapping continuously, with the raw leaves in their hands. The house was full of the rhythmic sound of clapping.

The workers were constantly being instructed by the tea makers on the correct procedure. Charles started noting everything down; he was preparing a report on tea production. After going through the whole process, the leaves finally became dark and dry and bitter to taste. Charles followed the experts to the drying sheds.

In another shed, the tea was being packed in crates. The labourers first pressed the leaves with their hands. Then, with socks on, they stuffed the tea in the crates with their feet.

Night had fallen by the time Charles climbed onto his horse to return to Tingrai.

Just a few hours before this, after a long and arduous voyage, the ship that carried Ho Han and Ho Yen arrived at the Calcutta port.

Seven

A phaeton pulled by horses was leaving Bow Bazaar in Calcutta and going towards the shipyard. Seated on the buggy was a thin, middle-aged Chinese man. On his lap he held a medium-sized wooden box. His name was Lum Kwa. He lived in the area and was an expert in Chinese medicine. He was on his way to the Hooghly harbour, where the ship carrying Chinese coolies had just docked. He had been entrusted with the responsibility of looking after these men.

A trader named Yi Kan had brought over these labourers. The Assam Company counted on him and a few other men to bring Chinese labourers from Penang and Singapore.

Lum Kwa, who had been appointed manager and interpreter by the Assam Tea Company, would take the Chinese to Upper Assam.

At the entrance to the Armenian dock, an aged Chinese man stopped him.

'I came to see you. Where are you going? Have you eaten your meal?'

Lum Kwa smiled gently in reply and said, 'A lot of Chinese coolies have come in today, to work in the tea gardens. I have come to receive them.'

'Yes, I know. How long will you have to stay here?'

'I don't really know,' Lum Kwa replied. 'As long as these coolies keep arriving. They don't understand any language other than their own.'

'Where will they be put up? We will come to see them.'

'There is a coolie depot at the docks. But perhaps they will be kept in Howrah. You will have to cross over if you want to visit.'

'Why do they have to be sent there? There are depots here, too.'

'Last time they were here the Chinese picked a quarrel. But tell me, how is your leather factory doing?'

'Things are fine. But we will have to employ more men. A leather factory needs a lot of workers. And to make shoes we need even more. Besides, I have started manufacturing other things too. So, I'm planning to bring my brothers. I might bring other men from my village as well.'

'With a ship plying between Calcutta and Kwangtung, things have become so much easier, haven't they?'

'Yes, that's right. So many people migrating to these parts. It's a hard life in China these days.'

'But if you go to China, make sure you come back married. How long can you live alone? Our brothers here are all married and have families.'

'Yes, I suppose I'll have to marry in China. I don't want to marry any girl here. Neither do they know our traditions nor do they speak the language well. I actually came here to meet you. The police have taken away Ming Chiu and Kai Fung.'

'What for?'

'Yesterday, they were bursting crackers for New Year. The carriage horses got frightened and bolted. There was chaos in the street. When the police found out, they arrested the two. The crackers were still strewn in front of the shop when the police arrived. Ming Chiu pleaded that the shop was not his. That he didn't know anything about the crackers. Kai Fung showed the licence that he'd been given by the police. But the licence was for dancing and singing, not for fireworks, he was told. Is there anything you can do? They have sent me to request you for help.'

'Yes, I suppose something will have to be done,' Lum Kwa said. 'I'll drop in at Lal Bazaar later, if possible.'

It was noon by the time he reached the shores of the Hooghly. The huge schooner, the *Oriental Pearl*, had just docked at the port.

On the deck stood coolies from Singapore, Penang and Macao. According to the terms of their contract, they had all been paid an advance for the voyage. This advance had to be returned once they started earning. After the fare and the food were paid for, Yi Kan felt that he was left with very little profit. So he lined up the men on the deck, and forced them to return a part of the advance they had been given. The men were unhappy about this but they did not protest because this was a new place and they knew no one but him.

On the deck, clutching their bundles, stood Ho Han and Ho Yen, curiously taking in their surroundings.

So, this was Calcutta Port!

They stared at the Hooghly Bridge in amazement. They were surprised to see the huge houses along the river, as well as the various boats that lined the shores, and the teeming crowds. It was not as though they had never seen a city, but it had been a long time ago. They no longer remembered how many years had passed since they left that city in South China where Ho Han and Ho Yen had worked from daybreak to sunset as slaves to the butcher. The days, months and years seemed jumbled up.

All they did was slog. There wasn't time for tears either. Perhaps, if they had stayed on with the meat seller, they would have found freedom. Ho Han might have had his own shop in the Thirteen Factory marketplace. It was because they ran away that they had met with such disaster.

After that first night of horror, they had stayed another three nights at Lintin Island and each night new recruits were brought in. Finally, when there was no more space left at the bottom of the ship, their voyage began. They were given one meal of rice and water every day. There was no air, and no light. In between, the armed guards came and took away the dead and the dying steeped in excretion and vomit.

Ho Han had no idea where they were going. The waves of the South China Sea rocked the ship and caused havoc among the captives. Their insides rattled with every movement. Finally, when the iron lid to their hellhole was opened, it was noon. The men climbed out towards the light, staggering from weakness. The guards with their whips and long muskets made them stand in a row.

Shielding their eyes from the intense sunlight, Ho Han and his companions walked forward, being pushed and ordered by the guards.

'What place is this?' they asked.

'This is the Prince of Wales Island in Penang. This is a British colony,' someone said.

Getting off the ship and inhaling the clean, fresh air, they thought their miseries had come to an end. But they were sadly mistaken, for an even worse plight awaited them.

Penang was a major distribution centre for the coolie trade. The group from the junk was taken straight to the coolie depot, which was nothing but a row of low window-less shacks that looked like cages. The cages were already full. After the men and women were shoved inside, the doors clanged shut. Ho Han and his companions found themselves in yet another prison. It was unimaginably filthy. Some people cried, others banged their heads on the walls to be let out. Those that shouted the most were taken out and given a whipping. They came back, their bodies covered in blood. Others, dead from the torture, were taken away to be thrown into the sea.

But Ho Han and Ho Yen and a few others survived this harrowing plight. And then one day, the doors of the cages opened. They were taken to the auction centre where labour agents with bags of silver hanging from their wrists were waiting for them.

Ho Han and Ho Yen were bought by the agent of a well-known family of Penang who owned tin mines. They were then taken to Phuket to work as coolies in the mines.

The coolies were housed in rows of shacks. There was a roll call every morning and then again in the afternoon. The shacks were watched over by guards armed with whips and muskets. The barracks were divided into small rooms without any ventilation. In each of these, two to three families were kept together.

Ho Han and Ho Yen worked alternately as tin-mine coolies, or under Cantonese blacksmiths and carpenters. They had no scope for rest, happiness or hope. They had no dreams for the future. Like animals, their day began and ended with work. Sleep came instantly to their fatigued bodies. Countless days and nights passed by in this manner. In utter despair, many of the coolies committed suicide. Many took to opium and destroyed themselves. When Ho Han started thinking that his life would end in the tin mine, Yi Kan arrived. He chose Ho Han and his companions from amongst the Chinese coolies and made a new agreement with them to take them to Calcutta. In the last few years they had become proficient in wood and iron work. On what terms the owner of the tin mine agreed to hand them over, they did not know.

Of the people that were picked by Yi Kan, some were ordinary coolies, some were good at wood and iron work, while others were proficient in tea cultivation. They were told that they would have to go to Calcutta, and would be better off than the other coolies. They got an advance of three months' salary from which Yi Kan deducted the cost of their food, although this was against the rules.

As soon as the transaction was complete, the coolies disembarked. Besides Lum Kwa and the manager of the coolie depot, there were others who waited to receive them. These included the field assistant of the gardens in Assam, Daffield, and the third assistant Powell. Yi Kan was also with them. These were important and expensive coolies. Losing even one would be a loss for the company as well as for Yi Kan.

Just before this another ship had docked at the port and a number of young British women wearing loose gowns and hats had got off. They, too, stood around looking at the scene before them with unabashed curiosity. Then they boarded the phaetons that were waiting to receive them.

'These are unmarried British girls who have come here to get married,' Lum Kwa explained to Ho Han and his companions, who were staring wide-eyed at the women.

'They've come here to get married?' Ho Han asked in surprise.

'British girls come here quite often. Many of the Britishers who come to work here are bachelors. Where would they find British girls here? That is why the girls come, knowing full well they will soon find a husband.'

'But how will that happen?' Ah Chin, one of Ho Han's companions asked in surprise.

'There will be dances and if the men and women like each other, they will get married.'

'Hai ah! Hai ah!' they all nodded.

Pointing towards another ship, Lum Kwa explained, 'That ship is bringing in a lot of ice from a distant country.'

A number of men carrying palanquins stood around. These men were Oriya – they had shaved a part of their heads and made little knots with the long hair that remained. Some of them were already in knee-deep water, trying to attract customers coming down from the boats to their own palanquins. On the roadside under the shade of trees, men were playing cards. A few of the palanquin bearers joined them and played bagh-bandi. Some men with their dancing bears were amusing crowds of spectators for a little money.

Walking past these sights, Ho Han's group reached the coolie depot. These depots were better than the ones in Penang, and it was from here that the assembled coolies, from different parts of India, were dispatched abroad.

'Ho Han!'

Ho Han looked back to find Yi Kan waiting.

'Come here.'

As Ho Han drew close, Yi Kan said, 'Don't enter the depot just now. Go to this man's house instead. I will join you in a while. I have something important to discuss with you.'

'Only with me?' he asked in surprise.

'Yes, go with this man.'

Worried, Ho Han asked, 'What is it that you want to talk about?'

'I'll tell you at his house. Go quietly without telling anyone. There is nothing to be worried about.'

Ho Han tried to read Yi Kan's face. Was there any sign of deceit? It was difficult to tell.

'I'll tell just Ho Yen,' he said. 'Or else he will keep looking for me.'

Pondering for a moment, Yi Kan said, 'Alright. But no one else should know.'

Ho Han went to tell Ho Yen, after which he got into a phaeton and left with Lum Kwa.

'Are you worried?' Lum Kwa asked him.

Ho Han shook his head uncertainly.

He was looking around wide-eyed. The tall brick houses, Fort William, the headquarters of the East India Company, the huge fields, the clean, broad roads with their beautiful lamp-posts, the attractive horse buggies, the bullock carts, palanquins, and the highroads filled with pedestrians – Ho Han was spellbound.

'How did you first come here?' he asked Lum Kwa.

'That's a long story. I'll tell you another time. There are almost four hundred Chinese families here.'

'Four hundred families?' Ho Han was surprised. 'Were they also bought?'

'No, they were not bought. Why would the traffickers want to buy Chinese men? Can't you see how Indian coolies are bought to be sold in other countries? You have been brought here for cultivation. People here don't know about tea farming.'

'Then why have our Chinese people come here?'

'I've heard that in the eightieth year of the last century a Chinese called Yong Atchew first came here to live. He set up a sugar mill. He brought with him a hundred Chinese men who knew how to make sugar. But the mill was a failure and a few years later, Yong Atchew passed away. However, the workers stayed on. Some Chinese sailors who ran away from their ships also stayed on here and in this way a lot of people from China, especially from Kwangtung, came to be residents in this city. It's miserable there, with the ongoing opium wars. Now there will be even more people migrating. But there is plenty of work and people get enough to eat. Our people have all kinds of skills and can work hard. It's this opium addiction that is the root of all evil. Where was your home?'

'My home,' Ho Han stopped short. After a while he shook his head and said, 'No, I don't have a home. I was sold as a child.'

'Oh! Doesn't matter. There is always a quota of sorrow in everyone's life. Some have a little more of it and some have less. You can think of me as your relative. Maybe an uncle, or even your father.'

Ho Han looked at him in disbelief. Were there really people who could speak this kindly?

Uncomfortable with these emotions, he changed the subject. 'This place is not like Kwangchow – the roads are much wider.'

'There are narrow lanes too, you will see.'

The rhythmic sound of the horses' hooves and the tinkle of their bells punctuated their journey. The phaeton passed through the clamour of drunken menials and the prostitutes who stood on both sides of the road.

After a while Lum Kwa spoke, 'Our people have opened shoe shops in Calcutta. Most people here are crazy about shoes made by the Chinese. But there are still those who will not wear shoes made from calf leather.'

'Why?' Ho Han asked.

'Because the Hindus worship cows. In this country there are high castes and low castes. Only the workers from the low castes work with leather. It is difficult to find skilled workers to make shoes. It is due to this that our Hakka shoemakers are at an advantage. They are rich. They have their own factories, and have brought a lot of their own kin from China, to take advantage of the job opportunities.'

'Are there Cantonese here as well?' asked Ho Han.

'Yes. Most of them do woodwork. Apart from being good at making furniture, they also build houses. The Chinese carpenters here enjoy a good reputation. Do you know any carpentry?'

'Yes, a little.'

'That's good. I'll arrange for you to learn woodwork. When your contract is up, you can work on your own.'

'Everyone says that but they don't let us go. As soon as one contract is over, they force us into another.'

'They may not. It is too early to say. That over there is Lal Bazaar Thana. It's the Calcutta police headquarters.' They now entered Bow Bazaar. 'And over there is my medicine shop,' Lum Kwa pointed out. A two-storied wooden house stood beside the road. A young boy sat outside with bottles of Chinese medicines.

Getting off the phaeton, Ho Han followed Lum Kwa into a small lane. The ambience here was completely different. Light filtered out through the closed windows of houses on either side. From each of these, one could hear the beats of the tabla and the tinkling anklets on the feet of nautch girls. Well-decorated phaetons carrying aristocratic men stood before these houses, giving the place a rather mysterious air.

Lum Kwa and Ho Han went further inside into a narrow lane where Chinese families lived. Ho Han entered Lum Kwa's house to find Yi Kan seated there, drinking tea. Looking at Ho Han, he said, 'We have actually brought you here for a special reason. It was difficult to talk in front of all those people at the depot.'

'What do you want to talk about?' Ho Han asked, somewhat worried now.

Hesitating for a moment, Yi Kan said, 'Although we told you that your agreement was for Calcutta, you will actually have to go further.'

'Further? Where?' Ho Han was stupefied.

'There is a place called Assam some distance away, where there are tea gardens. That's where you will go. The people who have come with you may be reluctant. You will have to convince them. They all seem to listen to you. There will be no problems in Assam. As a matter of fact, you will be in greater comfort there. You'll know after you reach.'

Ho Han was stunned. He understood that once again they had been duped by the traffickers. Yi Kan told them that he was taking them to Calcutta. But he would take them to a wretched place for much harder work for sure.

Was there any use protesting now? They were indentured labourers bound by legal obligations. They had signed an agreement and had taken money in advance. They could not say no.

After a long while Ho Han looked up. Both the men were watching him intently. Ho Han slowly shook his head.

'If I tell them about going further, they will be very angry. I won't be able to reason with them. You do the reasoning. Why did you lie to us?'

Before Yi Kan could answer him, a local man arrived on the scene. 'The Chinese are fighting amongst themselves, as well as with all the people in the depot. It's difficult to make out what is happening,' he said anxiously.

Yi Kan stood up instantly and, looking at Lum Kwa, said, 'You better come too. I may not be able to handle this on my own.'

The Chinese at the depot were restless. They did not understand each other's dialects – there were Hakka, Cantonese, Hubei, Shantou and Shantung people among them. They had surrounded the depot manager and were creating a commotion. Some were arguing amongst themselves. In a corner, five injured men sat crying, while the armed guards started beating the coolies with sticks, trying to keep them away from the manager. In another corner stood a confused Daffield and Powell.

No sooner had Yi Kan arrived than the coolies pounced on him.

'We were told that we were to work in the tea gardens at Calcutta,' they shouted. 'Now we are being told that we have to travel for three more months, to a place called Assam, infested with wild animals, and without roads.'

'Who told you all this?' Yi Kan roared.

'Isn't this true?'

'You have to go to Assam. It's true. It is written in the agreement. But Assam is not a bad place. You will get much better wages there.'

'Why have you duped us? Why have you lied and brought us here? We will not go anywhere from Calcutta. Give us the money you have taken from our advance. Send us back to where we came from.'

'Where is Assam in the first place? What is the route? How far is it?'

Ho Han tried to reason with them.

'What will you do by going back? We have no right to go back. We have signed an agreement. If we refuse to go, they will punish us. They have spent so much money to bring us here. Do you think they will spend even more to send us back? They will kill us if we say we want to return. What will we do in this unknown place? Who will listen to us?'

The men bagan to nod slowly.

'Don't fight. What is the use of fighting? Yi Kan deceived us despite being a Chinese. For men like him we are nothing but commodities. We are coolies. Wherever we are, we have to work. What is the difference whether we work in Assam or Calcutta? No one will spare us, so try to understand. We have to live in amity. We have to look after ourselves.'

The men listened attentively to Ho Han. Their eyes brimmed with tears.

'Right. Right,' they nodded.

Lum Kwa came forward, 'Ho Han is right. You should all have looked at what you signed. If you refuse to go now, you will only end up in trouble. Assam is not like Calcutta. It is full of jungles. I live there now. I have come here only to take you along. There are already some Chinese people in Assam. Some of the locals look just like us. The place is also a lot like the interiors of China. So, stop fighting. Ho Han is right. Wherever you are, you have to work. You have already endured enough hardship. I think you will suffer less in Assam than in your previous place of work. You will be able to live more freely. At the end of your agreement, you can decide for yourself whether you want to go back or continue working there.'

Daffield and Powell came forward. Discussing the matter with them, Lum Kwa spoke again, 'To get back the money you have paid Yi Kan, these gentlemen have asked you to appeal to the court. They will tell you what to do. Meanwhile, they have asked you to stay quiet. They have promised to look after you.'

After this the crowd calmed down, and Lum Kwa turned his attention to the injured.

The shores of the Hooghly slowly became quiet with the onset of night. The boats and ships floating on the river and the lights from the surrounding houses lent an ethereal air to the place.

On the mud floor of the coolie depot, a tired and injured group of pigtailed youth, clad in hemp, sat down to eat. A team of armed guards waited outside to transfer them to the depot in Howrah.

Eight

Green. Green everywhere. On one side of the huge tea garden Ho Han was making furniture on the verandah of a spacious single-storied quarter made of wood, bamboo and thatch. There was a long wooden box full of Chinese tools next to him. This was the house of the tea garden manager. Ho Han built it with help from Ho Yen and another Chinese fellow named Ah Chin.

The manager's bungalow was quiet. A Kachari worker was repairing the bamboo fencing around the spacious compound. Another worker was mowing the lawn. Ho Han was working by himself with deep concentration. There wasn't any trace of joy on his youthful face. Hard work and lack of nourishment had shadowed it. A long time had elapsed since their arrival in Assam.

They were now used to this way of life. Having already picked up a smattering of Hindustani and Bengali in Calcutta, they were now trying to learn the local dialect. When they were at the Howrah depot, Lum Kwa tried to teach them a bit of the local language and impart some knowledge about Chinese medicines. It was not easy trying to teach them new things, for most of them had suffered terrible cruelty and hardships and had lost all inclination to learn.

At the end of their long boat journey over the Brahmaputra, the group had been taken to the company's headquarters and there they were assigned to different tea gardens. The men were put to work felling trees, digging trenches, plucking tea leaves, and building houses. They were sent wherever there was a need. In a new place, with unusual food, unheard-of diseases, and gruelling work, the men were exhausted and weak. They feared never seeing their homeland or their loved ones again. In the beginning, some of them rebelled and refused to work. Gradually they came to accept their fate and this place as their own. The world they had left behind was slowly passing into obscurity. They did whatever was asked of them without any protest. Their infinite sighs had mixed with the air of the tea gardens of Assam. A million drops of their sweat mixed with the freshly dug soil of the gardens. Uncountable days and nights had passed in loneliness, in the small thatched huts assigned to them.

Years had gone by since Lum Kwa's death. Charles Bruce was no longer with the Assam Tea Company. It had been quite some time since he had been dismissed. The scenario in Upper Assam had changed drastically. Large tracts of dense forest had been cleared and tea gardens had been set up.

Disturbing the peaceful quiet of the compound, the manager's horse stopped in front of the bungalow. In seconds, the stable boy came running from somewhere. The manager got off his horse and walked into the house.

'Hey Big John, come here. *Idhar aao*,' he called.

Leaving his job, Ho Han appeared before him with his head down.

'Go to the machine room,' the manager said and gestured with his hands. He explained through a mix of gestures and words that Ho Han was needed at the factory. He would know what it was once he got there.

Without uttering a word, Ho Han saluted and left. He walked through the small lane of the tea garden. On both sides, male pluckers were at work. The garden had been made by cutting the tea plants at the height of three feet. Now they were almost double the height. The workers plucking the leaves from those trees were soaked in sweat. They were all local labourers working under a local supervisor. Some distance away, a group of workers was cleaning and weeding a newly planted area. The European assistant manager was supervising with a short steel-tipped stick. He looked annoyed.

All the work had to be done with fewer workers. The local labourers did not want to work. They ran away whenever they got a chance. But the expansion of the tea gardens was in full swing. European tea traders were attracted to the tea business after Assam tea had been accepted at the London tea auction. Many European traders came to Assam after that to start a business in tea cultivation. The East India Company began to lease out thousands of acres of wasteland to European traders and a few local people who were interested in tea cultivation.

But as the number of plantations increased, the company began to face a shortage of labour. The region was sparsely populated. The locals were unwilling to work and difficult to manage. The Chinese coolies and carpenters were expensive.

There were not many Chinese tea makers at the time. Of these, some were experts at making black tea, while others were good at making green tea. The other Chinese were a mixed lot – packers, lead-canister makers, carpenters, and the rest coolies. In the beginning, a skilled Chinese tea grower had been a necessity. But now that some locals had already been trained by the experts, the tea traders did not feel the need for skilled Chinese people now. Since Lum Kwa was also not there to manage the Chinese workers, whom the tea planters considered aggressive and rigid, the company had stopped bringing in Chinese coolies.

The European tea planters were desperately on the lookout for labourers. In place of the Chinese workers, the recruitment of coolies from different parts of British India was on. The Indian labourers would be arriving in a day or two. Ho Han and his group had constructed rows of thatched houses with the help of local workers for the new recruits.

Ho Han and the others remained indispensable because of their unmatched dexterity. The making and maintenance of tea garden machinery and tools was done by the Chinese. There was no work as such that Ho Han could not do. As a result, the manager gave him some importance and whenever Ho Han demanded something, he paid attention. A Chinese tea grower called Ah Mong had set up the first experimental tea plantation in Chabuwa, where he taught Ho Han the nitty-gritties of tea cultivation. Ah Mong had bought this garden from the company. Unable to maintain it, he sold it to a trader called James Warren. This happened after Ho Han had left Chabuwa for Keheng.

Ho Han met a group of labourers returning from work. They looked at the short, slant-eyed, fair Chinese man with a pigtail who looked as much a stranger to them as the fair-skinned Europeans, though not as scary. He was also a labourer like them.

Ho Han smiled gently at them.

'Where are you going?' one worker asked.

'Machine room. How are you?'

'I'm well, how about you?'

'Good, good.'

'Hey Chinese brother, Ah Chin is going to die from smoking opium. Control him.'

'He doesn't understand. No way out.'

'Take care of him,' a worker said as the group moved on.

Ho Han turned right to go to the factory. He felt bad about Ah Chin. His health was going from bad to worse. He didn't listen to anyone. These days, he would smoke opium, silently perform his tasks, and sit around hopelessly.

Ho Han entered the factory. Ho Yen, who was standing there, smiled at him.

'What's the problem? Why has the manager sent me here?'

Ho Yen took him to the rolling table and showed him the problem. In ten minutes Ho Han had repaired the machine.

'Where is Ah Chin?' he asked.

'He has gone away. He did not want to work today, so the manager beat him. He said he would throw Ah Chin in jail if he continued like this.'

'I think that was the reason I was asked to come here. Where has he gone?'

'I don't know. Perhaps to smoke opium,' Ho Yen answered sadly.

Ho Han was worried. He found Ah Chin adjacent to the garden in an opium den, a small, dark hut where a group of men were smoking silently. They were skin and bones in dirty clothes. Seeing Ho Han, they smiled. One of them asked, 'Have you come to join us?'

Ho Han did not answer. Silently he sat beside Ah Chin. This was the first time he was in an opium den. He looked around curiously.

The people sat, or lay asleep around the fire. One of the smokers was chopping large betel leaves on a block of wood with keen concentration. Another was dicing a banana stem. Taking a small amount of diced and smoked betel leaves from the hanging cane tray above the fire, one of the opium addicts kept it near him. Then placing a tiny piece of cloth smeared in opium on a ladle, he started to boil it in a little water. After draining out the water, the cloth was lifted out and placed on a banana leaf. All the opium smokers looked on attentively. The water evaporated, leaving a sticky opium residue in the ladle. The man placed a bit of minced betel leaf in the ladle and tossed it over with the skewers. And then began the ritual. The man lifted a bamboo tube that had turned black with smoke and smooth from regular use. At the bottom of the tube was water; a hole was carved two and a half inches above it. Another short and narrow tube was fixed to it. The man took a small portion of the opium-smeared betel leaves and placed it on the mouth of the small tube. Then he took a log of firewood from the fireplace, lit the diced leaves with the burning red embers and immediately sucked in the smoke from the big tube. After a moment or two, he slowly released the smoke. Then he lifted a bowl of tea. Taking a sip and nibbling on a piece of jaggery he offered the tube to another person and sat leaning against the wall.

Ah Chin sat there with downcast eyes, leaning against a pillar.

'Ah Chin,' Ho Han softly called out.

'What?' he looked at Ho Han with watery eyes.

'Come, let's go home.'

Ah Chin stared at him and then looked away.

'Come, let's go.'

'I like it here. You go ahead. I'll come later.'

'No, we'll go together, come on.'

'You go ahead, Ho Han.'

'Why are you doing this? How many times should I tell you? You don't listen to me. Should anyone end their life in this way?'

Ah Chin sat silently for a while. Then he said slowly, 'But I don't want to live. What should I stay alive for?'

'I have been telling you to save money all these years but you don't seem to listen. We will also help you. You will be able to return home one day.'

Ah Chin's eyes filled with tears.

'No, I can't. You are just trying to console me. I know I'll never be able to return home. I will never be able to see my parents, or my children and their mother. I don't want to live like this. Not even for a day.'

The others sitting around watched the two men in pigtails talk in a strange language. They said nothing. They were all aware that the manager had thrashed Ah Chin today with his steel-tipped cane for refusing to work.

As long as Lum Kwa had been alive, Ah Chin had some hope for the future. Just like his fellow prisoners, he had come in the same Chinese junk as Ho Han, leaving behind his family in China. Since the day he boarded the ship, no one had seen Ah Chin smile.

Lum Kwa had told him that he would arrange for his return to China. He had started saving some money for the journey.

But after Lum Kwa's death everything went awry. Shortage of money, the absence of someone who could speak for them and escort them back to China – many people like Ah Chin had remained confined to the tea gardens.

Losing all hope of seeing their families again, men like Ah Chin were heartbroken. Some of them were now destroying their lives with opium.

Ho Han placed a hand on Ah Chin's shoulder, 'We have to live. We have to survive. Just think about the days in the tin mines. We are much better here. Here our work has value. If we work hard our life will be better than what it is now. You must try to accept this place as your home.'

Suddenly, a boy entered the room in a huff. His face was red with excitement.

'They have come. They've arrived,' he said breathlessly.

'Who?'

'Lots of people. Very dark people. People like ghosts. Scores of them. Oh my God! I cannot make out whether they are human or ghost.' The boy smiled hesitantly.

'Maybe it's the coolies,' said one of the smokers.

'The days of the local workers are over then,' another opium smoker added, chuckling.

'Come, Ah Chin, let's go and have a look.'

After getting Ah Chin to chew on a piece of ginger and drink some rice-washed water to reduce his intoxication, Ho Han took him outside. A stream of people were going towards the coolie depot instead of their quarters. They had all heard of the new arrivals but had no idea what they would be like.

They were stunned. The newcomers really were ghost-like people of all ages – covered in dirt and grime, hair matted with dust, and their dirty faces stained with tears. All of them were ill, weak and skinny. Everyone huddled together in one place with their dirty little bundles. A few of the local workers poured black tea in the bowls and other utensils that they had brought with them. Others distributed flattened rice and jaggery. The smaller children looked around in fear and hungrily ate with their dirty fingers.

They all looked cheerless, hopeless and scared. But the onlookers were in for a big surprise. Women would now work in the tea gardens! This had never happened before. It made them happy. The presence of women in the all-male tea garden would provide them some relief.

Ho Han was watching. His past was repeating itself before his eyes. He could understand the agony and anguish these people must have gone through. He knew fully well how bonded labourers were collected and transported.

'Ah Chin, we too came like them,' Ho Han said.

Ah Chin did not answer. He kept watching them.

'We are not the only ones who have suffered. There are many people like us. Look, look carefully.'

The assistant manager arrived on horseback with two gunmen.

'Move back, move back!' The gunmen shooed the people away.

The labour agent, who had come with the assistant manager, busied himself getting the coolies organized. With the arrival of these coolies, their profits would soar. These bonded labourers were not independent like the local workers – they were almost slaves. They could be employed with very low wages and their upkeep would be very cheap.

Coolies from outside Assam had started pouring in. The new chapter of the coolie supply to Assam from different parts of British India had begun. The manager beamed with satisfaction.

The assistant manager came and sat happily in his chair. His work would start after the registration of the coolies was completed. He would make the single males in the group live together with the single females whether they were willing or not. This would save on money and space. And in the future, the coolie population would also increase. This system was being used in the other gardens.

A clerk with a thick logbook, quill pen and ink pot sat on a cane stool in front of a table to register the names and addresses of the newly arrived coolies. In the garden filled with the smell of freshly plucked tea leaves, a sombre dusk set in.

Nine

'Hey Monglu! Are you dead? Aren't you going out to work? Hurry up or else I'll beat you till your skin peels off!'

It was morning. The cracked voice of Budhuwa sardar shattered the quiet of the Bilashpuria line in the coolie quarters. Everyone who belonged to the line started coming out of their rooms instantly. A fearful voice reverberated through the quarters in the labour line.

'Hey Badhna, hey Raibari, hey Masiram! Hurry up, the demon has arrived!'

The number of coolie quarters had increased considerably. Now there were women and girl pluckers alongside the men. Young boys worked as cowherds or in the nurseries to collect seeds and young girls were also put to work in the nurseries. The men did everything, including plucking.

The workers picked up their tools and the baskets. Some of them tried to leave stealthily, evading the notice of the sardar. While the labour line rose to a clamour, Phulmati sat outside in the tiny courtyard, in the warmth of the sun.

'Will you be able to go to work? Why are you sitting in the sun? Has your fever increased?' asked Suhagmoni worriedly, on her way to work.

'My head hurts, I'm cold. I don't feel well at all.'

Placing her palm on Phulmati's forehead, Suhagmoni cried out, 'Oh my God, you are burning with fever! What will you do? The sardar is shouting!'

Before she could finish, the sardar arrived.

'Phulmati, what happened? You are sitting as though you have grown roots into the soil.'

'I can't go out to work. I have a fever,' she said, sounding exhausted.

'Won't go to work? You have to. Come on. Get up. It's always "can't go to work" with you. Always excuses! Get up if you don't want a slap.'

'How can she go to work? Can't you see she is burning up with fever?' Suhagmoni pleaded with the sardar.

'You don't talk. Go to work! Go!' Budhuwa sardar shouted and sent her away.

'This sardar is not human. Only work, work and work. Whether it is fever or an upset stomach, one has to work. These people will make even the dead work to get tips from the sahabs,' Suhagmoni muttered angrily under her breath.

'Oi Phulmati, get up. I am asking you one last time. Or else I'll drag you by your hair.'

Phulmati stood up slowly and, putting her basket on her head, followed the line of workers. The sardar went to the next coolie line. For every coolie, the sardars received a commission, something between one to two paise. This was taken out of each coolie's daily wages, so even if the coolies were sick, they were forced to work. This was profitable for both the manager and the sardar.

The sardars were ex-coolies who worked as middle-men between the coolies and the management. They would often go back to their home states to recruit more coolies. With the commissions they received for each new recruit, they were richer than the other coolies. Many even owned land and cattle.

Walking slowly, Phulmati went to the section where plucking was in progress.

'The sardar did not listen, did he?' Suhagmoni asked angrily.

'Why would he listen? There will be peace only if I die.'

'Don't ever speak of such things,' said Dukhi, who was plucking leaves nearby.

'I don't have anyone. It will be good if I die.'

'Who do you think we have? There are many people like us who have no one. Our sorrows are the same. But all of us don't say that we want to die,' admonished Suhagmoni.

Phulmati didn't utter a word. Among the crowd of women and young girls, she kept plucking tea leaves with a gloomy face. The basket on her back was slowly filling up. The pressure of the strap on her forehead, from which the basket was hanging, had started to weigh her down. Emptying out all the leaves into a bigger wicker basket nearby, Phulmati started plucking again.

Next to her, Dukhi was immersed in her own grief. When the people of the famine-stricken village met the labour agent for the first time, they felt as if some angel had arrived to save them from poverty and hunger. The man dressed in fine clothes and gold accessories told them about a land named Assam where gold was found underneath trees. He also told them that there was no dearth of food and work in that land. They believed the man and followed him onto a boat. After the boat ride, they had boarded a ship. And right at that moment they understood that they had been tricked. Once the ship was stuffed with people, a journey of indescribable hardship had begun. Even now, whenever Dukhi remembered those days, she would wilt in shame. On that ship, with no privacy, Dukhi and the rest were compelled to answer the call of nature in front of everyone. Having very little to eat, they became emaciated. They withered under the sun and got drenched in the torrential rains. One after the other they fell sick: fever, cholera and the pox. Without any treatment, Dukhi's husband and her three children passed away like many others. Along with the dead bodies, the dying were also thrown into the waters.

And those coolie depots? Men and women all placed in the same rooms filled with urine and faeces that flowed through the holes. Half of the captives died. But Dukhi survived. She had survived to die a slow death.

Time had gradually made them accept their reality. The environment of the garden had changed to a great extent in these years. Now there were rows of coolie quarters, staff quarters and spacious thatched bungalows for managers, assistant managers and superintendents. Beautiful nahar trees were planted by the roads. The manager, doing his rounds on horseback with his shining steel-tipped whip, was a common sight and the whip spared not a soul who tried to stay away from work.

The Babu lines, where the clerks and the in-charges of different departments lived with their families, had nothing to do with the coolie lines; there were strict rules prohibiting any kind of close contact between them. It was the same with the managers and assistant managers – a distance had to be maintained at all times between different hierarchies. The only exception to all these rules were the Chinese. In most of the tea gardens, there were just three to four Chinese men. They operated and repaired garden machinery, made furniture and built houses. They were housed separately with special amenities.

The Chinese were now a relatively contented lot. Some started doing contract work in the tea gardens and brought in more Chinese workers to help them. They often had get-togethers at which they cooked Chinese food. Gradually the place began to feel like home to them. Most of the workers had started speaking a different dialect: a mix of the languages of different provinces of British India along with the local language and Hindustani. This made communication easy between the Chinese and the Indian coolies. The first marriage between a Chinese and an Indian coolie, Ah Chin and Dukhi, was due to take place. Ho Han was the main coordinator of the wedding. He had become popular in the coolie lines because of his patience, earnestness and gentle nature. Everyone sought his advice in times of crisis.

Today, everyone was joyous in the garden. No one had any objection to the marriage. Rather, everyone was happy that two lonely people had found their partners. The labourers, even though they were busy with work, were eagerly looking forward to the festivities. The happiest was Ho Yen. He was still the same quiet slave who used to follow Ho Han. He still did whatever Ho Han asked him to do. These days Ho Yen didn't work in the factory. He looked after the saw mill of the garden which had been brought from England a few years back. It was actually a saw bench, run with the help of a steam engine and a boiler. This was used to make planks for the tea chests and to make materials for the construction of houses. At this moment Ho Yen was working in the shed.

'Hey, Ho Yen, Ah Chin hasn't come for work, has he?' one of the workers asked.

'No. The burra sahab has given him leave for today,' answered Ho Yen.

'The old fellow must be very happy.'

'Very happy.'

'What will they look like together? One as fair as milk, and the other black as coal!' a worker said, laughing heartily.

'We belong to the same community. We are the community of bonded labourers. What difference does colour of skin make?'

A group of women passed by, leaving the smell of plucked leaves in the air. Suhagmoni and her friends were among them. They'd been standing and plucking tea leaves for hours on end and their ankles were swollen. It was hard work, yet the girls always remembered to have a good time.

Leaving their work aside for a moment, Ho Yen and the other workers looked at the girls. They, too, stared back and giggled, nudging each other. Their faces were glowing, their eyes bashful.

Apart from Phulmati, the other women were busy chatting and joking with the men.

'Hey! See how Ho Yen is staring at Suhagmoni.'

Ho Yen smiled shyly, embarrassed, while the other boys teased him. People in the garden were aware of the intimacy that had developed between them. Lately, it seemed as though people were making an effort to be happy and forget their sad past. One could hear the sound of drums floating in the air, and the sweet, maddening notes of the flute at night. Slowly but steadily, people began celebrating their own traditions and festivals. During weddings and pujas, they would decorate the mud walls of their homes in the age-old way, with natural colours mixed with the gum of the dhatura plant. They planted sage, hibiscus and other local flowers in their gardens. Boys and girls meeting secretly under the nahar trees that lined the roads had become a regular affair.

In a house near the sawmill, Ho Han was making wooden tea chests with the help of a number of Indian coolies. Winter was round the corner and it was in this cold season that tea could be put into chests.

Ho Han and the others had learned to make fine tea chests.

Chinese people continued to arrive, especially from South China. Among them, the Cantonese were skilled in wood and iron work. Most of the Cantonese came to Assam. The Hakkas were experts in leather work; most of them stayed in Calcutta. Only a few went on to Assam. Many tanneries had sprung up in Calcutta along with a number of Chinese shoe stores. A few Chinese dentists had made their way to Assam. They did not stay in the tea gardens but lived outside, opened their own clinics and came to be known for their dexterity.

Ho Han and the other Chinese workers now had considerable freedom to move around. However, the garden manager kept a watchful eye on them, so that other tea companies would not seduce them with better offers. A number of tea companies had sprouted in Assam and competition was stiff.

After finishing his work, Ho Han went to the section where Phulmati was working. She was waiting along with the others near the weigh house with her basket of tender leaves. They were all busy picking out the mature, hardened leaves from wicker baskets. Ho Han came up to Phulmati, and asked in a low voice, 'Why don't you ever smile?'

The girls standing near her smiled, but Phulmati flared up, 'I'll do as I please. How does it matter to you?'

Ho Han smiled gently, 'Don't you understand how it matters?'

Phulmati looked at Ho Han for a moment, then moved away. Ho Han waited there for a while before walking towards the manager's bungalow. A strange emotion stirred somewhere deep down in his heart for a girl from an unknown, unheard-of place.

Almost all the workers were standing in front of the manager's bungalow. The workers from the factory would be here after their shifts.

Today was pay day.

The European manager appeared on the verandah of the bungalow and stood there. The workers were not supposed to look up at him. There was a long tin pipe tied to a rope hanging from the verandah about two and a half feet above the ground. Below the verandah sat a clerk. One by one, he called out the names of the labourers. As each labourer came up to the pipe, he held out the upper part of his garment to receive his salary, which came hurtling down the pipe. Earlier, when they had just arrived, Ho Han and his companions also received their wages in the same humiliating manner. Now, they were paid with the other employees of the garden. On each salary day, Ho Han felt helpless with anger and frustration. Today, seeing the labourers receiving their wages in this demeaning way, he felt the same restlessness. He stood watching for a while, and slowly walked away.

Ho Han, Ho Yen and Ah Chin lived together in the same house. Today, for the first time after coming to Assam, Ah Chin seemed happy. Dressed in new clothes, he looked tidy and clean. Seeing Ho Han, he smiled shyly. Soon, other Chinese workers from the neighbouring gardens started pouring in, each bearing a gift for Ah Chin. The Chinese man who had come to Assam from Calcutta and had started working as a contractor, arrived with his family. Another Chinese man came with his wife – she belonged to the local Kachari community. The canister-makers and paper-makers, too, brought their families. A few of them had been to Calcutta to marry Chinese girls while some had been to China to marry or to bring back their families who'd been left behind. Many had married local women. All of them were now in Ah Chin's small house.

After tea they all headed towards the Ranchi line. It was filled with people in their best clothes waiting to welcome Ah Chin. Dukhi's house had been given a makeover. The walls of the house had been freshly plastered with mud and decorated with various colourful drawings of flowers. Hibiscus garlands hung on the door front and a charpoy covered with a sheet awaited the bride and groom, while the guests were all seated in the verandah. Dukhi, wearing a sari dyed yellow with turmeric, sat on the charpoy. Her forehead, arms and neck were adorned with various kinds of silver jewellery. These were pieces that she had secretly brought with her from her village home. She did not let go of these even under the most dire circumstances – these were her most cherished possessions.

Dukhi looked beautiful in her finery, but painful memories, still unhealed, engulfed her mind. The young girls sitting around her were giggling amongst themselves.

Right in front of her eyes, in Gualundo and thereafter at the Dhubri coolie depot, one after another, Dukhi's two children and husband had died. Only her little boy was alive. Holding him to her bosom, Dukhi had prayed to every deity she could remember to keep her son safe.

But two days after boarding the ship at Dhubri, suddenly big watery blains had appeared on the boy's body. Immediately a wave of terror had spread on the entire ship.

Small pox! Dukhi's child had small pox!

Slowly, the blains had spread. Most of it had appeared on his face. Because of the blains that had appeared inside his mouth, he couldn't eat anything. The little boy, who was unable to see, would cry, groping around for Dukhi. Eight days later, at midnight, the boy left the world. Before dying he asked for milk. Dukhi could not fulfil his last wish.

The giggling girls seated nearby couln't have guessed her misery. With all her strength, Dukhi tried to keep her composure. What was the use of telling them? No one talked about their sorrows nowadays. They tried to be happy. They tried to carry on.

Two torch flames were lit near the spot where the bride sat. People were drinking home-brewed liquor, a few of the older men were smoking hookahs, while the young girls went around serving fried fish and fried tea flowers on bits of banana leaf.

'It's difficult to understand the doings of these blasted foreigners,' Monglu grumbled to himself. Hearing this, Chomra, who was already half-drunk, giggled.

'Hey Mongla, are you drunk already, that you are grumbling away?'

Monglu lifted his drooping head and spoke, 'No, brother, it's nothing to do with getting drunk. You would be flabbergasted too, if you heard what happened.'

'Tell us.'

'Yes, I'll tell you. Do you remember Tejuram Paniwallah of Bilaspur line? Our burra sahab went and fetched a girl for Paniwallah's son from the Itakhuli garden.'

'Our burra sahab did that?' everyone joined in, surprised. They all flocked near Monglu.

'That's exactly what happened. When he heard of the match, the burra sahab of the garden was livid. Calling the girl's father to his office he told him in no uncertain terms that he couldn't get his daughter married to a man from another tea garden.'

'Really?'

'Hearing this Paniwallah was livid, too. Who was more powerful? Was it the burra sahab of Itakhuli Garden or our burra sahab? Paniwallah took his complaint to our burra sahab. He was furious. "Who the hell says so," he roared. "I'll go and get that girl for your boy."'

'Oh!'

'Our burra sahab rode all the way to Itakhuli and thundered at their burra sahab. "You've got to let that girl marry our boy. Our labourer had spent money over her." Then he called the girl's father and asked him if he was agreeable to the match. He said, "Yes, sir." Our burra sahab then held the girl by her hand and placed her on his horse. After that it was straight to Paniwallah's house. He deposited the girl there – that's it!'

'Wah sahab!' they all chorused.

'So much trouble for Paniwallah?'

'What are you talking about? This has nothing to do with caring for Paniwallah,' Monglu continued. 'All that the sahab cares about is getting more labourers. Don't you understand? This way he gets one more worker. Soon, there will be children and their grandchildren. There will be more labourers.'

'I see!'

'Yes, I tell you. Lakiya, Soronga, Asmai of the Saora line and the others have been smuggled in by bribing the clerks in the coolie depots,' said Monglu.

'You mean they've been stolen?'

'Yes, of course, that's how it goes.'

After some time, Ho Han arrived with the bridegroom. Instantly the atmosphere changed, with the people milling around Ah Chin and his party. Ah Chin was made to sit beside Dukhi, while the rest of the bridegroom's party sat on the charpais around, covered with clean sheets of cloth. Since there were no formal rituals, soon Ah Chin would simply place vermillion on the parting of her hair and take her away. Everyone was staring at the short, slant-eyed, fair-complexioned Chinese men, with their pigtails. Ho Yen and Suhagmoni were shyly exchanging glances.

'Jhawru bhaya, take up your drum,' somebody said to a boy in the crowd.

Dithering for a while, Jhawru went out. Soon, he returned with his drum and started beating it. It seemed as though waves of joy, so long obstructed and dammed up by sorrow, were suddenly let loose and everyone burst out singing and dancing. In the midst of this merrymaking, however, Phulmati sat quietly, immersed in her own thoughts. Suhagmoni called out, 'Hey! Phulmati, come on, you too must sing!'

Ho Han was looking at her. Glancing at him for a moment she started singing,

'*Nisuti na guni guni*
Dehiya sukhaire
Kohobo kake dukhoker batiya
Kohobo kake kohobo dhoni
Kone potiyai re
Guni guni
Mor dehiya sukhaire guni guni ...
My body withers

To whom will I speak about my sorrows?

Who will believe in my tales?

My body withers ...'

The gathering became quiet. After a while, Suhagmoni broke the silence and said, 'Phulmati, you mustn't sing such a sad song today.'

Phulmati sat quietly for a few minutes. Then, without looking at anyone, she got up and left.

Jhawru looked at Phulmati as she left. Then, with renewed vigour, he beat his drum. The people around resumed singing wedding songs with greater enthusiasm.

In the midst of all this, Ah Chin and Dukhi became husband and wife. Ho Yen and Suhagmoni quietly retreated from the wedding venue and faced each other; they stood behind a tree lest somebody saw them.

'Have you decided to never come near me?' Ho Yen smiled.

'Don't I have any other work than to come after you? Tell me what you want to say.'

'You look ill. You look thinner, too.'

'Should I be looking fat? I haven't slept a wink these last few nights,' Suhagmoni snapped.

'What happened?'

'Phulmati was ill. She has no one. So I stayed with her.'

'Is Phulmati still going to work?'

'If she doesn't go to work, what will she eat? I will go to work too, even if I have a fever. I don't have anyone either.'

'Where are you from?'

'I don't know.'

'Why don't you know? Tell me.'

'They hit me on my head. I don't remember anything. What else do you want to ask?' she smiled at him.

'You are lying. You remember. Tell me.'

'What is the use of telling you?'

'If you tell your own people, your sorrow will become less.'

'Are you my own?' Suhagmoni laughed.

'Don't laugh. If I am not your own, then who is?'

'My own is Budhuwa sardar!' Suhagmoni laughed aloud.

Looking at her smiling face, Ho Yen asked gently, 'You have a lot of sorrow, don't you, Suhagmoni?'

Suhagmoni stopped smiling. After looking at Ho Yen for a few moments, she answered gravely, 'If a bonded labourer doesn't have sorrow, who else will? The sardars or the sahabs? You are also a bonded labourer. Don't you have your own?'

'Yes. Lots of sorrow.' Ho Yen's eyes brimmed with tears.

'Don't cry. It's no use.'

'I know. When you were not here, there was a lot of sorrow, but now ...' Ho Yen's voice trailed off.

'What has happened now?'

'Don't you know?'

'How would I ...'

'My companions here tease me about you. Do you mind?'

'Why should I mind? I like it. Don't you?'

'Yes, I like it too.'

Ho Yen became silent. He didn't have enough words to express his thoughts. He still hadn't learnt the common language properly. His eyes filled with tears. Looking at his crimson face in the moonlight that filtered through the trees, she said softly, 'If you don't have anything more to say, I will go.'

'There is. There are things to say.' Ho Yen became restless. Then gathering all his courage, he said, 'I have been thinking of telling you for a long time. I don't really know how to say it. I want to marry you. Don't say no, Suhagmoni.'

Suhagmoni looked at his face for some time before she spoke. 'You like me very much, do you?'

'Yes. Very much.'

'Can you leave this country for me?'

'What? I don't understand.'

'You will, when I tell you. Can you leave?'

Ho Yen looked at Suhagmoni's eyes for some time and said slowly, 'Wherever you live, that is my country.'

Suhagmoni looked at his flushed face for a long time.

'I will tell you something. Will you listen?'

'Why not? Tell me.'

'I once had a mother and father, brothers and sisters. On a dark night, that evil contractor captured and brought me here. He gagged me and hit me on the head. I fell unconscious. When I regained my senses, I was on the boat. I want to go home. Will you take me back to my home?'

For a while Ho Yen looked at her, then asked slowly, 'Where is your home, Suhagmoni?'

'Raipur. Will you take me?'

'Yes, I will.'

The wedding venue was now full of excitement and happiness. The Keheng tea garden resonated with the sound of the drum. In the middle of the night when Ho Han was about to return home with Ah Chin and Dukhi, a whispered rumour spread across the Ranchi line – Ho Yen and Suhagmoni were missing.

Ten

The room wasn't too large. The floor was quite even. On it lay two planks of wood and placed on top of the wood was a square tile, on which was glued a very fine sheet of paper, without edges or perforation. Chalk had been rubbed on the paper to smooth out any rough edges. Another similar tile was placed over this, facing downward. Only a bit of the topmost part of the tile protruded. On that side sat Ho Han. He was making lead sheets.

In front of him, to the right, was a huge kiln. The mouth of the kiln was slightly raised from the ground. A large iron wok was placed there, in which a mixture of lead and tin was poured. After the mixture boiled, the work would begin.

Ho Han was looking at the wok with concentration. Two Chinese and two Indian coolies stood by, ready to help. These sheets were necessary to line the insides of the tea chests. While some of these sheets came from England, the rest were made locally. A long time ago the government had sent Chinese paper makers and lead-sheet makers to Charles Bruce. One of them had trained Ho Han. Now, with the old canister-maker having left for another garden, the entire responsibility was on Ho Han's shoulders.

These days the Indian labourers did all the work in the garden. The Chinese had started working under contractors. Ho Han was now the head fitter in Keheng. Ah Chin had become an expert in papermaking, which was needed to wrap the tea chests, like those in China.

Ho Han had trained two Chinese labourers to make lead sheets, and with their help, along with a few other Indian coolies, he started making lead sheets, lead canisters and tea chests. Since it was not plucking season yet, Phulmati had been coming to help him on some days. Ho Han felt like pouring his heart out to Phulmati but could not because of her impenetrable silence.

Lead sheet-making demanded absolute concentration. Phulmati's job was to remove the scum from the top of the boiling mixture with a sieve attached to a long handle.

When the metal mixture began to boil, Ho Han took half a ladle of it and, holding the upper tile with his left hand and pressing the protruding part with his heel, poured the molten metal between the two tiles. Letting go of the left hand and loosening the heel instantly, Ho Han pressed down hard with his foot, and the upper tile came down with a bang. With a steady hand, lifting the upper tile, he took out a thin lead sheet. He slung it in a corner and repeated the action.

Nobody spoke while working. In a minute Ho Han was able to prepare three lead sheets. There was no time to look around. A slight shuffle could cause the molten mixture to spread out and lead sheets could not then be made as required. He was bathed in sweat and Phulmati who was near him, by the fire, was flushed from the heat. She kept looking at Ho Han's tired face; her heart went out to him.

After working non-stop for two hours, Ho Han stopped. Phulmati, also exhausted, came outside and sat under a tree. Two coolies brought salted tea in a tin drum tied to a pole. Phulmati took a mug out from her cloth bag and filled it. She then took out some flattened rice and a lump of jaggery. Ho Han came and sat by her side. He did not like salted tea. He carried his own tea in a small container.

'Here, have some chura,' Phulmati said, passing him a handful of flattened rice.

Accepting the snack, Ho Han smiled and said, 'You don't talk, you are always angry, but you also ask me to eat chura. What is the matter?'

'Why does it bother you?'

'You know everything, yet you act as if you know nothing. How will this work?'

'Whatever will be, will be. Why does it matter to you? If you feel like eating, eat, or else go.'

'What you are saying is not from your heart.'

Ho Han smiled and got up.

Phulmati looked at him anxiously – had she hurt him?

'I am going to Makum. Do you need anything?' Ho Han asked.

'No.'

Ho Han left in a bullock cart owned by a Marwari, which was going to Makum to bring back goods for his shop. The two carts stopped in front of Nandalal Shah's shop. Nandalal had come from Bihar to do business in Makum and his shop sold everything from rice to salt. With his frequent visits, Ho Han had become friendly with him. In his free time, he had made all the furniture for his house with the help of two Chinese carpenters who stayed at Nandalal's residence. They had constructed their house on Shah's land at the back of his residence and had continued to work independently from there.

'Come in, Ho Han!' Sitting on the cotton mattress inside his spacious thatched shop, Nandalal greeted Ho Han with a welcoming smile.

He spoke in the mixed language used by the tea garden labourers, as Ho Han did not know Bhojpuri. Nandalal's employees started loading the cart with bags full of provisions for the garden. After watching for a while, Ho Han bought some vermillion, coloured ribbons, sweetened tobacco and a few necessities for himself.

Nandalal's wife, her head covered with her sari, brought milk tea for them in brass tumblers. Offering Ho Han a plate of sweets, Nandalal said, 'Here are some special ones. Taste and tell me if you like it.'

Ho Han picked up one of the sweet balls and put it in his mouth.

'It's very good! What is it?'

'It's a special sweet from Bihar that we call motichur. Have some more.'

After some small talk, Nandalal said, 'Why don't you give up the garden job and settle down here? With your skill in carpentry, you will make very good money. I have a lot of land at the back of the shop. You can come and settle there. All you have to do is pay me an amount at the end of the month and the land is yours.'

Ho Han smiled, but didn't comment. Nandalal had been making this offer to him every now and then but he'd always taken it lightly. Slowly, however, a new dream had started playing hide-and-seek in his mind. Sipping his tea in silence for a while, Ho Han asked, a little hesitantly, 'May I take a few of these sweets with me?'

'Of course! Why not?'

The cart had already been loaded. Ho Han picked up his bundle of purchase and, bidding Shah farewell, he went to the hut adjacent to the houses of the Chinese carpenters at the back of Shah's house. Suhagmoni emerged with a little boy. Gone was the glow from Suhagmoni's face. Instead, a sickly and gloomy woman stood before him. Four long years had passed since the night Suhagmoni fled from the garden with Ho Yen. They had not consulted Ho Han before taking the hasty decision.

The manager of the tea garden had a secret understanding with the caretakers of the ghats of the different rivers. They were given a substantial commission for each runaway coolie they caught. Ho Yen and Suhagmoni were unaware of this understanding. They were caught right away and taken back to the garden. A law had been passed to punish the runaway labourers. The planters had the right to arrest a runaway labourer without any warrant within the district. The managers also retained the right to arrest and punish them. Armed with the law, the manager of the Keheng tea garden brought Ho Yen and Suhagmoni to his bungalow. In the presence of workers and the other staff, he caned and whipped them both black and blue. Ho Han tried his best to save them but failed. Both of them were sent to jail. Ho Yen died in jail. Suhagmoni returned completely destroyed, physically and mentally. She was pregnant by then. The manager threw her out, for he did not want a pregnant woman without relatives. Ho Han took her to Nandalal Shah's house in Makum, where she delivered a baby boy. Suhagmoni now worked for Shah.

After chatting with her for a while, and giving her a little money and the things he'd brought for them, Ho Han left. By the time he reached Keheng, the work in the garden was winding up. Getting off the cart in front of the crowded opium store adjacent to the garden, Ho Han went to the house where the withering of tea leaves was in progress. He looked around for Dukhi. She was coming out after finishing her shift. She now looked so beautiful – there was a contented glow on her face. With their three-year-old daughter, Dukhi and Ah Chin lived on a different side of the garden now. She had succeeded in slowly weaning Ah Chin off his opium addiction. He now smoked tobacco in a hookah. He had also visited his old home, near Kwangchow in China. Dukhi had slowly changed his life for the better.

'What is it?' she asked brightly, coming forward.

'Finished your work?'

'Yes. I'm on my way to get my ration from the burra gola. Ah Chin will also be coming.'

'I'll go with you,' said Ho Han. They walked in a companionable silence for a little while.

'How is Ah Chin?'

'Don't ask me about him. Perhaps it would have been better if he hadn't gone to China after all.'

'Why?'

'He keeps weeping. He talks of his children back in China and weeps. He remembers his parents who died long before he went there and weeps. Then he remembers his wife in China and weeps. If he keeps on weeping like this, he will land himself in the opium den again for sure. I've told him – if you are bent on weeping, go ahead and weep. If you want to go to China one more time, do that. If you want to bring back your wife and children with you, do that too. But if I ever see you again near the opium den, I'll play the Nagara drum on your back.'

Ho Han smiled.

In most of the coolie lines now, the Marwaris had opened up shops. The locals and the coolies called them 'keya golas'. In every garden, there was a big shop known as 'burra gola' which was responsible for distributing rations on behalf of the tea garden management. The company also used them as bankers.

There had been a great increase in the number of coolie lines. Coolies were still coming in from different parts of British India. With the number of the coolies increasing at a rapid pace, the exploitation of their lot had also intensified. The insides of the coolie lines were shadowed by dissatisfaction. Clashes between the managers and labourers had become a daily affair. The managers were in favour of controlling any rebellion with an iron fist. For them the coolies were nothing but slaves who could be whipped and kicked at will.

Only two months ago, a manager of a tea garden had caned a runaway coolie woman to death. In Keheng itself, the manager had thrashed two coolie boys as he suspected them to have secret liaisons with his coolie keep. The same manager, after a few days of that incident, kicked another coolie, who died on the spot.

A new manager had joined after that, but he was worse than his predecessor.

The coolies who were compelled to live in subhuman conditions in the gardens tried to tolerate the torture. They knew they were on the weaker side. Neither the owners of the gardens nor the law or the administration was sympathetic towards them. Even the smallest protests resulted in torture.

Dukhi and Ho Han halted in front of the ration house near the burra gola. There was a long queue of labourers in front of the house; there was no door to go inside. In its place was a big tube made of tin. The broad mouth of the tube was inside the house. The labourers had to bend to collect their rations coming down the tube, as it was placed two and a half feet above the ground.

They found Ah Chin standing outside holding his daughter's hand. Ho Han and Ah Chin were delighted to see each other. He gave the two packets to Dukhi, one containing vermillion and coloured ribbons and the other containing sweetened tobacco.

'This one is for you and Mini, and this one is for Ah Chin.'

'So many things!' Dukhi said, smiling broadly. 'You haven't come to our place for a long time. Make sure you come soon.'

'I will.'

After chatting with them for a while and fondly stroking the little girl's hair, Ho Han left. He walked on absent-mindedly. His mind was occupied with thoughts of Phulmati. Slowly, the image of a home and a family with Phulmati had started to take shape in his mind. The loneliness had become unbearable. He had to speak to her as soon as possible. She, too, was confined in the deep darkness of sorrow. She had lost all desire to live. Ho Han could understand that. He wanted to bring all the happiness of this world to her and wipe away her tears.

Suddenly, a shrill cry that seemed to come from the direction of the manager's bungalow brought him back from his thoughts.

He rushed towards the bungalow to find a large group of people standing around.

'What happened?'

'Burra sahab is flogging Jankee, Birosmoni and Phognee.'

Pushing his way through the crowd Ho Han went forward to see three women tied to a post in the verandah of the bungalow. In front of the fearful eyes of the entire crowd, the manager, red with rage, was flogging the women.

'Speak again, I say, speak again! Why are you silent now? Why don't you speak?'

There was complete silence except for the sound of flogging, the manager's growling and the women's howls for mercy.

'*Maph koro hujur. Maph koro*. Forgive us.'

Watching the scene for a while Ho Han asked the man by his side, 'What's the matter?'

'I don't know for sure.'

After sometime, the manager stopped. Standing silently for a few moments, he turned to the chowkidar.

'Hey! You! Come here.'

The chowkidar stepped forward, trembling with fear.

'*Kapra uthabe, kapra*. Hey, lift their clothes,' the manager commanded.

The chowkidar was stupefied.

'Lift their clothes. Now.'

With trembling steps he walked towards the women. They looked at him, eyes wide with fear and wailed, 'Don't do it, chowkidar. Don't do this to us.'

The chowkidar looked at the women for some time and made them bend forward and lifted their clothes up to their waist. In front of the uncountable eyes, the manager started flogging the bare buttocks of the three young women.

The labourers were in utter dilemma. Some lowered their heads. Some stood still with stiff faces and tight fists. The women laboures started weeping. Watching silently for a few moments, Ho Han stepped forward. He stood in front of the manager and said calmly, '*Mot maro, hujur*. Don't flog them.'

The manager turned around and thundered, 'What did you say? Don't flog them? Who the hell are you?' Then recognizing Ho Han, he stopped for a moment and bellowed again. 'Oh, it's you! But I will flog them, what can you do about it?'

Ho Han looked him in the eye, and calmly answered, 'I'll stop making lead sheets.'

The manager stood still in shock. Ho Han was the tea garden's one and only lead-sheet maker. He was the head fitter too. The manager could neither provoke nor antagonize him. Throwing the whip away in disgust, he walked inside the bungalow.

Ho Han released the women. Covering their faces with their hands and sobbing wildly, the women walked out, utterly drained. The women and girls who were assembled outside came and surrounded them. The situation changed instantly. The coolie lines became agitated. After sometime, the enraged labourers came out of the lines with their bows and poison-tipped arrows. The manager called the police. The sardars entered the coolie lines to pacify the labourers. In all this commotion, Phulmati and Ho Han were not to be found. They were sitting on the quiet banks of a nearby river.

'Everything there was in order. Ma was there. Baba was there. Two brothers and one sister too. I couldn't even imagine that I would come to such a country. One day, our Jagnu uncle came and told me, "Let's go to the fair." Ma said, go! Who could think this would happen? Had I not gone out with my uncle, nothing like this would have happened to me. Jagnu mama sold me to the trafficker Arkathia. And then everything went downhill ...' Phulmati cried her heart out. After some time, Ho Han took her hand and said,

'Don't think like that. Who doesn't have sorrow? Still, we have to live. Think about these tea bushes. Don't you think they're sad? A tree which was as tall as four men put together is cut to the size of half a man. But the tea tree did not die of that sorrow. Instead, it branched out from its sides. The tree did not die. It lived. We too have to live.'

Gently, he took Phulmati into his arms and said, 'Look at me. My own parents sold me. Look at the mark on my forehead. With a hot iron, my master stamped me as slave. I too have no one in this world. I too have a lot of sorrow. But I don't tell anyone.'

A flood of tears, held back for more than three decades, flowed from his eyes. 'Will you marry me, Phulmati? I can't live alone anymore.'

Someone rang the doorbell.

Lailin looked towards the door, confused.

It was a new day outside. How many hours had passed? She looked at her watch. It was half-past seven. It took her a while to understand where she was. Wiping the tears from her eyes, Lailin looked at Arunabh's book.

The bell chimed once more.

Marking the page with a pencil, Lailin went to the door. Standing outside was her father. A thin and frail old man in dishevelled clothes, he looked at Lailin from head to toe. Then, in a grave voice he said, 'Where is Mei Lin? Call her!'

Part Two

One

January, 1962. Makum, Upper Assam.

A thousand days and thousand nights had gone by. Crossing the scales of time, the chariot of history had arrived at another century. The nineteenth century was in the distant past. It was now fifteen years after India's independence.

Assam, which was under the Bengal Presidency during the days of the East India Company, was now a part of a free India. It was also no longer under the rule of the Ahom royalty. It was now a state made up of the old Assam together with the principalities of a host of native tribes like the Motoks, Koch, Singpho, Khamti, besides many other ethnic communities.

On the eastern border of Assam was a region named the North-East Frontier Agency, directly under the central administration of India. Bhutan, China and Burma were NEFA's immediate neighbours. The events of the past had changed the entire scenario of the region. A new style of governance, new laws, and new ways of life had replaced the antiquated ways of the past. Presently the state, particularly Upper Assam, was beginning to preen with the advent of modernity. Despite the changing times and fading memories of Charles Bruce, Ah Mong, Lum Kwa, Ho Han, Ho Yen and Ah Chin, tea gardens like Keheng, Chabua and many more continued to thrive.

Along with the tea gardens, the beautiful houses built by skilled Chinese carpenters remained. The Assam Railway and Trading Company, which constructed the Dibru-Saikhowa railway line, still existed. The Digboi refinery, the coal mines, the famous brick kiln of Ledo made by the British and many other establishments had stood the test of time. Until recently, licensed labour agents had been employing various means to bring labourers from different parts of India to the gardens to work in indentured servitude. The society of the tea garden labourers was now spread across the entire region of post-independence Assam. The small Chinese settlements alongside the labourers' societies were also branching out. Small and big Chinatowns were sprouting up in various parts of Assam.

Years ago, Nandalal Shah had come from far-flung Bihar to set up his shop in Makum. Two Chinese carpenters brought in by Ho Han had settled down in his backyard. Then came Suhagmoni, who was pregnant with Ho Yen's child. After that came Ho Han and Phulmati. Ho Han started constructing houses and making furniture. Ah Chin decided to stay on the tea garden. Over the years many more Chinese came to settle in Nandalal Shah's backyard and the vicinity. As the number of tea gardens added up, the demand for Chinese workmen adept in wood and iron work increased. Quite a few such skilled Chinese carpenters had come via Calcutta and Burma. Along with them had come a large number of Chinese labourers to work under Chinese contractors and carpenters. The migrants were an impoverished lot affected by famine, drought, flood and political unrest in their homeland. For food, clothes and shelter they bartered their skills and toil.

Makum now had the biggest Chinatown, known as Cheenapatti.

It was just after daybreak. Leaving the pleasant somnolence of the early morning, this peripheral region of Assam was gradually becoming abuzz with activity.

It was not only the meeting point of two railroads – it was also the intersection of two important highways going east and south. One road turned right over the level crossing, went through Digboi, Pawoi, Margherita, Ledo and Lekhapani and entered the Tirap Frontier Division of NEFA. Beyond that was Burma. The other road went ahead, parallel to the railroad and, turning left, it went beyond Doom Dooma to the last station, Dangori. This was the road that entered the Lohit Frontier Division of NEFA. The Lohit Frontier Division ended at the border between India and China, separated by the McMahon Line. In both these metre gauge lines, the trains were pulled by coal-fired steam engines. Even though Makum was a small town, it was strategically important because of its location at the intersection of two roads from where one could reach the border of two neighbouring states. The town grew around the Makum junction, the last in Upper Assam.

The marketplace was close to the level crossing. Compared to other places, Makum bazaar was a hive of activity during the day. On the right side of the train track was a row of shops. Among these were four shoe shops owned by Chinese people.

A tall, handsome young man was walking towards the shops. He was a clerk at the Samdang tea estate of the Doom Dooma Tea Company. His name was Pulok Baruah. He had come to meet Lee Chang, his friend and one-time classmate; they also belonged to the same football club. They had celebrated the wedding of their classmate Narayan Sarma's sister together just the previous night. Pulok was dressed in a black-and-green check poplin shirt with terry cotton trousers. His hair was parted to the right with a little wave in front and he sported a thin moustache. His thoughtful face and dreamy eyes glowed with youthfulness. His entire persona exuded a hassle-free life.

There was hardly anyone who didn't know Pulok and his team. They were all good football players. The superintendent of the Doom Dooma Tea Company, William Addison, who was a patron of their Seven Star Club, had personally offered him the job.

None in this area was as good in making customized shoes as the Chinese. Though the shops were small, the Chinese shoemakers were well-off. They had their own house and land in Cheenapatti. One of the shops belonged to Lee Chang's father. Lee Chang had joined the family business two years ago. He had his own shop in Tinsukia. He looked after this shop in Makum in the morning and went to Tinsukia in the afternoon.

'Hey Pulok. Come, come in.' Lao Thien Lee, the middle-aged owner of the first shop called out, smiling broadly. His small bright eyes were buried in his plump, rosy cheeks.

'How are you, ako?' Pulok asked.

'Very well, very well. Have you eaten?'

'Yes. What time did you come back from Narayan's house last night?'

'About eight o'clock. Do you know that it is Chinese New Year tomorrow?'

'Yes, yes, of course. I'll come over tomorrow.'

'Have dinner with us. In fact, after bringing my wife from China, I haven't had the opportunity to invite anyone over for a meal. You all must come tomorrow.'

Lao Thien Lee started discussing football with great enthusiasm, leaving his customers to be handled by his Chinese employees who could speak both Hindi and Assamese.

'Has Robin come home on leave?' he asked.

'Yes.'

'Well then, Seven Star will be champions again. Because of him we were able to score four goals last year, remember?'

'Robin didn't score a single goal. Liang scored one, Lee Chang two, and Tung Chin scored one goal. Don't say it was because of Robin that our club scored four goals, Lee ako – Tung Chin and the rest will thrash us.' Pulok chuckled.

'Ah ha! Who is going to say it in front of them? You also don't understand?' Lao Thien Lee whispered, laughing heartily.

After some time, Pulok left for Lee Chang's shop.

'You had quite a chat with the old man, ha!' Lee Chang laughed. 'It must have been about football, right?'

'Does he talk of anything besides football? He heard that Robin has come. He is sure that Seven Star will be champions again!' Pulok laughed loudly.

'You will go to Akong's house in the evening, won't you?'

'Yes. What about you?'

'So will I. We haven't met in a long time.'

'I've called Mei Lin to Chitta's house. Give me the bag.'

Lee Chang took out a packet wrapped in paper from under a wooden box and handed it to Pulok. Opening it, Pulok was delighted to see an exquisite purse made of beads and thin strips of polished leather. Inside, it had a velvet lining.

'Do you like it?' Lee Chang asked.

'Yes, very much. It's beautiful. Did you make it yourself?'

'Yes. It's a masterpiece. I won't make another – don't worry!'

His heart filled with joy, Pulok left the shop and took the road towards Doom Dooma. A reputed Chinese carpenter named C Hoi, was standing in front of the Chinese Club, a Chinese-style one-storey house. Seeing him, Pulok stopped. It was bustling with activity. The house was like a community centre for the Chinese people of Makum and nearby areas. It was often used for hosting marriages and other festivities. Chinese people from various places often came to stay here during the holidays and on festive occasions. They would have their get-togethers there and eat and dance and make merry.

'Come to our house tomorrow for the New Year as well as the house-warming party,' C Hoi said happily.

'We've been looking forward to seeing your new house. We'll be there for sure. What is happening at the club now?'

'We have a Chinese society meeting. A teacher from Calcutta has come to see our school. He is staying at my house. He will come here after some time. The guardians of the hostel boarders are here to take them home for the holidays. We will be having a meal together. When will the football matches start?'

'They should start by the end of this month.'

'Our club must become the champions this year too. You must play well.'

They chatted for some time and then C Hoi went back into the clubhouse. Pulok went on his way. Cheenapatti was at a bit of a distance from the Chinese club. Before he reached, he passed two small shops standing close together. One of them belonged to Chitta Biswas, the other to Johori Khan. Chitta Biswas and Pulok used to study together. Chitta was from a poor family and left his studies midway to start a business. Saying hello to Johori Khan, Pulok went to Chitta's shop.

'You didn't get any sleep, did you?' Chitta asked.

'How can one sleep? The bride left only a while ago. You got a chance to sneak out early because of your shop.'

'You'll come to our place, right?'

'Yes. Have you seen Mei Lin?'

'She has gone to Kaushalya's place. She'll be here any time now.'

'Okay, I'll be on my way then. You want to come with me?'

'I'll go after my brother arrives,' said Chitta.

After Chitta's, the two establishments were Mahabir Prasad Shah's grocery and cloth shops. Mahabir Prasad was the grandson of Nandalal Shah, who had died a long time ago. This was the oldest and biggest store on the road to Doom Dooma. Alongside the store was the big house where Mahabir Prasad Shah lived with his family. One of his sons, Thakur Prasad, was of the same age as Pulok.

'How are you? Haven't seen you in a long time!' Mahabir Prasad welcomed Pulok.

'I am well, uncle. Where is Thakur Prasad?' Pulok walked inside.

'Oh, don't ask me about Thakra. He is busy the whole day with wrestling, practising stick fights and spending time with the policemen. Only he knows why he does all these things. I am planning to get him married this year. Hope it will set him right!'

'Everything will be okay, uncle. Don't worry.'

'There is a lot to worry about. You are of the same age. You've studied. Now you are working. You also play football. Everyone knows you, loves you. You don't get yourself involved in meaningless hassles. If only my son had been like that!'

'You should make him sit in the shop with you.'

'Make him sit in the shop? If he sits in the shop who will get into brawls! My other sons are good. They are working and are settled. I tell him, not only the people of Makum, but people from far and wide knew my father and grandfather. The people loved them. Always keep in mind their respectful position. But he does not listen. Only bad stuff!'

A middle-aged Chinese woman entered the shop. She was wearing long trousers and a long top. Mahabir Prasad stopped talking and looked at her.

'I want a bar of Sunlight soap,' the woman said with a courteous smile. She took the soap, handed Mahabir Prasad one anna and left the shop with silent, graceful steps.

'That was Ho Wang's wife. They don't have children – it's very sad.' Mahabir Prasad sighed.

'I'll take your leave, uncle.' Pulok stood up to go.

'Alright. Come again.'

Pulok stepped out. This happened whenever he came through this road. Exchanging pleasantries with everyone took up a lot of his time. While crossing the lane he looked towards his left. The road through Cheenapatti was lively with people. A few Chinese women were chatting in front of their houses.

Many Chinese inhabitants had gone to the market to shop for the New Year festivities. The Makum market would be crowded with Chinese people today. Everyone knew that the Chinese loved food. In fact, many shops in the market depended mostly on the Chinese customers.

Almost facing each other, on either side of the main road leading to Doom Dooma, were the two lanes of Cheenapatti. On the other side of the railway line stood the Chinese school.

Pulok looked at the school. There were a few people on the verandah talking amongst themselves. A group of young children were playing in the courtyard. The shop-cum-restaurant owned by Mok Min near the school was full of customers.

An ex-tea garden labourer named Raghuwa Mahato, who lived inside the Cheenapatti lane, came out carrying two tins of paint. These days he cultivated his own land and did odd jobs.

'Is everything okay?' he enquired with a wide grin.

'Yes, uncle. Where are you going with these tins of paint?'

'To K. P. Lee sahab's bungalow. His wife called me. She asked me to bring two tins of paint. Yesterday, I painted Ah Fuk's sister's house and Ho Chang Ho's house too. It's going to be fun,' smiled Raghuwa.

Across the lane was Ming and Company's factory, owned by Ming Ho, one of the wealthiest Chinese men of Makum. Besides repairing tea garden machinery, the company also retreaded the machines. Next to it was K. P. Lee's factory. K. P. Lee lived with his family in the same compound.

'Lee sahab is going to buy another new car, I have heard. I don't know what he will do with so many cars. He already has two Plymouths and a Jeep. He has such a huge factory. Just go in and have a look, your head will start reeling,' Raghuwa muttered. Saying goodbye to Pulok, Raghuwa entered the compound. Several Alsatians barked from inside. Leaving the factory behind, Pulok turned left to enter a narrow lane towards Chitta's house. Chitta's wife Bela was seated in the courtyard, busy rubbing oil on her baby's body. Noticing Pulok, she covered her head with the throw of her sari.

'Please sit down, dada, while I bathe the baby.'

Chitta's mother came out of the kitchen and sat beside him. She had seen Pulok grow up. Chitta's sister Jhuma was in the kitchen garden. She hurriedly came in holding her sari and, after speaking with Pulok for a few moments, left to make tea.

At that moment, Mei Lin was talking to Kaushalya outside her house. Kaushalya was the local collector's daughter. The house stood on the right side just beyond the entrance to the lane adjacent to the Chinese school. Many Chinese families lived in this lane too. Mei Lin's friends, Siu, Alan and Mei Hang, also lived here – all three slowly arrived.

'We have just been to your house,' said Alan. 'Have you forgotten that we have to go from house to house to help make the New Year snacks?'

'Will it be okay if I come after an hour?' asked Mei Lin.

'Where are you going?' Mei Hang asked, faking gruff seriousness.

'To Chitta's house.'

'All of a sudden?'

Mei Lin's face turned red. 'Pulok asked me to go there.'

'When will you return?' Siu asked.

'She may not,' Mei Hang teased.

'Dhet,' Mei Lin smiled shyly.

'Okay, then come to our house after you're done.'

'Is this a New Year tradition – this snack-making?' Kaushalya asked.

'I don't really know. Many Chinese people here don't know how to make traditional Chinese snacks. So we help each other and also learn from those who know how to make them,' Alan said. 'You better go now, Mei Lin. Remind Pulok of our names. He might have forgotten.' Mei Hang laughed.

Mei Lin left her friends and went down the lane. On the right, in the front of the school courtyard, some students of different age groups were playing.

'Mei Lin ache ...' A little girl came running out of the compound to meet Mei Lin. 'Where are you going, ache?' asked nine-year-old Yiu Yi; her face was red and shining from exertion.

'Why have you come out? Sir will be angry,' Mei Lin said, stroking Yiu Yi's hair.

'No, he won't. School is closed today. We are just playing.'

'Do you know that your Sipahi dada is here?'

'Really? Who told you, ache?' Yiu Yi asked excitedly.

'I met him yesterday at Narayan's sister's wedding. He came just after you left.'

'Will Sipahi dada come to Makum today, ache?'

'I don't know.'

'I'll ask Chitta dada then. Oh, but if I go to Chitta dada's shop he will give me toffees and Maa will scold me if I take them.'

'Why?'

'She says I should pay for them. It's such a small shop, she says. It will close down if I keep on taking free toffees. Can a shop close down if I take a couple of small toffees? Maa doesn't understand. Chitta dada feels bad if I pay and Maa gets angry if I don't. Bohut tiktali,' she said, unable to pronounce the Assamese 'digdari'.

Mei Lin laughed too, as Yiu Yi went back to the school. In a bright mood, she crossed the railway track to reach the road.

Pulok was talking to Jhuma. Hearing the creak of the bamboo gate, Jhuma got up. It was Chitta. Asking Jhuma to make tea for three, Chitta sat down. After a while, Mei Lin walked in.

Mei Lin was wearing a mekhela-chador today. She let her straight, jet-black, plaited hair fall over her shoulders. Walking in the sun, the shyness and the excitement made her blush deeply. Pulok looked at her enchanting face with fascination.

Their eyes met for a brief moment. Mei Lin smiled and lowered her head. After chatting for a while over tea, Chitta left the room. Immediately shyness overcame Mei Lin.

'I'm seeing you after a long time,' Pulok said gently.

'Eighteen days!'

'You counted?'

Mei Lin looked at Pulok. A few moments passed in silence.

'I've spoken to my father about us,' he said quietly.

She looked at Pulok with apprehension.

'He doesn't approve of our marriage. Maa has also tried to reason with him but he refuses to listen.'

The glow on Mei Lin's face disappeared. After a few quiet moments, Pulok spoke, 'If my father doesn't agree, I will take you with me. Addison sahab has promised to give me family quarters in the tea garden by August or September. We will wait till then. Before that, if Deuta agrees, well and good. If not, I'll marry you the Chinese way if needed and take you with me to the garden.'

Mei Lin looked at Pulok with deep longing and said, 'You are the only son.'

'I know. I have never done anything to hurt my family. I've always listened to them. But this is my life, Mei Lin. I won't be able to live without you. Look at me. Tell me, can you live without me?'

Tears filled Mei Lin's eyes, 'Don't you know?'

'I can't sacrifice my love just because I am the only son. You may be able to do so, but I can't.'

'September is still some time away. You can try to reason with your father again.'

'I'll definitely do that. But if he persists in being unreasonable, then after getting the quarters, I'll take you away. Don't object then.'

Mei Lin did not answer. After a while she stood up. 'I'll go now. I feel shy talking to you like this for long.'

'Will you feel shy even after we are married and I take you around with me?'

'You are impossible. I am leaving.'

'Will you not allow me to even hold your hand?'

'Dhet!'

'What kind of a girl are you?'

'A Chinese girl.' She giggled. 'I must go now.'

'I have something for you.' Gently lifting up her hand, he placed in it the bag he had brought from Lee Chang's shop.

'It's for you.'

Holding the bag with both hands, Mei Lin looked at it closely for a few seconds. She felt herself blush. Then, hugging the bag, she slowly walked away.

Two

In an Assam-type quarter of the Babu line of the Raidang tea estate, Pulok and his friends sat in Akong's house. Akong worked as a fitter in the garden. All of them played for the Seven Star Club, and with the exception of Liang and Rameswar, the rest were childhood friends and classmates as well. Tung Chin supervised the business of Makum's famous contractor, Ho Yen Kee. Liang was an apprentice carpenter in Samdang tea estate. Yao Sen had his own garage. Narayan was a teacher at Ganga Bishan Chowkhani High School. Rameswar had a cycle shop, while Robin was a junior officer with the Assam Rifles. Robin had come home after a long time and hence every one had gathered at Akong's place.

'I won't be able to play this time,' Robin said suddenly.

'But why?' they all chimed in.

'I won't get a long leave. There is a lot of tension at the NEFA border.'

'What kind of tension?'

'For a long time there has been a border dispute between us and the Chinese. The problem seems to have grown more complicated. No one knows what might happen next.'

Everyone fell silent. They were not worried about the border problem. Their only concern was Robin's absence in the coming football matches. They were very disappointed.

'Won't you be able to come even for Pulok's wedding?' Rameswar asked, breaking the silence.

'Has his wedding been finalized?' Robin smiled.

'He has told Mei Lin that if his father doesn't agree to their marriage, he will marry her the Chinese way and take her away to his quarters in the garden,' Rameswar said.

'Let's think of a Chinese name for him,' Robin said.

'Let Mei Lin agree first. I know her. There is very little chance of their getting married soon,' Akong commented.

'Everyone can't elope with a girl from the market, as you did!' Tung Chin teased.

'You are no better, Ramakanta! Do you think we have forgotten the way you brought Xonpahi?'

They always teased Tung Chin by addressing him as Ramakanta. Ramakanta was Tung Chin's formal name. Lee Chang's formal name was Haranath. The headmaster of the lower primary school, finding it difficult to write the Chinese name of the little boy, changed it to Ramakanta with the title 'China'. Remembering that incident, his friends never tired of teasing him.

'Tung Chin!' the headmaster pronounced. 'What kind of name is that? Do you go around making a bell sound – toong, toong?'

The little boy stood still in utter shame and anger, while his friends were almost in tears, trying to control their laughter.

Next was Lee Chang's turn.

'Lee Chang!' the headmaster called out. 'From which chang, which raised platform, have you jumped down? One goes crazy hearing the names of the Chinese progeny! How difficult to pronounce! There were some more before. Thank God they have left school. What names!'

They listened to the headmaster with their heads lowered. It was almost impossible to look the fearsome man in the eye.

'As of today, your name is Haranath. Haranath China. Do you understand? Forget that your name was Lee Chang.'

That was a very sad day for Tung Chin and Lee Chang. As they walked back from school, the boys teased them, calling them by their new names. From then on, whenever their friends wanted to provoke them, they addressed them by these names.

The two boys pleaded with their parents to meet the headmaster to correct their names in the school register. But their parents didn't agree. To challenge the decision of the headmaster, whom they held in high regard, was beyond imagination.

'It has been good in a way. At least one child will have an Assamese name. Somewhere at least my identity will remain,' Tung Chin's mother Pramila Gogoi said, laughing, when she first heard the new name.

Although hardly used, the names stuck. Their friends, however, called them by their original Chinese names. Lee Chang changed his name back to Lee Chang through an affidavit. Tung Chin did not.

It was after a long time that they were teasing Tung Chin again. Everyone burst out laughing. Akong's three chubby little sons peeped shyly from behind.

'Your boys have perfect Chinese complexion. But no one will believe you are Chinese. What a complexion!' Rameshwar commented, patting the dark-complexioned Akong on his back, as they all went inside laughing.

The entire family sat around a table. There was Akong's father and his two brothers. The three little boys also joined them shyly. Akong's mother was arranging tea and snacks on the table. She was dark-complexioned with curly hair tied up in a high bun. Wearing a red-bordered white sari, she stood near her short and fair husband. It was difficult to ignore the contrast in their looks. 'You all have come after a long time,' said Akong's mother.

'We hardly ever get time these days,' Pulok said.

'Have dinner before you go.'

'Not today. We are going to have a discussion about the football game at the club,' Narayan said.

'But there is a meeting at the club,' one of Akong's brothers said.

'We will have our discussion after the meeting.'

'The person who has come from Calcutta is not reliable. I know him. His name is Liang Ching Wan. He has been here a couple of times before as well. He was persuading us to get Red China passports. He says it will be useful for us.'

'Don't you have Indian citizenship?' Pulok asked with surprise.

'No, we don't.'

'Why? You came here so many years ago, didn't you?'

'Yes. It was during British times, way before the Second World War.'

'Even then you don't have Indian citizenship? Why?'

'I don't know.'

'We were born here. Even then we don't have citizenship,' Akong said. 'We don't know under what terms we are here. Papa has some old papers that the tea garden manager gave him. We have some papers as well. Papa used to go to the Foreigner's Registration Office earlier. He doesn't anymore. No one has asked anything regarding this. No police enquiries, no difficulties, nothing,' said Akong.

'You better apply for citizenship. You might get into trouble later.'

'What trouble? We have married local girls. We came here years before the World War. We never went to China after that. We have almost forgotten about China,' Akong's father said.

'Why didn't you ever go back?' Narayan asked.

'You need money to go! We were very poor. My brother-in-law came to work here in the tea gardens. My sister had followed. And one day, I came as well. What could we have done staying in China? There was no work. There was no food. Only violence and bloodshed. It was much better here. Even though the freedom struggle was going on here, people had enough to eat.'

'And then what happened?' asked Pulok.

'I came and stayed with my brother-in-law near Pabhoi tea garden in Tezpur. I searched for jobs, but was unable to get any.

They didn't want Chinese labourers. They wanted carpenters. I didn't know much carpentry then. Besides, I was young. Who would want to employ me? My brother-in-law worked as a carpenter under a contractor for a pittance. With eight children of their own, they hardly had enough food. How could they feed another mouth? In spite of his hurtful abuses, I had to keep quiet. I had nowhere to go. My elder brother worked as a labourer under the contractor. He used to contribute a few bucks as well. Even then, my brother-in-law abused him. My brother finally became an opium addict and died. I realized that if I stayed there for very long I too would die. My sister also pleaded with me to leave. I came to Silghat. It was very difficult to survive. I suffered a lot. One day I came to Makum with a contractor. I was married and had two children at the time.'

'The old man then had a long pigtail,' the mother said with a chuckle.

'Not pigtail! Plaits,' said the younger son.

'It's the same thing. My friends used to tease me, "Hey Sukmati, you married a girl or a boy?"'

The room was filled with laughter.

'Tell us about yourself, aunty,' Rameswar said.

'How different would my story be? It's the same as all the other labourers. I am also one of those poor people whom the contractors tricked into coming to this land. We were tricked by that traitorous contractor, that bloody trafficker. My father was too naive. He trusted the man. He said, "Let's go to Assam. There is comfort in Assam. We won't have to suffer from hunger." Forget about comfort, my father died of cholera on the way. Mother also died, leaving me and my two brothers behind. We only cried in those days. In the coolie line, we barely managed to eat one square meal a day. Eventually my brothers became cowherds and I got a job as a nanny in the bungalow. The memsahab was a kind-hearted woman. She treated me very well.

Her complexion was like milk, believe it or not. This cunning old fellow was working as a carpenter in the bungalow then. He seduced me with his fair complexion and married me.'

The room was again filled with laughter. The sadness and incredulity that had engulfed the air a short while ago vanished in the merriment.

It was late afternoon by the time Pulok and his friends finished tea. Cycling together in a row, they all reached Makum. As they went past Cheenapatti lane, they stopped when they saw Yiu Yi.

She had come running out from the lane in a flowery pink frock. Her short, straight hair was tied on either side of her head with pink ribbons, which bobbed with each step. She was holding a jute bag. She stopped when she saw Pulok and the others.

'How are you, Yiu Yi ache?' Tung Chin called out.

'Ugh! Why do you keep calling me ache? I'm still small,' she tried to sound angry but could not supress her laughter.

'You are right. This fellow is getting really naughty. Where are you going, Yiu Yi?' Narayan asked.

'To Mok Min uncle's shop.'

Robin was at the back. Noticing him, Yiu Yi glowed.

'Sipahi dada!'

'Hey Yiu Yi, what do you call a Sepoy's bride?' Tung Chin asked.

Pinching Tung Chin on his arm, Yiu Yi ran away. Her plump pink cheeks turned red. They were still laughing when they reached Mok Min's shop. Mok Min's shop was neither a trinket shop nor a grocery shop. It was not a hotel either. It was a mix of all these. The shop was another attraction of Makum. In the front was a small eatery. On the other side was a grocery store. Apart from daily provisions, here one could get Chinese food items. The shop also stocked items required by the Chinese community. Everything came from Hong Kong to Calcutta, and from there to Assam. Chinese people from the surrounding areas came to

Mok Min's shop for their requirements. It was another meeting place for them. Not only Chinese, there was hardly anyone in the neighbourhood who had not stepped into Mok Min's shop.

Mok Min was fat and reserved. He was one of the richest Chinese men in the area. There were several other like Ho Yen Kee, Man Chung Ho, Ho Fuk, A. C. Chow, K. P. Lee and others who belonged to a higher social order. The labourers, fitters, carpenters and the shoe-makers constituted the lower and middle classes.

Mok Min's shop was always crowded. Older Chinese men were seen sitting here, sipping tea, talking or playing Mahjong. Smoke from pipes, cigarettes, bidis always filled the rooms. Opium smokers often sat around watching the games or dozing in some corner.

When Pulok and his friends reached the shop, Mok Min was sitting quietly at the cash counter looking serious as usual. Yiu Yi stood outside and began to recite her shopping list in a bright and loud voice.

'Wow, our little fairy knows the names of so many things!' Pulok whispered in her ears.

'Of course I do. I even know how to cook,' Yiu Yi said with a smile.

'Really?'

'Yes, I'll cook tomorrow. All of you must come.'

'Surely we will,' Robin said, and stroking her cheek. They went inside.

The old opium smokers were drinking tea indifferently. The place was filled with customers. C Hoi was reading the *China Review* out loud while a few others listened. Unlike the bundles of other newspapers that arrived from Calcutta at regular intervals, this one took weeks. There were not many people who could read or write Chinese. Although there were some who could speak Chinese, the majority of them were illiterate. The teachers of the Chinese school, C Hoi, Mok Min, A. C. Chow, Ho Chang Ho and a few others, knew the language. Some students in the school knew a little bit of Chinese, but their knowledge was not enough to read a newspaper.

C Hoi was reading the news regarding the ongoing border dispute between India and China and explaining it to the others. This was when the officer-in-charge of the Tinsukia police station arrived in his jeep. There was a party today at contractor Ho Fuk's house. Mok Min was to accompany the officer to the party. Everybody in the shop stood up in respect as the officer entered. He silently nodded at everyone, acknowledging their salutes, and walked inside with a certain sense of self-importance.

After Mok Min and the police officer left, C Hoi went inside the Mahjong room carrying the newspapers in his hands. Inside, Tung Chin's father, Yiu Yi's grandfather, Lee Chang's father and father-in-law were seated on wooden stools playing Mahjong. Passing on the heap of newspapers to Yiu Yi's grandfather, the oldest member of the group, C Hoi said, 'It seems that the India-China friendship will not remain the same anymore.'

'Why? What's wrong?' Yiu Yi's grandfather asked, pausing between puffs.

'Just look at the paper. Nehru says the Chinese troops must be pushed back from the border.'

Their faces instantly became serious. Reports regarding the border dispute between India and China were appearing in the newspapers for some days now. It was clear that there was an increasing sense of bitterness between the two nations.

'It seemed that Chow En Lai and Nehru were friends. Then why does he talk like this?' Ho Wang asked.

'God knows!'

Tung Chin's father stood up. 'There is no point discussing this. Let's go to the club and listen to what the teacher from Calcutta has to say. It's almost time for the meeting.'

A large Chinese crowd of various age groups gathered in the spacious club. The teacher from Calcutta, Liang Ching Wan, was seated in front, delivering a talk. Some people were listening attentively while others were talking amongst themselves.

'When I first came to Calcutta, I was only twenty-five,' Liang Ching Wan said. 'At that time there was a battle going on between Chiang Kai Shek and Mao Tse-tung. Mao Tse-tung won the battle and the Communists removed Chiang Kai Shek from power and formed a new government. Chow En Lai has become the Prime Minister.'

'I know, I know. Then there was friendship between Nehru and Chow En Lai. There was Hindi-Chini-bhai-bhai.'

'Yes, after that friendship, the position of the Chinese in India became much better,' said Chi Fu Hai in a low tone from the last row.

'Prior to Chow En Lai, when the Kuomintang government of Chiang Kai Shek was in power, India and China were friends. Do you know Chiang Kai Shek even visited India?'

'Really?' Ho Wang asked in surprise.

'Don't you know that?' the man next to Ho Wang asked.

'How would I know? I don't know how to read and write. I don't even know where exactly China is. I sell pork in Makum market. Ask me about the price of pork.'

They laughed, but not very loudly; the teacher from Calcutta was looking at them with irritation.

'Everything's a joke to you! Listen to what he is saying,' Mei Lin's uncle said, barely able to suppress his own laughter. For a while there was silence. Liang Ching Wan spoke about the same things each time he visited Makum. After some time the people felt bored and started to murmur again.

'The teacher is wrong. The Chinese in India were living in peace in Chiang Kai Shek's time. There were no harassments from the government's side. All this trouble started only after Mao Tse-tung came to power.'

'Is that so?'

'Yes, of course. Don't you remember how China was in turmoil when Mao Tse-tung fought against the Kuomintang? Lots of Chinese came to India at that time.'

'Yes, I remember. Lots of suffering. Violence and bloodshed. The supporters of Kuomintang were in serious trouble. Considering that there was friendship between Nehru and Chiang Kai Shek, lots of people left China and came over to India. They thought they could live in peace here. But then trouble started here as well. Nehru extended his friendship to Chow En Lai. The supporters of Kuomintang who were in India suddenly found themselves in hot water.'

'Friendship with Chow En Lai meant enemity with Chiang Kai Shek!'

'Chiang Kai Shek moved to Taipei and tried hard to oust the Communist government. Many Chinese in India helped him with money. They sent applications to the Indian government stating that they wanted to stay in India and become Indian citizens. But what happened then? The Indian government ultimately supported Red China. And none of us got citizenship.'

'Chandu Apak and his family were in Calcutta. They faced a lot of issues. The CID were constantly keeping tabs on their whereabouts. If the CID knew that someone supported Kuomintang they were harassed in all sorts of ways. Chandu Apak told us some were even deported to China.'

'Who is Chandu Apak?'

'That old man, Chi Fu Hai Apak, who else?'

'You call him Chandu Apak because he is an opium addict?' C Hoi laughed.

'Listen to what the teacher is saying, will you?' Yiu Yi's grandfather said sternly.

Ching Wan continued, 'When I was in China I learnt to read and write Cantonese. In India it was of no use. And then the Chinese diplomat Yuan Xiao Yuan came to Calcutta. She was China's first woman diplomat. She taught a lot of the Chinese in Calcutta how to read and write in their language. She engaged me and a few other people for the job. There was no Chinese school then. We would identify suitable places and teach people there till a Chinese school was built. Our Red China government is very good. They have done a lot of good things for the Chinese in India.'

The teacher went on. Some people listened intently. Others gazed at him indifferently. Some started discussing other issues in low whispers.

'The problems started because of these new government relations.'

'What problems?'

'Big problems. When Nehru sided with Red China, the Chinese in India were in a serious dilemma about whether to support Taipei or Red China. Supporting Kuomintang meant trouble. But most of them did not want to support Red China. People were divided into two groups. The supporters of Red China began to persuade the others to get themselves passports from the People's Republic of China. Thinking that Chow En Lai was trying to convert the Chinese in India to Communists, the supporters of Kuomintang agitated and started the Anti-Communist Nationalist Salvation Movement. But the effort was futile. In 1954, Nehru visited China. On his return the editor of a Chinese daily along with another person were arrested and deported to China, accused of being supporters of Taipei.'

'I know, I know. Another Taipei supporter was also arrested and jailed.'

'Is it? But the editor was against the Communists! He should not have been deported to China!'

'Nehru never thought about what would happen to those people once they were deported to China.'

'Nehru should have given protection to the Chinese living in India. But he didn't. He tried to appease Chow En Lai.'

'Do you know, just to maintain a good relationship with China, Nehru kicked around the Chinese in India like a football?'

'Hey! Hush! Hush! You will get into trouble.'

'I am telling the truth. Why should I be afraid of telling the truth? Listen to what happened after that. The football match scheduled between India and Hong Kong in 1958 was cancelled by the Indian government because the Hong Kong team had a few players who supported Chiang Kai Shek.That's it. After this the Chinese in India got scared. Even the Taipei supporters pretended to be in favour of Red China. Many went to the extent of getting new Chinese passports. They thought this would please Nehru and the government would not trouble them further. But this won't work, I tell you.'

'You talk too much! It's going to get you in trouble. Now listen to what the man is saying,' Mei Lin's uncle scolded.

The youngsters quietened down. The teacher from Calcutta continued, 'After that the first ambassador of the People's Republic of China came to India. The Chinese living in Calcutta gave him a grand reception.'

'Pack of lies! Except for a few Communists, every Chinese participated in that reception out of fear, fear of Nehru!'

'Oh, shut up, you!'

'After that China was offended again because of the Dalai Lama issue,' Ching Wan continued. 'If the Indian government had not given Dalai Lama political asylum it would have been much better. After all, Tibet is a part of China. It is not right to say that China had captured Tibet forcibly.'

A deep silence fell over the Chinese club. The teacher was not surprised. Not only the Chinese in Assam but all the Chinese living in India did not want to discuss this strained issue. It was even more sensitive for the Chinese living in Assam because the Dalai Lama had come to India through this route.

'Agent of Red China!' Akao Ho whispered. His friends giggled.

'Now he will tell us to apply for Chinese passports. I won't. I'll take Indian citizenship.'

'It's been over ten years since you applied. Have you received it? The Indian government does not trust us because we are Chinese. Everyone else gets citizenship. We are the only ones who don't.'

'That's true.'

'The teacher should be told not to say all these things. If someone comes to know there will be trouble. The situation is not good. There is no point getting into trouble for no reason.'

They started discussing the matter in whispers. Pretending not to notice the teacher went on, 'In Calcutta alone, 8,127 people have registered themselves as foreign residents till now. Of these some have Red China passports and some have Kuomintang passports. Thousands of other Chinese people have no passports at all. No papers. Not even birth certificates. It's the same in Assam. That is why I have come to see the school. Tomorrow, if there is any trouble who will look after us? The Red China government has sympathy for the Chinese in India. Our children can even go to China to study. After all China is our motherland. We should never forget that. I am not saying that you should hate India. I am also not telling you to harm India. I only want to say, along with India we should also keep China in mind.'

At that moment Pulok and his friends were at Mok Min's shop, busy discussing the forthcoming football matches. Every Chinese home in Cheenapatti was preparing for the New Year. The snow-clad India-China border was slowly heating up with animosity at the same time. Hidden from the public eyes, both the countries had begun sharpening their weapons to confront each other.

Three

Makum's Cheenapatti looked festive that day. It looked as though the entire neighbourhood had been spring-cleaned. On both sides of the neat lanes stood Chinese houses fenced with bamboo. The wooden beams of most of the houses wore fresh coats of bright red paint. The courtyards had been cleaned and the small gardens had been weeded and manicured to show off the colourful flowers. The main doorway of each house was decorated with red posters and couplets with auspicious golden lettering on them. All of Cheenapatti was decorated with red lanterns and festoons.

Robin, Pulok, Chitta, Rameswar and Narayan were on their way to C Hoi's house. Wrapped in a shawl all over from his waist up, Thakur Prasad stood at the entrance of the lane. Seeing them, he chuckled, 'New Year fever? Whose house have you been invited to?' Though he asked the question with an innocent face nobody could mistake the sarcastic tone they were well acquainted with.

'Why do you ask?' Robin replied sternly.

'Just like that. I'll be going to Dulal Yem's place myself. He is a good friend of mine.'

'Dulal? Your friend?' Chitta laughed.

'Why did you laugh?' Narayan asked.

'Ask him what kind of a friend Dulal Yem is to him. Hey Thakra, shall I tell him?'

'Oh ho! Why must you spill everything? I don't want to get into meaningless issues.'

'Oh really! Then why do you spend your time at the police outpost?'

'Leave it. Let's go,' said Rameswar.

'Wait, wait. Let's hear the story first. Thakra, tell them what happened.'

Thakur Prasad didn't speak, but his eyes twinkled with sarcasm.

'He won't. Let me tell you. Everyone knows about his friendship with Dulal. But, do you know what he did? He betrayed Dulal's father in court.'

'Why shouldn't I betray him? His father called me a government agent. Should I sit idle after that? When I got the chance, I paid him back,' retorted Thakur Prasad.

'He said nothing of that sort. I was there when he said that,' Chitta said. 'Whenever he gets a chance he taunts the Chinese. That day he was taunting Dulal's father. Dulal's father got angry and said, "You say all this because you are a government agent." That was all. If Dulal's father had known that this man would take it to heart would he have taken him along to court?'

'Why did he take him along?'

'Thakra, you tell him.'

Smiling, Thakur Prasad said, 'The Chinese who have residential permits have to go and report at the Foreigner's Registration Office regularly. When their permits expire they have to renew them. Dulal's father didn't report this in time. They served him a notice. Dulal's father took me along to identify him. When I was asked whether I knew him, I said, "I've never seen him before." He was fined three hundred rupees and jailed for two months.' Thakur Prasad burst out laughing. 'Measure for measure.'

'That was really unfair, Thakra,' Pulok said gravely.

'Why is it unfair? You can't imagine how wicked these Chinese are. I know what they do. They are not at all trustworthy. I didn't pick a fight with him. He called me a government agent. I showed him what a government is!'

'Are you on talking terms with Dulal now?'

'Why not? He is my friend.'

'What a friend!' Everyone laughed except Robin.

'Let's go,' he said.

They left the place promptly. Robin was a tough and uncompromising man. He might have hit Thakur Prasad.

'Thakra is a peculiar chap. I don't like him,' said Narayan.

'Yes, he is strange,' Chitta nodded in agreement, 'You can never tell whether he is serious or joking.'

On the left, just after Thakur Prasad's house was C Hoi's house. He was waiting for them on the front verandah. His eyes glowed with happiness.

Pulok and his friends looked curiously at the house – small, with a slanting roof. The front veranda was spacious. This was where, he did his woodwork. They could see some half-made furniture and tools in the corner. On the right was a forge. There was no fire in the forge. The factory was closed that day.

Pulok and his friends were slightly disappointed. They never thought that C Hoi's house would be so simple. He was a famous carpenter in the region. He was very skilled and people came looking for him from far and wide. He'd devoted a lot of time and care to build this house. Pulok and his friends had expected to find something stunning. The place had been hidden from view by a high bamboo wall for a long time. Today the wall was down, and in its place was a beautifully designed short wooden fence.

Pulok and his friends looked around. There were paper lanterns and couplets like other houses, arranged for the New Year. The children of the house, who were out in the courtyard in their new clothes, stopped playing to stare at Pulok and his friends. Their entire persona reflected the glow of good health and the happiness of a secure life. Dressed in the usual ankle-length pants and waist-length flowery top worn by Chinese women, C Hoi's wife and his mother were busy shifting household things. They smiled shyly at the visitors.

Entering a doorway, Pulok and the group stood transfixed. What looked like a tiny house from outside was actually a large two-storeyed structure!

After a long pause Narayan said, 'Salute, C Hoi dada! You have built the house in a really different style.'

'But nobody can see the house from outside,' Rameswar complained.

C Hoi shook his head, 'What is the need of showing it to others? It should only be comfortable to live in. Come, I'll show you the upper floor.'

Near the courtyard was a polished staircase to the upper floor. Step by step, they saw how artistically C Hoi had built his house.

'Who reads all these books?' Pulok asked, noticing two cabinets full of Chinese books.

'I do. These were my father's books. He was a learned man. When he came to India from China he stayed in the house of his father's elder brother in Calcutta. He learned carpentry there. My father told me that some Chinese doctor in Calcutta taught his father's elder brother how to read and write. His name was Lum Kwa. My father knew so many things but I could not learn anything from him,' C Hoi said, submerged in the past. 'My father told me that most of the old bungalows of Assam were constructed by Chinese carpenters. My father was very skilled, yet he never had enough money. His whole life he worked under a contractor. I feel sad whenever I think of him. He never got a chance to live in a nice house.' C Hoi sighed.

Around Cheenapatti, people from other communities also lived together with the Chinese. The Bihari mason Bholu Singh, Raghuwa Mahato, the carpenter Gati Karmakar, village headman Ramlal, and Banarasi Prasad Jaiswal also lived in this area. There was a Kali temple nearby.

A few yards past the Kali temple lived Banwari Lal Chowkhani, the owner of burra gola – the big all-purpose store that everyone knew as Murli Gola. Just opposite the house was a large walled compound owned by the Chowkhanis, enclosing a big cowshed and a godown to store tea seeds. The police station was near the main market as well. When Pulok and his friends reached the area, Thakur Prasad and his friend Rajendra were coming out of the police station. Both were startled to see them and hurriedly retreated. Pulok and his friends laughed and went on their way.

Like all other houses in Cheenapatti, in Yiu Yi's house, preparations for the festival were in full swing. After cleaning the entire house and bathing the children, Yiu Yi's mother was busy decorating. In a corner of the spacious front room was an altar at which offerings of tea and fruit had been laid. Candles had been lit and incense was burning.

Yiu Yi's uncle had come with his family from Tinsukia. He had married a girl from Shillong who was half-Chinese, half-Khasi. They had six children. Another uncle had come from Silghat with his wife and five children. This uncle had married a girl from the tea garden community. The house was alive with the sounds of the children playing and running around.

Yiu Yi's father entered the room with a bundle of paper packets. He was a famous carpenter and ran an independent business. The house had been built by his father. He was a famous carpenter too.

Yiu Yi's grandparents, their three sons and all the other family members sat together near the altar. Her grandfather distributed the clothes that her father had brought. Her grandmother was busy putting money into small red envelopes to give to all the unmarried youngsters the next day.

'Like every year, let me tell you where we came from,' Yiu Yi's grandfather said.

'We had a house in China a long time ago, didn't we?' asked Babu.

'How do you know this?' Yiu Yi asked him enthusiastically.

'I know everything. My papa told me. But my mother's house was not in China. It was in India – Bilaspur.'

'Bilaspur?' Yiu Yi's brother asked in surprise.

'Yes, Damodara village in Bilaspur, to be precise. A contractor brought her here. That is why she always cries. She has no one here. She can't even go back home. She doesn't remember the address of the village properly.'

'Why did he bring her here?' Yiu Yi asked, looking at her aunt's sad face.

'I don't know. Ask my mother.'

Yiu Yi's grandfather, who was listening to their conversation said, 'Many years ago, we came here from China. "We" meaning my grandfather came from China – from a place called Canton. His name was Ho Yen. Canton is in South China. We call the place Kwangtung. My grandfather was the slave of a meat seller in Canton. With him was another slave. His name was Ho Han. Do you know who he was? He was Mei Lin's father's grandfather – her great-grandfather. They were very close friends. Mei Lin's great-grandfather was very fond of my grandfather. They were like brothers and went through immense hardship together as slaves.'

'What is a slave?'

'A slave is a person who is bought by another.'

'Bought? Dhet! Can there be people for sale?' The children laughed in disbelief.

'Yes. There were human markets in those days. It was from one of these markets that the meat seller bought my grandfather. The meat seller branded his forehead with a hot iron.'

'My grandmother's name was Suhagmoni,' Yiu Yi's grandfather continued after a brief pause.

He narrated Ho Yen and Suhagmoni's story. Everyone listened in rapt silence. Babu's mother Parbati, however, kept wiping her tears. After he finished the story he turned to his wife and said, 'Go and get the box.'

Yiu Yi's grandmother brought a small, beautifully carved wooden box which had been kept near the altar. Her grandfather took the box, sighed and began again, 'One day, my grandfather met a man in the market ...'

He went back to the days of his ancestors, to the early period of tea cultivation in Assam. The images of Canton Port, Thirteen Factory, Chinese junks, the South China Sea, Prince of Wales Island and the coolie depots came alive, as did the images of pain and anguish of the people confined in the junk.

'I have faint childhood memories of my grandmother Suhagmoni. After my grandfather passed away, Mei Lin's great-grandfather, Ho Han, looked after her. Tung Chin's father's grandfather, Ah Chin, came along with our ancestors. That is why we consider ourselves part of the same clan. You should also live like kin. Never fight amongst yourselves. My grandfather came with nothing but a bowl and two chopsticks. He didn't even have a tool box when he came. My father made this box to hold the bowl and chopsticks. He had asked us to revere this as a relic of our ancestors. Mei Lin's family has preserved Ho Han's bowl and chopsticks. They keep it near the altar of the gods and ancestors. You must continue this tradition.'

Opening the box to show the children the blue, flower-inscribed china bowl and the chopsticks, he said, 'Your parents know this. You all must also remember this as we have remembered, or else we will forget where we came from. We have already forgotten our language.'

'I'll write it all down, ah yeh,' said Yiu Yi's brother.

His mother stroked his adolescent face and smiled. 'It's good if you write it.'

'If we don't write it down, slowly everything will be lost to oblivion,' Yiu Yi's grandfather said.

'Now go, play,' Yiu Yi's mother said to the children.

The old year was passing in peace and tranquillity. In every house and lane of Cheenapatti lanterns had already been lit.

The Assamese-Chinese community was ready to celebrate the New Year. What they could not imagine was that in the inner courtyard of the foreign ministries of both India and China, a different future was being planned for them.

One by one, the windows of the Chinese houses in Cheenapatti opened. The light of red lanterns and candles illuminated every house and everyone sat together for the reunion dinner. On this special day, happiness and contentment filled their hearts. The stream of life that had begun with the long years of pain and the anguish of slavery and indentured servitude had reached the plains of peace and joy. They lived a happy life in a free country. The bad times were a thing of the past.

After dinner, they moved to the front room of the house.

'I am going to open the door now,' Yiu Yi's grandfather announced.

The moment the front door was opened the children jumped with joy. They went out and lit the firecrackers hung outside. All of Cheenapatti, including the compound of K. P. Lee, Ming and Company and the Chinese Club, reverberated with light and sound. Most of the non-Chinese neighbours also came out to join the festivity including Pulok and his friends. The Chinese New Year ushered the message of good luck, happiness and prosperity into every home.The jubilant sounds of the children filled the air.

'Hey, Ramlal, sing a song for us,' someone shouted to the village headman.

'Eh, what will I sing? Why don't you ask Lilu? He knows a lot of songs.'

Ramlal's brother Lilu, when pressed to sing, feigned bashfulness for a minute, before starting soulfully:

'*Dhoni re, chole jay jeeban boro dukhe.*
Chara din kaam kori,
Khun ke pochina kori,
Tobu bhore paino dui chokhe.
Dhoni re, chole jay jeeban boro dukhe.
Life goes by in sorrow.
I toil away
With the sweat of my brow,
Yet my eyes don't see fulfilment.
Life goes by in sorrow.'

The crowd became quiet.

'Don't sing sad songs today. Sing something joyful,' Lee Chang said.

'Joyful songs?' Lilu stopped for a moment, then started a different song. With unsteady steps the men danced the jhumur. The girls laughed watching them dance.

'Sing a Bihu song. Hey Pulok, sing a Bihu song.'

Pulok looked at Mei Lin. She was looking at him, her eyes bright with amusement. Staring at her for a brief moment Pulok started to sing merrily,

'*Porbotor dhekia thorali oi thorali*
Thorali oi thorali
Hatee powaliye khaai
Ratir pore pore
Toloi monot pore
Toloi monot pore
Chokulo bagori jai ...
Every hour of the night I think of you
Think of you
My tears roll down ...'

'Aai oi, dehi oi – O my dear, O my darling –' a youngster in the crowd cried out while the rest cheered. Sounds of laughter touched the sky. Mei Lin blushed and hid her face. Pulok was also blushing, but he stood there with a smile on his face. These were his own people. These were Mei Lin's people.

Yiu Yi's aunt Parbati was leaning on the doorway absentmindedly. Her face was clouded in utter grief and frustration. Yiu Yi walked over to Parbati. Stretching out a hand full of toffees, she said slowly, 'Have some toffees, ah sam.'

Parbati picked up a toffee silently with a gloomy smile.

'Take some more, there are lots. Sipahi dada brought them for me.'

'Who is Sipahi dada?'

'You've forgotten. It's Robin dada, the tall military man with the big moustache! He has given me a doll as well. You bought this sari for New Year? It's beautiful.'

'Yes, your uncle gave it to me.' Parbati said, her mind still far away.

Yiu Yi held her hand and asked softly, 'You are thinking of your family, aren't you?'

'How do you know?'

'I can tell from your expression.'

'Yes. Always listen to your parents, Yiu Yi,' she said suddenly. 'I didn't listen to mine.'

'What did you do, ah sam?'

When Parbati didn't answer, Yiu Yi pressed harder, 'Tell me. You'll feel better, I promise.'

'We were very poor people. Without land of our own to cultivate, we were at the mercy of the zamindar. One day a man came to our village and told us about a place called Assam, a place with plenty of work and no zamindar. My parents didn't believe him. But I did and left with him. It was only after boarding the train that I realized I was a "girmiteeya", a bonded labourer. The contractor engaged me in Silghat tea garden. My job was plucking. I used to pluck the tea leaves and cry. That is where I met your uncle. He loves me a lot. He is a very good person. Everyone in your family is good. God has been merciful to me.'

'You could have gone back to your home with my uncle. Why didn't you?'

'I couldn't remember the address. I'll never see my family again, Yiu Yi!'

Yiu Yi hugged her aunt and wiped her tears with her little hands. 'Don't cry, ah sam. We are all here for you. Maa says the place which feeds us is our own. That place is our mother.'

Cheenapatti was still celebrating. Holding on to Yiu Yi's hand Parbati stood silently. It was almost dawn when the festivities wound down. The people, exhausted from the celebrations, had gone to sleep. The only person still awake was Thakur Prasad Shah. Wrapping a shawl around himself, he went about stealthily tearing down the lanterns and the red posters with golden lettering hanging over the lane. He trampled over the lanterns that were strewn everywhere. There was no trace of guilt on his face. Instead, it glowed with the blaze of vindictive happiness.

Four

'Five stars are flying high in the sky.'

Ganga Bishan Chowkhani High School resounded with the chorus of a song praising Red China. Today the campus was alive with activity. Like every year, the Ganga Bishan Chowkhani High School and the Makum Chinese School had jointly organized a function to celebrate India-China friendship. All the important people of Makum had been invited. On the tastefully decorated dais had been placed photographs of Chow En Lai and Nehru. In the front row sat local political leaders and honourable guests like Banwarilal Chowkhani, K. P. Lee, Ho Yen kee, A. C. Chow, Ho Chang Ho, and other leading members of the Chinese community. Behind them sat students from both schools and their guardians.

At the gate stood Ananta Baruah, a class ten student at GBC School. He was staring at Ahlin, his classmate, who stood on the opposite side of the entrance. Ahlin, aware of his gaze, was blushing profusely. Her friends Alan, Siu, Mei Hang and Kaushalya were teasing her.

The deteriorating relations between India and China had not affected the students yet. Only those who were aware of political developments were beginning to get worried about the border dispute. Both sides had been exchanging official protest notes on the border issue from time to time.

There had been minor skirmishes and some exchange of fire. On the border of the Kameng Frontier Division of NEFA, near the India-China-Bhutan tri-junction, the situation was far from peaceful. The fire of a potential conflict had been lit, and it carried with it the possibility of a full-fledged conflagration. As a result, an unimaginable crisis had descended on the Chinese living in

India. The Chinese living in Assam and West Bengal were in even more trouble. Though the teachers of the Chinese school had attended the function today, their faces were shadowed with worry.

The local authorities had suddenly imposed restrictions on the movement of the Chinese people and anyone of Chinese origin as well. They could no longer leave their towns. Upon receiving this news, the president of Makum's Chinese society, Ho Chang Ho, had called everyone to the club. After discussing the matter there, they had come to the school.

Forgetting about their duty to receive the guests, the teachers of the Chinese school joined the discussion. Lao Thien Lee, who owned a shoe shop, was worried. 'What will happen to us now? The Chinese government has not done the right thing. What will China gain by taking more land? They have already captured Tibet.'

'Why do you say so? How do you know what China has said is not right?' C Hoi countered.

'Quiet, quiet! You should not say such things. If the CID people hear you, they will put you in jail,' Chi Fu Hai said fearfully.

'This old fellow is a scaredy cat!' Ho Wang laughed.

Forgetting all their worries for the moment, the others joined in the laughter. The news they had heard in the club was disturbing but they had not seen any change in their surroundings. Everything seemed as usual. There had been no untoward incidents anywhere.

Makum was a peaceful town managed by a police outpost of eight constables without firearms and a sub-inspector. Here, one did not feel like an outsider, but as if they had been here for ages. The bones of their ancestors were buried in this soil.

The headmaster of the Chinese school came towards the group.

'Don't discuss this issue here. We could get into trouble.'

Asking everyone to take their places in the temporary shed, the headmaster returned to his seat. He was deeply worried about the hostel boarders. He wished he could send them home during the puja vacation. But now it had become uncertain whether their guardians would be able to come pick them up or not.

As one local leader of the Communist Party of India walked in, the headmaster went forward to welcome him. The guest said happily, 'Today's arrangements seem to be grander than other years.'

The headmaster smiled as the students ushered the guest to his seat. The other dignitaries exchanged greetings with the CPI leader and resumed talking politics.

A Praja Socialist Party leader looked at the CPI leader and said, 'We were discussing the border issue. The way the situation is deteriorating, it seems a war is inevitable.'

'How can you say that?' the CPI leader asked.

'The tune in both the camps is changing. China has said that the situation has reached the most critical point. There is every chance of war in the Chedong area because India has become increasingly aggressive. On the other hand, the Indian government has said that India has been using arms only for self-defence so far. Now the commanders have been ordered to expel the Chinese encroachers.'

'India has done the right thing. If China encroaches on Indian territory, should India sit idle? China should be taught a lesson. After occupying Tibet, China has become supercilious,' said a leader of the Indian National Congress.

The CPI leader's face turned serious. He said gravely, 'With other neighbouring countries the Indian borders have been properly demarcated. But the border between India and China is not that clear. It is difficult to say clearly which area is on which side. The McMahon Line is controversial. That's why it is not correct to say outright that China has encroached upon Indian soil.'

Just as the discussion was heating up, the member of the legislative assembly of the state representing the constituency arrived on the scene.

After he was welcomed by the headmasters of both the schools and the objectives of the meeting were announced, Ananta Baruah took over the microphone.

'This is a special day for the students' community of Makum. As a sign of India-China friendship, the function will begin with a song which reflects the friendship between the two countries. The song will be performed by the students of Ganga Bishan Chowkhani High School and Makum Chinese School.'

Ananta left the dais. Immediately two rows of students came from opposite ends of the stage carrying the flags of the two countries and sang, 'Hindi-Chini bhai-bhai, Hindi-Chini bhai-bhai. Long live India-China.'

As the song went on, the dignitaries returned to talking politics.

'Here we are shouting Hindi-Chini bhai-bhai, while bit by bit China is encroaching upon our land. This is useless. I don't understand why we are still organizing these programmes. First improve the border situation, then do all this Hindi-Chini bhai-bhai stuff. But it seems that the government is not at all concerned about the issue,' the PSP leader muttered in a low voice.

'Yes, you are right. The government has not taken the issue seriously. The government is telling the public that everything is alright on the one hand, and on the other hand sending protest letters to China. Sit with China. Discuss. If the McMahon Line is right then why are you not able to convince China?'

'True, absolutely true. The government has said that Indian defence is absolutely alright, at least on the NEFA border. That the Indian Army has taken best defence measures. There, the

Chinese troops cannot advance an inch without a fight. Then what has happened?'

'It was because of Nehru that things went wrong. Being a Congress leader you may not like my words, but I must say Nehru made the gravest mistake by trusting China.'

'Why do you say that? Nehru is a big-hearted leader. That's why he believed China. He has no greed for China's soil. He believes in peaceful co-existence. What should he have done according to you? Should he be waiting, pointing the gun at China in anticipation that China may attack?' the Congress leader said indignantly.

'Yes, he should have done exactly that. It is alright to believe in peaceful co-existence. It is wise to maintain good relations with the neighbours. But does that mean that you won't even check your borders? Will you allow your neighbours to break through your boundary?'

'See what our Prime Minister has done! There are problems going on at the borders and he has gone to London!'

'What option did he have? How can our Prime Minister avoid the Commonwealth Prime Ministers' Conference?'

'You are right. Nehru is not only the leader of India. He is a leader of Asia, too. After choosing the path of non-alignment, he has become one of the great statesmen of the world. We just don't recognize his worth.'

'We do recognize his worth. But does that mean we can't point out his mistakes? We must speak the truth. He has gone to London, that's alright. But after that he will be visiting a few countries in Asia and Africa and will return only after two weeks. It is his responsibility to return to India as early as possible and take action against China. Then only will we say he is a leader.'

'And our Defence Minister, Krishna Menon? He, too, has gone to London at this crucial time. He says, "There is no cause for worry," otherwise he would not have gone to London! Why should they panic? You live in comfort in Delhi. It will take many days for the Chinese Army to reach Delhi after crossing the NEFA border. What is there for you to worry about? If the Chinese attack, the people of Assam will be in danger. Our people will be killed. And what does Krishna Menon say? "Necessary steps have been taken." God only knows what kind of necessary steps he is referring to.'

'We see him visiting foreign countries most of the time. If both the Prime Minister and the Defence Minister stay outside the country in this time of crisis, how will things work out? Forget about that; tell me, what is our Assam government doing? Our Chief Minister is almost silent on this matter, apart from sending out a few weak press releases. How will he be able to impel the central government to take action against the invaders like this?'

'That's why we need a leader and a Member of Parliament like Hem Baruah. He said right to Nehru's face that the Chinese invasion was a national indignity for us. The sooner Nehru realizes this, the better for him and the country. One needs guts to say this to his face. I must say that the PSP has got a really strong leader.'

A group of little girls appeared on stage to perform a dance. The dignitaries continued their conversation.

'There is a bigger agenda hidden behind the activities of China, you see.'

'What's that?'

'They want to occupy Bhutan, Sikkim, Ladakh, Nepal and NEFA. They consider these places the five fingers of the Tibetan hand. It means that Tibet is China's hand and these places are the five fingers of that hand. I read it in the newspaper. Haven't you?'

'There is no proof of what is being said. If China had any ulterior motive, they would not have proposed talks next month. China has said that talks should be held between the officials of both the sides. That's not unreasonable,' said the CPI leader.

'Not unreasonable? How can you say that? China has proposed that both the parties should move back twelve miles from the border till any solution is reached.'

'Do you mean to say what China has said is reasonable? Why should India move back? China has already occupied our land. If we agree to that, we will be agreeing to their claim that the encroached land is theirs.'

'Forget all that. All we are worried about is security. What is the use of living in a free country that cannot provide security? The central government might be thinking NEFA and Assam are not a part of India.'

'That's true. What have we received in these years after Independence? The central government has always looked at us with a stepmotherly attitude. Forget about other things, we had to struggle even for our own language. Think about the NEFA border – till recently the Assam Rifles were deployed there. The paramilitary forces were tasked with safeguarding the border! Huh! They couldn't even properly demarcate the border all these years, because they don't consider Assam or NEFA parts of India.'

Another announcement was made – 'Now, Srimati Kaushalya Dutta will render a Chinese folk song.'

'Do you think the Chinese living here are unaware of what is going on?' one of the dignitaries commented.

'They may be unaware. Most of them are illiterate. Manual workers. They don't keep track of what goes on in the world.'

'Oh sir! Your notion is wrong. It will take time for you to understand these so-called timid people. They are not as simple as they pretend to be. They read Chinese newspapers that come from Calcutta, did you know? They listen to Radio Peking. They have information of what is happening around but they feign ignorance.'

'They may do that, but they are not what you have said they are. My son has a few Chinese friends. I have not seen anything bad in them. They are just like our children. They are not different in any way, even though they are Chinese.'

The leading people of the Chinese community who were seated near the other dignitaries wore a glum look. The whispers of the non-Chinese dignitaries had worried them.

After the cultural programme was over, the speeches started. The first person to come on stage was Radha Krishna Khemka, the legislator.

'I am happy to be here today. We Indians believe in the principles of Panchsheel. We want to maintain good relations with our neighbours. As a token of our friendship we sing "Hindi-Chini bhai-bhai". We want to live like brothers forever. But if someone comes to attack our sovereignty we cannot sit silently, without doing anything. Today our neighbour China has encroached upon our land. Honourable Prime Minister Nehruji has said this will not be tolerated ...'

'What is he talking about?' Ahlin asked Ananta, perplexed.

'I don't know. Forget it. When will we have mooncakes?'

'Come anytime. What is he saying? Is he talking about us?'

'Are you Chinese? Then tell me how to say I love you in Chinese.'

'Dhet!'

'What dhet? If you are Chinese you have to know the language. I will have to learn it too. Or else, how will we teach our children?'

'You are impossible. How can I know Chinese? We speak Assamese at home. Our mother is Assamese.'

'Then what is the need to pay heed to such useless discussions? Come closer to me. I have something to tell you.'

'What is it?' Ahlin asked, blushing.

'You won't come closer? Shall I say it loudly?'

'Hey – no – I am coming. Now tell me,' Ahlin said as she walked up to Ananta.

Ananta looked at Ahlin and slowly uttered, 'Wo ai ni.'

'What does it mean?' Ahlin asked.

'I love you. I am learning Chinese. I will need it in the future.'

'Dhet!' Forgetting that there were people around, Ahlin burst out laughing.

On stage, Radha Krishna Khemka was speaking at that moment.

'Chow En Lai has to understand. Our Nehruji says we still consider China our friend. Hindi-Chini bhai-bhai ...'

After a long speech he left the dais to the sound of applause.

A student leader stood up to speak next.

'Today we are making merry together with the Chinese inhabitants of Assam. We are very happy. But today in the Kameng Frontier, Indian soldiers are fighting to resist invasion. The Chinese troops must leave Indian soil. We must overthrow all the conspiracies of China, a country that wants to devour our land. We will never forgive this aggressor nation. We are still saying Hindi-Chini bhai-bhai.'

'What is this person talking about?' Mei Ho whispered to Anjali sitting next to her.

'Perhaps they are saying that they don't like this Hindi-Chini song. Let me ask Yiu Yi. She knows about a lot of things.'

'Hey, Yiu Yi, why are they saying "Cheena Cheena" so angrily?'

'The grown-ups usually talk like this. We hear a lot of big people talk like this on the radio. I don't know what kind of people our fathers are. Nowadays they only sit in the house, listen to the radio and then they smoke cigarettes, drink tea and talk and talk. They don't allow us to go near them. These days Maa and the others don't get a chance to listen to the radio. They are very angry with our fathers. Yunlin ache has been here for some time. She is also angry because of this. She says it would have been better if she stayed in Ledo. But she cannot now.'

'Why?'

Yiu Yi pointed to Ko Fuk and, with her finger on her lips, gestured to Mei Ho to keep quiet.

'I know why she can't stay there,' Mei Ho said with a mysterious smile. 'Yunlin ache is going to have a baby. Isn't she?'

'Yes,' Yiu Yi smiled like an experienced woman. 'Her appearance has totally changed do you know? What a huge tummy!'

The group of children giggled. Everyone looked at them. They suppressed their laughter and tried to pay attention to the lecture.

By the time the meeting was over, it was evening. The main street of Makum became lively with the laughter and merriment of the students who were exiting the school premises. There was no trace of any tension; the coarseness of the words uttered against China was absent.

'Yiu Yi!' Pulok called out.

Yui Yi, engrossed in talking with her friends looked at Pulok, and said goodbye to her friends. She got on to the front of Pulok's bicycle with a glowing face.

She was in her school uniform, dressed in a black skirt and white blouse. Her thin frame looked like a toy with Pulok's strong arms on the handles of the cycle. She was humming the song that had been sung at school.

'Hindi-Chini bhai-bhai – long live India-China.'

'You like this song?' Pulok asked. 'Why are you singing it over and over again?'

'Oh! We sang it today – it's stuck in my head, that's why.'

'Is it? Do you know what it means?' Pulok asked.

'Our teacher said that the Indians and the Chinese are brothers.'

'Is that so? But what are you? Chinese or Indian?'

'Grandpa says we were Chinese years ago. Now we are Indians. Both my father and my grandpa say that my grandpa's grandpa came here from a place called Canton. I know lots of thing about us, Pulok dada. I will tell you later. What are you, Pulok dada? Where did your grandpa's grandpa come from?'

'We, too, came from some other place, much before your great-great grandpa's time. It could have been from China, I don't know. We are called Ahoms, also Assamese, and at the same time we are Indians too. When I marry Mei Lin, I will become half-Chinese.'

'When are you going to marry Mei Lin, ache?'

'Let's see. That's why I am here. My mother has come, too. Want to come with me?'

'Let me tell my mother or she will worry. I'll come in a moment,' Yiu Yi said and ran off.

Cheenapatti now was full of people returning from the meeting, and from work as well. Pulok's mother and a few of the neighbourhood ladies were seated in Mei Lin's house. Mei Lin's father, uncle and aunt were also with them.

'We should have visited you first,' Mei Lin's aunt said apologetically to Pulok's mother.

'Please don't think like that. We would be lucky to have a girl like Mei Lin as our daughter-in-law. We also feel that our son would be the right match for Mei Lin. They understand each other very well.'

'But would it be right for them to marry, hurting Pulok's father's sentiments?'

'We will not do that. He has agreed now. At the beginning he made some fuss about Pulok marrying a Chinese girl. We tried our best to convince him. I told him it is Pulok who is getting married. It will be your son's family. We should think only about his happiness. They have grown up together. They studied in the same school. We have been there for each other through thick and thin. You are no less than our own. What is the use of thinking who came from where? Don't think about Pulok's father. Let us get them married this month, or else Pulok might elope with her. He said he has got a quarter in the garden,' said Pulok's mother.

'This month? That gives us very little time,' said Mei Lin's father.

'That's not a problem. It will all work out.'

'Our relatives are scattered in Silghat, Tezpur and other places. We will have to send people to invite them. We care for her a lot. We wanted to have a grander wedding.'

'Then send people to invite them,' Mei Lin's aunt said.

'But nobody can come now,' Mei Lin's uncle told his wife.

'Why not?'

'We are not allowed to move about freely, don't you know?'

'What are you talking about?' Mei Lin's aunt asked with surprise. Her husband did not want to talk about the problem in front of Pulok's family.

'I'll tell you afterwards. We can do without the people from outside. We have a lot of our people in Makum and Tinsukia.'

'You are right. You have your own people here. We are also there. Pulok and Mei Lin's friends are also there. Can there be any closer people than the ones staying near you?'

Pulok and Yiu Yi arrived on the scene. Mei Lin brought in the tea along with their special moon cake made for the moon festival. Although somewhat shy, Mei Lin was reasonably at ease with this family she had always known.

As they were having their tea, they heard some noise outside.

'Seven Star must have won,' Pulok said in excitement.

'Who did they play against today?' Mei Lin's father asked.

'Against the Rovers.'

Pulok looked at his mother. 'Maa, can I go now? They might feel bad if I don't. I neither played nor watched the game today.'

'OK, go. But don't be late.'

'Please take Yiu Yi back, Mei Lin.' Pulok looked at Mei Lin for a brief moment and went out happily.

'Hip hip hurray! Hip hip hurray!'

Boys in dirty jerseys, their faces glowing, were getting off a truck in front of Mok Min's shop. Pulok joined them.

At that time, the temperature at the India-China border at NEFA and Ladakh had dipped below zero. A thin layer of snow covered the high hills and dense forests of the frontiers. The Indian soldiers from the Kumaon regiment, JK Militia, the Sikh regiment, Gorkha regiment and Assam Rifles, clad in cotton uniforms, and the Chinese soldiers, clad in uniforms padded with cotton wool, were engaged in fierce fighting. The blood that sprung from the bodies of the soldiers created floral patterns on the great white canvas. Leaving behind the tangled web of diplomacy, the two countries were fast moving towards a deadly conflict.

Five

'What is this? What the hell is this, Burra babu?' the manager of Samdang tea estate, William Addison, was pointing at a specific portion of the Kamjari book and yelling at the head clerk, Radhanath. His voice was ablaze with anger; it was as if a tiger was roaring.

Radhanath's heart was pounding in apprehension. What had gone wrong today? It was a routine matter to place the Kamjari book before the manager every day. The book was a daily record of every job done during the day in the estate. Every detail of the sequence of work had to be recorded. The number of labourers noted in the book had to be tallied with the number of labourers actually working in the garden. It was easy for the head clerk to manipulate the log book and earn some extra money. But it was not possible with William Addison. He was a hawk-eyed manager. The slightest mistake could cost the head clerk his job.

'Here, what have you written here? How come the number of cowherds in the book doesn't tally with the number deployed? There are four extra in the book,' Addison said, pushing the book towards the head clerk. 'If these kinds of irregularities continue, you will lose your job, remember that. Now leave.'

Radhanath picked up the Kamjari book with trembling hands and left the room pale-faced. Addison picked up the phone and instantly transformed from a tough tea garden manager to a fun-loving young man.

The final match between the Seven Star Club and Duliajan Club was to be played today. Leaving the office, Addison went to the huge bungalow where he lived alone. It had been ten years since he had come to Assam from Scotland, at the invitation of the Warren Brothers. He was twenty-one years old then. Now, he was the manager of Samdang tea estate, which belonged to the

Doom Dooma Tea Company. He led a fast life, keeping himself busy with sundry activities like angling, hunting, golf, tennis, reading and drinking. Of late, there had been a new addition. It was Peggy Cowie, a girl with twinkling eyes full of dreams. He met her in a small village in Scotland when he went home on leave after working continuously for seven years. During that long vacation they had grown close. He was returning to Scotland at the end of the year, or at the beginning of next year. He had decided to formally propose to her this time.

Addison changed his clothes, finished his tea and went off in his Willys jeep. When he reached, the match was about to begin.

The Doom Dooma field was jam-packed with spectators. On one side of the ground was a canopy where the local dignitaries were seated, along with O'Connor, the superintendent of the Doom Dooma Tea Company and the managers of different tea estates. They were all peers and knew one another.

Pulok and his friends tried to maintain some distance between themselves and the managers even though their behaviour was friendly – especially Addison, as he did not usually follow the dictates of hierarchy. He was quite popular in the garden. As soon as he arrived, the players and supporters of the Seven Star Club went crazy with excitement. Waving to the players, he sat down under the canopy.

Pulok's team was getting ready to play. Many of the Seven Star Club players were from Cheenapatti. But the enthusiasm was missing today. Though they were having fun, it seemed as if they were somewhat conscious and uncomfortable with themselves. As the game hit fever pitch, the spectators were fervently discussing the war, to the extent that the match became a mere sideshow.

'Nehru is constantly vacillating. On the one hand, he talks of discussion and on the other he says, if necessary, India will apply force. I think he should refrain from using provocative language. See how China is talking so diplomatically. They speak as if India is in the wrong. India should also expose China's bad deeds. What is the use of saying we will use force, we will do this and that? Do what is needed.'

'It is not that. At times we need tough talk as well. Won't China think us weak otherwise?'

'Our Jan Sangh has told the government to take action to oust the Chinese. But the government has failed to do so. What we have read in the newspapers only indicates that the Chinese army is more powerful.'

'Just because they have attacked an auxiliary post doesn't mean that we should jump to conclusions. Had it been a regular post then it would have been a different matter. This post had been set up just for the use of the patrolling parties. Think carefully, how many soldiers and arms and ammunitions could be there at such an auxiliary post?'

'It seems that you spend the entire day reading newspapers and listening to the radio.'

'What to do? We have to keep track of things. Our country is in danger. The Chinese army has encroached, no doubt, but they won't be able to stay for long. Our army is not weak at all.'

'I don't think Krishna Menon is doing the right thing. It seems he has no idea about what is happening at the border. He is only visiting foreign countries. Doesn't he have any sense of responsibility?'

'No doubt he is a learned man. But I think he is overconfident. Perhaps he is sure that if there is a war the Chinese will be defeated. That's why he hasn't taken the issue that seriously.'

'But I think things will be a little different now. A special taskforce has been formed with its headquarters at Tezpur. It will only look after the NEFA frontiers.'

'Go-o-o-a-l!'

Lee Chang had scored. The audience turned boisterous. All political discussions came to a halt. Forgetting the war, they got engrossed in the game.

'We will win this time, too. Had Robin been here we c ould have shown them our mettle. We coaxed Ming and Hong to join Seven Star Club, but they didn't agree, you know,' someone said.

'I also told them, "All the Chinese players are in Seven Star Club. Why don't you join too?" Oh! He was so angry! He said, "Why do you call us Chinese all the time? I will play for Duliajan Club. All my friends are there." I said, "We too are your friends." Do you know what his answer was? "You are my friends? Huh! No way. You are our enemy. All the players of Seven Star Club are our enemies."' Narayan laughed.

Sipping beer, Addison and his friends watched the match, their faces red with excitement. Manager Daman Singh, Addison and a few others supported Seven Star. O'Connor and the others supported Duliajan. Each time, they divided their support in this way to encourage both the parties. They paid all the expenses of the football matches with the help of the garden fund.

'Go-o-o-a-l!'

This time the cheers were for Duliajan. A young boy of fifteen or sixteen was running in celebration. The supporters of Duliajan filled the air with their cheers. O'Connor and his group were also clapping enthusiastically.

With an aggressive strategy, the players of Duliajan were advancing towards the goalpost, overpowering the defences of Seven Star. The spectators watched with bated breath. Under the canopy, Addison and the others were on the edge of their seats with excitement. The whistle of the referee created the excitement of a war zone.

'He is readying for a shot!' a group of people shouted. The ball flew towards the goalpost.

'Pulok! Pulok!' the supporters of Seven Star shouted out to the goalkeeper. With both hands outstretched, Pulok caught the ball, but lost his balance and fell to the ground. The field resounded with applause again.

Ten minutes later, Liang of Seven Star scored a goal just as the referee blew the whistle for half-time.

The supporters of Duliajan were heartbroken. They had hired a couple of good players this time but still had no chance of winning. It was quite hard to beat Seven Star.

'It's time to close this Chinese club!' someone in the crowd said.

'Hong and Ming should not have been asked to play. They are Chinese. It is obvious that they will favour their own people.'

'Ming just scored a goal. Stop talking rubbish.'

'I am not talking rubbish. Why could Hong not catch Lee Chang's ball?'

'Hey, keep quiet. They will hear you!'

'Let them hear. What will they do? The very sight of these Chinese people annoys me these days.'

'What have they done?'

'Don't you know what they are doing at the border? Look at their faces now. Anyone can see how happy they are. And why wouldn't they be? If they beat us today they will feel as if they have occupied India.'

'Let them win today. We will thrash them in such a way that they will go back half dead.'

'What nonsense is this? Have they done anything to harm you? There are other non-Chinese players in this club too,' Ananta flared up after he overheard the conversation.

Ananta was a student leader and everyone knew him. The man looked at him in surprise and asked, 'Do *you* trust them?'

'Why does the question of trust arise? They are not at fault – they are football players. Why are you mixing up two completely different things?'

The man kept quiet. He did not want to antagonize a student leader.

'Don't talk like that, Ananta da,' another student cautioned him. 'The situation is not good at this moment.' There were a lot of comments coming through. Some volatile, some reasoned.

'It's obvious he will say that. Everyone knows about his affair with Ahlin. How can he take criticism against the Chinese?'

'In the next conference of the students' union we will have to remove him from the post.'

Lao Thien Lee, the shoe shop owner, heard the comments. His excited, happy face clouded over instantly. After a while, he got up and went to the field.

The players of the Seven Star team were sitting together, drinking lemonade. Lao Thien walked towards them and quietly said, 'You Chinese fellows, come along with me for a minute.'

'Chinese fellows only? Why?'

'Chinese fellows or only Hakka fellows?'

'What about those who want to marry Chinese girls? Are you calling them, too?'

'Don't joke now. I have something important to say,' he said gravely.

The Chinese players felt awkward and hesitantly went with Lee. What would the others think? Pulok and the others watched from a distance as Lao Thien spoke. The players' faces turned glum. After a while, the whistle sounded. Lao Thien Lee stood aside and the players returned with fallen faces.

'Pulok, Lao Thien Lee also wants to talk to you. Go quickly. We don't have much time.'

Pulok went over and asked, 'What is it, Lee ako?'

'Something serious has happened. Listen carefully,' he said, explaining the situation as best as he could.

'Don't be afraid, Lee ako,' Pulok said. 'It's not so easy to beat someone up.'

'No, Pulok. I've heard the conversations clearly. In any case, during the game people get aggressive. The situation is sensitive now because of the India-China problem. People are angry. So, if a Chinese club wins, anything could happen.'

'This club has other players too. Let someone lay hands on us. Then we will see.'

'No, Pulok, don't pick a fight. From a small issue, it may grow into something serious. I will tell you something. Please don't mind.'

'Tell me quickly.'

'Let Duliajan win today.'

'What?'

'There is no way out. It's no big deal. In any game, one team has to win and the other loses. You can win next time. There may be big trouble today if someone incites the crowd.'

After looking at Lao Thien Lee for a while, Pulok said, 'Do you think our supporters would allow anyone to get away with insulting or assaulting you? The border problem is a different issue. Don't mix the two. We can't let our club lose! When the ball comes to the goalpost, I'm going to catch it, no matter what.'

'Try to understand, Pulok. There will be many more matches in future, and we will win again. We know that everyone doesn't feel this way but we can't take any chances, can we? If we win, these people are bound to create trouble. And if there is a clash they will spread rumours that the Chinese people have beaten up the Indians. There is a possibility of strong repercussions after that. I am only telling you all this. Please don't discuss this with others.'

Pulok looked at him. Lao Thien tried to smile, suppressing his sadness. Pulok returned to the field with a heavy heart.

The Chinese players of Seven Star were heartbroken. The players of Duliajan were advancing without any resistance. They were surprised at the sudden change of mood in the opposing team. What had happened?

One after another, Pulok missed three saves. Seven Star Club lost the match. No one knew why.

Some expressed frustration at the missed saves and vented their anger on Pulok. The Seven Star team came to receive the runners-up trophy glumly.

The Duliajan players, with their dirty jerseys and glowing faces, shook hands with the losing team. Hong kept looking at Pulok while shaking hands with their opponents.

'Come to my wedding,' Pulok said gently, looking at him.

'Yes, I'll come. I'll come before the wedding too. Why did you do this, Pulok?' Hong asked sadly. Pulok did not answer him.

'I think I know why,' Hong said after some time.

Pulok was quiet. He was filled with a helpless anger.

All the players shook hands with O'Connor. Addison and his group clapped and smiled while both the trophies were handed over. Ming was declared man of the match.

'We didn't enjoy the match today, Baruah,' Addison said to Pulok. 'You all played very badly after half-time.'

No one answered.

'Next year, make sure you play well. Our club must win.'

Pulok's team went to the cycle stand to get their bicycles and return home. As they approached the stand, the victorious team, along with their supporters, was getting into the truck to return to Duliajan. The entire area resounded with loud cheers from the moving truck.

'Hip hip hurray! Hip hip hurray!'

Six

The preparations for Pulok's wedding were in full swing. All his friends had come to his house. Hong and his younger brother Ming had also arrived from Tipling, a small town near Duliajan. Pulok was getting married on 11 October. While everyone else laughed and joked, Ming sat quietly in a corner of the room reading an Assamese novel.

Pulok's two sisters had come with their families to help with the wedding preparations. Other relatives from distant places had also arrived. In the midst of all these joyous activities, the only person who remained aloof was Pulok's father Minaram Baruah. He was sitting alone in the verandah with a droopy face. He didn't greet his son's friends, pretending not to see them when they passed by.

Minaram Baruah's mind was not at peace. Earlier, he used to like his son's Chinese friends. Now he felt disgusted by the very sight of them. Perhaps they were responsible for bringing his son closer to the Chinese girl. There was no one as gentle and responsible as his son. But what spell had this Chinese girl cast upon him? How could he say bluntly to his father's face, 'If you don't let me marry her, I'll elope with her. I'll leave my home and take her to the quarters in the garden.' He had tried his best to dissuade his son. Had his wife not sided with Pulok, the marriage would never have taken place. This was the first time after their marriage that his wife had openly defied him, actively getting involved in the entire arrangement of the wedding.

There was no way out now.

'What is the matter? Aren't you going to listen to the news?' his wife asked.

He came to the living room. Minaram Baruah stopped for a moment, then took the radio to the room adjacent to Pulok's and increased the volume.

'Just look at what deuta is doing. He is doing this to annoy you,' Pulok's sister said as she walked into Pulok's room to serve him tea.

'Don't say anything. Just let him be.'

'Since I've arrived, all I've seen him do is read the newspaper, listen to the news and abuse the Chinese. Since you are out most of the time, you don't know what goes on in the house. Who knows what he might do to your wife! You better not give up your quarters. You might not be able to live here once you're married,' Pulok's sister joked.

Pulok's father was listening to the radio with a frown on his face.

'No talks under duress ...'

'China must first pull out of NEFA ...'

'India has firmly told China that there can be no talks or discussions on the border question, until the latest Chinese intrusion into Indian territory in NEFA is terminated. India has also made it clear that the coming talks will have to be confined to measures for reducing tensions and restoring the status quo in the western sector of the India-China border, which has been altered by force in the last few years. India's position on the talks with China has been set out in a three-page note handed to the Chinese embassy yesterday and released for publication this evening ...'

Pulok's room turned silent as his father had expected.

'Lt General L. P. Sen has already arrived in the NEFA region. Lt General Umrao Singh has already inspected the forward position and spent a night there ...'

For quite a while after the news, no one spoke. The joyous atmosphere had evaporated. Putting an end to the silence Tung Chin said, 'If things continue like this, there is bound to be a war.'

'If a war breaks out, there will be lot of trouble,' Narayan said.

'We've heard our elders discussing that we might already be in trouble,' Lee Chang said.

'Forget it. What trouble can there be? You haven't attacked India, have you? Now come on, let's go.' Rameswar stood up to leave.

Ming was still engrossed in his book.

'If you want any books, take them,' Pulok said.

Ming's face brightened as he looked at his brother for permission.

'You don't have to look at him. Just take them,' Pulok repeated.

'Can I take these three?'

'Go ahead,' Rameswar said, laughing. 'Pulok is not going to read books for some time, don't worry.'

Pulok and his friends went out. They were all going to Makum to see the Durga puja celebrations. After that, they were to go to Ho Wang's house for dinner.

The puja pandal reverberated with the sound of drums. Holding earthen pots, with the smoke of resin rising in the air, two young boys were performing an arati in front of the goddess. The area was filled with shops selling balloons and sweetmeats.

Yiu Yi was inside the pandal. She came running when she saw them; her face was gloomy.

'How are you, Yiu Yi?' asked Tung Chin.

'I'm very sad today, ako.'

'Why?'

'I am feeling bad for Anjali.'

'Who is Anjali?'

'The girl who studies with me. She cried a lot today, did you know? Mei Ho also cried. Achun, Wong Choy did too. Their parents have not come to take them home, that's why.'

Pulok and his friends were aware of this. They had already come to the school and discussed the matter with the teachers. They bought new clothes for the boarders to wear during the festival. The families of Cheenapatti had also invited the boarders to have food in their homes.

'Today we have been invited to Ho Wang uncle's house for dinner. Ko Fuk and their friends are very thankful that you all gave them new clothes. "Your brothers are very good," they said.'

'You are a very good girl,' Pulok said fondly.

'Have you met Mei Lin ache? There she is! Shall I call her?'

'It's alright. Don't call her.'

Pulok would meet Mei Lin in Ho Wang's house anyway. Since their engagement, Pulok also felt a little shy to talk to her in the presence of others.

A group of girls, including Kaushalya, Mei Hang, Alan, Siu, Ahlin, Chitta's wife Bela, his sister Jhuma and Mei Lin, were watching the arati.

'Ahlin, look there, it's Ananta,' Mei Hang said, laughing softly. 'Go and talk to him, or he won't get any sleep tonight.'

Ananta walked up to them.

'What is it?' Ahlin asked blushing.

'You saw me. Why didn't you come and talk to me?'

'Don't you see how everyone is staring?'

'So what? Can't one talk with a classmate?' Ananta's eyes sparkled in amusement.

'Huh! As if you are meeting me as a classmate!'

'Then what are we meeting as?'

'You only keep joking! I am going. I feel shy!'

'I don't feel shy at all. Let us pray to the goddess and tell her about us.'

'Do you really mean that?'

'Yes, I do. Don't you want to?'

'Is it okay if I pray without folding my hands?'

'Why? Are your hands hurting?'

'Even though you know, you still ask me. People will see.'

'Alright, you need not fold your hands but let us move ahead a bit.'

Ananta took a long time to pray, while Ahlin, fighting back her tears, kept looking at the face of the goddess.

'Have you given up your studies on the pretext of the puja?' Ananta asked.

'No, I haven't.'

'Remember, you have to study at Cotton College with me. You must score good marks. Wherever we go, we will go together. If you refuse, I will take you with me anyway, got it?'

Ahlin smiled. Ananta placed a folded slip of paper in her hand.

Ananta was so fearless. And shameless too. With so many people around, he gave her a letter!

'Where is my share?' he asked with twinkling eyes.

Ahlin fled from the place, blushing profusely.

At that moment, in the sitting room of Manchung Ho, the leading contractor of Makum, a party was underway. Manchung Ho had invited a few high officials and big contractors on the occasion of the festival. He maintained a good rapport with powerful people for his own interests.

Today, Mok Min was absent as he could not leave his shop. The high officials also could not spend much time because they had to work longer hours during the festival. They had come because they couldn't resist the food and the hospitality of the family.

Picking up the bottle of Scotch, the executive magistrate laughed and said, 'Don't be vague. Ask for Haig!'

'The wine shop must have been emptied out today. Such sales!'

'Mok Min's shop is also full of customers. He can make his entire year's profit during the puja. Besides, the Chinese of the entire district rely on his shop for Chinese provisions. This is another reason for his wealth.'

'This time his business won't be that good. Chinese customers will not be able to come because of the restrictions on their movement.'

The free-flowing whiskey soon ensured that the barrier between government and non-government collapsed. The Chinese businessmen were cautious. Most of them were aware of the situation at the border. They listened to both All India Radio and Radio Peking and they read all the daily newspapers.

'The restrictions will not be removed easily. Secret orders have already come to keep an eye on the Chinese,' one of the officials blurted.

The Chinese businessmen became wary.

'Why are there orders to keep an eye on us?' A. C. Chow asked hesitantly.

'There may be spies amongst you! Are there any?' a government officer asked jokingly.

'How would we know? Most people go to work and come home to eat and sleep. Most of them are not educated. What kind of spying can they do, I wonder?' A. C. Chow said.

'But some can read I'm sure. I've seen Chinese books in your club's library. Who reads those books?'

'It's the school teachers who read them.'

'Some from Cheenapatti also read them, I am sure. You cannot say there is no spy among them.'

A. C. Chow kept silent. Everyone glanced at the officer. Was he drunk or was he pretending? It was hard to say. Most of the Chinese businessmen were smart enough to know that agents of government intelligence were around. But they did not think that their safety was at stake. There was nothing to worry about. Most of the government officials of that area knew them. They were not new settlers. The bones of their ancestors were buried in this land. They had toiled hard to climb the ladder of success to reach their present status, in which endeavour the government officials had also helped a lot. In return, they also gave whatever they could to these officials.

'The Chinese can cook wonderful food, I must say. What is this – chow mein? Why is it so long? It is difficult to eat.'

'We don't break up the chow mein into small bits because the length signifies longevity.'

'Oh that's why? I'll come some other day to eat properly. I have to leave now. I'll take this with me.' The officer picked up the bottle and walked out unsteadily.

At that time Pulok and his friends were on their way to Ho Wang's house. Ho Wang had invited the hostel students for a meal. Pulok and his friends had brought small gifts for all the children. Ho Wang had also invited all the Chinese who lived in the lane. They'd all arrived a little before Pulok and his friends got there. Ho Wang's quiet home suddenly became lively with the presence of all the guests, including the children. Ho Wang and his wife received the guests with glowing faces.

The children, clad in new clothes and shoes, were sitting beside Cha Mu. They looked sad and confused. Every year they went home for the puja vacation. Most of them lived in tea gardens. Durga puja was their favourite festival. But this time no one had come to take them home.

Pulok and his friends sat near the children.

'Thakra dada abused us today,' Yiu Yi said quietly.

'Why did he do that?' Pulok asked.

'While passing his house we were talking loudly. Someone in his house is ill. He rebuked us for making a ruckus.'

'Did he say anything else?'

'Yes, he did. He said, "Go on, make a racket. You won't be able to keep it up much longer in any case." What did he mean, Pulok dada?'

'Forget it, he was just grumbling. I will scold him.'

'Don't say anything to Thakra dada. We are all afraid of him. He goes around Cheenapatti with a huge stick. If we want to go out at night, Maa says, "Don't go, Thakra will come." Is he a ghost, Pulok dada?' Yiu Yi giggled. So did the others.

The women entered the room with food. Putting down bowls in front of the children, Alan said, 'Start with the soup.'

'Why haven't our parents come?' Ho Yin from Class 1 asked Mei Lin.

Mei Lin looked at his tear-stained face, not knowing what to say.

'I know. The police didn't let them come,' Ko Fuk said.

'Why?' Mei Ho asked.

'I don't know.'

'Why won't the police let them come, Mei Lin ache?'

Mei Lin had no answer. The children had their soup in silence.

At that time Thakur Prasad and Rajendra were roaming outside. Their faces and bodies were covered with a shawl. With a long stick in their hand, they were patrolling alongside the constables of the Makum outpost.

Seven

The Chinese Club in Makum had been transformed into a wedding venue. Large canopies had been set up outside the clubhouse. The place was full of people. It was Mei Lin's wedding day.

In a pure white silk mekhela-chador, she looked like a typical Assamese bride. Everyone who saw her was captivated by her beauty. She was sitting in a beautifully decorated room surrounded by her friends. The marriage was to be performed according to Assamese rites to fulfil the wish of Pulok's father. Everyone accepted that heartily. They all loved the gentle girl. They wanted her to have a good life. Having lost his wife early in his life, Mei Lin's father had busied himself with work and left Mei Lin in the care of his brother-in-law's family.

The relatives, who lived far away, could not attend the wedding. Those who were nearby and could return the same day had come. Mei Lin's father had invited all his friends and acquaintances for the wedding of his only daughter. Even the family of Akong's wife Phulmoni was invited. Yiu Yi's sister Yunlin and her family, who lived near Ledo, had come too.

Banwarilal Chowkhani attended the wedding with his entire family and so did the constables and the sub-inspector of the outpost. Everyone from Makum was there. Special arrangements were made to receive guests like the Officer-in-Charge of Tinsukia police station in a separate room at the Chinese Club. For all of Cheenapatti, this wedding became a festive occasion. No one remembered the border. At the wedding venue, only the hostel boarders were sitting sadly. Pulok was still at home looking after the guests wearing a white dhoti and kurta. His bright young face glowed with utmost happiness. All his friends were here. They would all go together to Mei Lin's house with him.

'Hey Haranath!' Rameswar called out, seeing Lee Chang as he entered. His friends rolled in laughter and delight.

Lee Chang walked up to Rameswar and held him tightly in mock anger. Minaram Baruah was furious, seeing their happiness. Unable to control himself, he vented his anger at a neighbour who was sitting near him.

'Look at the Chinese. Look at their joy. It is obvious that they will make merry. It is their day after all.'

The guest was surprised and asked, 'What do you mean by that?'

'Don't you know what is happening at the border?'

'What is happening?' asked the man who usually came to listen to the news in Minaram's house.

'There is a war going on between India and China at the NEFA border, don't you know?'

'No, I don't. How did you find out?'

'From the news, of course! The Chinese were silent for eleven days. Suddenly they have started attacking. The fighting is going on in the Dhola area inside the Indian border. China has said that our soldiers had attacked their troops! Wait, let me get the newspaper.' Leaving his guests, Minaram Baruah went inside to look for the paper.

'Something is really wrong with Baruah. Even on his son's wedding day, all he talks about is the border scuffle. I think his only son marrying a Chinese girl has hit him hard.'

Baruah returned with the newspaper in his hand and, pointing to an article, said, 'Listen to this, I'll read it out to you. A New China News Agency report alleged that Indian troops on 10 October attacked Chinese Frontier Guards in Southern Tibet and inflicted eleven casualties. The news agency said that the Chinese Frontier Guards near Chihtung were compelled to hit back and the battle was still continuing. According to China, in the Chedong area which is north of the so-called McMahon Line, the Indian Army has intruded and established a few posts in the north of the Kechilang River and injured Chinese oldiers near Chihtung. To maintain its position and in self-defence, the Chinese troops were compelled to retaliate. In the protest note delivered to our government, China said that if India did not stop armed aggression immediately, China would certainly take necessary action for self-defence. India will have to take complete responsibility for all the consequences.'

'Why should India take responsibility? Has India attacked China? They have crossed the McMahon Line and set up posts on Indian soil. They have fired at our soldiers,' one of the guests said angrily.

'You say that in such a way as if you have visited the border. Who knows what is happening actually!' a CPI worker shot back.

'What do you mean to say? China has not attacked us?' another guest confronted the CPI worker.

'Why do you get agitated whenever we criticize China?'

'When did I get agitated? Can't I say what I feel? If I can't share this with you who else do I go to?'

'That's true. But it is high time to shed our sympathy for the Chinese.'

'But Nehru himself has not withdrawn his sympathy for China. He is still talking about discussion. He should have already expelled the Chinese troops from Indian soil. China occupied Longju long back, in 1959. Chinese troops returned after that, but India did not reoccupy Longju. Even if they haven't reoccupied, they should have been alert. India should have realized that those who have attacked once might do so again.'

'Baruah is right. These days I too feel irritated at the sight of these Chinese. China has been disturbing us at the border and these Chinese are silent.'

'What are you saying? What can they do? Who will listen to them? They are Chinese *Indians*.'

'Indian? How do you know?'

'If not Indian, then what? We've seen them here since we were born. They have been here since much before Independence. Those who have been living here since before 1947 will naturally be Indians.'

'Not all of them were here before Independence. I have heard now and then that the Chinese are still coming, though less in number.'

'Don't advocate on their behalf. These are bad times. You can never tell what might happen.'

'It's time to move. We have to leave in thirty minutes,' Pulok's mother came and said to the group. Then she went away to inform Pulok.

'Let's wait for Robin, Maa.'

'Robin will go straight to the bride's house.'

'Why, what's the problem?' Pulok asked anxiously.

'I don't know.'

Pulok was worried. Robin had come to attend his wedding. Pulok wondered if he was in any trouble.

Everyone was waiting near the gate for Pulok. Dressed in his bridegroom's finery, he bowed before his parents. Then he joined the crowd to leave amidst celebrations.

The gate of the Chinese Club had been decorated with banana plants, mango leaves, earthen pots with grains of rice, and incense. Men and women waited near the gate with earthen lamps to welcome the bridegroom. While the women sang wedding songs and the children threw fistfuls of rice at Pulok, Tung Chin's mother welcomed the bridegroom.

Yiu Yi washed Pulok's feet and wiped them with a new gamosa. Then looking at Pulok she asked, 'How will we address you now, Pulok dada?'

Robin arrived just as the couple sat down in front of the fire for the wedding rites. All the friends gathered around him. Yiu Yi came running happily.

'Why didn't you dress as the bridegroom's best man, Sipahi dada?'

'Because he will be our Yiu Yi's bridegroom. She is dressed up like a bride today,' Tung Chin teased.

Yiu Yi's plump pink cheeks turned red. Robin extended his hand to pull her cheeks. Avoiding his hand she ran away, light reflecting off her white gown.

'I'll have to leave today,' Robin said. 'I have to reach Tezu by tomorrow morning. Tonight I'll stay in Saikhowa. I don't know where I have to go from there.'

'Is there really a war on, Robin?'

'There have been skirmishes. That is why we are not allowed to leave our stations.'

Mei Lin's father came in with Ho Fuk. The topic had changed.

A few tables had been arranged for the older people in a corner. Some played Mahjong, some smoked pipes and watched others playing. Some were engrossed in conversation. Ho Fuk and Mei Lin's father joined this group.

'We haven't seen you in a long time. How are you?' Tung Chin's father asked Ho Fuk.

'Everything is fine.'

'You are such a big contractor! Everything is bound to be fine,' Chi Fu Hai said, smiling.

'Oh! I am not a big contractor at all. Things are a little better now – that's all. Just remember our past. How difficult it was.'

Following Ho Fuk's comment everyone was engrossed in the discussion of the old days. It had become a ritual. Whenever the old people met at any function, they talked about their past. Remembering their motherland and the days of suffering, they became nostalgic. Ho Fuk was listening to the discussion but he was buried deep in his own thoughts. He remembered his mother and his brothers and all the relatives whom he had left behind in China.

He came to Assam during the Second World War, when the Allied forces decided to construct a road from Ledo to Kunming. He came with the innumerable Chinese labourers brought to work on the Ledo Road and entered into a life of untold hardship.

Then one day the war was over.

The commanders of the war packed up their ammunition. Fighter planes were no longer heard screeching in the skies. The military trucks no longer moved on the roads rattling the houses. The frightening groups of soldiers disappeared. The shrill sounds of sirens were not heard anymore. The papers pasted on the window panes to block out the light were removed. And the zigzag trenches that were dug as shelters were converted into mossy breeding grounds for mosquitoes. The rainwater washed away the clotted blood of the dead. The fields that were destroyed by the heavy boots of the soldiers had now turned lush green again. The long road from Ledo to Kunming was deserted and quiet. The war zone was littered with the scraps of war materials and empty cans of food, beer and wine. With the end of the war came the end of the demand for Chinese labour.

Holding his glass of whiskey Ho Fuk sat, totally lost in his own thoughts.

He could not ever return to China. After the war was over he started working as a labourer to survive.

Many years had passed. From a daily-wage earner he had become a big contractor after much hardship. He got married. He built his own house. He was well-settled now. Now he wanted to visit his old village in China once. He wanted to visit his parents' graves and offer prayers.

'You too came during the war, didn't you?' C Hoi asked.

'Yes. I was brought by ship to Calcutta, and then by train to Margherita. After that I was taken to a Chinese driving school in Ledo,' said Ho Fuk, 'where the Chinese were taught to drive and repair cars.'

'Those were difficult days for all. But more so for the Chinese. We were brought from remote villages of China. We were deprived of food, winter clothes and medicines. We didn't know any other language and had to communicate through signs. The most arduous jobs were dumped on us. Most of us cried all the time. But no one cared. It was utter misery.'

'It was terrible!' said Mei Lin's father.

'We had to build a long motorable road. We had to clear thick jungles and fell huge trees and cut through mounds of earth. The jungles abounded with mosquitoes, snakes and leeches, in addition to all kinds of venomous insects. Most of those who came from our village died of fever, malaria and blood dysentery.'

'How did this old man drive, ask him,' Tung Chin's father said, smiling.

Everyone coaxed Ho Fuk to tell the story. The alcohol was helping them feel lighter.

'The trucks loaded with food and other materials were sent to Kunming through Ledo Road. There were other drivers too. But the number of Chinese drivers was higher. The roads were very bad. On one side were steep hills, and on the other, deep gorges. A little this way or that, and straight down. People aside, not even a part of the vehicle would be found. That's why perhaps they used us. If anyone died, it would be the Chinese labourers. Nothing but slaves. There were many accidents. No one knows how many people died. If one vehicle fell down the gorge three Chinese would die.'

'How come?'

'Each truck carried three drivers. We used to drive the truck together. We were short. The vehicles were huge. The seats were high. When seated, our legs could not reach the accelerator. We looked like small children. One driver sat with his legs folded under him on the seat. He steered the truck. The second one sat on the left to change gears while the third one sat at the bottom to manage the accelerator and brake with both hands.'

'Oh!'

'Didn't you drive to Kunming?'

'I was supposed to be a good driver so I drove small cars too. One day, I had to take two young white military officers to Kunming. They were of my age. They sat at the back and we followed the convoy. Halfway there, our car broke down. The convoy sped on and it started snowing. I sat there with nothing warm to cover me. All three of us shivered in the cold. Then, one of the officers gestured to me to come to the rear seat. I thought they were going to kill me because the car had broken down, but no, they made me sit between them and covered us all with whatever warm clothes they had. All of us fell asleep. When we woke the next morning we were frozen stiff!'

'And then?'

'The officers shook me out of my frozen stupor. Even in the middle of such a calamity we started laughing.'

'Why?'

'I had turned black in the freezing cold. The officers thought I was dead. Then they looked at each other and burst into laughter again. They looked the same as I did. They were really very nice fellows, just eighteen or nineteen years old!'

'Then what happened?'

'We came back. I had a raging fever. After that, there was the bombing in Japan. The war was over. And so was my job.'

'This fellow had such a long pigtail then,' Tung Chin's father joked.

'Let me tell you that I was considered a handsome youth in China. The day I left, so many young girls cried along with my mother. After I came here, the local girls looked at me too and I thought it was because they found me handsome. But they looked at me from afar and fled.'

'Then how did you get Saraswati to marry you?'

'At first she ran away. Then she would laugh. What could I do? I cut my pigtail to please her, but that made her laugh all the more. Now when we quarrel, I threaten to grow my pigtail again,' Ho Fuk laughed. Everyone joined him.

By the time the wedding ceremony was over, it was late at night. Yiu Yi fell asleep on Ahlin's lap holding on to Robin's hand. As soon as the couple had gone inside, Robin picked Yiu Yi up and took her to her mother. Her mother, who was preparing tea, turned around and asked Robin, 'Is she asleep? Wake her up.'

'If I wake her up, she won't let me go.'

'That is true. She was after me to stop you from leaving. Put her in the other room. Come with me.'

Robin put Yiu Yi on the bed where many other children were asleep. Slowly removing her grip from his hand, Robin came out, smiling gently at her mother. Mei Lin and Pulok were seated in another room surrounded by their friends. Seeing Robin, Mei Lin's face glowed for a while and clouded over again.

Robin smiled and pulled out a string of beads from his pocket.

'This is for you. I had asked someone to get them for me. The girls in NEFA wear them.'

With tearful eyes Mei Lin accepted the gift.

'Let us also see. How beautiful it is,' the wives of her friends came forward to look at the beads.

Robin stood up and left the room just as Mei Lin's aunt entered to announce the beginning of the tea ceremony.

'I will not follow Chinese customs. You go and have the tea,' Pulok's father told his wife angrily, who had come to call him.

'Why? What will happen if you do? Everything has been done the Assamese way. Why can't we follow one of their customs?'

'It will be good if you follow them! After some days we will have to follow their rules. We will have to live under them.'

'You just keep quiet. These people have not attacked our country. While constructing your house you wanted a Chinese carpenter! To make your furniture you need them too. You require the Chinese to make your shoes. Now that China has attacked India these people have become alien to us? We have seen them since our childhood. They are like our own people. Please do not create unnecessary problems during the marriage, I tell you.'

Seeing his wife flare up he kept quiet and followed her inside. But from his face it was apparent that he was seething with anger.

Mei Lin and Pulok sat in a room arranged for the tea ceremony. The first people to be honoured were Yiu Yi's grandparents and Tung Chin's parents. Though they were not from the same clan, they were treated as family members; the three families were descendants of Ho Han, Ho Yen and Ah Chin.

Mei Lin and Pulok came to kneel before Yiu Yi's grandparents and offer them a cup of tea. They in turn gave them a lai si, filled with money. One after the other, according to the hierarchies, they paid their respects to all the senior relatives. As they came to Mei Lin's father, Mei Lin could not control her emotions. Handing him the cup of tea, she lowered her head to conceal her tears.

Her father remained still and silent for some time before he gave her a Lai si packet. Then, from a bag beside him, he pulled out the beautifully carved wooden box that held the bowl and chopsticks of his ancestor Ho Han. Placing the box in Mei Lin's hand and placing his own hand in blessing over her head, he said, 'This is a relic of your ancestors. Treat it with respect.'

He placed his hand on Pulok's head next and said softly, 'Look after Mei Lin well, baba!'

After paying their respects to all their seniors, Mei Lin and Pulok were now seated in their chairs. They would give a lai si to all the youngsters of the family before leaving.

At that time, Liang was taking Robin to Saikhowa ghat on his bicycle. Rameswar and Lee Chang followed behind.

Dawn was breaking outside.

Eight

'Come in,' Pulok called out, smiling.

'Are you really asking me to come in? Or do you actually want me to carry on? Tell me honestly.' Getting off from his bicycle Narayan Sharma smiled back.

'You've come to show me your writings, I am sure.'

'How did you know?'

'You aren't here just to look at me so early in the day!'

'You are living in a dreamland. How can I disturb you? But for how long will you hibernate?'

Pulok showed Narayan into the living room.

'Let me inform Mei Lin.'

As soon as Pulok returned, Narayan handed him a sheaf of papers.

'Read this and give me your opinion.'

Narayan, who had so far been a local newspaper reporter, had started to write political articles. This one was about the tensions at the border – 'Will Nehru be in trouble because of his ego? And with him, his India?'

'Can you write like this about our Prime Minister?' Pulok asked.

'Everyone seems to be using this tone now. Read it and tell me what you think.'

Will Nehru be in trouble because of his ego? And with him, his India?

At this moment this is a major question for which many Indians want an answer. Nehru's latest statement and the news published in the media relating to defence makes us feel that we are going towards that possibility.

The border skirmishes between the two countries are creating a sense of confusion and dissatisfaction among the general public.

Questions began to arise over the determination, foresight and commitment of the leadership of our state.

On 11 October, at Nehru's behest a meeting was convened with the top brass of the defence establishment. Defence Minister V. K. Krishna Menon, the chiefs of the Army and Air Force, the members of the Cabinet, the secretaries of the Ministries of Defence and External Affairs, the director of the Intelligence Bureau, B. N. Mullik, and other important personalities including B. M. Kaul were present.

Nehru had a discussion with Lt General Kaul, the commander of the 'Four Corps' formed to oust the Chinese intruders from the eastern sector of the Indian border, and Lt General L. P. Sen, the general officer of the eastern command, regarding the present situation and the defence arrangements.

According to the media, Kaul, who is stationed at the operational headquarters of the Four Corps in Tezpur, has been studying the ground situation. General Sen also surveyed the current situation in the NEFA area and Lt General Umrao Singh spent a night in the forward positions at the NEFA border as well. It has been reported that these higher-ups of the army had already informed Nehru in detail about the situation at the NEFA border. It is known that the information which was given to Nehru was totally different from what he had been getting before that. It is also known that after he was informed about the actual position, Nehru paused to rethink for the first time.

It is clear that the position of the Indian defence at the border is not favourable for India. When it comes to communication, arms and ammunition, and even more minor issues like proper clothing and food, India is not in an advantageous position. If India takes an offensive stance and tries to oust the Chinese soldiers, China may retaliate in both the eastern and western sectors.

After discussing the issue with the higher-ups Nehru had decided to maintain the present position. Nehru had also decided that India would not take an aggressive stance to oust the Chinese soldiers from the north of the Namka Chu river.

After this, Nehru departed for Colombo. At the airport, journalists surrounded him with a volley of questions. What is going on at the border? How many Indians have been injured? How many have been killed? Is it true that in the Dhola area six Indian soldiers have been killed, eleven have been injured and seven have gone missing? What steps has your government taken to expel Chinese soldiers?

What was Nehru thinking at that time? If he told the truth, would the journalists think that India had moved back fearing the Chinese? How could he contradict his own confident statements to the effect that India would oust the Chinese from Indian soil? What would that do to Nehru's image? Would Nehru, the undisputed leader of Asia, bow down before the Premier of Red China, a state that was established after India became independent? Would he let China lead Asia?

How can Nehru accept a lower position? Can Nehru, the chief spokesman of the Non-Aligned Movement, the proponent of Panchsheel, the leader of the Indian freedom struggle, admit publicly the truth that Indian defence was not adequate to challenge China? Can he tell journalists that he did not study the ground situation personally as he was busy with world politics? That his statements were on the basis of the reports provided by the Defence Minister Menon and the high officials of the Army who were Menon loyalists?

No, he cannot.

He cannot expose that weakness. The enemy will be encouraged. His position would become weak in world politics. The world's statesmen would look down on him.

Perhaps for this reason he made certain statements in the impulse of the moment: 'Indian Army has been ordered to drive the

Chinese troops from Indian territory on the northeast frontier ... There is no question of any negotiation with China till it stops attacks at the NEFA frontier.'

Was that a wise step? Did Nehru do the right thing? Will the statement given by Nehru not give a chance to the Chinese to attack India? Should one speak of war when one does not have the strength to fight? Was it right for Nehru to play with the life of common people and the soldiers just to save his image?

At this crucial moment we need a statesman who is determined and has forethought, instead of such emotional leadership and hollow speeches ...

Pulok looked up from the pages and said, 'It is very good, Narayan. When did you write it?'

'Last night. In my opinion, Nehru should not have told the journalists that he had ordered the army to oust the Chinese. What I have learned from the news is that if China attacks India at the NEFA frontier, the Indian army will not be able to offer any resistance. We are in a weaker position from all sides. Nehru made the entire nation emotional. He might have considered the India-China conflict to be something like the Indian freedom struggle. He has little experience of war, whereas the Chinese leaders have direct experience of warfare.'

'Don't you think you might get into trouble for publishing this? How did you get all this information?'

'There is every chance that I will be in trouble. But I could not resist writing it. All this has been published in various newspapers from time to time. I've just put the main points together. Right now India's defences are weak but we have not stopped blustering and talking big.'

'After Nehru's statement, do you think the Chinese will stay quiet?'

'No, they won't. They are just waiting for an opportunity to attack. With this, Nehru has presented them with the opportunity.'

Mei Lin arrived with tea. The discussion came to an end. She looked even more beautiful in traditional Assamese attire. As Narayan looked at her in awe, she blushed, while Pulok smiled with pride.

'Have your tea,' Mei Lin said.

Meanwhile, A. C. Chow was listening to Radio Peking, sitting in his tastefully constructed house. One could see the worry lines on his forehead.

'It is said in *The Peking People's Daily*, the official mouthpiece of the Chinese Communist Party, that a massive Indian attack is imminent in the eastern sector of the border. In the first page editorial of the *The Peking People's Daily* comments have been published regarding Nehru's latest statement. It is also said that being the representative of the Indian reactionary ruling circle, Nehru would not hesitate to use the lives of Indian soldiers to satiate his greed. They want a yard after taking an inch. Can China be so weak-kneed? No aggressor could overthrow the brave Chinese army from their own land. The editorial also commented that China still wanted to settle the dispute through negotiation. In the editorial the Chinese frontier guards were told to maintain vigilance constantly. Following Nehru's orders, the Indian army may come to expel you. You have to be prepared for that. It is your sacred duty to safeguard your national soil and overthrow all the attacks of the encroachers.'

Chow looked worried. After a while, he switched off the radio and went out. He had seen life in all its colours. From abject poverty he had risen to become a wealthy contractor. He had arrived after a long period of suffering. Unlike the Chinese carpenters, fitters and meat sellers, he was a man of repute and he understood that the situation was turning grim. These days, even the indifferent Chinese of Cheenapatti listened to the news daily and discussed the issue in hushed voices. A. C. Chow, however, stayed away from these discussions. He had made his money during the construction of the Ledo Road in the Second World War by supplying Chinese labourers. A few Chinese had earned money this way. Most of the Chinese became rich by repairing numerous houses that had broken down during the earthquake of 1950.

He had been living happily in India. He could not educate his children because when they were growing up he was completely immersed in work trying to make a life for himself and his family. This was not a foreign land for him. This was his own country. This land had given him a lot.

For the first time life had become complicated.

He did not know what to do. The situation was deteriorating day by day. The local people had begun to look upon the Chinese with a sense of mistrust and doubt. Town committees were set up to collect money for the soldiers on the war front. It was the beginning of a nationalist agenda. Anything could happen at anytime.

A. C. Chow decided that he had to keep his own position safe and for that he needed to keep his name in the government's good books. After a discussion with Ho Chang Ho, the president of the Makum Chinese Society, they had decided to hold a meeting to discuss the ways through which they could show their loyalty to India.

When Chow arrived at the Chinese club, many others, including the headmaster, Wang Shu Shin, Ho Chang Ho, Mok Min, Man Chung Ho, Ho Yen Kee, Ho Fuk and K. P. Lee were already seated there. Several copies of the *China Review*, published in Calcutta, and a few local newspapers, were lying in front of them. With the arrival of Chow, serious discussions began.

Firdaus Ali, the officer-in-charge of the Makum police outpost, was attentively listening to the news at that time. Thakur Prasad

Shah arrived on the scene, grinning. Gesturing at him to sit, Firdaus continued to listen to the news from the border. Thakur Prasad was getting restless for he had important news.

'Nehru made a statement in Colombo that there could not be the slightest doubt, historically and factually, that the territories occupied by the Chinese belonged to India. Even if the Chinese did have any claim to such territory, aggression was not the means of upholding it ... Mr Nehru said that it was extremely difficult to deal with the Chinese. "Each time we move about in our own territory, the Chinese keep on sending us protest notes saying that we have trespassed onto their territory," Mr Nehru said. "China has seized about 12,000 square miles in the Ladakh area, but not much in the north-east. But if we do not stop them, they will march further and further." He added, "Our mentality is opposed to this military conflict. Apart from the fact that it is a burden on India and we have to try and build up our country, we are not interested in fighting." He also commented that in a treaty between China and Burma, the Chinese also have, in effect, agreed to the continuation of the McMahon Line as the border of Burma. He said, "I think that applies to India, too. It is the same borderline." On the other hand, the New China News Agency claimed yesterday that two more Indian planes flew over Chinese territory. The agency alleged that the first plane flew over the Migyitun area of the Tibet region, repeatedly circled over and reconnoitred the sentry post and the areas behind it, before flying off. The report followed a Chinese protest to India about aggression on their border and a warning that Chinese troops will surely continue to strike back resolutely if it continued. Against that, in a protest note India has said that the allegation was totally baseless and no air space violation had occurred.'

Ali took out a packet of cigarettes. Pulling out one for himself and offering another to Thakur Prasad, he asked, 'What news have you brought? How come I haven't seen you for a couple of days?'

'It wouldn't be right for me to come every day.'

'Why?'

'The Chinese in Cheenapatti have perhaps guessed that I give you inside information. They look at me with red eyes. They have bad motives, sir.'

'What is new about that? They already know that you are our man.'

'That is true. Everyone knows that I go to you with cases of dacoity and theft. They always say that I am a government agent. But now whenever they see me, they stop talking.'

'Do you have any new information?' Ali asked, trying to mask his irritation.

'Yes. Last night, three or four Chinese men came to C Hoi's house, sir. They came quietly like thieves. I went to find out who they were but they wouldn't let me enter, the son of a ...' Thakur paused and looked at Ali innocently, trying to gauge his reaction.

'Is it? Who were they?'

'They are not from Makum. Today I have brought very big news for you. All the Chinese big shots are meeting at the Chinese Club. K. P. Lee, Mok Min, C Hoi, Ho Yen Kee – all the big people. Ho Chang Ho will be joining as well. All bloody Chinese spies.'

Ali listened to him and stood up.

'You can leave now. I have to go out.'

Thakur Prasad came out of the police outpost feeling satisfied. It felt good to speak against the Chinese of Cheenapatti. Now he had to find out what they had discussed in the meeting and plot his revenge. It could be the opportunity he had been looking for.

Nine

Today, China launched a massive all-out attack on NEFA along a twelve-mile sector. The Indian troops fought back gallantly for every inch of their territory but were overwhelmed by more than 20,000 Chinese invaders, armed with heavy mortar and medium machine guns. The Khinzemane posts fell in the morning and the main Dhola post in the afternoon. In NEFA, the Chinese invaders swooped down the Thagla ridge in successive waves along the twelve-mile stretch ranging from the Khinzemane post to Dhola. Heavy fighting was raging south of the Namka Chu River.

The solemn voice of radio newsreader Lily Das hurled the war updates like powerful bombs into Mei Lin and Pulok's room. They were about to leave for Makum. The news made Mei Lin stop at the main door.

South of Dhola, the Indian troops had to abandon Sangdhar, an important post. South of Namka Chu river, which was under the control of the Indian Army before the Chinese attack, fierce fighting continued despite heavy snowfall. A large number of Chinese soldiers equipped with heavy mortar and mountain guns have also attacked the Chip Chap valley of Ladakh. According to latest news, they have extended this attack to the Pang Gong lake area to the south of the Chip Chap valley. From two forward posts the Indian Army had to retreat to a defensive position. However, the main post of Daulet Beg Oldi and the Galwan post encircled by the Chinese are still under Indian control and have been reinforced.

'The war has taken a serious turn, I don't know what will happen,' said Pulok gravely.

Mei Lin did not answer. She was feeling frustrated. After this update, it would be difficult to put up with her father-in-law's sarcasm. At least once a day he would find an excuse to vilify the Chinese, and taunt her indirectly. Most of the comments against the Chinese were made by him when the neighbours gathered to listen to the news on the radio. Mei Lin felt that he had still not accepted her as his daughter-in-law. He ate the food she served but did not speak to her. She was scared to go near him because of his sour temperament.

'Let's go, Mei Lin,' Pulok said with a sigh.

A meeting had been organized by the Praja Socialist Party in Makum. Dropping Mei Lin at her father's house, Pulok went there. After the meeting, the people planned to take out a procession. Pulok, however, had decided to return home with his wife.

In the kitchen of the Chinese school, boarders between six and twelve years of age sat in rows to have lunch. The puja holidays were almost over. Not one of them had gone home. By now they had understood that something was very wrong. Cha Mu was supervising the boarders cheerfully. She could not reveal her anxiety before the children. Every night, Cha Mu became a mother to seven-year-old Ho Yin, who would squeeze into her arms and sleep feeling safe. In fact, she was now mothering all these children and it was the first time in her lonely and difficult life that she was happy to be alive.

At the ringing of a bicycle bell the children became alert. It was the familiar sound of the postman's arrival.

'Letters from home!'

The boys stood up.

'I'll go and see. You finish your food or else sir will get angry,' Cha Mu said and went out.

She was not worried for herself; she had no one in this world from whom she could expect a letter.

Her parents sold her when she was still a child. It was a long story of suffering. Finally, she met Ho Yen Kee in Hong Kong, who eventually brought her to Makum and engaged her as a cook in the hostel.

'Cha Mu ache, look at the number of letters today!' the headmaster said. 'Bring the children over to my room.'

When Cha Mu entered the headmaster's office with the boarders, all the teachers seated there wore worried faces.

Someone had opened their letters! It was the work of the CID for sure. They suspected the Chinese of Makum. They suspected there might be secret messages in the letters.

Everyone sat silently. It would not be wise to speak before the children.

The headmaster called little Ho Yin, who was holding on tightly to Cha Mu's clothes. Distributing the letters to the older boys, he opened Ho Yin's letter. A teacher started reading the letter aloud to him as Ho Yin had not yet learned to read Assamese well.

'My dear Ho Yin,

We send you our love. I hope you are well by the grace of God. We are also well. You must be wondering why your father has not come to take you. But don't worry. Due to some difficulties I have not been able to come. Very soon, I will come and take you. You must not be sad. Eat well and study properly. Respect your teachers and consider Cha Mu as your mother. We felt very bad that you were not here during the puja. We missed you. We did not go anywhere to watch the puja. We have not bought any new clothes. When you come ...'

Ho Yin's sobs touched all present as if this was not his letter alone but a letter from everyone's fathers. All the boarders started crying.

In another room, teacher Chiang Chi Chien sat quietly with a letter in his hand. His eyes were shadowed with immense sorrow. The letter was from his new wife, who was supposed to come to Makum shortly from China. Everything had turned upside down because of the war. He read the letter again.

'I haven't received word from you for a long time. I am worried about you. Don't worry about us. Write soon. We are all fine. Everyone keeps asking me, "When will he come?" I go to work in the fields every day. I also do the housework. Everyone loves me. But I feel sad that you are not here. When will you come?'

Chiang Chi Chien tried to compose himself when his colleagues entered the room.

'You look sad. Whose letter is it?' one of his colleagues asked.

'It is from my wife. I don't know what I should do.'

'Don't worry. Everything will be fine. But be careful what you write. I think the letters are censored.'

'Yes. That's true. The Indian government suspects us. It feels terrible.'

'They may not. These things happen during a war. There might be some bad people amongst us. In a way, it is good that they censor the letters. They will know what we are doing.'

'Headmaster says we should meet Ho Chang Ho and see if some arrangement can be made to send the children home,' said another colleague.

The procession organized by the PSP and other organizations was approaching the school at that time. Perplexed, Cha Mu quickly locked the school gate and returned. One could never tell when it might turn into a mob. She hurriedly took the children indoors.

'Down with aggressor China! Down! Down! Down! Down!'

'Get ready to save the country! Get ready! Get ready!'

'Chow Mao murdabad!'

'Nehru zindabad!'

A few Leftist leaders were watching the procession sitting in a house near the road. The Indian Leftist leaders and intellectuals were worried. The Left camp had been in a comfortable position so far because of the friendly relations between Nehru and Communist China and Russia. Of late, the pro-China stand of the Left camp had pushed them into an impossible corner. Even common people had started looking at them with suspicion.

'See how emotional the people have become. The love for their country is true, but it is impractical. Nehru had used our people in the freedom movement; now he is going to use them again in the same way.'

'What will one achieve with such an agenda? Will the Chinese army retreat seeing all this?'

'Forget all that. Think of how we can keep our organization intact. The way the Congress party is after us, no one knows what will happen.'

'But what can we do? We have to follow the directions of our leaders.'

The procession moved slowly towards Cheenapatti. There was not a single Chinese among the curious crowd of onlookers. A little while ago, a few of Chitta's Chinese friends were seen chatting in front of his shop but with the arrival of the procession they all went inside the lane. The Chinese people standing in front of Mok Min's shop also went inside.

Johori Khan left his shop to talk to Chitta.

'The Chinese are all scared. But they should not be. If Pakistan attacks India, should I be afraid because I am a Muslim? This is my country. Most of the Chinese are old settlers. Still they are frightened. I feel terrible about this, Chitta.'

'People may not think as we do. No point getting into unnecessary trouble,' Chitta answered.

After the procession left, everything appeared to become normal again. The school gates opened. Mok Min's shop was packed again with customers. Cyclists could be seen going towards the cinema hall. But the Chinese who sold pork in the market were absent. The shoe shops and the other shops owned by the Chinese were closed. The Chinese who came to the market every day were not there. The market, otherwise teeming with Chinese people, looked empty.

All the Indian posts north of the Namka Chu river are now under Chinese occupation. The Chinese army is advancing from the south of the Namka Chu, where they were positioned yesterday. In spite of heavy snowfall in some parts of the Dhola region, heavy mortar shelling continues intermittently. Today, after encroaching on the Indian border, China has for the first time fired at Indian supply planes in both the eastern and western sectors. China has also shot down an Indian helicopter engaged in rescuing injured soldiers.

Prime Minister Jawaharlal Nehru has firmly stated today that India will not bow down before China. There is no need to panic because of the advances in the northeastern frontier. It will not be difficult to reoccupy the places which China has occupied already. He has given assurance that the Indian Army will take actions to oust the Chinese.

Inside a room of the Chinese Club, leaders of the Chinese society sat looking worried. After the local news was over, Manchung Ho changed the channel to Radio Peking.

The New China News Agency has said that after India began anti-Chinese activities, it had started getting more aid from the United States. China has submitted a protest note against the attack of the Indian Army on the Chinese border. It is said in the protest note that in the western and the eastern sectors, the Indian Army had attacked fiercely. The Chinese Army had to retaliate in self-defence. The fighting is still ongoing. The Indian army has attacked China after long preparations. The Indian government will be entirely responsible for the consequences.

At that time, there was heavy snowfall at the NEFA frontier. Defying the snowfall in the twelve-mile sector down the Thag La ridge, troop after troop of Chinese soldiers started coming down – politically motivated, enriched with the experience of war, and prepared to attack.

The snow-clad frontier began to redden with the blood of the soldiers.

Ten

William Addison was speeding through the Samdang tea estate in his jeep. He was wearing a black t-shirt, white shorts and canvas shoes; his blonde hair was covered with a flat hat. The setting sun poured its golden yellow rays on his youthful body; he looked divinely handsome. The men and women returning from work saluted him as he sped by. Today was a special day for him. Not only had he received a letter from Peggy, he had also got permission to go to Scotland on leave.

He spent most of his weekends at the Doom Dooma Planters' Club. He felt a special attachment to the club. The authorities provided almost all the amenities available in modern Europe. With its billiards room, tennis court, swimming pool, dance floor, sound-proof cinema hall and well-equipped bar, the club was the centre of attraction for the officers of the neighbouring tea gardens.

On the tennis court, Joe Mathews and David were already playing a match.

'Hey Bill!' Victor called out to him.

Gesturing to say he would be back in a moment, he went into the club. A lot of repair work was in progress. Addison was in charge of the work. Liang, his brother and a few other workers were busy making shelves and cupboards for the library. Seeing Addison they all stood up. After giving them a few instructions he looked at Liang's older brother and said, 'Big John, I want you to make me a small wooden ornament box. Do you understand what I mean? There should be small compartments in the box.' He took out a piece of paper and drew a diagram. 'Something like this, understand?'

The carpenters watched attentively and tried to make out exactly what Addison had in mind.

'It's for my wife-to-be. Make it properly. It must be beautiful, understand?'

They nodded.

'Good. Come to the office tomorrow and tell me what materials you need.'

Smiling gently and patting Liang on his back, Addison left. The carpenters went back to work. After a while Liang said, 'I'll leave a bit early today, ako.'

'Why?' his elder brother asked, putting aside his saw.

'There's a meeting in the Chinese Club. Then I'll go to Tung Chin's house. They've invited me for dinner.'

'Don't stay out late. No one knows what might happen.'

'We have our papers, ako.'

'Never mind, I feel scared even with the papers. People say that the war has taken a serious turn.'

As Liang made his way to the Chinese Club, Addison sat with his friends sipping beer in the open verandah beside the swimming pool. The news of the war replaced their usual topics of conversation.

The overall situation was slowly becoming grave.

Most people were worried about the security of the country. There were public drives to collect money, clothes and other materials to help the soldiers. There were many more issues that had made the atmosphere heavy with dread. Although the situation was tense, day-to-day work in the garden went on as usual.

When Liang reached the office, bearers of the Chinese society of Makum and other important Chinese people of the area had already gathered at the club.

Lee Chang was reading out the war news from a newspaper. Everyone was listening to him intently.

'Some of the Chinese living in Calcutta seem to be loyal to the People's Republic of China. Some of the Chinese have taken

Chinese passports because of the constant pressure from the pro-China people. They have convinced only 2000 Chinese to take red passports so far. It looks as though the Chinese Consulate General in Calcutta is taking an active interest in convincing the Chinese in Calcutta to take PRC passports. A number of Chinese who were active in this effort have been deported to China for their anti-India activity. Of these, approximately eighty people have been pushed out through the Nathu La Pass and the rest asked to leave the country ...' Lee Chang stopped. He sat silently without looking at anybody.

Intense feelings of humiliation and sadness engulfed him. This was the first time that they had attended a meeting of this sort in the Chinese Club. So far, the elders had kept them away. Now the crisis had become acute. It had become necessary to get the opinion of the youngsters before taking any decision.

'What if they think of us as Chinese spies too?' Akong asked, breaking the silence.

'Why should they think like that? The government knows fully well who is involved in what. Their informers are everywhere, though we don't know who they are.'

'What if they think we are? Everyone should speak carefully or else we will be in trouble.'

'We should tell the government that we want to live in India. We have no one in China. Even if there is, India is our land. We were born here. We have worked here, married here. Our birth place is our motherland.'

'Anyone who attacks our motherland is our enemy. We are Indians and we will be with India.'

'People have started staring at us angrily as though we are the ones who have attacked India.'

'You are right. I feel so ashamed. I should not have listened to the teacher from Calcutta and obtained a Red China passport.'

'It's not wise to roam around too much now.'

'If we don't go out, how are we going to survive? What is there to fear? China has attacked India. Not us.'

'I have a hunch that things are going to get worse.'

'No need to worry right now. All our shops are running as before, including Mok Min's hotel. No one has said anything offensive so far.'

'What else does it say?' asked Yui Yi's grandfather.

'The government is worried about the presence of about seventy hardcore Chinese Communists in India. These people had been acting in favour of China among the Indian Chinese much before the war had begun. *The China Review* had been carrying propaganda that Indian soldiers had entered Chinese territory. The newspaper has also published fake photographs. The government also found some articles and editorials published in the newspaper as offensive. Local police have seized a few editions of the newspaper and banned the circulation of the same.'

'Oh! That's why the newspaper has not come.'

'Even if it has come, the CID might have seized them. They will harass the subscribers.'

'Didn't the Indian government deport the editor of the same newspaper to China because he supported the Kuomintang government, after China went under the Communists?'

'Yes.'

'What kind of a government is this? Why doesn't the government tell us what they want from us? One day the government will arrest and deport us if we don't support Communist China, another day they will punish us if we do.'

'Why can't they understand that the paper had been supporting Red China because India was Red China's friend?'

'Hey shhh! We will be put in jail if the CID hears this.'

'But the paper should not support China after China has attacked India. This is wrong.'

'Stop discussing this for a moment. What else does the report say?'

'As a part of security measures, strict vigilance is being maintained on the Chinese in New Delhi. There are three hundred and sixty Chinese in the capital and of them twelve have been expelled from India because of their undesirable activities. The Chinese government is spreading propaganda among the Tibetan refugees and trying to convince them to return. The agents who are engaged in this process have been arrested. Periodic screening of the refugees is going on. Interestingly, the authorities of Palam airport have intimated that in the last three weeks not a single Chinese person has arrived in or left India. Not even a diplomatic courier from China has arrived.'

After a short silence, Yiu Yi's grandfather said, 'Let the president of our society call a meeting. Let him invite the important people of Makum. We must express our support for India. Otherwise people will misunderstand us. And so will the government. This is for our good. What else have they written?'

'In the case of the stateless Chinese of Calcutta, no steps have been taken so far. After thorough examination it has been found that most of them are simple working-class people. They are mostly skilled artisans and factory workers who work independently. The news circulated widely that many Chinese people have left Calcutta, which according to the government is entirely false and fabricated. Some Chinese boys who had been to the Sibpur garden for a picnic were seen having tea at Howrah station. This led to talk about the Chinese leaving.'

'I told you, there is no cause for panic!'

'Discuss later. Let him finish reading first.'

'The government is now aware of China's attempt to infiltrate agents in Sikkim and Bhutan. In West Bengal, vigilance has been increased at the northern border. Professor Nirmal Chandra Bhattacharya, the General Secretary of India-China Friendship

Society has resigned from his post today because of China's unprovoked attack. He said that not resigning was equal to treachery. Yesterday a Chinese person was arrested at the Rangia rail station who was moving around suspiciously ...'

Outside the club house, Thakur Prasad Shah was prowling around keeping vigil with a smirk on his face. He had a lot to report to the outpost in-charge, Firdaus Ali.

Far away from Makum, at both the eastern and western frontiers, fierce fighting was going on between Indian and Chinese soldiers. At the Kameng frontier of NEFA, at the tri-junction of India, Bhutan and Tibet, crossing the border line and the Namka Chu river, Chinese troops were trying to advance towards Tawang, a small village surrounded by hills on three sides. With a population of 300 people, this was the first habitation this side of the border. A political officer was stationed in Tawang.

The road from Tezpur to the Kameng border ended here. There had been heavy snowfall and blizzards. On one side of the track were steep mountains, while on the other were deep gorges that seemed to disappear into an infinite nothingness. The rows of Chinese soldiers climbing the hillside were dressed in padded uniforms and snow boots. They carried food and other essentials in their backpacks with sophisticated weapons on their shoulders. Well-planned lines of communication had been built up with their base. A well-organized supply line had been supporting the soldiers. All arrangements were made ready for emergency evacuation.

The Indian soldiers, on the other hand, did not have proper supply lines, had limited arms and ammunition, hasty soldier deployment and very poor preparations. They were waiting for the enemy, their fingers on the triggers of the light machine guns or LMGs in frozen bunkers in the snow-clad mountains; dressed in cotton uniforms that were no match for the cold, and leather shoes that were unsuitable for the snow.

China had already constructed a road to the McMahon Line. On the Indian side, there were only mule tracks serving as roads. In some places they had to depend on air-dropped supplies.

Chinese troops had simultaneously attacked the India-Bhutan-Tibet tri-junction at the Kameng frontier, the India-Burma-China tri-junction at the Lohit frontier of NEFA, and the India-Pakistan-China tri-junction in Ladakh. Unable to sustain the fierce attack by the Chinese troops, the Indian troops had started retreating slowly.

After the meeting was over, Liang and the others gathered in Tung Chin's house with their families. Their usual cheerfulness was absent today. The war weighed heavily on their minds.

The ladies, however, had no time to talk about the war. Mei Lin was surreptitiously looking at Lee Chang's pregnant wife Wai Kwan. In a room, the youngsters were playing Ludo while the older ones listened to music from a radiogram. Tung Chin's mother was busy cooking. Pulok's mother, and Tung Chin's sister-in-law – Madhabi's mother, were helping her. Despite being a Chinese household, most of the customs observed were Assamese because Tung Chin's mother, Pramila Gogoi, was Assamese. She was from Sivasagar. She first met the young Ho Min Fuk when she had gone to an open-air cinema in the tea garden adjacent to her village. At that time, she had just completed her matriculation. She was a courageous girl and married Ho Min Fuk despite all opposition. They had been together for thirty-two years. She was now the headmistress of an Assamese lower primary school near Makum. All three of her sons were married and working. Her eldest daughter-in-law Madhabi's father was Chinese and her mother was from the tea garden workers' community. Her second daughter-in-law's name was Wenling, a Chinese woman from Dibrugarh. The youngest, Xonpahi, was an Assamese girl from Sivasagar. Of her two daughters, one was married and the other was engaged to a Chinese boy who worked in a tea garden near Siliguri in north Bengal. Once she was wedded, Pramila's responsibilities would be over. She bowed before God a thousand times for giving her a home full of peace and happiness.

Although dinner was going to be Chinese today, the daughters-in-law had made some Assamese sweets to serve with tea. Wenling brought these on a plate and placed it in front of Mei Lin.

'Tell me how you like it. The rice cakes kept breaking in the beginning. Now I've got the hang of it. But I hardly get the time with five children around,' she laughed.

'It's very nice. Maa has taught me how to make them too.'

The young women got busy with small talk. Tung Chin's youngest sister Mei Fung was also lost in her own dreams. She was to be married on 10 December. The boy came to meet Mei Fung after their marriage was fixed. They were in constant touch with each other through letters. Actually, she had written a pile of letters but had not posted them. She had planned to give them to him after their wedding, as a gift.

In the sitting room the men were listening to the radio.

The Prime Minister has appealed to the nation to be prepared to face the gravest danger since India's independence. He said that there can be no sacrifice bigger than the one made for one's motherland. Nehru commented that it was unfortunate that we had to carry out military operations extensively in the frontier regions after speaking of peace and the ideologies of the United Nations. But India had to take this step against her will. He again said that we had not gone against the ideology of the United Nations. We had not encroached on any foreign territory. What is happening is on our soil. He also said that India had to face a powerful state without any conscience. We had to prepare ourselves fully to face the situation. Praising our soldiers, he stated that even if we fail on some fronts, the final result will surely be in our favour. We will fight till we are victorious, India has said in a statement today: If China returns to the positions they held before the 18th of September this year, then India is ready to discuss the border issue. On the other hand, China has put forward a proposal that the troops of both the countries go back twenty kilometres from the Line of Actual Control. The Indian government said that this was China's strategy to confuse ...

'Is India losing the war?' Wenling asked gently after the broadcast was over.

Before anyone said anything, Rameswar flared up. 'Who said so? Of course we are not losing! Those who are hoping so will soon be taught a lesson.'

Everyone looked at Rameswar's reddened face in utter surprise. Wenling's eyes filled with tears. She looked at Rameswar for a brief moment and, without saying a word, walked away gloomily. Before anyone could speak, Tung Chin's mother arrived to call them for tea. Everyone was quiet. Rameswar apologized immediately for his sudden outburst.

A spread had been laid out on the large dining table. They all sat down for tea.

At the NEFA border, the Chinese soldiers had occupied three important posts – Lumpu, Boom La and Kibithu. They had started sharpening their glistening bayonets on the other side of Tawang.

Eleven

The Makum playground was jam-packed with students. They had all been asked to bring with them a piece of blotting paper, a small ball of cotton wool, a feather pen and a pin, but no one knew why. The general secretary of the Steering Committee of the All Assam Students' Union had appealed to the students to take an oath for safeguarding India's sovereignty. Ananta and his group had organized this meeting.

On a large table lay a sheaf of blank papers. Across the table sat the leaders of the student union with grave faces. The students were full of excitement and enthusiasm. The language movement of the 1960s was still fresh in their minds. Grievances were still alive against the central government for its step-motherly attitude towards Assam. But this time the tune was different. Now the student leaders talked about a united India. They talked about safeguarding India by uniting with the entire nation.

The student leaders had been delivering their patriotic speeches one after the other. Among the students were Alan, Siu and Kaushalya. The Chinese students had also come but they were not at ease.

The easy rhythm of life had been disturbed. Things seemed to have changed, almost overnight. They could see the change and the difference in the eyes of the students present in the field. Those were not the eyes of friends. Fear and confusion occupied their minds. Though no one said anything they felt an unfamiliar anxiety. They felt as if everyone was observing them. They felt like outsiders.

Ananta was looking grave. Although he looked at Ahlin and smiled, he did not talk to her. He had changed a lot in recent times. Whenever Ahlin wanted to know what had happened to him, he just avoided her.

'Hey Ahlin,' Mei Hang whispered, 'look, Ananta is speaking like a leader.'

Ananta was saying, 'Today our country has arrived at a critical juncture. China, whom we considered our brother, has attacked our country to devour our land. Our uncompromising troops are engaged in a life-and-death battle to save our motherland. The war is still in full flow. Yesterday, Tawang, an important post at Kameng frontier, fell into the clutches of the Chinese. In this moment of need, it is the duty of the student community to extend its support. Keeping this aim before us, students from all over Assam have decided to sign a letter swearing our support and send the same to the defence minister. As you all know, students from other parts of Assam have already sent their signed letters of allegiance.'

'No, we don't know. When did they do this?' one of the students whispered.

'Oh, keep quiet!' someone said.

The murmur subsided.

'In such a situation, the students of Makum should not hold back. Will you come forward to sign and engage yourself in this great effort?'

'Yes we will, we will!' everyone present echoed in unison.

'Jai Hind!' they all shouted.

Ahlin and her friends joined in too.

'Ananta is right. We are all Indians, and this is our country. We should throw out the Chinese army. I will sign the letter – a thousand times if need be,' Ahlin thought, as she tearfully raised her hand to shout 'Jai Hind!'

The first one to go forward was Ananta. Pricking his index finger with a pin he pressed hard till a drop of blood oozed out. Dipping the quill pen in the blood, he signed his name on a sheet of paper.

The students were stunned.

'Do we have to sign the way he did?'

'Yes, of course. No sacrifice is big enough for your country, Nehru has said.'

'We will have to sacrifice for our nation.'

'For that, is it necessary to sign in blood? Isn't an ordinary signature enough?'

'I love my country. I will do what is needed. But I cannot prick my finger with a pin.'

'You are afraid to shed one drop of blood and you say you will fight for the country? Huh! I know what you will do. If the Chinese army comes, you will either turn tail and run away or fall at their feet for mercy.'

'As if you are not scared! Why are you sweating so much then?'

The students slowly went forward to sign. Some were scared, while others were not. Some sneaked out from the queue in fear, compromising their self-respect. Mei Hang was scared stiff and kept staring at those who were signing.

'Oh God! How can I prick my finger? What if all my blood flows out? Hey Kaushalya, why did the Chinese have to attack our land? Oh! The Chinese are after my blood!'

The girls who were around burst out in laughter.

'Look at the way they are laughing. Absolutely unmindful of where they are,' a student leader commented in irritation.

'I know her. She is a Chinese girl, studying in GBC.'

'Oh! That's why they are laughing!'

'No, not for that. I know that girl, Mei Hang, she is very funny.'

'How do you know?'

'We studied together. She is a good friend of Ananta.'

'Is that so?'

Ananta was looking at the girls too. Slowly his face became serious. What was there to laugh about? How could Ahlin and the others laugh at such a serious moment?

Was it because they were Chinese? Was it because they would not lose anything if the Chinese subjugated India? Or did they not feel anything when Indian soldiers were killed at the frontier?

No. This could not be the reason. There were other girls like Kaushalya who were laughing, too. It was not just the Chinese girls. There must be something funny. He shouldn't have thought this way about Ahlin.

But he still wasn't feeling good – he did not know why. His friends used to tease him about Ahlin. He had enjoyed that. But now he could hear a mild echo of allegation in their teasing. He felt as if his fondness for Ahlin threw into question his loyalty towards India. He had become restless because of the tussle between his feelings. He needed to explain the situation to Ahlin. She would surely understand. She would not feel bad after that. It felt good to see her laughing. Ahlin was now close to him. Composing himself, he held the paper in front of her. He looked at her eyes with a loving smile.

'I'll come today,' Ananta said in a whisper.

The cloud that had gathered was carried away by her smile. The sky became clear. At that moment, her friends were imploring Mei Hang secretly not to joke, lest they laugh again.

It was late evening by the time the meeting ended. In Pulok's house, the neighbours had gathered to listen to the news. An agriculture bulletin was going on. Minaram Baruah was reading the newspaper.

'After prolonged and bitter fighting in the town's outskirts, the Chinese have occupied Tawang, the farthest road head in the north-western part of NEFA.

The Indian troops, who had fought gallantly for over twenty-four hours, withdrew on Wednesday evening in the face of a massive three-pronged attack by the Chinese. The withdrawal was according to plan and a large proportion of the local population, including the head priest and other priests of the local monastery, were safely evacuated. The monastery, it is officially stated today, is safe. It is not clear in which direction the Chinese troops are moving. But along with Tawang, Lumpu has also fallen into Chinese hands.'

The listeners became frustrated. They remained silent for a few moments then started commenting excitedly.

'Why has the Indian army moved back? Do they think we are fools? If they couldn't fight the Chinese, they should have had the guts to admit it. Why is the government trying to conceal the truth?' someone said.

'The government is talking big only to console us!'

'Don't say that! When thousands of Chinese soldiers come hurtling down the mountains in waves, how can our limited troops face them?'

'They can't come down like waves,' someone commented.

'How do you know that?'

'I've served on the NEFA border as a sepoy. I know the actual situation. The hills are not in a line for waves to come down.'

'People in my workplace were saying that it was difficult for our troops to fight, as most of them are unfamiliar with the hills and snow.'

'That's absolutely true. Those who are unused to heights have headaches due to scanty oxygen and water collects in their lungs. The Chinese soldiers don't have this problem. The Tibetan plateau is much higher than the NEFA hills. They have to come down from a high altitude; our soldiers become tired by the time they reach the frontier. Right up to last year, we managed with pullovers and greatcoats made with blankets and used balaclava hats to cover our heads. We were given leather boots which were no good in the snow. They would get wet in no time and our feet would be numb with cold. A lot of us end up getting chilblain and frostbite. Sometimes, a soldier's legs would have to be amputated. Our weapons and ammunition are outdated. They were used in the Second World War. The Chinese have automatic rifles while we have bolt action 303 Lee Enfield rifles, one bullet at a time and machine guns which we have to keep cooling with water. Our mortar are old-fashioned. Those do not go far. And our artillery guns are –'

'What are artillery guns?'

'Canons. Ours have a small firing range. I remember seeing a canon being carried by fourteen mules. That is the state of the Indian army! How can the Indian soldiers fight the Chinese, you tell me.'

'I think we will have to run away with our families! If things continue at this rate, it won't take them long to reach here.'

'Eh! We have enough time to worry about that. The Chinese army has only reached Tawang.'

'That is at the Kameng frontier. Here, in the Lohit frontier, the situation is not good either. What's going to happen if our army fails to resist the Chinese at this frontier? How much time will they take to reach Makum?'

'Have you noticed how the Chinese are living here comfortably? It seems they are happy about what is happening. Because they have nothing to bother about, if the Chinese occupy Makum or even India,' Baruah vented his anger. 'The Indian government will not do anything against them. The Chinese army will also not harm them, for sure. If the Chinese soldiers arrive in Makum, they will probably go and receive them with alacrity.'

'How can you say such things? They are not happy. They are ashamed and worried. My son has a lot of Chinese friends. That's how I know.'

'It's all drama, I tell you. We should teach them a lesson if we can. We don't have enough to eat, and yet look at them. They are filthy rich. After the Marwaris, they have the best houses.

They have sawmills, garages, factories, hotels, shoe shops and saloons. You name it and they have it!'

'They are hardworking people. Will anyone leave his own country if he has enough to eat and if he can live peacefully there? It is meaningless to blame them for the Chinese attack.'

'He is right, Baruah. You must control your unreasonable anger. And now that you have a Chinese daughter-in-law, you must be careful about what you say. She will be hurt if she hears you!'

'We can't afford to keep our eyes and ears closed,' Baruah continued. 'There may be spies among the Chinese here. The chief minister has asked people to report anything suspicious to the police. The police are keeping an eye on them. After all, they are Chinese. They might want to help the enemy.'

Hearing Pulok's cycle bell near the front door, Baruah fell silent.

After taking over Tawang, the Chinese troops were advancing on the small motorable road towards Bomdila. In between Tawang and Tezpur, at a place called Jang, a fierce battle was going on. In the easternmost sector of the Burma border, fifteen miles south of the McMahon Line, Chinese troops had almost reached Walong, on the bank of the Lohit River in the Lohit Frontier Division. They simultaneously attacked the Indian troops from two sides.

Those who were listening to the radio were astounded when this unexpected news broke out:

The President of India, Dr Sarvepalli Radhakrishnan, has declared a national emergency. An ordinance that is being called 'The Defence of India Ordinance' has been issued.

Twelve

A bamboo-and-cloth gate had been erected across the Makum–Doom Dooma Road with 'Welcome' written on it. A group of students led by Ananta were removing pebbles and filling up the potholes in the road with earth. Army trucks carrying soldiers to the NEFA border were passing through the town. A crowd had gathered on both sides of the road. They were waving Indian flags and throwing flowers to the soldiers and shouting 'Jai Hind!'

The military convoys had increased as more and more soldiers were brought into the region. Army and civil hospitals were full of injured soldiers rescued from the war front. Newspapers were full of reports related to the war. But how far those reports were true and how many of them were rumours was hard to tell. The more the news of failure of the Indian defence came in, the more the people became emotional. They had offered generous donations to the National Defence Fund. At the same time, frustration, insecurity and fear had slowly started eating into the nation's morale.

The international community reacted as well. America announced its acceptance of the McMahon Line. The prime minister of the United Kingdom had denounced the Chinese aggression. Speaking at the House of Commons, he pledged Britain's support to India and sent across arms and ammunition. Canada, too, offered military aid to India. The Dalai Lama, who had taken political asylum in India, also denounced the Chinese attack. Russia, however, expressed its support for China. Pakistan warned the Western nations who offered military support to India that their foreign policy might turn pro-Moscow if things continued like that.

In the internal sphere, there was a new development. Both the opposition and ruling parties stood against Defence Minister

Krishna Menon and demanded his removal and that India snap ties with China.

At the same time, people had started expressing their aversion against Communists in public. Incidents of stone-pelting at meetings organized by Communists, burning effigies of Chow En Lai and other Communist leaders and boycotting Communists became increasingly common.

While the student body in Makum led by Ananta welcomed the soldiers going to the front, all the parties except the CPI assembled at the Makum playground. Every speaker was jeering against the Communists, calling them fifth columns and anti-Indian.

At both these gatherings, there was no one from Cheenapatti. They had assembled in the Chinese school compound. The president of the Chinese society, Ho Chang Ho, had convened a meeting in the school. All the important people, as well as the heads of all the organizations of Makum and the government officials had been invited. Ananta and the other student leaders were also among the invitees. All the Chinese, and the people of Chinese origin of Makum and the surrounding areas, were present at the meeting. They were sitting on the tarpaulin spread out in the courtyard with a worried look. Ahlin was waiting for Ananta. She hadn't seen him in the last ten days, although she had been to the school every day to attend the coaching classes.

'Ahlin!' Chow Chi Yong, the headmaster, called out.

'We have to take down these photographs. Call a few of the boys for help.'

'Why do we have to take them down, sir?'

Chow Chi Yong did not answer.

'What's happened?' Alan asked her.

'Sir wants us to take down these pictures.'

'Why?'

'I don't know. Let us call Dulal ako and some others.'

After a while Dulal Yem and Hong came up to the verandah.

'Oh God! Look who's here – my heart is going to break any minute!' Mei Hang cried out.

Hong turned to look at the group of girls and spotted Mei Hang hiding behind Siu. He smiled. He knew what was on her mind. But she didn't know what was in his.

'I will let her know,' Hong thought to himself, as he went up to the verandah.

Meanwhile, Dulal and the others were busy taking down pictures of Mao Tse-tung, Chow En Lai, Karl Marx, Liu Shao Qi. They were all kept hidden behind the almirahs in the office room.

Dulal was now taking down Nehru's photograph.

'Hey, don't, dont take that down,' Ling Kwang Tung cried out.

Dulal stopped. Looking at Ling Kwang Tung's face for a moment, he got off the stool with a grave face.

Nehru remained alone, smiling, on a wall full of empty and clean squares, which until sometime back had been covered by framed pictures.

In the office room, Ho Chang Ho, K. P. Lee, Yiu Yi's grandpa, Ho Fuk, Mok Min and the headmaster Chow Chi Yong were discussing the war situation with utmost seriousness. Many things had happened of late. The license given to the Bank of China in Calcutta had been cancelled by the Reserve Bank of India. The Chinese Consulate in Calcutta as well as the Chinese Embassy in Delhi constantly faced demonstrations by student groups and politicians. News of arrests of Chinese people under the ordinance that had been put in place during the Emergency was coming from all sides.

As soon as A. C. Chow entered, the discussions came to a close. These days, he seemed to be on very good terms with the government so they didn't want to air their views in front of him.

Hong came in. 'It's time for all of you to go outside. The guests have arrived.'

Ahlin and her friends stood near the gate to welcome the invitees. The first to arrive was Gangeswar Sharma, the headmaster of GBC School. Gradually, the others came in. The last to enter was Ananta. Ahlin's face brightened at the sight of him, while her friends smiled at her.

'You are late,' Ahlin said to him but he did not answer or smile. He looked at her for a moment and headed straight to the dais. He could not exchange smiles with a Chinese girl in public. He was not a common boy. He was a student leader.

The smile disappeared from Ahlin's face. She went to Mei Hang, her head hanging low, and sat there with tears in her eyes.

Mei Hang held her close and said slowly, 'Don't cry. Try to understand.'

They had noticed that these days Ananta did not talk to them as he did before. Although he smiled at them in acknowledgement, he no longer joked with them. They understood how busy he was with collecting donations, training people for emergency duties, collecting woollens for the soldiers and holding meetings. But he had stopped involving the students from Cheenapatti in his activities. They knew all these activities were against China. The people of Makum who had come from China had no right to take part in these exercises. They were slowly beginning to feel demoralized. It seemed that the love that had earlier bound the people of this small township had vanished.

At that moment, Hong went onstage to explain the objectives of the meeting. Forgetting everything, Mei Hang gazed at him.

'In the first half of the nineteenth century, the Chinese came to Assam – which was then under British rule – to work in the tea gardens. Most of them were forcibly brought as indentured labourers by human traffickers. After that too, many people came to this land willingly, in search of a good life. Most of them had married local girls and settled down. They made it their home. The people of the Chinese society of Assam, which is composed of the second, third and fourth generations of those indentured labourers and early migrants, have no other place to go. This is our motherland. This land never let us suffer. It has fed us, has given us shelter and security. Here, we have found love!'

Hong, who was an undergraduate student of Kanoi College, Dibrugarh, spoke fluent Assamese. The audience looked at this gentle, handsome boy in admiration.

'We have received so much from this land. Perhaps we could not give much in return. But we have given our toil and loyalty. We have mixed our identity with this soil. True, we came from China. But we can never betray this land. To us, this is our motherland. Our janam jaga. Today, our people are full of fear. They are afraid that someone might question their loyalty. After much thought, our elders have decided to call this meeting to express our love and loyalty towards India and to ask for advice from the wisest among us about the appropriate course of action.'

As soon as Hong finished, Ho Chang Ho stood up to speak. Hong came down and stood near Alan and the others. His heart became turbulent with intense emotions, with the feeling of deep humiliation and sadness. His tearful eyes filled Mei Hang's heart with an inexplicable desire to be close to him.

After Ho Chang Ho, the headmaster of GBC School delivered his speech.

'It is very sad that a meeting of this kind had to be organized here today. I would like to ask, why is it necessary for the Chinese people here to prove their loyalty? I would like to point at this boy, Hong, and ask just one question. If he is not an Indian, then who is? We have many Chinese children in our school. I cannot see any difference between them and the other children.'

Ananta was looking at Ahlin secretly. He did not hear what the speakers were saying. His heart was filled with an eerie sadness. What had that girl, sitting with her head down, done wrong? What should he do now?

His friend and other student leaders had started mocking him about his relationship with a Chinese girl with a mixture of relentless hatred and disrespect. The district leaders had cautioned him to not get involved with Ahlin.

At the behest of the president of the meeting, Ananta came to stand near him. On behalf of the entire Chinese community, Ho Chang Ho placed a thousand rupees in Ananta's hands. C Hoi's mother placed a bundle of pullovers knitted by the women of Cheenapatti.

It was evening when the meeting finally ended. The meeting at the Makum playground was also over. Workers of all political parties took out a procession. People carried placards and the air was full of slogans.

'Down with Russian duplicity. Down. Down. Down. Down.'

'Enemy's friend is enemy.'

'To hell with the Indian Communist.'

'Expel Defence Minister Krishna Menon.'

The procession halted in front of the Chinese school. The people of the procession looked at the Chinese who were crossing the road.

Whose people were they? Those who studied in the Assamese-medium school and spoke fluent Assamese?

Could there be any fifth columns like the CPI hidden among them? Could there be any Chinese spies? Traitors? Who could tell?

'We have to keep an eye on these people,' someone said. 'Have you heard? The police have arrested a Chinese in Jorhat who spoke six languages. There was a Nepalese man with him. They came from Kalimpong. He must be a spy.'

'What nonsense are you talking? Do you think only a Chinese spy can speak six languages? Listen, even our Chinese folks in Makum can speak four to five languages. Nepalese, Hindi, Bengali, Chinese, English, not to mention Assamese. Some can even speak six languages. This is a cosmopolitan society. You hardly ever come across a pure Chinese here.'

'Still, you can never tell.'

'If they are Indian, why do they establish Chinese schools?'

'Why do the Bengalis and the Hindi-speaking people open their own schools here? Every community wants to preserve their own language. They do it because the government allows it.'

'Chow En Lai murdabad!'

'Down with fifth columns, down, down!'

'Don't shout these slogans! Please don't,' a leader of the PSP yelled as he quickly walked past the procession.

The procession gradually went quiet.

At that time, all the posts in the western sector of the India-China border were being overrun by the Chinese army.

Thirteen

About 200 women and children – families of men belonging to the Assam Rifles – made a long and arduous trek back to safety from the forward areas in NEFA, according to UNI's special correspondent with the Indian forces in NEFA.

They began moving back when the posts in the forward areas came under massive assault by the Chinese. Assam rifles personnel are allowed to have their families even in these areas.

In small batches, these women and children walked about seventy-five miles from Lumpu to Jang via Tawang. Some of the women carried their babies on their backs. They could bring very few of their belongings with them and had to go practically without food on their hazardous trek to safety. They are now lodged at a camp near Misamari, about sixteen miles from Tezpur.

They are being given rations as well as financial and medical assistance.

In the jungle, some of the children were separated from their mothers but most of them were reunited in the camp.

'People will get angrier now,' Yiu Yi's father commented with a sigh.

Nobody reacted. The silent room became heavy with the sighs of sadness and frustration.

Everything was quiet in Mok Min's shop nowadays. The sound of the Mahjong dice had been silenced. Only the elders sat quietly, looking worried and despondent. A few Chinese people came to listen to the newspapers read by someone and to find out what was happening.

Today, like other days, people had come to listen to the newspapers being read out. Mok Min was also there. He looked gloomy. Chow Chi Yong began to read again.

'The answer to the three-point proposal of ceasefire sent by Chow En Lai to Nehru on the fourth of November was handed over to China's Charge d'Affaires in Delhi after ten days, where it is said that the McMahon Line cannot be the issue of deliberation. All the Latin American countries have responded favourably to India's appeal for support in the Sino-Indian war. Offering aid to India, some of these countries have condemned China's actions. Argentina has even offered to send volunteers. Brazil is the lone country whose stand is not clear. Brazil has expressed hope of a peaceful settlement. Cuba has not expressed her stand either. The response of the Eastern European countries is positive. Except Yugoslavia and Albania, the others have reflected the Soviet standpoint. They have not promised anything except hope of an early solution to this problem through discussion.'

'What is the use of reading all this?' Ho Wang said irritably. 'Read what is written about us.'

Leafing through the pages, Yiu Yi's father said, 'Yesterday there was a long discussion about our issues in the Parliament. Lal Bahadur Shastri –'

'Who is Lal Bahadur Shastri?' Ho Wang asked.

'Don't you know anything? He is the home minister. Now don't ask who or what a home minister is,' C Hoi snapped.

'What or who is a home minister?'

Everyone present there laughed. But the laughter was not hearty like before. It was subdued now.

'Home means house. That particular minister is in charge of the home, meaning India. He looks after the internal affairs of his home,' Mok Min explained patiently.

'There must be a minister, then, to look after the outside affairs?'

'Yes, there are all kinds of ministers. Tell me, who is the chief minister of Assam?'

'Everybody knows? Bimala Prasad Chaliha.'

'How did you know that?'

'I've heard that on the radio in the last few days. These days I feel very scared. People say all sorts of awful things in the marketplace.'

'Don't listen, and don't comment.'

Yiu Yi's father picked up the paper again.

'Home Minister Lal Bahadur Shastri today informed the Lok Sabha that if any Chinese living in India creates any threat to the security of India, stern action will be taken against them. Speaking to H. V. Kamath, Shashtri said that sound security measures have been taken. Kamath, on the other hand, pointed out that the loyalty expressed by the Chinese living in India may actually be a ploy to cover up their intentions.'

'What was that? I don't understand,' said Ho Wang.

'Remember, the Chinese in India expressed their loyalty to India?'

'Yes, I remember. Then what?'

'One important person has said that we, the Chinese living in India, are manipulative people. We don't support India from our heart. We only pretend that we are with India. They don't believe us.'

'The big people think like that? Aiyah!'

The listeners looked sad. Yiu Yi's father looked at their faces and started again.

'The home minister informed the House that the government has ordered to impose restrictions on the Chinese living in India.'

'He talked about the restriction of movement that has been imposed on us. We cannot leave our places till the war is over.'

The listeners became gloomier.

'Even God does not know when the war will be over,' Chi Fu Hai commented with a sigh.

'The home minister has informed the House that strict vigilance will be kept on people who seem potentially anti-Indian.'

'What does that mean?'

'It means that the government has put CID agents after those who can harm India and who are not good people.'

'It says here how many Chinese have been chased away so far.'

'Really? Read it out. Let us hear.'

'B. N. Datar had informed Jashpal Singh that, between the 30th of June and now, twenty-four Chinese citizens have been given notice to leave India. Of these, five left immediately. Special steps will now be taken about the remaining nineteen, as well as those Chinese living in India who are considered undesirable.'

'The home minister said that the government will do something against those Chinese whom the government does not want.'

'Aiyah! They said that?'

'What did he mean by "do something"? Chase them away?'

'He didn't say they will be chased or thrown out. He said "special steps" would be taken.'

'If they throw us out, where shall we go?'

'What else is written? Keep reading, ako.'

'Indrajit Gupta wanted to know how many of those who have been given notice were Chinese citizens, how many stateless, and how many Indian citizens. The home minister said he couldn't give details. But they were all put in the same category. Any measure which the government would take against one would be taken against all.'

'Aiyah! That means they are all the same – those who came long ago, those who have just come, the ones with PRC passports, Kuomintang passports, Indian citizens with papers and without papers?'

'An Indian and a Chinese citizen are the same? That is unfair. How can this be?'

'Look, they have written about our Chinese school here!'

Excited and worried, heads hovered over the newspaper trying to locate the specific section.

'What is there to see? Read it out to us,' Ho Wang said.

Yiu Yi's father resumed, 'In answer to a question by P. C. Baruah, regarding the presence of a Chinese Buddhist school, Shashtri said that a close watch was being kept on the school ...'

'They have put the CID after our school too!'

'Aiiiyaah!'

The people were speechless. Before anyone could comment, they heard a noise. They looked at each other, and then went out to see what had happened.

The non-Chinese customers were already waiting outside. Chitta, Rameswar and Johori Khan were also there. All the customers looked at the sad and worried faces of the Chinese people. These were familiar faces they saw every day.

'A procession is coming,' someone said with a dreary smile. Vibrating the air with slogans, a long procession of students was coming forward led by Ananta and other student leaders.

'Communists murdabad! Murdabad! Murdabad!'

'Down with fifth columns! Down down down down!'

'Death to China government!'

'Chow Mao murdabad, murdabad!'

'Nehru zindabad, zindabad!'

The Chinese looked puzzled, sad and uncertain at first.

Then panic overpowered them. A student procession, furious because of the continuous defeat of the Indian army at the hands of the Chinese, could turn into a mob at the slightest pretext.

'Come inside, all of you come inside!' Mok Min called out to the Chinese fearfully and went in.

'Why are you scared? Don't be,' said Johori Khan.

'We are with you. No one can do anything,' Chitta assured them.

'Don't be scared – you've done nothing wrong.'

The people stood still. They looked at each other, feeling unsure.

'No, but we are still frightened,' Ho Wang said and went inside hurriedly. Others followed suit.

The procession had reached Mok Min's shop by now and slowed down. Someone from the middle of the procession shouted, 'You Chinese people, go away!'

After a moment's silence, all of them started shouting.

'Go away, go away!'

'We won't tolerate China's vandalism.'

The procession slowly moved forward. The faces of the boys at the end of the procession were blazing with anger, hatred and a manic excitement.

Suddenly, a stone flew past the people's heads and landed on the roof of the shop. It made a tremendous sound and came hurtling down. The people assembled there looked first at the stone and then at the boys. Then the pelting started in earnest. A glass jar on the counter shattered.

Chitta and his companions went forward.

'Hey, hey you, why are you throwing stones? Who are you trying to attack?'

The boys stared at him in disbelief and then shouted back insolently, 'Can't you see? The Chinese – who else?'

Chitta looked at the boys. They were not from Makum.

'Don't throw stones,' Chitta yelled at them to stop. 'They haven't done anything.'

'Have you come to advocate for them? Because they buy betel nut at your shop?' they shouted back.

'Hey you, betel-nut seller! Are you a Chinese spy too?'

'What did you say? Let me hear that again! Who do you think you are talking to? I'll break your jaw with one blow!' Chitta and his companions chased the boys, seething with anger.

'These are not the Chinese who have attacked us. They are our own people, understand? Our own people. Go join your processions. But if you harm these people, we will make mincemeat of you.'

The boys who were pelting stones didn't know what to do. There was hardly anyone in Makum who did not know Rameswar and his friends. It wouldn't be wise to antagonize any of the football players in Pulok Baruah's group, the boy knew. In Makum, no one spoke disrespectfully to their elders. Someone in the procession asked the boys, 'What are you saying? Don't you know them? Let's go or you'll get into serious trouble.'

The procession had now reached the Chinese school. At Chow Chi Yong's instructions, Cha Mu had locked the front gate even though lessons were going on in the classrooms. But the children couldn't concentrate. They were excited by the loud slogans the procession was chanting; they wanted to go outside and have a look. Ko Fuk stood up to ask the teacher's permission.

'Sit down,' the teacher said. 'There is nothing to see, don't go out.'

'Why, sir?'

The teacher did not answer. The entire class looked at him expectantly.

'I know. If we go out, they will abuse us. We are Chinese. The Chinese have attacked India. Even Ananta dada dislikes us now,' Yiu Yi said.

'We can't even go home. Our parents can't come to see us. I feel frightened all the time, you know?'

Slowly the noise quietened down. The procession had entered Cheenapatti now. The lane was completely vacant. The Chinese were all behind closed doors. The only two people waiting outside were Thakur Prasad and Rajendra. Thakra's face was glowing with perverted happiness, his cruel eyes glittering.

Ahlin was at home with all the others. For the last few days, her parents had not allowed her to go to school, in case she was humiliated. She had not met Ananta even once. As the procession was passing by, Ahlin's brother whispered, 'That is Ananta dada's voice, shouting slogans.'

Ahlin who was sitting with her head on her knees, looked up, startled. Looking at her brother's eyes for a brief moment, she stood up and went out.

'Don't go out, Ahlin!' her mother cried out, but she did not listen, as if she was in a daze. She wanted to hear what Ananta had to say. Why had they come to Cheenapatti? What had the people of Cheenapatti done? He knew that his Ahlin, his very own Ahlin lived here.

'Ungrateful Chinese! Go away, go away!' Sparks of hatred flew from the procession.

Ahlin looked at the students. Numb. Motionless.

Who were Ananta and his group accusing of being ungrateful? Ahlin and the others? The people of Cheenapatti?

Most of the faces were familiar to Ahlin. Most of them were her friends, schoolmates, childhood companions.

A strange fear gripped her. Her family had come out and stood near Ahlin.

Ananta stopped for a moment.

This was a home he had visited so often. These people were like family. Ahlin and Ananta looked at each other. Ananta wanted to smile at her, but he held back.

Slowly he looked away from Ahlin, spat on the ground and shouted, 'Chow Mao murdabad, murdabad! We won't tolerate Chinese vandalism!'

Leading the procession, Ananta went past. Thakur Prasad was following him. He looked at Ahlin with a sly smile. Ahlin's family quietly went inside.

Lying in bed, Ahlin wept inconsolably.

Her very own Ananta had spat in front of her to show his hatred. China had attacked India and Ananta made her his enemy.

Yiu Yi came to Ahlin and sat beside her.

'Don't cry, Ahlin ache,' she said slowly.

'He abused us. He asked us to leave, Yiu Yi. I will surely leave. I will surely go away from here. And later, even if he cries and looks for me, I won't come back.'

Yiu Yi said sadly, 'Don't cry, ache. Ananta dada is difficult. I'll scold him.'

'Why has Ananta dada asked us to leave?' Ahlin's little brother asked.

'I don't know. I'll have to find out,' said Yiu Yi.

'Don't ask him. He will get angry.'

'He won't be angry with me. But okay, I won't ask him; instead I'll speak to Sipahi dada. He will scold Ananta dada. Don't cry, ache.'

Slowly the children returned to their own little worlds, blissfully oblivious as they were of the growing political tensions. Slowly Cheenapatti limped back to normalcy. But not with the laughter and happiness that had once filled the neighbourhood.

Fourteen

'Will you be returning early?' Mei Lin asked Pulok who was on his way to the tea garden.

'Why? Do you want me to come back early?' Pulok drew her close.

'Always naughty things on your mind!' she said and smiled.'We should have gone to Cheenapatti once.'

'When do you want to go? Today?'

'If you return early, we could go today itself. I'm so worried. I have heard that people start abusing and throwing stones at the sight of a Chinese person.'

'Who told you this? I'm sure it's my father, isn't it?'

Mei Lin looked away. She didn't have the heart to tell him that the moment he left for work, his father read out all kinds of horrible news and abused the entire Chinese community.

'He has exaggerated. There is nothing to worry about.'

Mei Lin said nothing. After a few minutes, Pulok said, 'We'll go out in the evening. I'll try to return as early as possible. Don't go out to serve tea to the people who come to listen to the news. I'll ask Maa to handle that.'

He pulled Mei Lin close again.

'Do you remember what you have to do in case of an air raid?'

'Yes, I do.'

'Don't think twice. No matter how much deuta gets angry, run to the trench the moment you hear the siren. The Chinese planes will not know that there is a Chinese girl in our house.'

He released Mei Lin from his arms and left.

Though he assured Mei Lin that there was no cause for worry, Pulok himself was troubled. The Indian troops were being defeated repeatedly in both the eastern and western sectors of the India-China border. Crossing NEFA, the Chinese army could enter Assam any moment. Defence Minister Krishna Menon had resigned. Nehru had now appointed Y. B. Chavan in his place.

Rumours about the Chinese advance abounded and the common man was gripped with fear.

Not a single Chinese soldier had been captured by the Indian Army so far. On the other hand, the Indian Red Cross confirmed that China had captured 927 Indian prisoners of war. Brigadier Dalvi was among them. The Chinese Red Cross had assured India that all the prisoners were fine. Most of the people from outside Assam had already sent their families away and were themselves in a state of preparedness. Helicopters had started taking off from the small helipads of various tea gardens, carrying the high officials. The window panes of the houses had been covered with thick paper, so as not to let out light and crooked, zigzagging trenches had been dug. The civilians had been instructed about what they needed to do in case of air raids. All the European families in the neighbouring tea estates had left. So had the Indian officers. As a result, work in the tea gardens had come to a halt, and the gardens wore a deserted look. Even though work had stopped, Pulok continued to go to the garden. The officer-in-charge of the Planters' Club had also left with his family. It was now Pulok's responsibility to look after the club.

When Pulok reached the club, the atmosphere there was completely different. He found Addison and his fellow managers busy digging a trench in the tennis court with purpose.

They had decided that they would not let the club go to the Chinese without a fight. So after they sent their families away, they pitched their tents there. They had sourced their own arms, gathered the arms of the officers who had left, and were preparing for battle.

As soon as Addison saw Pulok, he asked him to call Liang and the other young officers at the garden. Pulok was stunned at Addison's childish enthusiasm, but he went to call the officers anyway. They all started digging trenches and filling bags with sand to make bunkers. Slowly, Addison's zeal infected the entire group. The war made them forget about rank and traditions, all hierarchies were wiped out.

The club's bar was now without a bartender to keep a tab on the number of drinks Addison and his friends were downing. Cigar in mouth, a few of them were cleaning the barrels of their guns.

'Hey John, will you have a whiskey?' Addison asked.

'No, sahab,' Liang smiled hesitantly.

'Why not? Have a drink, you'll feel good. Come on, I'm a soldier, not a manager today.'

All the other young managers were smiling indulgently. Had it been any other time they might have been offended by Addison's behaviour. Today was different. The war had touched them with all its madness. Many serious day-to-day matters had become unimportant in the light of self-defence.

Liang was digging. His face looked grave. His otherwise simple mind, which did not dwell on complicated matters, was now occupied by many different issues. He had never imagined that a day would come when his identity would be in question, that people would look at him with mistrust and suspicion. All of a sudden, many of the things which he believed to be true had become untrue. All those people whom he considered his own had become strangers. He had discovered that he was an outsider. When he saw people looking at him and making harsh comments, misery clouded his mind. But when he met Pulok and his other friends, he felt as though nothing had changed.

Addison had noticed Liang's sadness.

'Hey John, come over here!'

Putting the shovel aside, Liang went over.

'China has attacked India, that is why you feel bad, right, little John?'

Liang lowered his head. He did not answer.

'Listen, our prime minister Harold Macmillan has condemned the Chinese aggression. The British are with India. America is with India, too. Kennedy said, "The entire world is with India." But India's enemy Pakistan is not with India. Russia is also not with India. Although the British have left India, we are still friends. We have business relations. If China attacks India, we will not spare China. Right, little John?'

Liang was quiet. Noting his distress, Addison continued, 'India is now your country. It's my country too. We will fight together. Go and call everyone. We will teach you how to use rifles.'

Addison stood up. There was work to be done, there were men to be trained.

Far away from the club, Robin was walking along the treacherous route between Hayuliang and Walong in the Lohit Frontier Division. Along with him were a few soldiers of the Assam Rifles, the base superintendent of Hayuliang, B. N. Chowdhury, and his assistant, Biren. They were carrying ammunition on requisition from the higher authority of the army. In spite of the extreme cold, the men were sweating profusely. The wind dried it quickly though, leaving a thin layer of salt on their muscular bodies. Chowdhury's backpack was filled with bullets, while Biren carried his provisions. Robin and the others carried bullets and grenades along with their backpacks.

In the neighbouring areas of Walong, a fierce battle was in progress. The Chinese troops attacked the Indian post in the Kibithu-Walong tract, crossing the rapids in rubber boats. The Gorkha soldiers were trying to resist the Chinese troops with all their strength. Their ammunition was slowly diminishing. The bunkers were being destroyed one after the other. Despite repeatedly requesting reinforcements, no support was forthcoming. In the face of the vast Chinese army, equipped with modern armaments, the small number of Gorkha soldiers became helpless. Slowly, the sound of their war cry was dying down.

Walong was a small hamlet located near the tri-junction of Tibet, Burma and India. It was a small but strategically important place. It was the headquarters of one of the circles of the Lohit Division of NEFA. It was manned by an Assam Rifles post with a small airstrip; only Indian Air Force Otters and Caribous could land there. Air drops were the only way to support this sector. There was a dilapidated ancient trade route used by porters and it was this route that Robin and the others were using to carry the ammunition to Walong.

But there was no porter today. All of them had fled in fear. So Robin and his fellow soldiers were under orders to carry the ammunition to the war front.

By the time Chowdhury's group reached Walong, the Chinese had started to attack all the forward posts. Under the leadership of Brigadier N. C. Rawley, the Indian troops were engaged in a fierce battle. Dumping part of the ammunition in the underground bunkers, Robin and a few others went out to hand over some of the ammunition to the fighting soldiers. Although Chowdhury was not allotted war duty, he too was at the battlefield.

After some time the communication with Robin's group failed. Chowdhury went into a bunker that had a wireless set.

The enemy was slowly advancing. Slowly, the ammunition was getting exhausted. The number of soldiers was also decreasing. A deep darkness was setting in.

The hills of Walong rattled with the sound of artillery and mortar shells, mine explosions and machine gun fire. The battlefield was deafening, filled with the agonizing howls and the battle cries of the warring soldiers of different regiments.

No reinforcements had reached yet. No ammunition. No new soldiers either. Nor any new orders.

The artillery and mortar shelling had destroyed the entire communication system at the war front. There was a complete breakdown of the command and control system. There was no means of communication at that moment. No action had been taken to support the fighting from the back. There was no properly organized system of prepared defence. There was no advance reconnaissance. Hurriedly deployed, most of the soldiers had no clear idea of the area. Chaos had overpowered discipline within the Indian army. The words transmitted by the wireless set carried pictures of the battlefield in bits and pieces. Against the innumerable Chinese troops were a handful of Indian soldiers. There were mortar, but no ammunition and no commands. There was also no pre-cooked ration suitable for war in the hills.

The voice of the soldiers asking for support and directions could be heard on the wireless set.

'We have only pouch ammo now. Enemy is firing mortar. We need mortar and machine guns.'

The soldiers who were fighting with limited ammunition became frustrated – they finally understood that there was no chance of getting mortar or any other kind of support.

'What are our orders? It seems like they have surrounded us from all sides. We can hear them advancing and firing small arms.'

'Don't leave your positions. As long as you stay put, the enemy cannot advance.'

The subedar ordered, 'Fix your bayonets and fight.'

The soldiers stopped retreating and confronted the advancing enemy, knowing fully well that death was inevitable.

The Chinese troops slowly surrounded the remaining Indian soldiers.

The ground became damp with blood and littered with bodies.

The wireless set again echoed with the subedar's voice. 'Our communication with the company commander has broken down.

Before that, we heard the sound of mortar and machine gun fire from that place. Sounds like he became a martyr.'

The Indian troops were becoming weak. The signs of defeat were evident. All the bunkers were empty now. The ammunition store was empty, too. The commanders became silent.

No orders for withdrawal had come yet. The enemy was advancing. The wireless echoed repeatedly with the voice of the soldiers asking for orders.

'What is the next order? I don't have any ammunition with me. What should I do? Should I withdraw?'

'There have been no orders for withdrawal yet.'

The wireless operator looked at Chowdhury and said, 'You go, sahab. It's not your job.'

Chowdhury did not answer. With an impassive face he looked outside the bunker.

'What should I do, sir? We are only three. All the others are dead. Should we retreat, sir?'

'I can't say anything. I have not received any orders.'

The eyes of the wireless operator turned red with helpless anger, frustration and grief.

'Say something, sir. The other two are dead. I am alone. I don't have anything to fight with except the bayonet. Should I withdraw, sir?'

'What should I tell you, subedar? Please forgive me.' The operator looked at Chowdhury.

'Go, Chowdhury sahab. Or you will not survive.'

'Sir, the enemy is advancing. I have no arms. How can I fight, sir? Say something, sir – should I withdraw, sir? I –'

Suddenly, the wireless set went silent.

'Leave, Chowdhury sahab. You are a civil officer. Why do you want to die?'

'Come with me. What will you do here with this wireless set?'

'No, sahab. I can't move. You go, sahab. Please.'

Chowdhury did not leave. He sat with an LMG by the side of the operator.

By the time the withdrawal orders came, it was far too late. The troops were not organized enough to convey the withdrawal orders to all the soldiers. The soldiers had already been surrounded by the enemy.

Many of the confused and helpless soldiers had fled into the dense jungles. Those who did not receive the orders kept on fighting. They fought till they were bathed in blood and dropped dead.

Amongst them were eight of Robin's compatriots. Robin had survived. So had Prahlad, Abinash and Amarendra. Taking the injured Amarendra with them, they returned to the air strip in Walong.

Evacuation was in full swing at Walong and the airstrip was packed with people from the army as well as civilians. Soon after Robin and his comrades reached the airstrip, an Otter that could carry six passengers landed. Robin, with the help of the others, tried to take Amarendra to the plane. A scuffle broke out between the army and the civil officers. Not a single civilian succeeded in getting into the Otter. In all of the Otters that landed on the airstrip, only army officers got in and flew to safety. The low-ranking officers and support staff of the army and civil administration kept looking on.

Tired of waiting, some of the dejected and frightened people fled on foot. Brigadier Rawley and other responsible officers, however, did not desert their soldiers. They did not board the Otters.

Robin and his group returned from the airstrip. Their faces brightened seeing Chowdhury walking towards them from the opposite direction.

'Where are the others?' Chowdhury enquired anxiously.

Before Robin could answer him, a mortar shell landed right near them. There was no time for talk. Quickening their steps, they reached Chowdhury's government quarters. As soon as Chowdhury entered, he asked Biren, 'Is the food ready?'

'There is just rice and daal, nothing else.'

'Just serve that. Let us all eat whatever we can.'

Chowdhury gave Amarendra first aid, then told everyone to eat and pack as many provisions as they could carry in their pockets and bags. In fifteen minutes they were ready to leave. There was just one thing left to do. They had to set fire to the godowns that were filled with their supplies.

Chowdhury started with the government papers and the godowns of food supplies located at the centre of Walong, now almost deserted. Robin and the rest came forward to help. There was no one now to give commands to. They did not notice the local people who had come out from the villages. They came to the godown with dao blades in their hands. As the godowns burned, the villagers became ferocious.

'Hey, sahab, why are you setting fire to the godowns? Why are you burning the rations? Give them to us. We will take them for our families.'

'The rule is to not give the rations to villagers. The rule is to burn down the godowns before abandoning a place. We can't keep anything for the enemy.'

'We are not enemies. We are Indians. Give us the rations. We won't give anything to the enemies.'

The villagers encircled Chowdhury.

'Move back!'

'We won't. What will you do? If you burn the godown, we will use our arms.' They took out their glistening daos from their scabbards.

Robin and his group came forward. Seeing their arms the villagers slowly backed away.

The godowns and the government offices slowly went up in smoke. Creating big holes in the ground, mortar shells and canon balls had started to drop.

By the time the Chinese troops entered Walong, the place was completely deserted.

A group of Chinese soldiers kicked open the door of Chowdhury's thatched hut, which had not yet been destroyed. They fired aimlessly and kicked his stove and utensils, scattering them all around. One of the soldiers spotted the small pocket-sized *Bhagavad Gita* that Chowdhury had left on his bed. The soldier tore it to shreds and flung it on the floor. Seething with hatred, he stamped on the scraps of paper and walked out.

Downhill from Walong, a chaotic retreat had begun.

Fifteen

Yiu Yi's mother had come out of her house with a bag in hand.

The previous night, her elder daughter Yunlin had delivered a baby girl. She was going to Ledo to give the good news to Yunlin's in-laws. Her family had asked her not to go without informing the police but she refused to listen.

'How will the police get to know? I'll travel by train. Yunlin's in-laws will mind if we don't give them the news. It's only for men that the police have imposed restrictions. It's alright for women to move about,' she argued.

She couldn't contain her excitement. This was her first grandchild.

She met Ahlin's mother on her way.

'I'm going to Ledo. Take care of Yunlin.'

'Sure. Don't worry. You'll be back today, won't you?'

'I will.'

Before Ahlin's mother could say anything, Thakur Prasad arrived on the scene.

'Where are you off to at this early hour? To the Chinese government?' His face was grave but his eyes were glittering with menace.

Ahlin's mother flared up instantly.

'What did you say? Say it again. Huh! What can you say, after all! You are nothing but a government informer.'

'If I am a government informer, what are you? A Chinese spy?'

'Yes. I'm a spy. What are you going to do? Beat me?'

'I don't have to; the government will take care of it.'

'Now don't pick a quarrel,' Yiu Yi's mother said softly.

It was morning and the Chinese residents of Cheenapatti were leaving for work on their bicycles. Though they feared going out, the people who worked in the tea gardens kept at it. The situation was not favourable. The Bihari fitters were jealous of them. Whenever they got a chance, they tried to engage their people and replace the Chinese.

Yiu Yi's mother looked at the Chinese school. Cha Mu was sweeping the large compound. It was quiet now. The students who used to play under the shade of the trees were absent.

Yiu Yi's mother walked towards the station. Many families were also going to the station with their luggage. They were shifting to a safer place as they feared the Chinese army could reach the area any moment. From the opposite direction, an armed patrol group was approaching them. Yiu Yi's mother continued to walk but with a feeling of uneasiness.

By the time she reached Ledo, the situation in Makum had become grim. The number of police patrolling the roads had increased rather significantly, and so had the number of government vehicles on the roads.

The children of Cheenapatti had been attending school regularly, but they had lost all interest in their studies. Everyone could sense that something was wrong. When they asked the elders what was happening, they did not get answers. The saddest and most worried were the hostel boarders. Anjali and Mei Ho, who stayed with their relatives, were miserable too, as no one had come from their homes to take them as yet.

'Why are so many soldiers walking on the streets? They stared at me when I was on my way to school. I felt so scared! I just shut my eyes and ran away,' Anjali said.

'They stared at me too. Oh, I'm so frightened!' said Mei Ho.

'I have also met a lot of soldiers. They have big rifles,' Yiu Yi joined in.

'Is it? Oh God! Did they say anything to you?'

'No, they didn't. They had moustaches *this* big and big eyes too. They looked like the Durga puja demon,' Yiu Yi giggled.

The other children joined her but their mirth was muted.

'Maa asked me not to go to school,' Yiu Yi said. 'But I came anyway. Yunlin ache gave birth to a little girl last night. How cute she is! Maa has gone to inform her in-laws. She will come back in the evening.'

As Ling Kwang Tung entered the classroom, the children took out their books. The teacher looked grim and worried. After roll call, he went to the blackboard absentmindedly. Writing in the Chinese script, he looked back at the children and said, 'Repeat after me, "Ni hao ma?"'

'Ni hao ma?' the children said.

'Ni hao ma means "How are you?" Do you understand?'

'Yes, sir,' the children answered in unison.

'Anjali, did you understand? No? In Assamese it would be "Aapuni kaney ase?". Yes?'

'Yes, sir,' Anjali answered.

'Now say in Chinese: "What is your name?" Ko Fuk, you tell me.'

Ko Fuk stood up and tried to put the words together.

'Ni jiao shenme mingzi?'

'Good. Now children, open your books. We won't do anything new today. We will read from the earlier chapters. Ko Fuk, come here and read this story out for everyone.'

Ko Fuk came forward and started reading. The first page had a picture of a river and a bridge over it. A black dog and a white dog were facing each other on the bridge and fighting. On the facing page, the two dogs had fallen into the river. As Ko Fuk turned to the next page, she saw a river with a bridge going across. Here a black goat and a white goat were facing each other. In the picture below this, the white goat had backed out and made room for the black goat to pass. The next picture showed the two goats going their separate ways to the two different banks of the river.

'So what do you think?' the teacher asked after Ko Fuk finished reading.

'The dog is a bigger scoundrel than the goat, sir,' a boy replied.

The children roared with laughter. Looking at the children for a while, the teacher said, 'The moral of this story is that we should live in harmony. There is nothing to gain by fighting.'

'Why is China fighting with India? My elder brothers say this is not a good thing.'

'China is fighting with India for land. I have heard it on the radio. Our father and the others discuss it in hushed voices. They are worried.'

'Nowadays they don't let us go outside to play. They say, don't go, they will beat you.'

'Ahlin ache cries all the time. Ananta dada and the others scolded her because she is Chinese. They say Chow Mao murdabad. Who is Chow Mao?'

'Don't you know about Mao? Chairman Mao. Chow En Lai. Didn't you see them in the pictures in our school verandah? They are fighting with India.'

'Why do these old people fight so much? I think they don't know the story of the dogs and the goats.'

'They should have studied in our school. Sir could have told them the moral of the story.'

'Stop talking. Read another story. You read, Ko Fuk,' the teacher said indifferently.

The ever-smiling teacher was cheerless today. He was engrossed in his own thoughts. Suddenly one of the boys called out, 'Sir, there are police outside!'

Police!

The teacher got startled and went out. The headmaster was already outside. There were two policemen at the gate. One of them said, 'Sir, Ali sir has asked you to close the school for the day.'

'Has something happened?' the headmaster asked worriedly.

'We have heard that some orders have come from Shillong. We don't know what they are. Send the local children home. Don't let the hostel children and the teachers go out. You, too, shouldn't go out.'

After some thought, Chow Chi Yong asked the teacher to send the children home. Then he said to the policemen, 'But we have to go home, or our families will be worried.'

'There is no way out. The orders are that no one should go out. I'll try to inform one of the households from where everyone else will get the information. Tell me which house to inform.'

'Just inform Lee Chang. When will we be allowed to leave?'

'I don't know that.'

One of the policemen left but the other stayed behind.

The children who were coming out from the classrooms were surprised and confused. They were not laughing and chatting like on other days. They were looking back at the school, at their teachers, and were trying to understand what was going on.

After they left, the teachers gathered in Chow Chi Yong's room. At that time, Cha Mu was busy preparing the evening snacks and dinner simultaneously. She had a strange feeling that something bad was going to happen today.

Kaushalya was standing outside her house. She waved to the boys from the Chinese school and asked why school was over so early. Ko Fuk gestured to say that he didn't know. Kaushalya was worried.

Today, two government officials had come to talk to her mother. She did not know what they had discussed. But she felt that something was going to happen. Kaushalya asked her mother but the older woman did not answer. Kaushalya, Siu and Alan used to study together but today they were not together.

'Come inside,' her mother said.

'Can I go for just ten minutes to Alan's house?'

'Why?'

'I'll come back in a moment – I'm so worried. Why are there so many policemen?'

'You don't need to know. Come inside.'

'Please, Maa.'

Her mother considered for a while and said, 'Okay, go. But come back soon.'

As Kaushalya hurried to Alan's house, two cars were coming into the lane. There were eight stern-faced men inside.

Eight executive magistrates!

Alan and Siu sat in Alan's house. They looked worried. Seeing Kaushalya, their faces brightened.

'Why didn't you come?' Kaushalya asked.

'Our parents told us not to go out. Didn't you see how many policemen there are on the road?'

'Why is that?'

'I don't know. Everyone is so frightened!'

'I too am scared, you know. The Chinese troops must have arrived. I saw a lot of people going to the station this morning. Everyone is fleeing. I wonder where we will go! I asked Maa. She didn't answer. Where will you all go, Alan?'

After chatting with them for some time, Kaushalya stood up to leave.

'Now I have to go, or Maa will scold me. If someone says something, come straight to our house. No one will dare to do anything to you if you stay with us.'

Kaushalya said her goodbyes and left.

In their lane too, the armed policemen were doing their rounds.

The people living in the neighbourhood had returned to their homes much earlier than usual. The men who used to gather every day at Mok Min's shop and the Chinese Club had also returned home. Looking at the armed police guarding the entrance, they went inside their houses. They were worried now.

No one knew what was happening.

Evening set in. Together with the cold and the mist, a grim fear hung over the lanes of Cheenapatti.

Sixteen

Now the borders lay open.

The Indian Army had fled, accepting their defeat. There was no resistance left.

People were sitting silently in their houses. Nobody knew why the armed police were guarding the lanes of Cheenapatti and why they were not allowing anybody to go out. Everyone was listening to the news over the radio on low volume. It was the news of India's defeat.

Yiu Yi was busy in the kitchen, preparing the evening meal with her grandmother. Her mother was yet to return from Ledo. In between her tasks, Yiu Yi went to Yunlin's room to see if she wanted anything. Yunlin was fast asleep with the baby beside her. Her father and grandfather were sipping tea in the front room, while her brothers were studying in their own rooms. The atmosphere became serene with the smell of incense lit before the altar.

Having finished her work in the kitchen, Yiu Yi came to Yunlin's room to play with the doll that Robin had given her. Right at that moment they heard someone striking on the front door with a baton. Startled, Yunlin got up and held her baby. 'Maa is back,' Yiu Yi ran to open the front door.

'Yiu Yi! Wait!' her father said in a hushed voice.

Yiu Yi stopped and looked at her father.

'Go inside,' he said.

'Hey, open the door,' someone shouted in a harsh voice, hitting the door again. Yiu Yi's father looked out of the window. A group of policemen were standing in the dark.

'Open the door!'

His hands shaking, Yiu Yi's father opened the door. Instantly, without waiting to be invited in, an officer in civil clothes entered the house. He was followed by three armed policemen and another officer in plain clothes.

'Namaste,' Yiu Yi's father greeted them with folded hands. Yiu Yi's grandparents stood beside him in trepidation.

The officer didn't reciprocate the greeting. Looking around, he said gravely, 'Call everyone to this room.'

'What happened, sahab?' Yiu Yi's father asked meekly.

'We have orders. You will have to leave this place now. For two or three days.'

'Where do we have to go, sahab?'

'All the Chinese people are to be collected in one place. Don't ask questions. Call everyone. Quick. You have ten minutes.'

'But why, sahab?'

'We don't know. Go, go,' the officer almost pushed Yiu Yi's father inside.

'But my children's mother is not at home. She has gone to Ledo –'

'That's alright. When she returns, we will bring her as well. Now go and call everyone.'

It was not necessary to call them. The children had heard the entire conversation. With trembling hands, Yunlin was hastily putting some clothes in a bag. Yiu Yi was standing near her speechlessly, holding her doll. Her two older brothers were stunned into silence and the younger one clutched Yiu Yi and started crying.

'We haven't even eaten. There are children in the house. Please give us half an hour. My parents are old –'

'No. There's no time. Hurry up. Move. Move. Move outside. Take only your papers with you. Nothing else.'

The officer then turned to one of the constables.

'Hey, call Rajendra.'

Rajendra entered diffidently, his eyes shining greedily.

'Leave this house in his custody. Sign this paper. When you come back, you will get everything just as you left it. Till then, the house will remain locked.'

There was no scope for protest. Yiu Yi's grandfather signed the paper with downcast eyes while her father went inside.

The magistrate looked around the room. He looked at every piece of the beautifully carved wooden furniture, fascinating decorative articles and the altar admiringly.

Yunlin came out with the baby, following her father. Yiu Yi, too, followed with the bag and her doll, while her younger brother held onto her. The rest of the brothers had also come. They all looked at the men in fear.

'Leave the bag. No permission to take anything along, except your papers. Don't take anything with you,' one of the policemen said harshly.

'There are clothes for my baby in the bag,' Yunlin said.

'It doesn't matter what it contains. You can't take it. That's all.' The policeman snatched the bag and the doll from Yiu Yi's hand.

'I will take this doll wth me. Sipahi dada gave it to me,' Yiu Yi started weeping.

Yiu Yi's grandma took Yiu Yi in her arms and said, 'No one will take your doll away. You will get it when we come back. Don't cry.'

'I'll tell Sipahi dada,' Yiu Yi said, trying to control her tears.

'Move. Move.' The policemen shouted harshly, almost pushing them out of their home. Speechless and shaken to the core, they walked out.

A similar scene was playing out in every Chinese home.

Lee Chang had just got home and was having tea with his family. Hearing the sound of the baton, they opened the door.

In an instant, everything changed. Anger, fear, uncertainty, surprise and untold sadness had replaced the environment of peace and happiness.

'You have to leave this place.'

'But why? And where will we go?'

'We don't know. Go. Get ready. If you have a passport or other relevant papers, take them with you. Don't take anything else.'

Lee Chang's mother started to cry. His father stood stupefied. Trying to control his overwhelming emotions, Lee Chang looked at the magistrate and said, 'How can I take my wife along – she is heavily pregnant.'

'She will have to go. There is no other way. Go, get ready. Don't worry. This is all for your safety. If you stay on here, you might be in danger.'

Looking straight into the eyes of the magistrate Lee Chang asked in a calm voice, 'What kind of danger, sir?'

'The public may attack you. You can see how angry they are.' The man looked away to hide his uneasiness.

Lee Chang became silent.

The images of the 'public' of Makum came to his mind. Who were the public anyway? Chitta? Johori Khan? Pulok? Narayan? Rameswar? And who else? The friends who used to support him in the football matches and rejoiced in his glory?

Yes, yes! Ananta and his groups hated them! The PSP hated them! The Congress hated them! PSP – Rameswar was a member of the PSP! Would he attack Lee Chang and the others? Who knew!

With tears in his eyes, Ganga Sagar Rai took custody of Lee Chang's house as the entire family left, turning back again and again to look at their home.

Perplexed and in shock, some were walking silently. Others looked around terrified or walked on with eyes downcast.

Near Ho Chang Ho's house, Thakur Prasad stood with some policemen. Seeing them, he chuckled. A devilish smile spread across his face.

Seeing the smile, Dulal Yem's mother flared up.

'You! You've done all this. I know. You want to finish us. You want our land. You won't get it. You won't get anything. When I return, I'll finish you first. I will drink your blood. You bloody government informer!'

'Shhh, quiet,' Dulal's father intervened fearfully.

Thakur Prasad did not say anything; his smile only became sharper.

Holding Dulal's mother, who was frothing at the mouth, Dulal's father walked past Thakur Prasad.

'Don't take anything. Move. Move.'

The sound of wailing spread across Cheenapatti. The air was heavy with lamentation and sighs.

One after another, trucks carrying detainees had started entering the lane teeming with armed police. They were moving towards the cowshed of the Chowkhanis, which was known as the Murli Gola cowshed. This is where the Chinese people who had been arrested from Ledo, Margherita and the other neighbouring towns, villages and tea gardens would be held.

Tung Chin had not yet returned from work. His mother was busy correcting school notebooks. The daughters-in-law and Mei Fung were busy cooking. The children were all studying in one room, while his father and two elder brothers were listening to the news.

But this was not to last.

As soon as the door was opened to a knock, a group of stone-faced men entered the house. They stood with their shoes on in front of the altar and enquired harshly, 'How many people live here? Call them all.'

Everyone came out and gathered in the room.

Hearing the magistrate's order, Tung Chin's mother asked, 'Are we in danger, sir? I am an Assamese; my name is Pramila Gogoi.'

The magistrate looked at her for some time and said, 'How many Indians in your family?'

'All the members of our family are Indians. We have Indian citizenship, sir.'

'No, I mean how many in your family are local people?'

'Our youngest daughter-in-law here is Assamese. Her name is Xonpahi Bora. This is my eldest daughter-in-law, Madhabi. Her mother is from the tea garden community. My husband's great grandfather had first come here. They had all married local girls. We have been settled here for generations, sir.'

The magistrate wrote down the names and addresses of the parents of the daughters-in-law. Then he looked up and asked,

'Where is your youngest son, Tung Chin?'

'He has not yet returned. He works in the garden under the contractor Ho Yen Kee.'

The magistrate sat silently. He looked both confused and sorrowful.

The policemen noted his discomfiture and looked on curiously. After dithering for a while, he said, 'We have orders to take only the Chinese persons amongst you. Ho Min Fu, his three sons, Wenling, and Wenling's five children will go. The rest will stay back. Our people will come to take Tung Chin later.'

Pramila looked at the officer in disbelief.

'What are you talking about? What kind of justice is this? If my husband is Chinese, I am Chinese, too. If I am Assamese, so are my children. If my son is Chinese, how can his children not be Chinese? If you take one, you will have to take us all.'

'We won't go. What do you think of us? We are Indian citizens, just as you are. We haven't attacked India. We are not India's enemies,' Wenlin flared up.

The rest of the family was standing in uncertainty. The faces of the police turned rigid.

The enemies were talking big, standing on Indian soil! Chinese spies were showing their temper! The police personnel felt an unbearable urge to shut the enemy's mouth. But the magistrate remained calm.

'Don't be angry,' the magistrate said. 'We have to follow orders. Please get ready quickly. We can't give you much time. Only those whose names I've read out will move. Don't take anything with you. You have no permission to do so.'

'On what grounds have you divided us? What kind of government rules are these? If China has attacked, fight with China. Why are you taking out your vengence on us for your defeat?' Wenling burst out in anger.

'Why do you say we are taking revenge on you? This is all for your safety.'

'What safety are you talking about? Who will harm us? Are we fighting for China or spying for China? You are lying so you can take us away.'

'She is right,' Pramila intervened. 'I've lived with my husband for thirty-five years. None of us have any ties with China. We have never seen China. There are no Chinese spies in our house. Arrest us all, if you have to.'

One of the policemen came forward.

'What are you saying about the government?'

Holding on to their mothers, the children started crying.

'Let me do the talking. You go and wait outside. The children will get scared.'

'Do you know these people?' the policeman looked at the magistrate.

The magistrate became cautious. If these police reported to the seniors, he might be arrested for having links with the enemy. His face hardened, as he spoke firmly. 'If you don't cooperate we will have to apply force. You will be considered agents of the enemy. Then you will be in real trouble.'

'He is right, Pramila,' Ho Min Fu said in a steady, quiet voice. 'Don't argue. Since they have come to take us, we have to go. Besides, it will only be for a couple of days or so.'

Pramila Gogoi looked at her husband with tears in her eyes.

Finally, the magistrate lost his cool. The policemen came forward. Madhabi held her husband tightly and started crying.

'I won't let him go. I'll also go with him. Take me along, sir. Sir, don't do this to us, sir …'

Without waiting for the magistrate's order, one policeman pulled Madhabi's husband from her and dragged him outside. In the midst of Madhabi's distressing wails and the screams of the children, Tung Chin's father, his two elder brothers, his sister-in-law Wenling and their five children left their home. The armed constables pushed them down the road, which was teeming with a crowd of curious neighbours.

Mok Min closed his shop early. Hearing that the police had surrounded Cheenapatti, the people who were sitting in his shop had left in a hurry. Mok Min went to Manchung Ho's place. There he found the officer-in-charge of the Tinsukia police station, A. C. Chow and Manchung Ho engrossed in deep conversation.

'Come on in, we were talking about you,' the OC grinned.

After taking his seat, Mok Min asked politely, 'The police have surrounded Cheenapatti. I have heard that they have arrested some people. What has happened, sir?'

'President's rule. These things happen. If anything would have taken place, would I be sitting here?' the OC grinned again.

'Will there be any problems for us, sir?'

'What problem? You are an old settler. You have no reason to worry. You have such good ties with the higher-ups. Who doesn't know you? You are involved in so many social activities. That day in the meeting, you were the first to sign on the declaration of loyalty. Why would anyone harm you?'

After talking to them for a while, Mok Min stood up.

'I'll take your leave now, sir. The family will be worried.'

'Yes, go ahead. Send me two bottles of ginger ale and a tin of cheese, if you can,' the OC said.

'Sure sir, I'll send them over immediately,' Mok Min said.

Feeling a little relieved, Mok Min went back to his shop, while the other three remained immersed in their secret discussions.

Mok Min sent over two bottles of ginger ale, a tin of cheese and two tins of wafers as well, and went home. The children were all home. Everyone was worried.

'Are they going to arrest us too?'

'The OC says we have nothing to worry about. We are old settlers.'

After freshening up, Mok Min took a stroll around his house. He had a lot of money in the bank. But he also hoarded a great amount of money and gold in his house. He hid that money behind walls and inside photo frames and secret drawers. He even dug holes on the floors to bury cash and gold. He inspected the secret places and returned to his room. Shedding his worries, he sat down to do the accounts of the shop. And at that very moment, he heard a heavy knock on his door.

As soon as the door was opened, the crying began. Leaving his hard-earned wealth behind and his beautiful house in the hands of his neighbours, Mok Min walked towards Cheenapatti with his family, silent and shocked.

In their house in Tipling, Hong, Ming and their parents sat, numb. The second officer of the Duliajan police outpost, and a football fan, said to them with tearful eyes, 'I don't understand why I've been asked to arrest you. If you want to get away, do that. I don't care if I lose my job, but I'll help.'

'We won't run away. Why should we? We haven't done anything wrong. Are we thieves? Are we dacoits? No, we won't run away. Let them take us away.'

The anger and resentment of the two brothers shattered the air, their eyes filled with tears of despair.

'Don't be angry!' the father consoled. 'We are Chinese. That is the reality. Even if we live here for a thousand years, this will be our identity. They will not consider us one of them. Come, let us go.'

Wiping her tears their mother said, 'Please don't mind what my sons said. They were born here. They think of this place as their own.'

'I understand, baideu. I don't know why God has entrusted me with this sinful responsibility. You are not permitted to take anything with you. But never mind. Take all your valuables. Take a plate and bowl each. Take some clothes too. Orders are that you will be shifted for two days. But who knows; it could be more that that. The war is still on. And our soldiers only know how to flee. What do you say, sir?' the second officer looked at the magistrate.

'Keep the seizure list safely, so that you can claim whatever you have left behind, when you return,' the magistrate said gravely.

The second officer helped the family pack. The father tucked some money into the folds of his clothes, while the mother made a small bundle of her jewellery and tucked it in her waist. Ming put some essentials in a bag and then put in the books he had borrowed from Pulok.

'Why are you taking those?'

'I haven't finished reading them, ako.'

'Leave them behind. We don't even know where they are taking us.'

'Let me take them, ako.'

The magistrate, the witness and the neighbour who took charge of the house, were deeply saddened by the sight of the Assamese books.

The two most popular youths of Tipling and their parents climbed into the jeep surrounded by policemen. With tears in their eyes, the speechless onlookers watched their Chinese neighbours being taken away.

The small township of Tipling fell silent.

Not a single goodbye was said.

Slowly the two vehicles disappeared round the bend. The people left behind were still silent. The neighbourhood women wept quietly while the air filled with the heavy sighs of the men as they returned to their own homes.

The compound of the Duliajan police station had started to fill up with the Chinese who had been brought from all the neighbouring areas.

Seventeen

Addison and his friends were still waiting at the Doom Dooma Planters' Club. They had been at the club for the past two nights. Keeping loaded guns at hand, they were drinking to their heart's content and keeping a watch over the tea garden.

The Chinese soldiers were yet to arrive. Wallong had already fallen. The Indian soldiers had fled, leaving the border area of Lohit Frontier Division in the hands of the enemy. But there was no sign of the enemy yet. They were tired of waiting. It would have been better if they had come!

They had dug trenches in the tennis court without permission. If the Chinese didn't come, they would have to repair the court at their own expense. They would also have to pay for all the liquor they'd consumed over the last two days.

It was evening. Liang and the others who were waiting to fight the Chinese had left a while ago. Pulok would also leave after some time. He had been given leave for four hours today as he had to take Mei Lin to Cheenapatti.

Pulok became alert when he saw the guard of the club gate running towards them.

'Someone is running towards us,' he informed Addison excitedly.

Everyone looked at the gate anxiously. Arjun sardar!

After a while, Arjun sardar reached the club, breathless. Saluting Addison, he said, 'Sir, the police are picking up the Chinese people from our garden.'

'What?' the playful managers turned serious.

Pulok's heart missed a beat. Who had they arrested? Was it Liang or his brother? Or Tung Chin?

'But why?' Addison asked.

'I don't know, sir.'

'Where is the head clerk?'

'He is in the office with the police.'

Addison discussed the matter with his friends and came out with Daman Singh. Pulok followed on his bicycle with Arjun. He forgot all about going home.

When Addison and Daman Singh arrived at the tea garden office, a police jeep and two trucks were parked in front of the office. A number of people were sitting in the office courtyard cordoned off by the police. Seeing Addison, they looked relieved.

He walked into the office. An officer of the Doom Dooma police station, Tileswar Baruah, was seated inside to take permission from the manager to arrest the Chinese. It was just a formality. If they arrest without informing the European managers, they might create problems later.

Addison and Daman Singh sat on the chairs. Addison looked at Tileswar Baruah angrily.

'Yes, officer?'

'The public is furious. The Chinese are facing a security threat. Order has come from Shillong to shift them to a safer place for two to three days. They will return when the situation normalizes,' Tileswar Baruah explained, forwarding a copy of the government order.

Addison went through the papers.

'Okay, tell me officer, in which safe place are you going to keep them?'

'I don't know. It would be better if you speak with the officer-in-charge.'

Addison thought for a while and then went out to talk to the detainees.

Pulok had reached by then. He stood anxiously near the crowd.

'Pulok's here!' someone in the crowd shouted.

Hearing Pulok's name, Tung Chin looked up. His face glowed in relief.

Pulok ran to Tung Chin, held his arms and stood still, speechless.

'I don't know what is happening at home. You'll have to find out,' Tung Chin said quietly, breaking the silence.

'I'll do that. Where is Liang? And Akong?'

'I've seen them getting off just now. Akong is over there. Only his father and his brothers have been arrested. Others from his family are left behind.'

'I will go and see,' Pulok said and hurried towards the two trucks.

Liang and Yao Sen were standing under a tree. Liang's brother and his sister-in-law were standing a little distance away with their children. Pulok went over and asked anxiously, 'Where is Kam Ling? And your children?'

'They didn't arrest them. I am Chinese. That's why I have been arrested,' Yao Sen answered with a brave smile.

Before Pulok could say anything, a policeman came up to them. He looked at Pulok and asked harshly, 'What are you doing here?'

Before Pulok could answer, the policeman saw Yao Sen and Liang. He looked at Pulok again and asked bitingly, 'So, you have come to enquire about your bosom friends?'

He was reeking of cheap liquor. Pulok remained quiet, not knowing how to react.

'What happened? Why are you silent? Are you heartbroken because the Chinese spies have been arrested?'

'Whom are you calling Chinese spies? Think before you speak,' Pulok flared up.

'What did you say? Think before I speak? That's what I have done. If they aren't spies, then who are? Could China defeat us without their help? We are also keeping an eye on you. Playing for the Seven Star Club, you've become their slaves. Or have you also started betraying us like them? Go. Leave right now, or else –'

After swearing at Pulok, the policeman, a fanatical supporter of Doom Dooma's Rover's Club, laughed madly, delighted at having the Chinese players of the Seven Star Club in his hold. Pulok looked at him and said coolly, 'Or else what?'

'Do you want to find out? Have you seen this stick? I'll push this in and churn you.'

Pulok turned red with anger.

Hearing the commotion, a few armed guards came forward to ask what had happened.

'This man is creating a problem. He is with the Chinese.'

Pulok was immediately surrounded by the guards.

'Son of a swine. Supporting the Chinese.'

'Arrest him, too. Advocating for the Chinese! Son of a bastard! You are also a Chinese spy, or probably a Communist. We will rip your insides out.'

Addison heard the commotion as he was coming out of the building.

'Hey Baruah, don't fight. Don't fight.'

'I'm not fighting, sir, this constable is –'

'It's okay. It's okay. Now come,' he pulled Pulok away.

The detainees were then being moved into the trucks.

'Where are they taking Liang and the others, sir?'

'To the Doom Dooma police station. After that, I don't know where they will take them. Go home now. I'll see what can be done. I'll talk to the higher authorities.'

Addison left with Daman Singh. Pulok decided to go to the police station.

Pulok's father was waiting outside the Makum police outpost.

Everyone at the outpost was busy. Everyone looked serious. For the first time, the outpost had been assigned a big responsibility: the arrests of the Chinese. The Makum area had the largest concentration of Chinese people and people of

Chinese origin. The military and the paramilitary forces had also been employed for the same task.

After hesitating for a while, Minaram Baruah went to a constable and said, 'Sir, it is important to meet Ali sir.'

Gratified at being called 'sir', the constable measured Minaram Baruah from top to bottom and said, 'Why? What's so important?'

'I have some information about the enemy,' Baruah whispered.

The constable became alert.

'Is that so? What is your name? Where have you come from?'

Minaram Baruah answered in whispers. Thinking for a while, the constable said, 'Alright. You wait here. I will inform sir.'

The other constables who were standing nearby heard Minaram Baruah's whispered words. They came forward.

'What happened? What's the matter?'

'I have come to meet Ali sir. I have some information.'

'Oh really!' The constables didn't look impressed.

Many had been streaming in with information for the last few days, after the chief minister's appeal to inform the police about anything suspicious. Most of the information they brought with them was imaginary, unfounded.

'You have done very well, arresting these enemies. They live in our country and spy for China. Everyone should be chased away. Let them go where they have come from. Ungrateful people!' said Minaram Baruah.

The constables had just returned from the day-long assignment of arresting the Chinese. They were depressed.

'They shouldn't just be arrested, they should be finished off. They came as coolies and became kings. They have taken away our wealth, and grown fat and –'

'Shut up! Keep quiet! I am really pissed off. I don't know what I will do with you. Get out of here. I say – go –' one of the constables yelled at him.

Minaram Baruah was about to leave, scared out of his wits at this unexpected reaction, when the first constable came back.

'Sir has called you.'

Swallowing hard, Pulok's father went in.

'What news do you have?' Ali asked Minaram Baruah.

Rubbing his hands, Baruah said, 'It's a secret.'

Ali thought for a while and asked the constable to leave. Then he looked at Minaram Baruah.

'Now tell me what you have to say. I have very little time.'

'Please don't tell anyone what I tell you, sir. Not even my family. If they get to know, it will be a big issue, sir. My daughter-in-law is a Chinese girl. She secretly talks to Chinese-looking people. Unknown people. No one in our family knows about that. Only I have seen her. But I am scared to say anything. She is educated. She writes letters and passes them on to those people. I have seen this with my own eyes. Now, when our country is in danger, sir, it would be a crime if I didn't inform you.'

Ali thought for a while and then looked at Minaram Baruah.

'Can you give it to me in writing?'

'Will I get into trouble, sir?'

'Why would you? You are doing this for your country. These matters will not be made public. Don't worry.'

Handing him paper and pen, Ali sat down in anticipation.

Eighteen

After Tawang and Jang, Se La also fell.

Today, in answer to a house adjournment motion and a call attention motion in the parliament, Nehru informed the house that Walong and Se La, important mountain passes in the Kameng frontier, have fallen to the Chinese. He also informed the house that, bypassing the Indian army, the Chinese troops have cut off the road connection to Bomdila, a strategically important place, eighty kilometres from Se La pass. He said that, although this is bad news, we are determined not to surrender. We shall keep fighting till the Chinese are ousted from our land.

'Hey Tileswar, what kind of people have you arrested? I told you to arrest only the Chinese and not their local wives and their children. Why have you picked them all up?' The voice of the officer-in-charge of the Doom Dooma police station subdued the voice of the newsreader on the radio.

Tileswar Baruah, the second officer, came and stood near the officer-in-charge.

'What to do, sir, no way out. All are mixed up. It is very difficult to segregate. Whoever we could, we have left behind.'

'What do you mean "mixed up"?'

'A Chinese man has a local wife. His sons also have local wives. Whom to arrest and whom to leave behind? We have left their local wives. Few local women have come clinging to their husbands. Some of us brought them out of sympathy. There are some who even wanted to leave the Chinese behind.'

'Okay. No need to criticize others. Call them one by one. I didn't think there were so many Chinese here. It is really difficult to identify them as Chinese. Most of them don't look Chinese at all.'

'You have assigned me a very bad job, sir. It's very difficult to pull people away from their loved ones. I might have sinned, sir.'

'That's true, sir. They cried a lot. We had to pull them away by force. Some of them didn't have any idea what was happening. When we went to arrest them they asked why we were arresting them. They don't know the Chinese language. They have not even seen China. They don't even look Chinese,' another sub-inspector added.

'Forget about it. You have only done your duty. Now bring them in. Otherwise it will take us till morning to finish.'

The first to come in was Liang. Looking at him, the officer's face turned gloomy. A very familiar face! A very popular footballer!

'Sit down, Liang.'

Liang slowly sat down on the chair and looked at the floor.

'Let me see your papers.'

Liang handed over his papers. The officer glanced at the papers and then looked at Liang with surprise.

'I thought you were an Indian citizen.' Liang said nothing.

After examining the papers, the officer asked Liang, 'Why did you all do such a thing?'

'Meaning?'

'Your year of birth is 1941, your brother's is 1938, and your father came here in 1932. And yet you did not take up Indian citizenship! Why? Was it because you hoped to go back to China some day?'

Endless grief filled Liang's eyes. Meanwhile, Pulok had entered the room and stood near the officer. He intervened.

'Don't say that, sir.'

The officer looked up at Pulok. He knew of Pulok and his friendship with Liang, as members of the same club.

'Oh, it's you! Why have you come inside?'

'Please let Liang go, sir. He has not done anything wrong. These people are not aware of anything, sir. I know them very well. They are not our enemies. They are not Chinese spies. They are our own people, sir.'

Pulok was overwhelmed. Liang looked at him for some time, then lowered his gaze. The room fell silent.

'Why do you think they have been arrested for spying? We have brought them here just to shift them to a safer place. Don't worry. Your friends will be safe. You better go now. CID people are roaming around. If they come to know that you have pleaded for their release, they will put you in jail under the security act. Do you understand? Please leave now.'

The officer resumed his work. But Pulok did not leave. He stood in a corner and watched. At that moment, Robin got down from a jeep in front of the police station, frustrated, exhausted and shattered.

He had just arrived at Doom Dooma with a contingent from Tezu. Without glancing at anyone, he walked into the police station compound. He had just returned from the war fields of the distant mountains, leaving behind his fellow soldiers, who had died fighting.

Robin entered the officer-in-charge's room. Seeing him, Pulok's face brightened.

'When did you arrive? Look, they've arrested Liang, Yao Sen, Tung Chin and others. They have arrested Akong, too.'

Robin said nothing. He just stared at Pulok's face. Pulok looked at the officer.

'Sir, he is a friend of ours. He is Robin Dohotia, sir. Do you recognize him? He is the centre-forward of Seven Star Club. Ask him what kind of people Liang and the others are –'

Pulok turned to Robin again. But Robin was leaving the room, stone-faced; he had come to assist in the shifting of the detainees.

'Go outside now. There is nothing we can do. The intelligence people are around. Not only will you get into trouble, I will also lose my job,' he said to Pulok quietly.

Wiping his tears, Pulok left the room.

The teachers of the Chinese school were still sitting inside. Armed police guarded the entrance of the school and patrolled the roads. The Chinese families were moving towards the opposite lane, group after group. The laments of the captives could be heard throughout the area. Slowly everything became vacant and quiet. Only a few curious onlookers gathered at the entrance of the gully.

Just then, a group of armed police with a civil officer entered the school. Startled, all the teachers stood up. The officer spoke, 'All of you along with the hostel children have to leave with us right away. Get ready, headmaster.'

The faces of the teachers turned pale.

'Why are you arresting us?' Chow Chi Yong asked gently.

'We are not arresting you. But if you resist, we have orders to do so. Where are the hostellers?'

'They are in the hostel at the back.'

'Let us go there.'

Without waiting to be led, the officer and the policemen walked towards the hostel.

In Pulok's house, the neighbours were sitting before the radio. The news had just ended. Pulok's father had not returned yet. Mei Lin was helping her mother-in-law in the kitchen. She was waiting for Pulok to take her to Cheenapatti.

She looked worried. The hurtful comments of her father-in-law and the news that came over the radio had made her sad and tense. She hadn't been able to talk to Pulok properly for a few days as he went out very early to the garden and returned late at night.

'Tell him today, there's no need to guard the club anymore. It is enough. All the big commanders failed and he has gone to fight! Addison sahab is crazy. He wants to fight the Chinese with an air-gun. God only knows what he plans to do. Pulok's father hasn't returned yet. I am really worried. He usually doesn't return so late. Don't know what is happening. Most of the people in our village have left their homes to safety. It would have been better maybe if we had have gone too.'

Pulok's mother talked to Mei Lin while cooking. Mei Lin kept listening. She was very fond of her simple and loving mother-in-law.

Minaram Baruah returned after some time. Greeting the neighbours who were waiting to listen to Nehru's speech on the radio, he went to freshen up.

'Where have you been?' Pulok's mother asked in irritation. 'Both father and son are the same. Pulok also has not come yet. Mei Lin is waiting to go to Cheenapatti with him.'

'Why are they going there? At this late hour?' he asked cautiously.

'What are you saying? Don't you know that his in-laws live in Cheenapatti? Where were you? Have the Chinese soldiers reached this place? Have you heard anything about it?'

'No, I haven't.'

Minaram Baruah went inside. By the time he finished tea, Nehru's voice came floating on the radio.

Huge Chinese armies have been marching in the northern part of the North-East Frontier Agency. In the north also, in Ladakh, in the Chusul area, the Chinese have been attacking fiercely. They have been held. Now what is happening is very serious and very saddening to us. I can well understand what our friends in Assam must be feeling because all this is happening on their doorstep, one might say. I want to tell them that we feel for them and that we shall help them to the best of our ability.

Everyone was listening to the speech intently. Minaram Baruah came and sat down, his mind filled with fear. He was sitting absentmindedly among the guests.

We shall not accept any terms that they may offer, because they may think that we are a little frightened by some setbacks. I want to make it clear to all of you, and more especially to our countrymen in Assam, to whom my heart goes out at this moment.

A vehicle stopped at the gate. Startled by the sound, people got up and went to the doorway. Switching off the radio with trembling hands and wiping the sweat from his face, Minaram Baruah came out diffidently.

'Police!' someone said fearfully.

A group of armed policemen got down and walked towards the house.

'Why have the police come here?' Minaram Baruah's wife, who had come out, whispered.

Minaram Baruah looked at his wife and said sternly, 'Why have you come out? Go inside.'

'Why have the police come?'

'How should I know?'

In the meantime, the policemen reached the verandah. The guests returned to the sitting room and stood against a wall.

The magistrate entered and looked around the room.

'Who is Minaram Baruah?'

'It's me, sir. Namaskar, sir,' Minaram Baruah said fearfully with folded hands.

'Call Mei Lin, your Chinese daughter-in-law.'

It was as if a bolt of lightning had struck the house. The people were speechless.

'What are you waiting for? Go. Call her here.'

'What has our daughter-in-law done?' Pulok's mother asked from behind the door.

'We will tell you later. Call her. If you refuse, we will have to go in.'

'Go and call her,' Minaram Baruah swallowed hard and told his wife.

Pulok's mother went in, with tears in her eyes. Mei Lin had heard the entire conversation and was standing inside, petrified.

'They are asking for you, child. Did you hear what they said? Come. Otherwise they will come in.'

Mei Lin came out. The magistrate observed her from head to toe and asked, 'Are you Mei Lin Ho?'

'Yes. But now I'm Mei Lin Baruah.'

'Is your home in Cheenapatti?'

'Yes.'

'Give us the names and addresses of your parents and the rest of the family.'

The magistrate sat on a chair. After writing down all the information, he said gravely, 'We have come to arrest you. Here is the arrest warrant.'

'What are you talking about? You've come to arrest her? What has she done?' Pulok's mother cried out.

'There is an allegation of conspiracy against her.'

Conspiracy!

Everyone looked at the magistrate in utter bewilderment, including Mei Lin.

'Someone has given you false information, just because she is Chinese. She has done nothing wrong, sir. Our daughter-in-law is a very good girl. Please don't take her away, sir.'

'It's not in our hands. We have to carry out the orders. Get ready, Mei Lin Ho. You have five minutes. Take all your papers with you and a few essentials in a small handbag.'

'Her husband has not returned from work yet. Please wait till he comes back,' Pulok's mother appealed desperately to the magistrate and then turned to Minaram. 'Why don't you say anything? They have come to take away our daughter-in-law. Why are you silent?'

Minaram Baruah lowered his head. Pulok's mother looked at her husband intently for a few seconds and asked, 'Where did you go today?'

'To play cards. Where else?' he answered awkwardly.

'That's a lie. Today you didn't go to play cards. Tell me, where did you go? You have asked these people to come, haven't you? You want to get rid of our daughter-in-law. Don't you?'

'I – I – why should I –'

'How could you do this?' Pulok's mother broke down.

The neighbours were speechless. They looked at Minaram Baruah in confusion.

'Alright, I'll go with her then. I can't send my daughter-in-law alone to the police station at this hour of the night,' she looked at the magistrate.

'No one can accompany her. That is the order. If you protest, she will get into more trouble. There is a definite allegation against her. In the present situation this is a very big allegation. We will see that she does not run into any more trouble. Now please go in, we are already late.'

'Come Maa, let's go in,' Mei Lin said gently.

Pulok's mother broke into helpless tears.

'Your father-in-law has done this. I know for sure.'

Mei Lin did not react. She entered her room and looked around. Then she opened her wooden cupboard and took out the leather purse that Pulok had given her and the carved wooden box that her father had given her. She put them in a small bag. She also put in it a small brass pot of vermillion. She removed their wedding photograph from the photo frame, rolled it in a piece of paper and put it inside the bag. Then she turned to her mother-in-law and said softly, 'If I've done anything wrong, please forgive me. And tell your son, too.'

'Don't say things like that! You will come back soon, child. As soon as Pulok is back, I'll send him to the police station. He will get you released. Don't worry.'

Mei Lin said nothing. Pulok's mother put a few essentials in the bag, weeping all the while. When Mei Lin got ready to leave, she embraced her and cried.

'All this has happened because of your father-in-law. I know. What will I say to you, child?'

Mei Lin gently removed herself from the embrace and said, 'They have arrested me because I am Chinese. What is his fault?'

Kneeling to bow in obeisance to her mother-in-law, Mei Lin calmly walked out of the room.

Pulok was on his way home from Tung Chin's house at that very moment. He had heard that his Chinese friends who were arrested would be taken to Cheenapatti. He had decided to go there after meeting Mei Lin. As he approached his house, he saw the police jeep drive out. Getting off his bicycle, he watched in surprise. Why had the police come to their house?

Mei Lin!

Mei Lin saw Pulok and called out to him.

'Who is that man?'

'He is my husband. Please stop the car for a moment. Let me say goodbye to him before I go.'

The magistrate looked at the policemen. It was risky to stop the car. Pulok could create problems. The villagers might also come out. There was every possibility that the situation might go out of hand.

'Let me just talk to him once. Please stop the car for a minute. I haven't committed any crime. Why don't you try to understand? He is my husband. My –'

Ignoring Mei Lin's desperate pleas, the jeep sped ahead.

Nineteen

The gate of the huge Chowkhani cowshed had been closed.

Inside was a spacious courtyard, a small house on the right to store tea seeds and a big cowshed in the front. The house and the cowshed had been emptied today. The entire premises were filled with the Chinese detainees.

People squatted in the courtyard. Most of them were talking impatiently. Some were crying. Every now and then, the gate was opened to let in more captives.

Cheenapatti was absolutely quiet now.

After dusk, even the non-Chinese were not allowed to use the lane leading to the cowshed. Only the magistrates and the people who took custody of the Chinese people's properties were moving around.

People like Bholu Singh, Ramlal the village headman and a few others were taking charge of the properties of their much-loved neighbours with heavy hearts.

Chinese soldiers had been captured. Chinese spies had been arrested, too.

There were rumours doing the rounds. Some people gathered at the entrance of the lane to look at the so-called spies. Some of the onlookers resisted the urge to attack the Chinese enemies who were coming in the open trucks. Any moment, the crowd could transform into a mob.

In all of Cheenapatti, only two people were happy today. They were Thakur Prasad and Rajendra. They were stealthily moving about in the neighbourhood. There was no one who could stop them now.

Chitta and Johori Khan's shops were closed. Both of them were standing gloomily at the entrance of the lane. Ananta was beside them. All his doubts had cleared, especially the ones about his love for Ahlin. More intense was the sense of guilt. The guilt of spitting on the lane, showing his hatred. Now there was nothing he could do.

The Chinese people of Makum had become the people of the enemy camp, a threat to the security of India. He tried to enter the lane but returned, getting a strong reproof from the armed guards.

Trucks were entering the gully, one after another, the captives looking around in total confusion, trying to figure out where they had been brought.

Seeing Liang and Tung Chin on a truck, Chitta got carried away. He ran after it, calling out their names.

The onlookers reacted in different ways. Some were sad, some angry and others made sarcastic comments.

Rameswar came running to Chitta.

'What's happening here?'

'They are arresting the Chinese. Everyone, including the hostel boys.'

'Why? What had happened?'

'I don't know. Everyone is saying that they have captured Chinese soldiers and spies. But whom have they caught? Are Tung Chin and the others spies?' Johori Khan said.

'This must be something very serious. They arrested Narayan too, a little while ago.'

'But why?'

'I don't know. They have arrested many others. I have heard they are arresting the Communists too.'

'What will happen now? What should we do?'

Yiu Yi's mother had just returned from Ledo. She was pleading with the armed guards to let her go into the lane. Chitta and the others went to placate her. Seeing them, she cried out.

'They are not letting me go in. What has gone wrong? What will I do now?'

'Hey, you. Move back,' one of the armed guards shouted.

'Let her go. Her house is on this lane. She has little children. Please let her go, sir,' Johori Khan pleaded.

'I can't permit that right now. I can't let her go. Go away.'

'Arrest me too, sipahi sahab. My whole life is here. My home, my kids, the father of my kids –'

At that moment Pulok arrived.

'They have arrested Mei Lin. They said she would be taken to the police station. But she is not there. What will I do now? They said that she has conspired against the country.'

'I've heard that all of them have been taken to Chowkhani's cowshed. She might be there. But they are not allowing anyone to go in.'

'They have to let me in. I'm going there right now.' Ignoring Chitta's caution and defying the guards, he entered the lane. The guards surrounded him immediately. They started kicking and beating him. Chitta, Johori Khan and Rameswar ran towards him and brought him back, pacifying the guards. Blood dripped from Pulok's head, mixing with his helpless tears.

Inside the cowshed, Mei Lin was sitting on the floor. Yunlin was beside her with the baby on her lap. The baby had been crying ever since they had been brought to the shed and Yunlin did not know what to do. Mei Lin took off her shawl and passed it to Yunlin.

'The baby might be catching a cold. Wrap her with the shawl.'

Yunlin took the shawl and looked at Mei Lin with moist eyes. Wrapping the baby in it, she held it to her bosom.

Liang, Akong, Yao Sen and Tung Chin came to sit near them.

'Did you see Pulok before they took you?' Tung Chin asked.

'I saw him. Called out to him too. He didn't hear. I requested the police many times to stop the jeep. But they didn't.'

'Don't worry, he will do something. Where is your father? And what about your uncle?'

'I haven't seen my father. No one knows where he is. But my uncle and aunt are over there somewhere.'

'Wait here. We'll go outside and look for them.'

'Don't go out. They will abuse you.'

'Let them.'

Tung Chin and his friends went out to the courtyard.

Almost all the people from Makum and the nearby areas had been confined to the cowshed. Only A. C. Chow and Manchung Ho were not among them. They were now busy in a closed-door meeting with the government officials. They were safe as they had sided with the government. Both their family and property were safe. How could they afford to lose their hard-earned property? What was wrong, if they gave the government some information about Cheenapatti?

'You will have to talk to your people once,' one of the officers said.

'Which people?' A. C. Chow asked, taken aback.

'The people in the cowshed. They might create trouble. They respect you. If you tell them that they have been arrested for a few days, it will be easier for us to handle them.'

'They don't respect me like they used to. If Ho Chang Ho goes, it may be better.'

'He has been arrested. How can he convince them? You will have to do the talking. Come on now, let's go,' the officer said in a commanding voice.

A. C. Chow stood up without any protest.

There was no one now at the entrance of the lane except for the armed guards. A little distance away, some of the families of the detainees and few locals were waiting. The night slowly deepened, bringing with it an unkind darkness. A couple of hours had passed after the last truck had entered the lane.

Breaking the silence and the darkness of the lane, a military jeep came to a halt at the entrance. Robin and two other men in uniform got off the jeep. Seeing him, Xonpahi ran towards him and cried out, 'It's me, Xonpahi, Robin dada.'

Robin looked at Xonpahi's tear-stained face. His stiff expression remained unchanged. Meanwhile, Yiu Yi's mother, Madhabi, Phulmoni and Chitta moved closer. Xonpahi was crying.

'Do something Robin dada – no one is listening to us. We are not allowed to go inside. Where are they taking our families?'

Robin looked at her silently. His face still showed no emotion.

'Hey, Robin, why are you silent?' Chitta shouted in anger.

'Is he a friend?' one of the army men looked at Robin with suspicion.

Inside the lane a different situation was playing out. Robin looked around. While some government officers were sealing Chinese homes, many others were busy looting them. Among them were Thakur Prasad and Rajendra.

Robin entered C Hoi's house first. The beautiful house was now in shambles. The armed guards were loitering around inside while a police officer and a magistrate known to Robin were questioning C Hoi. His entire family was crying loudly in a corner. Seeing Robin, C Hoi cried out, 'Robin, look! They think I'm a Chinese spy. They beat me. Tell them I've done nothing wrong. I am only a carpenter. I haven't done anything, Robin.'

'Hey, shut up! If you are not a spy then what are you? Do you know this man?' The officer looked at Robin.

'Yes, I do.' Robin answered gravely. 'What happened?'

'Go and have a look at his house, upstairs,' the magistrate said.

'I've seen it.'

'When?'

'When I was invited for the housewarming.'

'Have you seen the secret passage?'

'Secret passage?'

'Yes. Go and see yourself. He is definitely a Chinese spy. We haven't checked the other houses yet. There may be others too. These Chinese people are treacherous!'

Robin walked up the stairs, ignoring C Hoi's cries. He entered the bedroom, which was a mess. Looking around for some time, he went to the adjacent room. There was some furniture and two cupboards with books and other paraphernalia. The books that were in Chinese lay scattered on the floor. Behind a cupboard was a passage through which one could drop down.

Robin looked in disbelief. Why had C Hoi built this secret passage? Did he really have a secret life? Did C Hoi, who had become rich within only a few years, have any secret liaison with China?

It was difficult to believe. Why would a Chinese spy spend his entire life's earnings to build a beautiful house in another country? Robin wondered if any other Chinese homes had a secret passage. One by one, the faces of his Chinese friends flashed before him. He stood absentmindedly for some time near the passage and went down through it. He fell into a tiny chamber which could not be seen from outside. On the southern wall of the room was a hole, big enough for a grown person to pass through. On the other side of the wall, just at the beginning of the passage, there was a water tank, which obstructed the passage from view. Robin came out and found himself in C Hoi's backyard. Next to the courtyard, was the neighbour's kitchen garden. Bypassing the garden, Robin went to the Kali temple in Murli Gola lane.

Thakur Prasad and Rajendra, with their faces covered, laden with loot from empty houses, were sneaking out. Seeing Robin they dropped their bundles and ran. The looted items lay scattered on the road. Robin stood in shock for some time, then went to a nearby house. There he found Raghuwa Mahato and a few armed guards.

'This house is in my custody,' Mahato said sadly. 'The poor people could not even eat before being taken away. They have left the place as it was. People have already started lifting their things. They don't listen to anyone.'

Before Robin could reply, he saw five constables coming with bundles of looted goods. They intended to hide the stuff in a small hut behind the house. They would pick up the loot at a convenient time. One of them was carrying Yiu Yi's doll.

'Where did you get this doll?' Robin asked.

'Why? Do you want it?'

'Yes. Give it to me.'

'Why, brother? Will you give it to your sister?' the constable asked sarcastically, stuffing the doll into his bundle.

'I said, give it to me,' Robin said. Snatching the doll, he slapped the constable.

The constable was shocked and stared at Robin. Patting the man on the back, another constable said, 'Let it go, friend. It's enemy property. Let him keep it.'

Robin did not react. He walked out of the house with the doll in his hand. He went into the cowshed and stood there, looking for his friends.

He felt extremely uneasy. He was sweating. He felt like running away. The conflict between anger and love became unbearable.

There was nothing he could do. He was also a captive to duty and patriotism. The destiny of these people had already been written. Nothing could be done to change it.

Controlling his emotions, Robin left the courtyard and stood at the doorway. Inside, Mei Lin was trying to feed Yiu Yi's brother the food provided by the Chowkhanis. The child was still weeping. Everyone was shivering in the cold. The workers of the Chowkhanis who had come to distribute food gave their shawls to the detainees. These warm shawls were spread on the floor for the children. Those who had been able to bring some warm clothes from their homes, thanks to the kindness of a few magistrates, spread these over the children who were asleep.

Handing the doll to a guard, Robin pointed to Yiu Yi and said, 'Go and give this to that girl over there.'

'Why, sahab?' he asked suspiciously.

'I have seen her drop the doll on her way here. She is just a child. Return it to her,' Robin said and, without bothering to see the guard's reaction, walked away.

Just then an officer walked into the compound, followed by A. C. Chow.

The officer stood in front of the people sitting in the courtyard. Chow stood behind him. The officer asked all the men to come out of the shed and sit in the courtyard. When all the men had assembled, he said, 'Please remain quiet. There is nothing to fear. You all know that China has attacked our country. The situation is tense. Anything can happen at any moment. Therefore, the government has ordered to keep you under police custody for three or four days. For your security. After the situation improves, you will all be sent back to your homes.'

A. C. Chow came forward.

'Don't worry. I've talked to the authorities. It is just a matter of two or three days.'

On seeing A. C. Chow, the people's fear turned to intense hatred. Surrounding the officer, they created a commotion.

'We have left our homes without locking the doors. We were compelled to leave all our money, ornaments and other valuables in our houses. We were not allowed to bring anything.'

'You'll get everything back. That is the government's responsibility. Don't worry about it.'

'But you have not arrested our women and children. Where will we go, leaving behind our families?' The men who were separated from their families continued asking questions.

Chow wiped his face with a handkerchief to hide his uneasiness. After a while the officer lifted his hand.

'Since we don't have the required facilities to keep you here, we will have to take you to a different place.'

The place fell silent immediately. The detainees gazed at the officer in complete surprise.

'Where will you be taking us, sahab?' Chi Fu Hai stood up among the petrified captives.

'I can't tell you that right now.'

Without anyone noticing, Yiu Yi had quietly come out. She looked at the officer for some time and then came towards him.

'Have you seen my mother, uncle? She has not come yet. She went to Ledo to inform about Yunlin ache's baby.'

'Where is your father?' the officer asked, looking at the child in surprise.

'There, the one sitting in the front row.'

The officer looked at her father. He called to him. The officer asked her father about his wife, jotted down her name and looked at Yiu Yi.

'I'll find your mother. Don't worry.'

The officer left the cowshed. Robin came forward with the armed guards.

'Come on, stand up and fall into line.'

'Sipahi dada!' Yiu Yi came over to Robin with hope-filled eyes and held his hand.

'Where were you all this while? I am tired of searching for you. Look how we have been brought here. We told them so many times that we have done nothing wrong, but they didn't listen. They were angry with us for no reason. I told them that I would tell you. Very bad sipahis! Have you scolded them? I know you did. That's why they have returned my doll.'

Robin did not react. He stood there stiffly. Slowly, Yiu Yi's eyes filled with tears. Trying hard to hold back her tears she said, 'Maa went to Ledo. She has not returned. Have you seen her, Sipahi dada?'

'Move. Move. Stand in line,' the guards were shouting.

The cowshed became heavy with wailing again. Yiu Yi's father came to her and said sadly, 'Come. Let us stand in line. Or else they will abuse us.'

Yiu Yi clutched Robin's hand.

'They are taking us away from here. How will Maa find us? Let us wait for her. We will go after she comes. Please tell them. They'll listen to you.'

Robin stood still. With tears in her eyes, Yiu Yi started shaking Robin's hand.

'O Sipahi dada, what's wrong with you? Why won't you talk to me? Are you angry with me?'

'Hey girl, what are you doing? Where is your family?' an armed guard shouted and came forward.

'She is my daughter,' Yiu Yi's father said fearfully.

'Then why are you standing here? Go and stand in the line.'

Trying to keep his composure, Robin said, 'Go and stand in line, Yiu Yi.'

Yiu Yi looked at him for some time and asked slowly, 'The sipahis are not allowed to talk to Chinese people, right, Sipahi dada?'

'Are you still standing there? Will you go or not?' the armed guard yelled at her.

'Come away, Yiu Yi, or he will hit you,' her father said and grasped her hand.

Mei Lin came forward and looked at Robin for a moment. Then hugging Yiu Yi to herself, she said, 'Come away, Yiu Yi. Don't disturb Sipahi dada.'

The armed guard, placing his hand on Mei Lin's back pushed her ahead.

'Move. Move forward.'

'Hey, don't you dare touch her,' Robin shouted in rage, forgetting his position.

'What do you mean?'

'I mean, don't touch her.'

The guard halted. Staring hard at Robin, he asked, 'What happened? So much sympathy? They are all bloody enemies of our country. They spit on the plate from which they eat. Ungrateful people.'

'Even then. Don't touch her.'

'Why? Is she your sweetheart?'

'Shut up. I say shut up. Or I'll break your teeth!'

'What's going on here? Go do your work,' the magistrate ordered. Robin went out without looking at Mei Lin.

'Move. Move. Move to the gate.'

The detainees were put on the trucks waiting outside the cowshed. After all the people were on board, the trucks left in a convoy.

The entrance to the Cheenapatti lane had been cleared. So had the main road. Pulok and his friends, who were waiting at the entrance to the lane, were all chased out. Beyond the police cordon, hosts of friends and relatives of the captives were waiting in fear and anguish for a last look at their dear ones.

The wailing, crying and pleading of the relatives and friends of the captives had turned the Makum sky into a pall of gloom and despair. The chaos was overtaken by the sound of the roaring trucks that were moving out.

The abandoned houses were sealed by then. On each seal was a piece of paper that said in red ink with bold letters: ENEMY PROPERTY.

Twenty

The situation at Kameng Frontier was miserable.

Bomdila had fallen. The Chinese troops were advancing towards Tezpur. Rescue operations were on. The helicopters carrying the Monpas and other civilians from the frontier region were landing one after the other on the Balipara helipad.

The newly arrived Indian troops were busy protecting the Tezpur airfield and making other arrangements. Now there remained only Chaku between Tezpur and Bomdila. If that fell to the Chinese, there would be no resistance left between the Chinese troops and the army headquarters in Tezpur.

The inhabitants of Tezpur and its neighbouring areas who could afford to leave had already evacuated the region. The Tezpur ferry pier was teeming with people fleeing from the hills of NEFA and the locals as well. The large ferries on the Brahmaputra were busy carrying people across day and night. There was almost no administration in the entire area. The train services had been closed down. All the employees had fled.

In the midst of the lawlessness, a few trucks were waiting outside the Tezpur police station. All of them were packed with Chinese people brought in from various places. The trucks had been arriving since evening. Each of the trucks carried uprooted homes, divided families, tears and anguish.

Those who had been arrested by kind policemen and humane officers were allowed to bring along basic essentials. Some had even managed to bring jewellery and money. But most of them came empty-handed.

Most of the people who were entrusted with the responsibility of arresting the Chinese were worried about their own safety. There was no time to think about humanity now. They had arrested as many Chinese people as they could. It was not possible to arrest all the Chinese people from such a large area in one day. Now they had to transport these detainees to the other bank of the Brahmaputra.

Manching, the student of the Chinese school in Makum, had been brought to the Pavoi tea estate. Manchung's older brothers were with them. But his mother and grandmother had not been arrested as they were not Chinese. His schoolmate Ho Yin's mother sat weeping, wondering where her son was.

They had no idea where they would be taken. They had understood only one thing – the situation was no longer favourable. The people they had known to be their own had suddenly become strangers. Gone were the peaceful, carefree days. Now they were guilty of being Chinese.

Suddenly Sangkakati, the superintendent of police, came out of the police station with a few senior officials. He gave the officer-in-charge a few instructions and got into the jeep. There was a lot of work to be done. The cabinet committee was coming from the capital. Most of the senior officers had left for secure places. The entire administration in the district had broken down. A handful of officers were working round the clock.

The officer-in-charge went to the trucks and announced, 'You will all have to cross by ferry to Silghat now. From there you will be taken to Nowgong jail.'

The row of trucks carrying the detainees from Makum had entered Dibrugarh.

The news had spread across town much before their arrival. The news had created tension among the people. Many people came out to see the 'Chinese soldiers and spies'. As soon as the convoy of trucks entered the town, the people waiting on the road started to abuse the detainees. Some started chanting slogans.

The detainees kept their heads low. The children started looking around in surprise. Driving through the commotion, the trucks reached Dibrugarh jail.

The detainees stared at the jail in surprise.

'They brought us to a jail! We will have to stay in the jail!'

A sense of deep sadness and anger occupied their mind. Some started crying, including the children. The people who had gathered outside entered the compound and charged at the detainees furiously. Armed guards from the escort trucks jumped down and, hitting the trucks with their canes, ordered the people to climb down as fast as they could.

As the prisoners climbed down fearfully, an onslaught of stones greeted them. The angry mob threw whatever they could lay their hands on. Some of the guards chased them, while others tried to hasten the entry of the prisoners into the jail. Walking through the dirty abuses and the rain of stones, the detainees entered the jail office. A few officers were seated gravely before a table. One of them spoke.

'Everyone's names will be put down in these registers. If you have any papers, keep them ready. Your valuables will have to be deposited in the office. As per jail rules, you will all be searched. You will get your belongings back when you leave.'

Outside, the people were still shouting. The compound was littered with stones and other things. The internees entered the jail slowly.

The jail was now packed with Communists and the Chinese. The Communists were kept like other prisoners in their cells, while the Chinese were kept in open spaces. The newcomers joined the prisoners who had arrived before them. Many of them had bandaged heads.

The first to enter the jail were the hostel boys and Cha Mu. The hostel boys were searching for their parents, clutching the

the grown-ups. After being scolded by the guards, they returned to their place, crying.

As night fell, dense fog and cold enveloped the open spaces of the jail. Towards the wee hours of the morning, food was served. By then people were exhausted and freezing. Some had started to fall ill.

It was dawn by the time they finished eating. One officer arrived on the scene and said, 'All of you stand in a line. You are going to be taken away from here.'

'Taken away? Where to, sir?' Yiu Yi's father stood up.

'We don't know. We have orders to take you to the railway station.'

Instantly there was a commotion.

'You have to tell us where we will be taken.'

'We were told we would be taken away for a couple of days to a safer place. And now, you want to take us somewhere by train!'

'Where are our valuables?'

'The person in charge has not yet come. You'll get them when you return.'

'All lies! We don't believe you! You have to return our stuff right now.'

Eventually, the officer lost his patience. Armed men came charging at the detainees, pointing their bayonets, their eyes inflamed with rage. The detainees were silenced. Wiping tears, they boarded the trucks.

The trucks moved through the foggy morning towards the Dibrugarh railway station.

At that time the superintendent of police and the deputy commissioner were having a serious discussion with the members of the cabinet sub-committee in Tezpur. Early that morning, Chaku had fallen to the Chinese. There was no resistance left between the Chinese army and the army headquarters at Tezpur. The eastern command in Kameng, Lohit and Subansiri frontier divisions had broken down. The command and control in the western sector of Ladakh had also been destroyed.

A portion of the Indian Army had already been shifted to Siliguri from Tezpur. The rest of the army was also preparing to vacate. Indian troops had started returning from Subansiri and Siang, abandoning their positions.

In the Lohit division, the process of shifting the Indian troops to Ledo had begun. From all the war zones of the eastern and western sectors of the India-China border, the humiliating and dangerous process of withdrawal without command and discipline had begun. The remote pockets of NEFA and Ladakh were strewn with the bodies of the soldiers who had died in the war or at the time of withdrawal.

The Chinese troops were only a few hundred miles away from Tezpur now. The situation in panic-stricken Tezpur was out of control; there was hardly any trace of administration.

All the shops were closed. Numerous bags filled with coins from the banks had been thrown into the Padum Pukhuri, the town's largest pond. Huge bundles of bank notes had been burnt, so had all the important papers in the town's government offices. In front of every office, fires were burning. The gates of the mental asylum had been thrown open; lunatics had started roaming around the town. The prison, too, was emptied out. In the midst of all this chaos, a group of people in Tezpur and its suburbs were looting houses and shops without restraint.

Suddenly, in the middle of this anarchy, Tezpur was blessed with unexpected news.

China had announced a unilateral ceasefire!

Twenty-one

Opening the windows was forbidden.

Opening the doors was prohibited.

All shutters had been pulled down. All doors were closed. There was no way to find out how far they had travelled and where they were. In the early hours of the morning a mysterious train sped on. On that train was a load of prisoners of Chinese origin who had no idea where they were going.

Mei Lin was seated near a window. The packed compartment was quiet except for the sound of the moving train. No one was talking. The passengers were exhausted beyond measure. They sat in their allotted places, motionless and silent.

The boys from the hostel and Cha Mu were in Mei Lin's compartment. Most of the boys had found their parents from among the many Chinese people who had boarded the train from various stations on the way. Ko Fuk, Manchung, Wong Choi, Aheng and Ho Yin were yet to be reunited with their parents. The families of Yiu Yi, Siu, Liang, Lee Chang, Akong, Yao Sen, Hong and Chi Fu Hai were also with them. So were the families of Mei Lin's uncle, Yunlin's family, Anjali's uncle's family and Mei Lin's father. People were sitting on the berths and also on the floor. A middle-aged man boarded the train along with his differently-abled son at one station. The boy was playing and drooling like a baby.

Khagen Baishya, who was in charge of the group, was sitting near the door of the compartment. He sat on his bed and watched the scene around him without speaking to anyone. That was the only space which was not occupied as no one dared to sit near him.

Suddenly the train came to a halt.

People became alert. Some of the passengers went to the windows to peep through the crack. Khagen Baishya opened the door a little to look out and opened it fully. A handsome young man entered. The guards who came to drop him helped him up with all his belongings and also gave him some food for the journey.

The platform was packed with curious people of all ages, who had come to see what was going on. They all looked at the train in surprise.

Suddenly, a sandal was hurled at the train. Just after that they started abusing and pelting stones at the train. The detainees, who were waiting on the platform, covered their heads and, holding their children close to them, hurried into the waiting train. Even after the doors were closed they could hear the stones hit the train.

The newcomer was looking around trying to find a place for himself. Everyone inside the compartment was looking at him and his luggage in surprise. What a lot of stuff!

'You can sit here,' Khagen Baishya spoke for the first time. 'What is your name?'

'Ameng Tham.'

'Where were you arrested?' Chi Fu Hai asked.

'In Jorhat.'

'Did they let you bring all this stuff?'

'Yes, the policemen were very kind. They even brought water and other stuff for me. They were very sad at the turn of events.'

'We were not allowed to bring anything with us. Even our gold and money was snatched away from us in the Dibrugarh jail.' Ho Fuk narrated sadly.

'Where is your home? Where is the rest of your family?' Hong asked the man, to change the subject.

'Jamugurihat. My parents and my five brothers live there. I am studying at Jorhat Agriculture University. It was from the hostel that they arrested me. Do you have any idea where we are being taken?'

'No. They have told us that we are being taken to a safe place for two or three days,' Hong said.

When Ameng was arrested there was no one at the hostel to bid him farewell. Every boarder had gone home as the university had remained closed. Ameng had been forced to stay back in the hostel because of the check on the movements of the Chinese. Perhaps because he was arrested in the hostel, they let him bring his luggage. Even though Ameng was calm on the outside, he was extremely disturbed. He kept remembering his family and the face of a lovely girl whom he had not been able to say goodbye to. All he could do was leave a letter for Meghali with the watchman. He had seen people taking down the signboards outside Chinese restaurants. The owners had taken them down themselves in fear.

After talking to Lee Chang and the others, Ameng spread out his thin mattress. Then he requested Yunlin, Lee Chang's wife Wai Kwan and Yiu Yi's grandparents to sit down. He also asked old Chi Fu Hai to sit there. He spread one of his blankets on the floor for the children and asked Yiu Yi's grandma to distribute biscuits and oranges among the children. Keeping aside two bed sheets for himself he sat along with C Hoi's and Yiu Yi's older uncle.

The inside of the coach brightened for a while.

Hong looked at Mei Hang. She had not spoken since her arrest. She was sitting with her eyes downcast. Hong asked Mei Hang to come with him and went to the door. Mei Hang got up and followed. No one noticed her go as they were all busy watching Ameng.

Mei Lin's uncle took out his Mahjong board from his bundle and placed it on Ameng's trunk. The elders looked at it in surprise. Slowly their faces brightened and soon they were completely engrossed in the game. The compartment had transformed into a home. After a few moments of hesitation, Chi Fu Hai took out a small bag which had opium and the paraphernalia required to smoke it. Yunlin's father-in-law drew close. The people around smiled in amusement. Chi Fu Hai would soon be in seventh heaven. Then it was Yunlin's father-in-law's turn – he had brought his own opium.

Hong was standing near the door.

'Why did you call me, Hong?' Mei Hang asked slowly.

'Is it possible to bring back your smile?' Hong asked her gently, looking steadily at her.

'It has gone to the battlefield. It hasn't returned yet,' she answered with the trace of a smile.

'Even though the smile knew that I was waiting?'

'Did you say that you were waiting?'

'I said so many times! But if someone pretends not to hear –' Hong looked at her. 'We have to live, Mei Hang! Have you seen our people? They are dying inside. It is you who can bring them to life. Bring back your smile, Mei Hang.'

'Just give me a little more time, Hong.'

In the midst of lifelessness, a small bud of hope was trying to bloom.

In the jail at Nowgong, pandemonium reigned. Shrieks of fear could be heard from the women's enclosure.

'Fire! Fire!'

A sudden fear gripped the men who sat eating in the courtyard of their enclosure. Leaving their food behind, the men ran to where the women and children were confined. Seeing smoke rise above the walls they began pounding on the doors and shouting for help.

People came running from everywhere as the alarm sounded. Someone opened the gates and the firefighters came to douse the fierce flames. The Chinese men, who had rushed in to help, were held back by the armed guards at gun point.

The train carrying the detainees had come to a halt. Khagen Baishya opened the door and looked out. At a distance, he could make out the twinkling lights of a station.

'Why has the train stopped here?' Ameng asked Khagen Baishya.

'I don't know. We have not been told everything.'

'What station is this?'

'Chaparmukh.'

Chaparmukh! They were close to Silghat!

Most of the detainees, including Yiu Yi's family, went hurriedly to the windows. Yiu Yi's youngest uncle lived in Silghat. He and his family would have to board from here. Anjali started crying, 'Let me have a look. We used to live here.'

But no one boarded the train. There was no sign of anybody outside. Slowly the people who had gathered near the windows returned to their places.

The commotion at Nowgong jail had simmered down. The prisoners returned to their enclosures and the doors to the women's quarters were closed. The women and children were now sharing space with the men in the open courtyard. Worried and anxious, they were talking amongst themselves. Something dreadful was going to happen, but no one knew what. The officials of the jail did not answer their queries. The standard answer to every question was a curt 'We don't know.'

After dusk, the jailer and two other officers came to speak to them.

'We have orders to take some of you away from here. I'll read out the list. Those whose names are called out must stand here in a line and the others will have to go back inside the prison.'

The people looked at the officer in confusion.

Should they protest? Should they stand together and say in unison that they wouldn't go? Would these officers listen? Did they have the authority to decide?

No. The detainees knew that they didn't. Their future had been fixed somewhere else. The detainees created a commotion by asking questions. The wailing and crying began. A large group of armed guards came and stood behind the officers. Gradually the commotion subsided.

The officer started reading out the names. The detainees were divided into two groups. The inside of the jail became heavy with the crying of the people whose homes had been broken.

Standing in line and wiping their tears, the people who were left behind returned to the prison. The others left the jail weeping. They boarded the buses waiting outside. Following the officers in their jeeps, they sped on, not knowing their new destination.

Nowgong town had become desolate.

It had been several hours since the train had stopped at Chaparmukh station. The internees were sitting restlessly inside the closed compartments.

They had not been given any food after the meal in Dibrugarh jail. The small children were now asking their mothers for food. Those who were too small to understand had started crying. The father of the differently abled boy was cooking barley on a stove. Smelling the barley, the children had started cajoling their mothers.

'Alen is ill. Let him eat. Don't disturb him. You will get food. You will get rice. Forget about the barley.'

'I am sorry, children. My son is ill, and there is just this little bit of barley,' Alen's father said sadly.

'We are not hungry, apak,' Yiu Yi said. Then she turned to the others. 'We are not hungry. Are we?'

'No, we are not.' They shook their heads. Only little Ho Yin said, 'I am hungry but I won't have barley. Give the barley to Alen, apak. My parents will bring food. I will eat then.'

Cha Mu brought the boy closer to her and covering her face with her hands, wept. Everyone was quiet, including the hungry children. Alen, however, was busy making funny, meaningless sounds, and playing with himself.

The wait to reach a destination, any destination, was becoming unbearable.

After some more hours, they heard the voices of many people outside and loud knocking on the doors and windows.

'Open the doors. Open the windows. Quick. Quick.'

Khagen Baishya opened the door. The others quickly opened the windows.

The station was packed with detainees. Some carried bundles, others were empty-handed. Each face was etched with the same fear, the same pain and distress. The hostel boys who had still not found their parents became restless. Standing before the windows and trying hard to look outside, they started crying.

'Manchung Tham, Makum Chinese School Hostel, Manchung Tham,' someone shouted outside.

'Hey Manchung, they have called your name.'

'Manchung Tham is here.'

Manchung's father came running to the window.

'Father,' Manchung cried out.

'Come out,' one of the guards outside shouted. Khagen Baishya came forward.

'Come, let me help you get down.'

Cha Mu hugged the boy and stroked his hair.

'Go,' she said.

'Anjali – Makum Cheenapatti.'

Crying loudly, Anjali got down too. Aheng and Wong Choi also found their families.

Ho Yin's family and Yiu Yi's uncle's family boarded the compartment.

'Take your food. Hurry. Hurry.' There was the sound of banging on the coaches.

Everyone rushed to the windows. They stretched their hands outside and took the Indian bread and jaggery brought from Nowgong jail. 'Close the windows. Close the doors. Don't peep outside.' The armed guards went on beating the coaches with their batons.

Khagen Baishya returned to the compartment after eating a good meal; he brought with him extra food in a tiffin carrier along with a big container of water.

'A passenger train is going to cross the Saraighat Bridge for the first time today. We have heard that they decided to test the bridge with this train.'

The new detainees spread the news in all the compartments of the train.

'Really? Is this really true?'

The detainees looked at the people who gave the news, stunned.

The Indian government had decided to test the bridge with them! Was the government so displeased with them? Would they be able to live in this country again after they returned?

No one knew.

It seemed as though the armed guards were made of stone. They simply wouldn't respond. Only a few words and the same instructions.

'No one should open the windows. Don't peep outside. Don't try to escape. Or else we will shoot. Just sit quietly.'

When the train finally began to move again, it was midnight.

Twenty-two

The sky was clear. There were open fields on both sides of the rail tracks. Carrying the captives inside, a ghostly train sped along, hissing through the free world outside.

After leaving Guwahati, the train had not stopped anywhere except at signals. There was no way of knowing where they were, or how far they had travelled. They had been travelling for hours. Slowly the compartments were getting dirty. The air inside became heavy.

Mei Lin sat on a wooden bench, her head leaning against a closed window. Beside her sat Cha Mu. Ko Fuk was sleeping with his head on Cha Mu's lap. He was running a temperature and was moaning weakly.

A little further sat the young boys, talking in hushed voices. Ming, sitting near them, was engrossed in a book while Hong sat deep in thought, his hand on Ming's shoulder. The elders were still playing Mahjong in a corner but their minds were not on the game. Chi Fu Hai sat on a corner, leaning on the side of the compartment. He was thumping his head slowly against it every now and then. Anyone could say that he was in pain. He had been itching all over since the previous day. He had become restless since his stock of opium had finished. He flared up at the slightest pretext and tried to quarrel.

They were not given anything to eat after Chaparmukh. All of them were extremely hungry.

Yunlin was unable to breastfeed her baby. Her milk had dried up. The baby was crying in hunger. The pregnant Wai Kwan lay listless. The children were silent, knowing that there was no use complaining.

Mei Hang sat on a bench with her chin on her knees. Overpowering her feelings of hunger, frustration and uncertainty, was her love for Hong. What other reason besides love could there be to live in this strange world? Amidst the sheer lifelessness of the compartment Mei Hang drifted into her own dream world.

'Water, ache,' Ko Fuk said in a faint voice.

Mei Hang looked at the tear-stained face of the little boy, and then at Cha Mu.

'There is no water,' Cha Mu said slowly.

'Does anyone have any water?' Mei Hang asked loudly.

Everyone shook their heads.

'I'll get some,' Mei Lin stood up. Carrying a bowl with her, she went through the crowd to the wash basin near the door.

'There is no water in the tap,' Khagen Baishya said.

Standing perplexed near the basin for a while, Mei Lin returned.

'Does anyone here have any water? Give some for the boy.'

Some shook their heads while others looked down. Mei Lin returned slowly.

'There is no water anywhere, Ko Fuk,' Mei Lin said.

Ko Fuk turned glum. Silently he placed his head back on Cha Mu's lap. Mei Lin stood for a few moments and then turned back. There was still some water in the toilet.

'Mei Lin, are you going to give him the water from the toilet?' Tung Chin looked at Mei Lin sadly.

'The child is so thirsty. What else can I do?'

Mei Lin returned with the water. Everyone sat motionless. The first who stood up to collect water from the toilet was Wenling. Behind her was Liang's sister-in law. It caused a stir inside the compartment. People made a beeline for the toilet.

After drinking the water, Ko Fuk looked at Mei Lin with feverish eyes and asked slowly, 'Why did the people abuse us? What is the meaning of "beiman"?'

'I know the meaning,' said Yiu Yi. 'Now there is no "Hindi-Chini bhai-bhai". China is now India's enemy. We are enemies. We are betrayers. Beiman.'

Yiu Yi's grandpa, who was playing Mahjong, turned around to look at Yiu Yi. Then leaving the game halfway, he came and sat next to the children.

'Do you want to hear a story?'

The children looked at Yiu Yi's grandfather. But their eyes didn't contain any happiness. He sat amidst the children and slowly began.

'This is the story of Leifeng pagoda. Many, many years ago, there was a boy who lived in a place called Hangzhou ...'

The train halted. The enthralled listeners were startled. They anxiously gathered near the windows to look outside.

They had stopped in the middle of a barren and uninhabited field.

What was going on?

The faces of the people turned ashen with fear. They had come to realize that they hadn't been arrested so they could be kept safe. There was some other reason behind it.

Many army men surrounded the train immediately. Some of them entered the compartments and started shouting orders.

'No one move. Stay inside.'

They selected a few young boys and ordered them to go down, saying, 'You will have to cook.'

'Hey, what are you doing?' one army man asked Alen's father, who had started cooking barley.

'My son is ill. This food is for him.'

'You were told not to cook. Why have you lit the stove? Who has allowed you to bring this?'

'The sirs allowed me. Because my son is ill.'

'Turn off the stove. Stop cooking.'

'Please don't do this, sahab. My child will die.'

'The son of a bitch will not die. You bloody Chinese will not die so easily.'

'Please don't say that, sahab. Don't call my son a dog. He has done no wrong.'

'What did you say? He has done no wrong? Then who has? Us?'

Slapping him hard, the guard snatched the stove away and threw out the saucepan, spilling the barley on the floor. On his way out, he ordered in a loud voice, 'Open all the windows on this side.'

'Now what will I do? My child will die.' Alen's father started crying.

Khagen Baishya came to him and said, 'Don't worry. I'll bring the stove back.'

The guards ordered twenty to twenty-five young men from different compartments to bring down huge cooking utensils, bags of rice, lentils and other material from the train.

'Only one hour! Cook khichdi,' an officer ordered, as he sounded his whistle.

It was not cooking but a battle. There was no time to wash the uncooked rice and lentils. Some of them collected water in huge saucepans from the nearby pond and ran to the train for everyone to drink. After their thirst had been quenched, they stretched their glasses, bowls, kettles, plates and whatever they had through the windows to get more water to take with them.

In exactly forty minutes the whistle blew again.

'Time over. Stop cooking. Serve the khichdi through the windows. Quick. Quick.'

The profusely sweating cooks looked up at the officer in surprise and said, 'The khichdi is half-cooked, sir.'

'Shut up, you,' the officer thundered. 'If it isn't cooked, so be it. You will have to eat it as it is. If you don't want to, throw it away. Finish serving within fifteen minutes.'

The cooks ran to the train with the huge saucepans. People emptied their utensils to take the food. Before everyone could be served, the whistle sounded again. The children and the old failed to get any food in the scuffle.

'Move. Move. Board the train. Put everything back in the train. Take your food with you. Quick. Quick.'

Mei Lin looked at the frustrated people who could not get their share and then looked at her own bowl. It was filled with khichdi.

Khagen Baishya returned to the compartment. Alen's father came to him and asked anxiously, 'Where is my stove?'

'I pleaded with them, but they wouldn't give it back. They said they would give it at the next station.'

The old man sat on the floor in frustration and cried out, 'My child will die!'

'You had a tin of baby food. Is it over?'

'There is just a little left. But it won't last even two days. Besides, there is no hot water around.'

Offering his flask, Khagen Baishya said, 'There is some hot water here. Use this to make some food for your son.'

Alen's father looked at Khagen Baisya with surprise. Then he took the flask from him with both hands and wiped his tears.

The train had just started to move.

Mei Lin looked at the children around her. Most of their hands were empty. Borrowing a saucepan lid, she poured a portion of her share.

'Come on children, come and eat khichdi.'

Everyone in the compartment looked towards Mei Lin. After a moment, Liang came forward through the crowd and without saying a word he added some khichdi from his share. Many others followed him. Yiu Yi's grandma and Yunlin's mother-in-law came to help distribute the khichdi among the children. Then they got more for the elders who had been unable to get it for themselves.

Khagen Baishya watched in silence. His own food had come in a steel plate with many sections. There was rice, lentils, vegetables and a few other things. After looking at Mei Lin and others for some time, he called out to the children. As they came hesitantly, he distributed his share of the vegetables among them. Then he divided the rice and lentils amongst the smallest of the children.

Chi Fu Hai came up to Baishya and said, 'Please take some khichdi, sahab. You are a good person.'

The army officer's family, who were in the special compartment, had just sat down for a sumptuous lunch.

Jalpaiguri was about four hours away. A large group of detainees from Darjeeling and the surrounding areas were waiting there to board the train.

When the train reached the station, Khagen Baishya looked outside and returned to inform the people.

'It's Jalpaiguri.'

Jalpaiguri!

Mei Fung sat up, startled. Jalpaiguri meant Siliguri was near! Her would-be husband lived here! Had he been arrested too?

'Ko Fuk. Makum Chinese School Hostel. Ko Fuk, Mal Bazaar.'

The detainees of all the compartments became restless. They opened all the windows.

Khagen Baishya ran towards the door, shouting, 'Ko Fuk is here. Here.'

Carrying Ko Fuk, Ameng came to the door.

'Baba!' Ko Fuk cried out. Outside the train, his father and two sisters were also crying bitterly. Holding out his arms he took Ko Fuk from Ameng and gently put him down on the platform.

Forgetting everything, Mei Fung went to the door and, looking at the armed guards on the platform, she cried out, 'Is Ting San Kong here? Ting San Kong? Please check. His home is in Siliguri.'

'Who?' a curious guard asked.

'Ting San Kong.'

'How is he related to you?'

For a second, she didn't know what to say. Then casting her shyness away, she said, 'He is my husband.'

The guard looked at a list that a plainclothes officer was carrying, and shook his head.

'His name is not in the list. He has not been arrested.'

'He is Chinese. Why has he not been arrested? Please check again.'

The guard walked away. He had neither the time nor the inclination to listen to the wailing of the enemy.

'San Kong! San Kong!' Mei Fung called out frantically, thrusting her head out of the door.

Where was Mei Fung's would-be groom? Why hadn't they arrested him? How could she live without him? What was the point of living?

'Hey girl, go inside,' a guard shouted angrily at her.

'Come along, Mei Fung. Get inside,' Tung Chin placed his hand on her shoulder softly. Mei Fung looked back. She broke down crying.

'What will I do now? O ako, what will I do?'

Suddenly they heard the crashing sound of stones being thrown at the train.

'Close the doors. Close the windows,' the guards shouted, hitting the train's compartments with their batons.

'There's water in the taps,' someone shouted.

Instantly, the atmosphere in the compartment changed and everyone stood up holding out their vessels. Just then Khagen Baishya climbed in carrying a big bundle.

'There are some kids' clothes here along with some medicines. I've brought food as well,' he said.

'Give me food. I am hungry. Give me,' Ho Yin's father cried out desperately.

The train began to gather speed.

Twenty-three

Yunlin was in pain.

Everyone had lost track of time. It was pitch dark inside the coach. It was as if a group of voiceless shadows were sitting in an ancient cave. There had been no light since the day before. The air inside the coach had become thick with the stench of urine and excreta.

There was no water for washing either.

Ameng's bucket, mug, two water containers, a few bottles of lemonade, glasses, bowls and a kettle were the only property on that coach that could be used to store water. This was nothing for a coach full of captives who became thirstier after eating half-cooked khichdi.

They had to stop at a station to refill the water tank. They didn't. Maybe they had no permission to stop. The news of the passengers in that ghost train was not published in any of the newspapers. Still, somehow, people living close to the stations got wind. At every station where the train stopped, people would gather. Some watched in silence, others turned violent. They pelted stones and shouted abuse.

The news in the papers was different – news of torture by the Chinese forces dealt out to the retreating Indian soldiers and civilians, and news of Indian martyrs and the returned POWs.

The general populace was in a state of hysteria.

Inside the train was an indescribable hell. The smoke from the coal engine and the coal dust had made the people black and dirty. Fever spread and many complained of stomach trouble. There was nothing one could do. The captives were turning into spectres. Barring the yelling and crying spells by Ho Yin's father, the feeble weeping of the children and the sighs of the elders, there was no other sound. People had forgotten to talk. The sound of Mahjong had stopped. Four days had since the opium had finished. Chi Fu Hai was manic with withdrawal symptoms.

Wai Kwan was crying in pain.

'What happened, Wai Kwan?' Yiu Yi's grandmother asked.

Lee Chang came and sat next to Wai Kwan, worry on his face.

The elders realized that a great problem was about to befall them now. Amidst this darkness and filth Wai Kwan was going to deliver a baby.

'I want some water. I am very thirsty,' Wai Kwan said weakly.

There were only a few mugs of water in the bucket. Yiu Yi's grandmother brought a mug and, letting Wai Kwan drink first, she distributed a little to each of the children.

Wai Kwan cried out again. The pain was slowly becoming unbearable. The gaps between the contractions were decreasing.

'Please switch on the torch, Baishya dada,' said Lee Chang.

Baishya turned on the torch and handed it to Lee Chang.

'No one look this way,' Yiu Yi's mother said.

Lee Chang stepped aside. Yunlin's mother-in-law and Chi Fu Hai's wife came forward. Siu and the others surrounded Wai Kwan. Khagen Baishya passed the hot water flask and said, 'There isn't much in here.'

Ameng offered his clothes. The women moved Wai Kwan towards the door. Khagen Baishya along with the other young men went to the other side and sat down.

Wai Kwan's cries grew louder. The children started wailing in fear.

When she finally delivered the baby, it was dawn. Wearing Liang's sister-in-law's clothes, Wai Kwan came and lay on her bed.

'I need water. Give me water or I will die.'

'There is no water, Wai Kwan. Please try to be strong,' Lee Chang said.

Yiu Yi's grandmother held up the newborn. The children came forward with curious faces, thirst forgotten for the moment.

The train suddenly halted. The captives again got anxious. Liang lifted one window slightly and looked outside. The train had not received the signal to proceed. A locomotive had also stopped on the parallel line. After some thought, Liang turned around and said, 'Give me the kettle. Quickly. I will bring water from the engine.'

Without heeding the warnings of his fellow captives, he jumped down with the kettle and started running in the direction of the engine. Showing the kettle to the driver, Liang started pleading for water. The army men who were on the train started shouting at him.

'Hey Chinese! Son of a swine! Move back or we will shoot you.'

Liang ignored them and kept on pleading. The driver looked at Liang with surprise and then at the train. He thought for some time and then released the engine water. Filling up the kettle with hot water, Liang ran back to the coach amidst the volley of abuses from the army men. The train had started to gather speed by then.

It would appear that life had returned to the coach. Cooling down the water, Yiu Yi's grandmother said, 'I will let everyone have a sip. Be patient.'

Everyone waited in restless anticipation. Only Ho Yin's father was impatient and started shouting, 'Water. Give me water.'

Inside the compartments played out scenes from hell, as the passengers hurtled towards a frightening uncertainty.

Twenty-four

It was afternoon. Without any warning, the train had stopped after seven days and seven nights.

No one had the strength to react. No one tried to look out of the window.

'Open the door! Open the door!' someone shouted from outside, banging on the door with a stick.

Khagen Baishya went forward sluggishly and opened the door. The armed guard who was looking to come inside was repulsed by the stench.

'Get down. All of you get down. You will have to go to another place.'

The platform was empty. It was cordoned off by armed guards. People slowly started disembarking. There was a huge crowd outside the station. They looked at the filthy group of people alighting from the train with curiosity and hatred.

Yiu Yi walked over to Khagen Baishya and gave him her doll.

'Police dada, take this. This is for you.'

'Why are you giving this to me? What will I do?'

'You have cared for us a lot. You are very good. Take this.'

'I cannot take this, Yiu Yi. Take it back or else I will feel very hurt.'

'Don't think like that. How will I get a chance to play with this doll? Give it to your children. It is a little dirty – just was it once.'

Without waiting for Khagen Baishya's answer, Yiu Yi got down.

Holding the handles of the door with his hands, Chi Fu Hai stood without moving.

'Get down, Baba,' his son told him from the platform.

Chi Fu Hai stood still, blankly looking outside.

'Baba. Get down. People are waiting.'

There was no answer.

'Hey, what's happening? Get down. Get down,' one guard shouted, banging his stick on the coach. 'Hey, old fellow. Get down I say.'

When Chi Fu Hai failed to respond, the guard pulled him down. Chi Fu Hai fell face down on the platform. People surrounded him. His son turned him around and cried out. He was dead.

A group of guards came forward.

'Hey. Move. Move. What happened?'

'My father is dead.'

'Move. Let us see.' They surrounded the dead body.

One of them poked the body with his stick and said to his companions, 'He is dead for sure.'

They stood silently for a while. Then one of them said harshly, 'Okay. We will take care of the body. Now you move along.'

'How can I leave my father behind? I won't go. I have to bury –'

'The government will bury your father. You don't have any business being here.'

The guards pushed the people forward. As soon as they exited the station, the abuse and the stone-pelting commenced. The captives silently boarded the buses. By the time they reached the high-walled compound, it was almost dusk. There were a few sentry posts on the perimeter of the compound, barbed wire all around, and a crowd outside. The captives looked at the compound with endless surprise.

'Do we have to stay here? In this walled enclosure?'

The captives stood in a line.

'Look! Chinese spies.'

'From where have you brought them? Thrash them properly.'

'Hey small-eyed people – you have destroyed our country.'

'Beat them. Beat the bloody betrayers.'

Wenling stopped and looked at the crowd, trying to control her anger.

'Why are you looking at me like that? Do you want to marry me? Go. Go. Your graves will be dug on the plains of Tibet.'

Wenling lost her patience.

'What did you say? Say that again. Come. Fight with me. Fight like a man. We are not thieves. Understood? You think I am scared? Come fight with this woman.'

Her husband pulled her back but she wouldn't stop speaking her mind.

'You are cowards. All of you. What does the Indian government think of us? That we are spies? My father may be Chinese but my mother is Indian. We don't betray our country. Got it? Now come and fight.'

The guards came forward angrily.

'Shut up, or else ...'

'Or else what? You will kill me? If we are the enemy of this country then come finish us.'

Wenling had forgotten her fear. The guards were confused. They could not decide what to do. Before anyone could say anything more, a calm-looking middle-aged person came and stood in front of Wenling and the others. Everyone fell silent. The man said with a smile, 'Why are you fighting, brothers? Let it be. There are old people and young children here. They have come from so far. Just look at their condition. It's pathetic. Why fight with them? Please leave. We will now take them inside.'

The situation turned peaceful. The captives went in a line to the office for registration. Some of the officials took down their names and addresses, while others frisked them. The middle-aged man sat in a corner.

'You faced a lot of trouble, didn't you?' he asked Yiu Yi's grandfather.

Yiu Yi's grandfather's eyes filled with tears. After staying quiet for a while, he asked, 'What place is this?'

'This is Deoli jail. We are in Deoli, Rajasthan. I am the doctor of this jail.'

'Will we get some water? We haven't had any since yesterday afternoon.'

The doctor looked at him for a while and went away. After some time, a group of people came out with buckets of water mixed with sugar and salt.

Breaking the queue, Ho Yin's father came running forward.

'Water. Give me water, or I'll die.'

'Hey. Why have you broken the queue? Go back or else –' A guard raised his stick.

'No! Let him be. Can't you see how thirsty he is?' the doctor said.

'Why do you care if he is thirsty? Are you a friend of China?'

'I am a friend of humanity. They haven't had any water to drink since yesterday. They will die. What will you do then? Will you take responsibility for their deaths?' he said firmly to the guards and passed a glass of water to Ho Yin's father.

Ho Yin's father started complaining again.

'He is not stable,' his son said fearfully.

'Everything will be alright. I'll look after him,' the doctor said and returned to his seat.

The people started entering the compound after completing their registration. Without knowing it, they had become internees in wartime India.

Part Three

One

It had been fifteen days since Mei Lin had come to Deoli. In those two weeks she had lost considerable weight. She looked pale and undernourished, with signs of sleeplessness. Her clothes hung loosely on her body. Still in the same clothes she had on while in the train, she came out of her room in Deoli Internment Camp, carrying a jug. All that the camp had provided was a plate, a bowl, a tumbler and a jug, along with a bedsheet, pillow and blanket. Their living conditions remained miserable from the very first day and no measures had been taken to make the situation any better.

The camp was attached to the main Deoli jail. It was divided breadth-wise into five sections. Each wing was separated by barbed wire and had a gate manned at all times by armed guards. Two sections lay to the left of the main gate, while the other three were on the right. The first one on the right was Wing 3: the Chinese from Calcutta, Darjeeling, Kalimpong and Siliguri were housed there. In Wing 2 were some Tibetans and those who had business ties with Tibet or were married to Tibetans. Wing 1 was occupied by a few rich, aristocratic families from Darjeeling, Kurseong, Kalimpong and Siliguri. On the left was Wing 4 which housed the Chinese from Silghat, Tezpur, Sootea, Balipara and other areas in Lower Assam and the north bank of the Brahmaputra. Wing 5 had people from the different areas of Upper Assam: Titabor, Jorhat, Golaghat, Sivasagar, Dibrugarh, Duliajan, Makum, Doom Dooma, Margherita, Ledo, Tinsukia and other places. Each of these wings was divided into two blocks. These were further divided into small rooms with long dormitories in between. A commander was in charge of each wing. He reported to a deputy camp commander who, in turn, reported to the camp commander.

The small rooms had been allotted to families, while the young men were put into dormitories. Mei Lin stayed in one of these small rooms with Siu, Mei Hang and Ahlin.

She shielded her eyes from the bright sunlight and looked around. Yiu Yi's grandfather was sitting on a charpoy in front of his room, his head hung low. Yunlin's father-in-law and Ho Wang sat beside him, placing their hands on their foreheads while on another charpoy sat C Hoi, Ho Chang Ho and Ah Fuk. The Mahjong board and its soiled dice lay abandoned on a wooden packing case nearby. No one was playing or talking. Everyone looked gloomy. Their bodies showed signs of malnutrition, sleeplessness, exhaustion and frustration.

Ever since they had arrived at Deoli camp, Yiu Yi's grandfather had sat like this for the most part of the day. The other older men sat like this as well. The children and the youngsters also joined them once in a while. He had become the guardian of their wing.

Mei Lin went to the open space between the two wings, where the children were playing. Everyone was wearing dirty clothes, their hair matted. The dusty dryness of the camp had absorbed all colour. Everything looked dull and faded. Yiu Yi stood beside the children absentmindedly. As Mei Lin approached her, she said with a smile, 'I didn't see you, Mei Lin ache.'

'What were you thinking about, Yiu Yi?'

'About Maa. Don't know when she will come. My little brother cries all the time. He refuses to eat or sleep. I told him to come and play. But he gets angry at me. Do you know when Maa will come, ache?'

'She will come. She will come soon.'

'If she comes, will she be allowed to enter? They have put us in this huge jail. They won't even let us go out.'

'They won't keep us here forever. We are kept here because the situation is bad.'

'If there is a war, it is always bad, isn't it, ache? All the sipahi dadas become angry. Ananta dada and the others become angry too. Was Pulok dada angry as well? Was that the reason he sent you away with us?'

'Pulok dada didn't send me away.'

'Then why hasn't he come to take you? It's been such a long time since we were made to leave our homes!'

'Everything will be alright. Come, let us go and fetch some water.'

'I can't come, ache. Yunlin ache has asked me to look after her baby for a while.'

At that time C Hoi was requesting the armed guard to open the gate of Wing 5.

'Let me go out. I need to go to the office.'

'It's lunchtime. Go have your lunch,' the guard said irritably. This man had been coming to the gate every now and then demanding to be let out. He had almost lost his mind.

But he wasn't the only one. Others had begun to lose their patience too. Some wept all the time. Some sat brooding and didn't want to talk or eat. They would attempt to cajole the guard to open the gate.

So far, no one had been permitted to go out. They were allowed to go out only if they needed to go to the hospital for medical attention. The doctor came by daily to see them and dispense medicines. There were some old people in the hospital with severe opium withdrawal symptoms and there were others who were unwell. The hospital was one only in name; a place of consolation for the sick, with the bare minimum facilities.

'Let me go, please. Do you know how big a house I have built? How much gold! How much money! I was allowed to bring nothing. We were sent here like beggars.'

C Hoi's wife was trying to pull her husband back. She looked irritated and frustrated. Seeing Mei Lin approach, her face brightened. Mei Lin went near the gate and said gently, 'Ako.'

'I have left the entire house open. Nothing was permitted to be taken. Everything will be stolen. I want to go to the office to let them know. But they don't listen. You tell them.'

'Okay I will tell them. But it is time for lunch. Now the office is closed. Let's go now, ako. We will come again after lunch.'

'Why don't they let me go? I'm not a CID agent from China. That teacher from Calcutta had asked me to keep a secret passage when I built my house. He told me to take a Red China passport. No one believes me. Not even Robin. He didn't even talk to me. I was very hurt, you know.'

'I'll explain the whole thing to Robin. Don't you worry, ako. It's just a matter of a few days. After that everything will be ok.'

Mei Lin brought him back and went to the side of the wing that housed a row of toilets, bathrooms and water taps. Nearby, in a temporary kitchen, food was being cooked.

Tung Chin was filling his jug absentmindedly. Standing near him were Ameng and Ah Fuk's son, Aman. They smiled when they saw Mei Lin. Giving his jug to Ameng, Tung Chin took Mei Lin's jug from her hand and started to fill it silently.

A whistle sounded near the kitchen, indicating that lunch was ready.

The people of Wing 5 had begun filing out with their aluminium plates. They looked as if they had come from an ancient and lifeless city.

There was no one in this camp without sorrow. Everyone had lost someone. Every family had been divided. Everyone had left behind their hard-earned property. Sorrow was an inseparable load attached to their existence.

Only Ameng had accepted this load with some ease. Having learned at the Nasirabad station that his entire family had been left behind in Nowgaon jail, he had been distraught, but he had wiped the worry from his face. No one could tell what was going on in his mind.

Mei Lin returned with Tung Chin and Ameng. Mei Hang came out chatting with Yiu Yi and the other children, their faces happy. Mei Hang must have said something funny to them. Ever since they had come to this jail, Mei Hang had tried hard to keep the people of Wing 5 happy and occupied. Along with Siu, Ameng and others, she would play with the children and tell them funny stories. Mei Lin and her companions knew that behind Mei Hang's cheerful countenance was Hong's support and love.

'I can't,' Hong had said to Mei Hang. 'But you can. Try to make people feel a little cheerful.'

Mei Hang could do it. She knew the magic of laughter in the midst of despair.

Tung Chin's sister-in-law, Wenling, and her children, and Liang's sister-in-law followed Mei Hang. Wenling went past Mei Lin without a word. No one had seen Wenling smile for a while. The smallest things triggered her anger. The harsh experiences after she was caught, the ordeal of camp life and the sufferings of her children had made her unstable.

Keeping the jug inside, Mei Lin returned.

People from both the blocks were standing in a line, waiting for food. They looked extremely uneasy. Ever since they had arrived at Deoli, they had been served only khichdi. They were tired of the same gruel day in and day out. The sight of it was enough to nauseate them. The elderly would somehow gulp it down, but the children wept and refused to eat.

Slowly, they were getting restless. They were not scared like before. They would create a commotion at the slightest pretext. Of course, it would have no effect on the management. Instead, armed guards were called in to discipline the inmates.

The soldiers' batons, their guns and stony faces forced them into silence.

The food was ready to be distributed. Craning her neck, Mei Hang looked at the food and cried out, 'Oh God! Hey Siu, Mei Lin, these days I only see tomatoes dancing in front of my eyes. Instead of killing us with bullets, the Indian government is trying to kill us with tomatoes –'

Waves of mild laughter passed through the crowd. But at the same time they looked disgusted. Khichdi with tomato! Again!

Mok Min became red with anger and burst out, 'Khichdi again? I won't eat it. Give us something else.'

K. P. Lee joined in.

'Yes. We won't have khichdi. Why are you serving this to us every day? What do you think of us? Animals? Beggars?'

'Why are you telling us? Tell them at the office. We are just obeying orders,' the kitchen in-charge replied angrily.

'Right. Right. You think we are spies? You think we are the enemy? That's why you are torturing us, am I correct? Listen – we are working people. We are not thieves or dacoits. We are not China's spies. But you say we are spies. Why? Is it because we are Chinese?'

People were getting excited. The little children clinging to their mothers' clothes looked on in fear.

In the middle of all the commotion, the deputy commander arrived on the scene. Holding up his hand for silence, he shouted, 'Please be quiet. Please say what you want to say peacefully.'

It took a while for the crowd to quieten down. Then, Ho Chang Ho spoke. 'I am the President of the Chinese Society of Makum. We have suffered a lot, sir. Our families ...'

The deputy commander listened attentively to what Ho Chang Ho was saying, but before he could finish, C Hoi, breaking the queue, went up to the deputy commander and asked, 'When are we going home?'

'I don't know. We haven't got orders yet.'

'I had a brand new house, you know. Absolutely new. It was completed on the new year.'

'Go and stand in line,' the commander ordered.

'I am not a Chinese CID agent. I make and sell furniture in Makum. Let me go home, commander sahab.' His voice became shaky.

Yiu Yi's father came forward, and holding him by his hand said, 'Come on, come and stand in the line.'

'No, I won't stand in line. Why did they say I was a Chinese CID agent? The teacher from Calcutta asked me to keep a passage to escape ...'

Yiu Yi's father took him back to the queue almost by force, as C Hoi smacked his own forehead and wept. The camp fell silent.

After a while the commander spoke again.

'The camp commander has called a meeting in Wing 1 at three o'clock this afternoon. He will listen to whatever you have to say. Only men will be allowed to come. Everything will be sorted out by tomorrow. Meanwhile, eat the food that has been served.' He left.

When the men reached the open area of Wing 1 they saw a lot of people already seated on the ground. Mei Lin's uncle sat beside Lao Thien Lee and asked slowly, 'Why have they arrested all the Dalai Lamas?'

'What do you mean by all? There is only one Dalai Lama.'

'Oh! I meant all the Bhutia people in Wing 1?'

'Where are the Bhutias? These are Tibetans and Chinese.'

'Oh ho! It's one and the same thing. Why have they been arrested? The Dalai Lama is a friend of India, isn't he?'

'I don't know. Besides, you shouldn't talk about all that. You'll get into trouble.'

The commanders of the five wings, their deputies, and the camp commander arrived on the scene and sat down facing the people. The camp commander began, 'I want you to speak openly about your problems.'

At first they were all quiet. Then a number of them started speaking at the same time.

'One at a time, one at a time please!' The camp commander stood up and raised his hand.

Everyone had the same complaints. There was no soap, no clothes, no food suitable for children. They were fed up with khichdi. There was no news from home and they wanted to communicate with their families.

After listening to everyone's complaints, the camp commander spoke. 'The government can feel your pain. That is why the government has taken some steps to address these problems. From tomorrow, you can cook your own food.'

Instantly everyone's face turned bright.

The commander continued, 'Every day, each one of you will get some amount of rice, along with vegetables. Each week, you will get some eggs and fish. Every month, you will get a coupon for five rupees, which you can use to buy your essentials from the canteen outside. The children will be provided milk. You will have the freedom to move about inside the camp but you will need permission from the wing commander to go from one wing to another, or to visit the canteen.'

'How long do we have to stay here, sir?'

'I don't know that. This is something that the government will decide.'

'Some of our family members are still in Assam. Someone's mother, someone's wife and children ...'

The camp commander raised his hand again to silence them.

'Look, I don't have an answer to this question. I can only tell you that the government will soon take a decision. Now, you can write letters to your own families.'

Having apprised the people about the rules of the camp, he stood up to leave and then stopped.

'One more thing. The Chinese Red Cross has sent things for you. Those things will be brought to your wing. I assure you that I will keep all your problems in mind. As long as you are here, you will have no difficulties.'

With the meeting over, the murmur quickly turned into chaotic noise. Along with a sense of joy came many questions.

'It's as if they have seen another side of reality.'

'Now we understand why the government has suddenly become so sympathetic towards us.'

'It is because the Chinese Red Cross has taken note of us.'

'Have you noticed one thing? Who has come to enquire about us? The Chinese Red Cross. No Indian organization has come forward to help. Everyone has abandoned us. Only the Chinese Red Cross has come. Because we are Chinese. Even if we lived here for a thousand years, we would still remain Chinese!'

'Had the Chinese Red Cross not come forward, we'd have continued being fed khichdi and provided with nothing.'

The internees went back, talking animatedly among themselves. Slowly, a sense of anger and distrust against India gripped their minds.

The Tibetans went back with a heavy heart. What difference did it make if the Chinese Red Cross came? Had the Chinese Red Cross come for them? Were they Chinese? Did they have Red China or Kuomintang passports? The Chinese were better off. Even if the Indian government detained them, the Chinese government came forward to help them. They returned to their wing, carrying in their hearts the helplessness of a people without a guardian state.

The officials, with the help of the wing commanders, were giving out the parcels to the internees. Each parcel weighed around three kilograms and contained t-shirts, undergarments, sandals, soap, toothpaste, toothbrushes, chocolates, medicines, mugs, cigarettes, etc.

The camp came alive. Simultaneously in every wing, those who could not read or write went to those who could write letters for them. In Ameng's dormitory, Mei Lin and her friends joined in to help write letters. People from Wing 4 also came to get their letters written.

Tung Chin entered the room cheerfully.

'How many does each one want?' Holding up a sheaf of paper, he asked with a smile. Then he looked at his sister, Mei Fung, and said, 'One will not be enough for you, I am sure!'

Without looking up from her writing, Mei Hang said, 'She will need reams – she is used to writing novels!'

Handing over two letters, Tung Chin went away.

Sitting next to Mei Lin, Ahlin was gloomily helping write letters for different people. A strong wave of emotion overcame her. The image of Ananta was floating in her mind. Her memories were bringing back the slogans.

'Chow Mao murdabad!'

'Chinese people go back!'

The image of Ananta spitting on the ground and walking away.

Could she write to that Ananta? Could she open her heart and show him the dark clouds within?

No.

Ananta was now someone else. He was a patriot, ready to fight for his country. And Ahlin? Who was she now? She was the kin of those who had attacked Ananta's country. No matter what India meant to her, to Ananta she was an enemy. Untrustworthy.

Ananta and the others did not want Ahlin and others like her in their country. They were undesirable, unwanted. They wanted them to leave India.

Everyone was busy writing to those they had left behind, but Ahlin did not want pity. She wanted love. She wanted true love built on mutual respect and trust.

Ho Fuk walked past them all, talking to himself.

'No use writing letters. We won't get to see anyone. We won't get anything back.'

Looking up at him for a moment, Mei Lin and the others busied themselves with writing again.

'I am alright. I am in jail. The journey was very difficult. It looks as though things will improve now. I can't see you. I can't see the children. I feel so sad. Don't worry too much. Look after the goats well. If you have problems, sell the goats. Write with all the news. When will I get to see you all again, Lakshmi – I think of you all the time ...' The man dictating the letter started weeping.

Mei Lin ended the letter with a sigh and looked at him. 'What address shall I put down?'

'Address!' He looked at her in surprise. Wiping his tears on his shirt sleeves, he said, 'Address? Write: "Lakshmi. Near Pavoi garden."'

'That won't do. We will need the district, post office, and so on.'

'I don't know all that.'

'My address is also like that,' said another. 'Write Jonaki Wong. Dafalagar garden.'

'With these addresses, the letters won't reach.'

'I don't know the full address. I'm the contractor's man. He knows everything.'

'Who is the contractor?'

'They have detained him. But he is now in Nowgong jail.'

After thinking for a while, Mei Lin went to Ameng and said, 'Help me with some addresses from your area.'

'Just wait for a moment. Let me finish this. It won't take much time. These people have the same problem. They don't know their addresses. I've tried to find out the districts and the post offices. I don't know whether these letters will reach their destination.' After finishing his work, he sat down with Mei Lin to sort out the problem.

After the letter writing was over, everyone in Wing 5 sat down, somewhat joyfully, to eat dinner. All the children were busy playing games, with chocolates in their hands, courtesy the Red Cross. The men got to smoke cigarettes after a long time and were chatting happily. The elderly sat playing Mahjong.

After many days, it seemed that the hands of time were turning again. A soft breeze had lightened the air of Deoli camp, heavy for so long with tears and sighs.

Smiling to herself, Mei Lin sat down to write her own letter.

Two

Ameng and his team were playing volleyball in Wing 5. The fiery hot day had started to cool down.

A visible change had come over the camp. The internees had received some more amenities. The government officials no longer treated them the way they used to.

The young boys now played volleyball every evening. The little ones would sit around Yiu Yi's grandfather to listen to stories while the women busied themselves with household chores.

These days, a boy named Chun Fu Thien from Wing 3, whose father was Chinese and mother Lepcha, came to play volleyball, and so did another boy named Ting Mok Kong from Wing 4; he was from a rich family in Shillong. They had become very friendly with the young boys from Wing 5 and, in fact, were very popular with everyone because of their jolly nature. Chun Fu Thien was also a proficient singer and was adept at playing the Chinese er hu. He enlivened the atmosphere whenever he visited Wing 5.

As the boys played, Mei Hang and her friends, Yunlin and Wai Kwan, came out with their babies.

Yiu Yi's grandfather and the other elderly people were busy playing Mahjong. Smoking cigarettes, others were watching them play. Some were busy talking among themselves. Like every other day, C Hoi and Ho Fuk were loitering near the gate. Mok Min, Ho Chang Ho, Ah Fuk, K. P. Lee and few others were discussing a number of things, sitting under a neem tree. Yiu Yi's older uncle had returned from the office with some news. Someone from Wing 1 had left the camp that morning. He was a prominent businessman who lived in Darjeeling and owned a string of restaurants, including one in Nepal. As he was a close friend of the king of Nepal, the king had requested the Indian government to release him. He was now leaving for America with his family. This news had been met with mixed reactions in the camp. Some were happy for him, some envious, while others just felt sad and dejected. Some of them were engaged in serious discussion to devise possible ways of escape. On the other side of the courtyard, some women were cooking in earthen kilns, burning dry leaves and twigs. There were some neem trees and thorny bushes in the compound. The women and the children collected ingredients from them and used them to cook.

Life in the camp was slowly acquiring the flavour of domesticity.

Slowly, the children were also getting used to life in the camp. Anjali, Mei Ho and Ko Fuk from Wing 4 often came to their wing. Yiu Yi and others, too, went over to theirs. The children from Makum were reunited again. They roamed around, played together and listened to stories. Only the children whose families had partly been left behind were sad and glum. But Yiu Yi didn't brood. Hiding her sorrow, she took care of her little brother and Yunlin's baby like a responsible guardian and also helped with the household chores.

Every morning, Wang Shu Shin and the other teachers from Makum School held classes for the children even though no one was really interested, including the teachers. One of Wang Shu Shin's brothers had been left behind in Calcutta. One of Ling Kwang Tung's brothers had also been left behind in Siliguri. Chow Chi Yong's wife and the children had come but the rest of his family was still in Calcutta.

'Letters have come! And this one's for me!'

Waving a letter, Akong came running happily through the gate.

Instantly the game and everything else came to a halt. Everyone made a beeline for the gate. When they reached the office, it was noisy. Many people had come from the other wings, too.

The wing commander made them stand in a line. Mei Lin stood at the end. She was filled with anxiety.

Had Pulok received her letter?

Tung Chin came out, carrying a heap of letters that had been opened and censored by the authorities. It did not matter to him. It was enough that he had received the letters. Seeing Mei Lin, he said, his face shining, 'Uncountable numbers of letters have come. Everyone from our families has sent letters. I have even received Chitta's letter. I am going. Have to distribute the letters. Everyone's waiting.'

Those who received letters were happy and excited, those who didn't were gloomy and tearful.

Mok Min came out crying. He had asked a relative to keep an eye on the gold and money he had hidden in his house. But the letter didn't reach his relatives. While censoring his letter someone had hidden it and looted his life's savings.

Alan's father and Yao Sen were happy after their letters arrived. Yiu Yi's father, however, returned worried. He had received a letter from Yiu Yi's mother, who was staying with Alan's family. She had written that someone had opened the back door of their house, left in Rajendra's custody, and looted all the valuables.

One after the other, people were returning from the gate, bearing news of happiness and sorrow. It was almost dark when Mei Lin's turn came.

The officer seated in front of a heap of letters asked, 'What's your name?'

'It was Mei Lin Ho before I got married. Now it is Mei Lin Baruah.'

'Baruah is not a Chinese surname. What community did you marry into?'

'Assamese.'

'Really? And yet they arrested you? Strange, isn't it?' the man remarked, as he looked for a letter addressed to Mei Lin Baruah.

'No, there is no letter for you.'

The spark in her face suddenly disappeared. Speechless, she looked at the man. He checked the letters again and shook his head, 'No, there is no letter addressed to Mei Lin Baruah or Mei Lin Ho.'

'That is impossible. Will you look just once more, sir?'

'Didn't sir say no letter has come? Why are you bothering him?' a guard standing beside the officer said harshly.

'Oh-ho! Be quiet. Can't you see how upset she is?'

Concealing her tear-filled eyes, Mei Lin returned slowly to her wing.

Some people happily shared their news with her. She feigned cheerfulness. There was no reason to ruin other people's moods with her agony.

All her friends were sitting in front of her room on a charpoy. Seeing them, she became cheerless again. She sat silently near Siu.

'You provided the house address on the letter, didn't you?' Akong asked her.

'Yes.'

'He may not have got the letter. I have come to know he hardly stays at home.'

'How do you know?' Mei Lin asked in surprise.

'Phulmoni wrote. After we were taken away, he left his house and went to live in the garden quarters. He doesn't visit his parents. Addison sahab had come to our house. He said that he and Pulok were trying to get you released. He told my mother that Pulok's father had reported you to the police. That is why it is difficult to get you released from here.'

Everyone fell quiet. After a while, Akong spoke again, 'Pulok is extremely disturbed. He hardly speaks to anyone. He visited our house just twice. He did nothing but weep. After getting my letter, Phulmoni went to his quarters in the garden, but he'd already gone to Shillong. Write to him tomorrow, and give the address of the garden.'

Trying hard to control the gush of grief that threatened to flood her senses, Mei Lin sat there silently.

'Don't worry. Everything will be alright again. With Addison sahab trying so hard, I am sure it will work out. A family has been released from Wing 1, did you know?' Yao Sen said.

This eased the tension. 'Hey Mei Hang, your mother asked me about Hong today.' Tung Chin looked at Mei Hang.

'Oh God, what did she ask?' Mei Hang's eyes twinkled with mischief.

'What else will she ask? You know it! I've told her everything.'

'I'll treat you to sweetmeats. Tell me, was she laughing, or crying?'

'She just let out a deep breath and said, "Thank God!" Perhaps she thought that you would never get married.'

The courtyard was brightened with the laughter of the group of friends. Chun Fu Thien arrived in the middle of all the laughter.

They chatted for a while. Mei Fung and Ahlin brought tea for everyone. After tea, Ameng said, 'Sing a song for us, Thien.'

'Alright, just wait. Let me go and get my erhu,' Thien said.

Lee Chang brought a tub and Tung Chin a plate. After Chun Fu started singing, all the men slowly started gathering near them. Finishing their cooking as fast as they could, the women joined, too. The children stopped playing and came closer. Thien's magical voice transported them to a different world. Slowly, tranquility descended on Wing 5. Gradually, as the night darkened, silvery moonlight enveloped them all. Siu was looking at Thien intently. Her heart was filled with intense love and longing for him. Hong took Mei Hang's hand into his own without anyone noticing.

Bringing them back to reality, a man announced, 'The deputy commander has come.'

They rushed to the place where the deputy commander was waiting. When everyone had gathered, he began, 'There is news for you. The Chinese government has said that they will take you back. They will send ships to take all of you back.'

It was as though a ball of fire had suddenly dropped down from the moonlit sky into the courtyard. They stared at him in shock as if they didn't understand what he had just said. The Chinese government will send ships! To take back the people imprisoned by the Indian government! How strange! How impossibly strange!

After some moments of stunned silence, the atmosphere turned noisy.

The deputy commander raised his hand.

'Another thing. Those who want to stay back and those who want to go must send their applications within a few days. The family members who have been left behind must do this as well.'

The internees listened in complete silence and then started throwing their questions at him. After answering as many as he could, he left.

The commander had thrown a pebble into a calm pond. Wing 5 turned turbulent. Doubt, confusion, fear and a host of questions were consuming everyone. They looked back on their past. Their society. Their own people. And they searched inside their souls. In which soil was their soul implanted? Which country were their hearts tied up with?

They were to be uprooted them from this country. China wanted to take them back to the land from which their forefathers had come. It's true that their roots were connected with that land. But that was far away in the past. An unknown land which most of them had never seen. The first place they had known when they had opened their eyes was this country.

How would they find out who was Chinese and who was not?

The Indian government seemed to know.

Post-war talks between the enemy countries were centred on a handful of prisoners. China had already returned their prisoners of war to India. Now the Chinese government wanted to take back the people of Chinese origin imprisoned by the Indian government. They wanted to accept those who had announced in open meetings that they were with India. They had said, 'You have confined them as they are Chinese. We will take responsibility for them. We will give them shelter. Send them back. We can't see our people suffering.'

Could they ignore this offer?

No. They couldn't. People shook their heads. At the same time other questions started to take hold.

What was the reason for this sudden interest? Was it just a sense of responsibility? Or was it sympathy for those whom the Chinese considered their own people?

Everyone was confused. Murli Gola cowshed floated in front of their eyes. And so did the inside of the train. The memory of the abuses and denouncements returned to haunt them.

The internees shook their heads. There was no place for them in this country! What would they do after returning home? Where were their homes? The blaze of the war had burnt down everything to ashes. It had destroyed the altar of love, trust and friendship. It had uprooted their identity, planted deep in the soil of this land. What was the point of returning?

On what vestige of faith would they live? A country that could smash all relations and the past under its foot and order them to leave, a country that could put them behind bars, suspecting them to be spies just because their forefathers were Chinese, a country that could lump together citizens and non-citizens into one, just because they were of Chinese origin – what was the meaning of citizenship in such a country? What security would there be?

'The Indian government was never going to allow us to stay in India. When we are freed even the public will not spare us. If there is a problem again, they will put us in jail. We are not going to stay here. We will go.'

People nodded.

'Who do we have in China? That place is totally unknown to us. From the time we were born we have only seen Assam. Maa is from Assam. Wife is from Assam. Even grandma is from Assam. I don't even know the Chinese language. What will we do in China? How will we live there?'

People were nodding.

'The Indian government has imprisoned us as enemies. Indian people pelted us with stones and abused us. After all this, you still want to stay in India? Don't you have any shame? I will go, if the Chinese government sends ships for us. I am not going to stay here anymore.'

'Want to go to China! What will you do there, tell me? Do you remember why we came away from China? Can you live under a Communist government?'

'Who came looking for us, when we were fed nothing but khichdi with tomatoes? Only the Chinese Red Cross. If they hadn't come, half the people here would have been dead by now.'

'It was not only the Chinese Red Cross that came. Others also came. There is no point thinking about all this. Will you be able to live as comfortably in China as we have been living here? If you don't know what is going on in China, you'd better ask someone who knows.'

'Have we been given any less pain here? Don't you remember how they put us in the cowshed? Don't you remember how we were caught? Can you forget how they snatched our valuables from us in the jail? And the awful train journey? Have you forgotten all that so soon? Have you forgotten the abuses? After all this, will you return like shameless people? People will spit on us, you see? People will abuse us, as ungrateful traitors – will you listen to that? If you can tolerate that, go ahead. I won't. I will go if the ship comes.'

'Have you heard the news? The Chinese consulate has closed down. Bank of China has closed down, too. After this, will we be able to live the same way as before? No matter what we do, no one will trust us. The CID will be after us to see if we are spies and put us in jail. After that they will tell us to leave. See how many people have been chased out! Some were not even allowed to take their children and wife with them. Some were pushed out through the Nathu La pass. So much suffering!'

'What will happen to our properties? And our money? Where is it all anyway? Our accounts with the Bank of China have been seized by the Indian government. I've heard that our houses and belongings will be auctioned as enemy property. There will be no security for us in this country. There is no choice but to toil hard in Communist China. At least we will not have to live in fear. No one will snatch our hard-earned property. No one will consider us enemies, traitors or spies.'

Mei Lin's uncle came and sat down, looking serious. 'I've heard that the Dalai Lamas of Wing 1 are writing to the Indian government, saying that no one in their camp wants to go to China. They are afraid.'

'How can they speak for us? We will decide whether or not we want to go.' All the assembled people were agitated.

'Let's go and ask them right now.'

'Don't quarrel, don't pick a fight,' Yiu Yi's grandpa shouted as they stood up to go. But no one listened to him.

Some people from Wing 4 also joined them. The people of Wing 1 had gathered in one place.

Seeing the inmates from Wings 4 and 5 in an aggressive mood, a group of young boys came forward to confront them.

'What is it?'

'Is it true that you are writing to the government?'

'Yes, so what?'

'What are you planning to write?'

'We are writing that we will not go to China.'

'What do you mean by "we"? You mean us as well, don't you?'

'Have you come to threaten us? We will write what we wish. Why do you bother? You go and write your own letters.'

In minutes, the open space turned into a sparring ground. The alarm went off, summoning the armed guards. The wing commander and the camp commander arrived on the scene. With their stout sticks, the armed guards jumped on the boys and brought them under control.

'Come on, you enemies of the country! Now you are all fighting to go to China! Go there. That's the right place for you, you ungrateful wretches. You've given us no peace since you arrived here. Take off your belt, you! Remove your belts.'

Beating the boys black and blue, the guards removed their belts and dragged them to the jail adjacent to the camp. Then dumping ten or twelve boys in each cell, they closed the doors on them. It became unbearably stuffy and hot with so many packed into a space meant for one prisoner. The confined boys became restless. Some of them wiped tears of humiliation and frustration. Others were filled with infinite anger.

'Did you see what the guards did? They didn't hit them. They are the Dalai Lama's people. They are India's people. We are not. They hate us. We won't live in this country any more. We will go to China. Whatever the consequences!'

There was pandemonium in Wings 4 and 5. Confusion and conflicting emotions had pushed the young men to the brink of despair.

Three

Not used to the tremendous heat of Rajasthan, the people were in utter torment. The young boys were constantly pouring water on the thick jute curtains on the doors and windows to keep the rooms cool. Life at the Deoli internment camp went on as usual. It had been three and a half months since they had been brought here.

In all these months Mei Lin had not received a single letter from Pulok. She did not know whether he had received the letters she had mailed him. She got information about Pulok only through Phulmoni's letters. All she knew was that he was in Shillong. Phulmoni could not write any more as the letters were still being censored. If she revealed anything more about Pulok, her letters would not be delivered by the authorities. Mei Lin was apparently guilty of treason. It was a crime to maintain contact with her. It was unlikely that Mei Lin would receive more news from Phulmoni, and keeping contact with an 'enemy' like her might create trouble for Phulmoni and her family!

Ho Wang's wife asked Mei Lin to help her stitch some clothes for Yunlin's child and Wai Kwan's babies. They had bought material from the canteen with the coupons allotted to them.

Both Mei Lin and Mei Hang were with Ho Wang's wife in their room. Mei Hang was holding Wai Kwan's baby. The chubby little child looked like Lee Chang, and had his father's sparkling eyes. He would be passed from one lap to the other like a doll. As soon as he saw a known face, his own would light up with a bright happy toothless smile. While Ho Wang's wife concentrated on stitching the garments that Mei Lin had cut out for her, Yiu Yi arrived there with her playmates, a rag-doll in her hand. She had received a letter from her mother and was feeling much happier now. But even so, she was nothing like the lively child she had been in Makum.

'Look, I've made myself a doll,' said Yiu Yi.

Surfacing from her misery, Mei Lin looked up at Yiu Yi.

She was wearing a shabbily stitched off-white dress made of markin cloth. Her silky black hair now hung limp and ragged. Her deep black eyes looked lifeless and her soft golden skin had tanned in the heat of the harsh sun. She looked like a doll that was old and frayed.

'What are you wearing?' Mei Hang asked.

'Grandma has stitched it. Don't you like it?'

'No, I don't. When our lovely doll wears such clothes, how can I like it? Don't wear this again.'

'But the dress I came here in is torn.'

'There are better clothes available in the canteen, Yiu Yi.'

'But they are very costly. Besides, there are so many children in our family, and everyone needs clothes. How can grandma buy material just for me? It's really alright, ache – what's the point of wearing good clothes in the jail anyway?'

Unable to bear her words, Mei Hang changed the topic and asked, 'Why have you come out in the scorching sun?'

'We were playing inside. We came running to meet Mei Lin ache as soon as we got to know she was here.'

Mei Lin drew Yiu Yi close to her and asked the other children to sit down.

'How do you like my doll, Mei Lin ache?'

Taking the doll from Yiu Yi's hand, she examined it for a while and said, 'It's beautiful. When did you make it?'

'I made it today. I have taken a piece of cloth from Yunlin ache's baby clothes. But there is something else I need.'

'And what does our fairy need?' Mei Lin asked.

'Can you give me a bit of vermillion? I'll draw her lips with it. I drew her eyes with the black remains of a burned candle. How do you like her eyes?'

'They are lovely. Will you let me do her lips for you?'

'Yes.'

Mei Lin took a clip from her hair, and some vermillion from her parting, and drew the red lips of the doll.The children gathered around her, looking on with interest.

'Make her look like a bride,' Mei Ho said.

Putting a dot on the doll's forehead with vermillion, Mei Lin smiled and asked, 'Isn't she beautiful?'

'Now we have to find a bridegroom for her,' one of the children said.

'Let's wet her face with water,' someone else said.

'What for?'

'She will look as though she's been weeping. Mei Fung ache weeps all the time because her groom is not here. Our bridegroom is also not here. He has also been left behind in Makum.'

'Yes, with Pulok dada.'

'Pulok dada has hidden him.'

'No, they are in the cowshed. Eating dry roti and sabzi. And weeping.'

'Ananta dada and the others will beat the bridegroom.'

'I'll give this to Maa. She has written that she will come soon.'

'Come with me, Yiu Yi. I'll comb your hair properly,' Mei Lin said, rumpling Yiu Yi's hair.

'All of you wait here, I'll give you some sugar,' Ho Wang's wife told the children.

And the children stayed back.

As she left with Mei Lin, Yiu Yi told her friends, 'After a while, come to Ameng ako's room. Grandpa said that he will come there and tell stories.'

In her room, Mei Lin combed Yiu Yi's hair and used hair clips to keep it in place. She then wiped her face clean and rubbed a bit of coconut oil on it. Mei Lin's eyes filled with tears. Where was the little fairy in her beautiful satin dress who ran around with her ponytail tied up with red ribbons?

The heat of Rajasthan had burnt her up. The absence of her mother had burnt her too. She didn't share her agony with anyone.

'Mei Lin – Mei Lin –'

Mei Lin came out from her room. Tung Chin was waiting outside, glowing with happiness.

'There is good news for you. There's a letter from Pulok!'

Mei Lin stood speechless as Tung Chin handed her the letter, which had come enclosed with his mother's letter.

'I'll come back later,' Tung Chin said. She had been unwell for the last few days. The discomfort of everyday life would often nauseate her. She was losing her appetite too and had started to skip her meals now and then. But her senses were now on alert.

Mei Lin went to her room and sat on her bed. With trembling fingers, she opened the letter.

It was Pulok's handwriting indeed!

She wiped her tears and, after composing herself, started reading.

There are no words to express my feelings. The sorrow, heavy like a stone, has blocked my expression. How can I tell you how I am? I know how you are. Knowing full well how you are, I am dying. The crime that my father has committed is killing me inside. I am desperately looking for a way out. I will definitely find a way. No one can take you away from me. No one. Just don't say that you want to go to China. Without you, how can I live? Can anyone live if his soul is taken away from him?

Tears rolled down Mei Lin's cheeks. The alphabets became hazy.

'Why are you crying, ache? Is Pulok dada angry with you?'

'No. He isn't.'

'Then why are you crying? Don't cry. Come, let us go and listen to grandpa's stories. You'll feel better.'

'I can't, Yiu Yi. You go.'

Yiu Yi wiped Mei Lin's tears and left, carrying her doll with her.

Rounding up the children loitering around, Yiu Yi's grandpa brought them inside Ameng's dormitory and started telling them a story.

'Many years ago in China, there lived a dragon king. He was the rain god and lived in a river. He had a close friend. One day, the dragon king made a bet that he would stop the rains for an hour and decrease the rainfall to one-tenth the usual amount, if he so wished. And so there was scanty rainfall that year. The officers of the emperor came to know that it was the dragon king who was responsible for the lack of rains. They informed the emperor. The emperor decided to try him in court. The dragon king was found guilty and condemned to death. The emperor ordered him to be executed three days later at three o'clock.

That night, the dragon king came to the emperor in his dream and told him the real story and asked for pardon. The emperor gave him his word that at the appointed time of execution he would keep the officer inside the palace.'

'Why?' asked the children.

'Because the officer could perform the execution only if he could go out,' Yiu Yi's grandfather explained.

'The emperor called the officer on the day of the execution and expressed his wish to play Mahjong with him so the officer would not be able to go out. And just before three o'clock the officer fell asleep on the Mahjong board. The emperor thought that the dragon king was saved. But –'

'But?'

The children looked at Yiu Yi's grandpa, eyex transfixed on his face.

'But the dragon king had already been executed at the appointed time! Because in his dream, the officer had gone and beheaded the dragon king.'

'Oh!'

'Then what happened?'

'That night the ghost of the beheaded dragon king came to the emperor's palace and started yelling and abusing him for having broken his promise. All the emperor's explanations fell on deaf ears. Eventually, the emperor came to believe that the officer had truly beheaded the king in his dream. After that, every time the emperor went to bed at night the dragon started to disturb the emperor, demanding his life back. Finally, the emperor fell ill because of lack of sleep. No treatment could cure him. Then one day the emperor's two trusted generals discovered that the emperor had fallen ill because of a ghost. So they told the emperor that they would guard his door dressed in full armour.

That night the ghost did not come in fear of the generals and the emperor slept soundly. After that, every night the generals kept guard by the emperor's bedroom door. His health improved by the day. The emperor felt bad for the guards. After thinking about it for a long time, the emperor came up with an idea. He asked his artist to paint two life-size pictures of the two generals and placed them on both sides of his door. The dragon king's ghost was fooled into thinking that the generals were still guarding the emperor. And the emperor became his old self again. When the people of the city found out about this, they too bought paintings from the artist and hung them up on their own doorways, to ward off evil spirits. Even today, lots of people keep these pictures to guard their doorways. Do you know when this happened? Two and a half thousand years ago!'

'That long ago?'

'Tell us one more story grandpa.'

Yu Yi's grandpa started telling them another story.

An hour later, Akong came in and said, 'The camp commander is here.'

The sun was just about to set. If the camp commander was coming to see them at this hour, it meant he probably had something important to say!

With a worried look Yiu Yi's grandfather came out. Everyone else was already outside. The camp commander and the deputy were accompanied by a large number of armed guards. In front of them, under the blazing sun, the internees stood in fear. After everyone had assembled, the camp commander stood up to speak.

'The ship from China has arrived.'

Those who had applied to go looked at the commander speechlessly. A distant scene had suddenly become prominent, like the bright sun! The officers had arrived to execute the decision.

They were to leave.

There was no way to refuse.

'You will be taken from here after seven days. The government has decided to send all of you to China. Anyone in your family who wants to go will also be sent. All the people who are outside the camp have also been informed.'

They gaped at the commander. A deathly silence had descended on Wing 5. But soon there were a hundred questions and arguments.

'How can they send everyone? We had applied to say we didn't want to go. All our relatives are in India. The government can't do this!'

'We can't change government orders. You have seven days in hand. If you want to reapply, you can do so. We will forward your applications. But the order is that all of you have to go. You don't have a choice. They have decided to send you in batches.

The first batch, whose names are on this list here, has to be ready to leave by early morning. I'll read out the list in a moment.'

In that unbearable heat, they waited with bated breath.

'We'll start with Mok Min and his family.'

Mok Min stood there unconcerned and unperturbed. What would he do in Makum anyway? All his happiness had been destroyed. He had nothing left. It no longer mattered to him where he went; China or India – it was all the same.

'After that, Ho Chang Ho and his family.'

'And what about his sons?'

'They will go later.'

'Go later? How can that be? If they go, they will go together, or not go at all.'

'This is what it says on the list – I can't change the list. Whichever names are here, only they have to go.'

This was not a list, but an order to break up families! Homes were being torn apart, one after another!

'There is no cause for worry. You can go in the second batch. Besides, another ship will arrive soon,' the camp commander tried to pacify them.

Mei Hang's family was third on the list. But not all of them. It was just Mei Hang's parents and all but one of her siblings. Her own name and that of her older brother were not in the list.

In the middle of all the cries and clamour, Mei Hang looked at Hong. Would his name be on the list too?

Mei Lin Ho was number four.

The crowd looked at the commander in utter disbelief.

'How can Mei Lin go? And why should she go? She's married to an Indian. What right did the government have to drive her away from her country?' Lee Chang and his companion stood up with reddened faces.

Mei Lin was petrified. She looked at the commander with dumb eyes.

'You keep quiet. Let Mei Lin Ho speak.'

Mei Lin stood up, controlling herself forcibly.

'My husband's name is Pulok Baruah. Does he know that my name has been included in the list?'

The camp commander checked the papers and shook his head.

'We have no information about your husband Pulok Baruah. No one has contacted us in this regard. And no one has applied to go with you.'

Mei Lin looked around in utter confusion.

'Mei Lin's husband is Assamese. How can she go? She is pregnant. You will have to let her stay back,' Ho Chang Ho stood up now.

'I told you before – everyone who is on this list will have to go.' Ignoring the protests, the commander looked down at the list again.

After reading out all the names on the list, the camp commander stopped.

'There are no more names. The rest belong to another batch. The families that were left behind in Assam will all be taken to Madras Port.'

People began to move back to their rooms. Suddenly nausea overcame Mei Lin again and she rushed to the side of a wall and began to throw up. Siu, Yunlin's mother-in-law, Koneng Lotha, Wenling and a few others stood near her helplessly, well aware of what it meant.

Mei Lin was pregnant!

In their house in Makum, Akong's wife Phulmoni was sobbing madly, 'No. I won't go. I won't go to China. That's not my country. This is my country!'

Her mother-in-law was trying hard to convince Phulmoni to accompany Akong to China, wiping her own tears.

'Whose children are these? Tell me – whose children are these? They are not yours alone. They belong to their father as well. How can Akong live without you and the kids? He will die. How will you live without him?'

'Oh mother – please forgive me. I have no answers to your question. I won't go. I won't go to China. China is not our country.'

The same tussle was going on in Tung Chin's house with Xonpahi.

'You can't go. Do you understand? We didn't oppose your getting married to Tung Chin. Now you want to follow him to China! Do you realise what kind of a country China is?'

After discovering that Xonpahi was leaving with Tung Chin, her elder brother, who had come to take her back, became furious.

'You can't go. Get ready to leave with me. Right now.'

'No, I won't come with you. I'll go to China with him. If his mother can go, why can't I?'

'Don't you compare yourself with her! Her people have allowed her to go. We are not allowing you to go. I have already put in an application to that effect. Now get ready and come with me.'

The tussle and the crying and wailing was playing out in innumerable homes.

Far away, in the courtyard of Wing 5 of Deoli camp, the internees sat in utter confusion. The fiery sun was scorching them. They felt extremely thirsty. But no one felt the urge to leave the courtyard, as if they had lost all the strength of their bodies and minds.

Mei Lin sat with her head in her hands, dumb and scared.

Ameng and Lee Chang came and stood near her.

'Get up, Mei Lin. You will fall ill sitting in the sun like this,' Lee Chang said softly.

Mei Lin looked up. After a few moments of silence, she asked slowly, 'Now what will you do, Ameng?'

'I'll put in another application. You should do that too.'

'Even my letters don't go anywhere, how will the application help? I did apply once. I am a traitor. A Chinese spy. It is meaningless to apply again, Ameng.'

'Ameng hasn't received a single letter from his family. He hasn't made any contact so far. But you have to keep on trying. Come, Mei Lin. Let's sit inside and talk.'

Mei Lin stood up. She said, 'Why did there have to be a war, Lee Chang?'

Before Lee Chang could reply, Babu came up running to them.

'Yiu Yi has fallen down. She is not talking.'

The silence of the courtyard was shattered.

'What happened? What has happened to Yiu Yi?'

'She had gone to collect dry leaves. I was with her. Suddenly she fell down. She stopped talking.' Babu ran back; the others followed him.

A fearful cry reverbrated through the wing.

In a corner of the compound, near a neem tree, lay Yiu Yi. Her eyes were closed and she was bleeding from the nose. Ho Wang's wife was shaking her, trying to wake her up. Her rag doll lay nearby.

'Let me pass! Let me see her!' Yiu Yi's father said, pushing through the crowd 'Yiu Yi, Yiu Yi, what's wrong with you? Wake up – please wake up –'

Yiu Yi did not open her eyes. Nor did she move. He lifted her in his arms and looked around in utter despair.

'Call the doctor! Somebody call the doctor!'

Carrying the limp child on his shoulder, Yiu Yi's father started running. A group of people ran with him through the gate that the guards had opened without any questions.

The hospital outside the camp was silent. Entering through the open door, Yiu Yi's father gently laid her down on a bed, while the crowd called out for the doctor. Hearing the commotion, a nurse came out and asked, 'What's wrong?'

'She isn't opening her eyes. She has fainted in the heat. Where is doctor sahab? Call doctor sahab –'

'The doctor has gone away. He will return in the evening.'

The nurse felt Yiu Yi's pulse, and suddenly her face darkened. Letting go of her hand, she lifted her eyelids and placing her ears on the child's chest, listened for her heartbeat. Then, she shook her head, and said, 'She is dead.'

There was absolute silence.

'Her heart has collapsed.'

Her father stroked her still body and kept listening for a heartbeat. He tried to wake her up by shaking her body. No one tried to stop him. After a while, Yiu Yi's grandfather came and stood beside him. Seeing him, Yiu Yui's father broke down.

Then, controlling his tears, he placed a hand on his son's shoulder. 'Let us take her away. What else can we do.'

They carried Yiu Yi's body back to their wing. Amidst heartbroken sobs they buried her near a neem tree in a corner of the wing. Someone planted a twig of a thorny plant with tiny white flowers over the grave.

Leaving the past in the grave, they returned. All the other internees had assembled in front of her room. The children sat there together. The space in front of the room was heavy with the stifled sound of sobbing. The people who had returned sat down, lowering their heads.

The camp commander and the deputy commander had just arrived with the camp doctor. The guard was not at the gate at that time. He was running towards Yiu Yi's room.

'That child who died today. Who is the father of that child? From under the ground there has been a voice calling out "Baba, Baba." That child is not dead.'

Everyone ran back to the grave.

Yiu Yi's father started digging like a madman. So did the others.

Yiu Yi was still, her body covered in soil. It was warm, as if she was alive. Only, it was still. Only, it was silent.

Had there been life in her body only moments ago? Did she regain consciousness in the grave after the heatstroke?

Holding her soil-covered body against his chest, Yiu Yi's father looked up at the doctor for a few moments before breaking down.

'Oh doctor, why didn't you come just a little earlier? My child is dead, doctor!'

A deafening silence descended on Wing 5.

Four

It was dawn.

Seven nights had passed, soaked with tears, heavy with the sound of crying.

Seven unbearable nights.

And then it stopped. There were no sounds coming from Wing 5. People went about their daily chores in silence.

It was as if Yiu Yi had taken away the life-giving breeze with her. One by one people were coming out of their rooms. Preparations began for the journey ahead. In a while, they would all leave for Madras.

All their appeals had been in vain. The government of India paid no heed to the captives imprisoned in Deoli camp. The heap of applications remained unanswered.

In her room, Mei Lin was combing Mei Hang's hair. Siu and Ahlin sat beside her. Mei Hang was getting married today. Her parents wanted to see her marry Hong before they left for China.

Mei Lin was wearing a deep green terry cotton mekhela-chador. She'd bought the material from the canteen and stitched it herself.

'If you somehow meet Pulok, tell him, Mei Hang – I didn't want to go,' Mei Lin said slowly.

Mei Hang grasped Mei Lin's hand. Letting the tears flow freely, they sat there in silence, their eyes downcast.

Into that frozen silence entered Mei Hang's mother, her eyes reddened with worry and sleeplessness.

'Come to Liang's room.'

A crowd stood waiting outside Yiu Yi's room. Sounds of crying were coming from the room.

In Liang's dormitory, Hong was seated on a charpoy in his old clothes. Mei Hang sat beside him in the same old cloth. The same faded look.

The elderly people sat around the couple, while Liang, Akong, Yao Sen, Lee Chang, Aman, Tung Chin, Ameng and Chun Fu Thien stood around. In the midst of the prevailing despair, Hong and Mei Hang were married. Each of the guests picked up a bit of fried flour mixed with sugar and biscuit as Hong and Mei Hang rose from their seats to kneel before Hong's parents and offer them tea. Next came Mei Hang's parents.

'She is our eldest daughter. We had dreams of a grand marriage. We could not fulfil them. We are going far away. Don't know whether we will be able to see you again. Take care of her, Hong.' Mei Hang's father said slowly.

Mei Hang embraced her mother.

By this time the wing commander had arrived.

'Let us go to Yiu Yi,' Siu said.

Yiu Yi's family was praying at her grave. Siu and the others knelt beside them. They lit incense and prayed together.

They then began to form a line in the open space between the two blocks with their baggage.

'Come on, get moving,' the deputy commander began shouting. Mei Lin and her companions arrived with their baggage to join the line.

Once again, the armed guards and the buses. Once again, the train. This time the mob was absent. So was the half-cooked khichdi. The Sino-Indian war had become an old topic now. It had been replaced by new events.

After travelling for a few days, they reached Madras; it was afternoon. At a hotel near the port, people from various places had been waiting anxiously for their relatives from the camp. These people were not being chased out by the Indian government. They had come here willingly, to accompany their spouses and families to China. They were women from different Indian communities with different surnames.

Outside the hotel stood a crowd of curious people – apart from the locals, people of Chinese origin were also present, each one carrying bundles of different items like food and clothes. They had come from Assam and West Bengal to see off their relatives. Rope barricades had been put up on both sides of the road. Armed police and army men surrounded the hotel. Standing outside the barricade, people were looking at the gloomy and frazzled faces getting off from the buses with curiosity as well as sorrow and helplessness.

As soon as the convoy of buses arrived, the people waiting inside the hotel came running out. Immediately, they were pushed back by the armed guards.

The internees from Deoli started entering the hotel. The people waiting outside cried out the names of their relatives. Only a few words could be exchanged as they moved along. No one was allowed to stop and talk even for a moment. Looking back and crying constantly, they moved forward.

The first person in the line was Mok Min.

He walked ahead with his head lowered. His family followed him. Then came Lao Thien Lee's family.

Pramila Gogoi was trying to find her family by pushing through the crowd. Where were they? She looked everywhere frantically but couldn't spot them.

Tung Chin was also looking around for his dear ones. Where was Maa? And where was Xonpahi? Where were Achin and the other members of his family? His elder brother too, was anxiously looking around for his family.

'Move aside,' a guard said harshly, pushing Tung Chin to the side. Tung Chin's father kept looking around for his loving companion of thirty-five years.

Pramila Gogoi came forward with Madhabi and the children. Tung Chin looked at everyone and asked his mother, 'Xonpahi? Where is Xonpahi, Ma?'

'She couldn't come.'

Couldn't come! Xonpahi!

'Why couldn't she come? Who held her back, Maa?'

'It's not her fault. They took her away forcibly.'

'But who? Who took her away forcibly?'

'Her elder brother. She cried a lot and pleaded with him to let her go. But he wouldn't listen. He took her with him forcibly.'

'My daughter-in-law did not come. She was afraid to go to China. That is not her own country, you know. Who would want to leave one's own country, tell me?'

'But you've come. Why have you come, Maa?'

'Everyone's mind is not alike. Don't think that she didn't come because she doesn't love you. She has asked for your forgiveness. And she has sent a letter with me.'

All of Yiu Yi's siblings embraced their mother, crying loudly. Seeing her ragged children, she too, broke down in tears, hugging and kissing them constantly.

After a while, she looked around and asked, 'Where is Yiu Yi?'

Yiu Yi!

Her children went stiff. The adults became silent. They all stood with their heads lowered. Surprised at their behaviour she asked again, 'Where is Yiu Yi?'

'She left with the previous group,' her husband said gently. 'The government organizes everything. Her name had come up so she had to go. There was no way out. Now come along, let us go to our room. We have to leave soon.'

Standing in a corner, Ameng was looking sadly at everything. He was going away to an unknown country, leaving everyone behind. He couldn't contact anyone. He could not say goodbye to anybody.

Oh Meghali!

Meghali hadn't answered a single letter that Ameng had written. No, she did once. She wrote a short letter in response to all his letters.

'Don't write to me. My family doesn't like it. Your letters are opened by the CID. Government officials come to our house to ask about you. My father is a government official. He may lose his job. They may even arrest him. Please forgive me, Ameng.'

Lee Chang came near him and said gently, 'Liang's parents did not come. They stayed back in Nowgaon jail.'

Ameng looked at Lee Chang. Controlling his emotions, he went with Lee Chang to meet Liang. Standing in a corner, Liang was weeping silently.

'Liang!' Ameng took one of Liang's trembling hands into his and said slowly, as if consoling himself, 'There is nothing we can do.'

The people outside were pleading with the officers to allow them to handover the things they had brought for their departing relatives.

'No, no permission. Go back. You are not allowed to meet them.'

Clutching the ropes of the barricade, they kept weeping. The bright day darkened under a shroud of sadness.

Mei Lin was numb. Her name was now on the list of deportees. She was now one of China's people. There was no way to strike her name off the list. There was no time. This country had told Mei Lin to leave. A country that could put these Indian women in a Chinese ship with sheer indifference and chase away the children of an Indian mother – what was the sense in appealing to that country, asking for space for a tiny foetus?

The ship was waiting. The government officials had ordered them to move out. The buses were ready to leave for the port.

Removing Mei Lin's hand, her father left without saying anything. All her friends left too.

'Move. Move. Hurry Up. Move fast,' the armed guards commanded.

Pramila Gogoi took Mei Lin in her arms.

'Let's go. There is nothing we can do to change things now.'

Rows of people went out of the hotel towards the waiting buses, while the people beyond the police barriers looked on in dismay. They were still holding the bundles they had brought.

'Move. Move. Keep moving. No permission to talk. Move, move!'

They were never meeting again! Their dear ones were leaving the country forever! No way out! Simply no way! They were nothing but particles of dust, undesired weeds in the great garden called the state.

Who would give them justice? Where was the humane leadership? Where was the wise guardian?

There was no one anywhere. There was no hope. Not even a speck of soil to stand on.

They looked from beyond the barricade to the procession of people fading out of sight.

Left behind was a part of their divided soul. A part of their divided heart and divided identity! This was a foreign state now, an enemy of China. No doors were left open for return! No passage back to their dear ones! No gateway to their own society!

One by one, the buses left. The people who were left behind looked at the buses, as if dazed. The bundles they were carrying became heavier.

As soon as they arrived at the port, they encountered a different situation.

There were two ships. Having boarded them, they could only look around in surprise. Most of them had not set eyes on a sea before.

The chief Chinese officer onboard came forward and said in a clear and stern voice, 'They have thrown you out like beggars and kept all your belongings. You have come aboard with these rags and utensils. Don't you feel ashamed? Throw them away. Throw out all the Indian stuff!'

People looked at him in surprise.

'What is this man saying?' someone asked.

'He has asked you to throw away all your Indian things.' Explaining what the officer said, Lao Thien Lee ended with, 'We are no longer India's prisoners. We are Chinese now.'

The teacher from Calcutta, Liang Ching Wan, came forward and threw his bundle into the sea in utter disgust. Some of the others followed him, but not all. Babu's father held his flask close; he had very cleverly hidden his passbook. There were a thousand rupees saved in the passbook.

'I will not throw my bag. There are papers. There are photos.'

'We, too, have papers. We will face problems later on.'

'Yes, yes. We, too, have papers.'

Most of those who had come from Assam held on to their bundles and bags. The Hindu women clutched their belongings desperately, as they contained vermillion, pictures and small idols of gods.

Mei Lin was clautching her small bag. How could she throw away the photograph with Pulok, taken just after they were married? How could she throw away the little pot of vermillion? Her silk mekhela-chador? The beads that Robin gave her? The bowl and the chopsticks of her forefathers? Pulok's letter?

Seeing her, Liang Ching Wan asked with a taunting smile, 'What's wrong? You still haven't shed your longing for India, have you?'

'Who told you I wanted to shed my longing?'

'What do you mean? Will you continue loving this country after all that has happened?' Without bothering to reply, Mei Lin moved away from Liang Ching Wan.

At that very moment Pulok arrived, permission papers in hand, to meet Mei Lin in faraway Deoli.

Five

In the deep blue waters of the South China Sea, two Chinese ships were sailing along majestically. Under the blazing sun the journey was nearing its end. They had almost reached the Guangdong province of South China.

Fourteen long days had passed.

Almost all the passengers were suffering from sea sickness. Their bodies had wilted, wasting away. There was no one to look after them. No medicine. Nothing.

The Chinese officers were not concerned about anything except providing food regularly. These were valueless returnees, thrown out by an enemy country.

Mei Lin was asleep inside a cabin. Siu and Ahlin were beside her. They were wiping her face with a wet cloth, soaking it in water now and then. They were sweating profusely in the unbearable heat of the cabin.

Although she was exhausted like the others, Siu looked happy and content. Her life had changed. Now she was Chun Fu Thien's wife. Their guardians had decided to get them married on the ship since no one knew what would happen once they reached China.

'You two go and rest. I will sleep,' Mei Lin said weakly.

'You can't be on your own.'

'I'll be alright. Don't worry. You've both been sitting here since morning. Now go and get some fresh air, or else you'll end up falling sick. Let me sleep alone for some time. I will be okay. Believe me.'

They left reluctantly. Mei Lin closed her eyes. She wanted some time alone. This merciless reality was like an illusion – understandable, yet so incomprehensible! A bud was blooming inside her body!

Hours passed. Mei Lin was not aware of her surroundings. It was as though she was standing between life and death, or in that foggy moment between dream and reality. As if there was no one else around. As if she were floating through the endless silence of death.

'Mei Lin – Mei Lin –'

Someone seemed to be calling her from a distance. Who could it be? She opened her eyes, reddened with the smoke of delusion. Two familiar but hazy faces were hovering above her.

'Sit up, Mei Lin. We have to get off the ship. We have arrived in China.'

China!

That undesired word hit her. Slowly sound and sight became prominent. Someone had placed a soft and cool hand on her forehead. Lee Chang was saying anxiously, 'She is burning with fever!'

'I want some water,' Mei Lin said slowly.

Liang hurried out and brought some water, while Lee Chang helped her sit up and made her drink it. Looking at Lee Chang, Mei Lin said slowly, 'I don't want to die, Lee Chang!'

'Everything will be okay. We will live.' Lee Chang's eyes became moist.

'I am so tired! I have travelled so much! We have left Makum far behind. How will Pulok find me? How will I see him again? I must return Lee Chang! I will return to Makum!'

Lee Chang looked at Tung Chin and Ameng. Mei Lin was delirious.

'Have some more water, Mei Lin. You are dehydrated. Please get up.'

Lee Chang helped Mei Lin sit up and drink some more water.

'Now we have to go out. We will have to get off.'

Lee Chang held her and took her out. Ameng took her bag. Meanwhile, the passengers went up to the deck to set eyes on the huge port.

This was China! They would have to live here till their deaths! Utter confusion and fear had paralysed their minds.

Would they be able to live in this tightly-regulated communist country? After living in a democracy for so long? They had to, they said to themselves.

Were they really living freely in India? Weren't they compelled to live in captivity?

At least they wouldn't be captives here. At least they wouldn't suffer humiliation. No one would look at them with suspicion. No one would shout hateful words at them.

Leaning on Lee Chang, Mei Lin came to the deck and stood with the others. She looked around with tired eyes.

'This is Canton Port,' someone said.

Over a hundred years ago, in this very place, their ancestors Ho Han and Ho Yen had been confined in the hold of a ship. They had only had a bowl and a pair of chopsticks to call their own. Today their descendants had returned to this land empty-handed. What was there to call their own in this land, except a handful of memories that weren't even their own?

'Let's go, Mei Lin,' Pramila Gogoi said quietly.

She touched her hand for a moment and then disembarked with the support of Lee Chang.

In order to rehabilitate the thousands of overseas Chinese returnees, the State Council of China had formed 'The Overseas Chinese Affairs Commission'. Under this commission, the 'National Committee of Receiving and Settling Returned Overseas Chinese' had been formed as well.

The officials of the Receiving Committee led the returnees from India to the registration office. Mei Lin and others stood in a queue in front of the registration office.

The locals slowly gathered there and looked at them.

This was not new for the locals. For the past few years, they had watched people from different lands disembarking at this port.

After the formation of People's Republic of China, the situation in southeast Asia had begun to change. With that, the position of the overseas Chinese, especially of Malaya, Indonesia and Vietnam, had also changed. Because of the political and economic pressures exerted on them, a mass return journey of the overseas Chinese had been set in motion.

The people who worked and lived near the port had become accustomed to such sights. Many people in China knew about these returnees. They had no sympathy for the returnees since they received special care from the Chinese government. Rather, they hated and envied them.

Yet, here they were to see the new lot of returnees. And this time, their faces reflected extreme surprise.

Were these the people who had been deported from India? Some looked Chinese, somewhat. But the others? Do Chinese people look like this? In China, they had never seen people wearing such strange clothes. Were they Indians?

Yes. Yes. They were. Enemies of China, Indians.

Huaqiao, huaqiao.

Gui guo huaqiao.

Many comments were heard. The returnees couldn't understand the words, but they had no difficulty understanding the tone.

'What are they saying?'

'Returned overseas Chinese.'

Slowly the faces of the locals became aggressive with hatred.

Hak gwai. Hak gwai. Black ghost. Black ghost.

'Hey foreign devils! Why have you come to our country? To eat without working? Go back to wherever you came from.

Aren't you ashamed to return to China after being chased away? Aren't you ashamed to return like beggars? Leave our country.'

The faces of the people who knew the language became crimson with rage and frustration, tears brimming in their eyes.

The tension in the air was palpable. This sort of behavior was not unfamiliar to them. It was dangerous to protest. Everyone lowered their heads.

The stern-faced policemen were checking their belongings and their bodies. They were removing everything which they considered doubtful. These people had come from a capitalist country. They were not trustworthy. There might be Indian spies hiding among these people. Most of them looked Indian. They had lived in India for a few generations. They might create trouble in China.

The officials of the registration office had taken a few returnees who knew the Chinese language with them. With their help, they started registering the newcomers.

Slowly the queue moved forward. After registration, they were sent to a three-storied hotel, a temporary camp for the returnees. The receiving committee had made good arrangements for them.

Yiu Yi's mother became restless to meet Yiu Yi.

'Were the people from the first batch brought to this hotel?' she asked her husband in a low voice.

'I don't know,' he answered absentmindedly.

'Ask someone then.'

'Whom will I ask now? Registration is going on. See how angry the locals are. Now you can't ask anyone. I will ask later.'

She became silent. But when she reached the hotel, she went to one official to enquire about Yiu Yi.

'Where are the people from the first batch?' She asked in broken Chinese.

'First batch?' the officer asked in surprise.

'Yes, that ship which came before, some days before? My daughter was there in that batch. Her name is Yiu Yi.'

'Who told you that a batch of people had come before this?'

'He told me. He is Yiu Yi's father.'

Looking at Yiu Yi's father for a few moments the officer asked him suspiciously, 'What is this woman saying?'

Yiu Yi's father lowered his head and answered slowly, 'I told her that our daughter had come in the first batch.'

'But this is the first batch. Why did you lie?'

'He lied?' Yiu Yi's mother turned to her husband. 'You lied?' She looked at her husband who stood with his head lowered. Then she cried out, 'Where is Yiu Yi?'

All the family members came running to them. The children embraced her.

'Where is Yiu Yi? Where did you leave her? Why are you not telling me anything?'

'She is no more. At the Deoli camp, because of the heat, she –'

Yiu Yi's father's words were muffled with the sound of her mother's heartbreaking lamentation. A loud, metallic voice announced, 'Go to your own rooms. Get some rest. Our officer will talk to you when needed.'

The people slowly moved inside.

The senior officers sat down for a serious discussion with the register of names in front of them.

Six

Another week had gone by.

The exhaustion had begun to fade.

They felt a little better after they had rested and eaten proper food. The sorrow lingered on but the frustration was diminishing. The care and concern of the officials had created an atmosphere of hope. They had started believing that they would be able to live in China comfortably. They had started to think that the bad days were over at last. Before, China had only been a land of tales. But in these seven days, the people started to feel a sense of closeness with this country.

The hotel rooms were filled with tears and laughter. Hearing about the Chinese from India, many people had come to meet them at the hotel, searching for connections with those who had left for India ages ago. They were entering the rooms in search of them. Old people with walking sticks came to find their brothers and sisters. Some found their nieces and nephews. They wept when they remembered their brothers who had died in India. They held them close and caressed them with all their love and offered them the home-cooked food they brought. Surprise, happiness and sorrow blended together.

'You have all been asked to gather in the hall downstairs. Please come down quickly. Only the adults are wanted,' the officers of the Receiving Committee announced.

They looked at each other with concern. They became worried.

What had happened again?

They put aside their joys and hurried down.

Mei Lin, too, walked down slowly with her father. She had grown thinner this past week.

As soon as everyone had assembled, one of the officers stood up to speak. Ho Chang Ho stood close to the officers as the interpreter.

'We would like to apprise you of the fact that many overseas Chinese from different countries of the world have returned to China already. To rehabilitate these returnees, our government has taken different measures. The returnees will have to follow the new rules and regulations of our country. Special arrangements have been made to get them acquainted with the system of the People's Republic of China. This is a communist country. Everyone has to work for a living. You will have to work, too. Keeping in mind that you can work in an organised way and can live together, The Overseas Chinese Affairs Commission of our State Council has formed some 'special category farms'. You will have to work there like the locals of our country who work in the state farms. You will get wages. However, you will get some extra facilities. For you the farms have already been arranged. One is in Jiayi. The other one –'

'But none of us knows any farming,' Mok Min stood up.

'If you don't, you will have to learn. We will provide experts. However, not all of you will be taken to the farms.'

Instantly an unknown fear weighed heavy on their hearts. This was a familiar tune! It was surely not an indication of anything good.

'At the time of registration we noted down details about each of you – your education, your work, your interests, etc. After sorting through the information, it has been decided who would be given what work to perform. However, temporarily, most of you will be placed in the farms. Later on, you will be placed in jobs suiting your ability. Now the list will be read out which will tell you who is going where and what work he will have to do.'

Holding a sheaf of paper, an aged man stood up.

'It is decided that the children below eighteen years, who have studied beyond class six, will be sent to study in Peking. Among the older students, only Ameng Tham, who is an agriculture student, will be sent to Peking University. If he wants to go, he will have to apply. Those with knowledge of tea farming will be sent to tea gardens. Those who are above eighteen will be moved to the factories. The rest will be divided into three groups and will be sent to the farms. The government will provide support for the rehabilitation of returnees, whom local relatives have agreed to keep with them. Old people will be sent to old-age homes.' The officer halted. After looking at the returnees for some time he said, 'You are probably not aware of the fact that China has been going through a very difficult time. We have not yet completely recovered from the famine of 1958. Because of this, we have to be extremely careful about our expenses. Keeping this situation in mind, you will have to cooperate with the government. All arrangements have been made. Everyone will be provided with a bundle of certain essentials. Everyone stand in a queue, sign on the resister and collect your bundles. Get ready. After four hours you will be sent to your respective places.'

The people looked at each other. They grabbed each other's hands.

Those who had come from Kalimpong and Siliguri would be sent to the farms in Jiayi. Siu would go away with Chun Fu Thien.

Mei Lin's father was sitting on his bed with Mei Lin's grandmother's and uncle's family. Mei Lin stood near her father, trying to appear as strong as she could. Her friends came in.

Mei Lin's father looked at them and smiled calmly.

'I might not be able to see you all again. Live always like a family. Do take care of Mei Lin. She doesn't have anyone other than you.'

No one said anything. After sitting in silence for a few moments Mei Lin's father stood up. Placing a hand on Tung Chin's shoulder, he said, 'Time never remains the same. Good days will come. Don't lose your patience, Tung Chin.'

Then he walked over to Ameng.

'In this land, you have your friends. There can't be anyone dearer to you than a friend. Never think that you are alone. I –'

The sound of a whistle came from the ground floor.

First to leave were the children. Then the returnees who were to go to the Jiayi farm. Ko Fuk's family and Siu went away with them, weeping. Tung Chin left to work in a cloth mill. Many other young boys also left to work in different factories. After the old people left for the old-age homes, Mei Lin and the rest got into the trucks to go to the railway station for their journey.

The days of the Great Leap Forward, and the dream of building a modern China, were not over yet. The agriculture sector was still under the absolute control of the government. Individual farming was banned. In its place, communes had been formed. This had changed the entire socio-economic system. The famine had also greatly affected society as a whole. Slowly, conditions were improving. The export of grains had been stopped. Imported grains had started coming in from Australia and Canada. The Great Leap Forward was still on, as it was attached to the 'five-year plans', but not with the same intensity as before. It would end this year. Change had come to the political sector, too. Mao was now the chairman of the Communist Party. Deng Xiaoping was the general secretary. Liu Shao Qi was now the chairman of the PRC.

After the train journey came the trucks, heading towards the farm. The returnees looked around with curiosity and surprise.

An unknown country!

Still, it didn't feel entirely unknown. Somehow the climate, the air, the nature and the people, was similar to Assam.

But, though life around them was in motion, something was missing. Most of the people they saw looked grave. The forests near the villages and towns they crossed were thin and sparse. They saw furnaces in every school and office compound. It appeared as if they hadn't been used for a long time. For rapid industrial growth, under Mao's direction, the whole nation became busy in producing steel. It had been quite some time since the days of hectic production of steel ended. Only the furnaces remained.

Slowly the line of trucks started climbing the hill.

Finally, they reached a place near a forest. The officials of the Receiving Committee got down from the first vehicle.

'From here you have to walk. The road is not motorable.'

The returnees got down without protest. Carrying their belongings and the small children, they began to walk. Before the curious eyes of the passersby, the line of gaunt people moved forward.

When they reached the farm, it was afternoon. To receive the returnees a few government officials and the local leaders of the CPC were waiting outside. Some local people were also standing nearby, watching curiously.

The returnees looked around with tired eyes. In front of them was a big compound inside which stood a line of brick-walled old barracks. On the left was a thin, sparse forest. On the right was a wide field, beyond which was the village.

'This is your farm. *Hua quiao Nongchang*,' said the Receiving Committee's official.

'"Nongchang" means farm. It's a farm for the overseas Chinese,' Ho Chang Ho said in a low voice.

'*Hak gwai. Hak gwai.* Black ghosts. Black ghosts.'

'*Indu ren. Indu ren.* Indians. Indians.'

The familiar words started spilling out of the mouths of the locals. Sheer hatred started to replace the curiosity.

The returnees took their allotted places in the long barracks, which were divided into small rooms. At that time in the hall, situated in the front of the compound, the manager of the farm, the members of the local CPC, the members of the Receiving Committee and the representative of the Overseas Chinese Affairs Commission were present. The returnees freshened up and congregated there. The meeting began.

After the introduction was over, the officer of the Receiving Committee stood up to speak.

'Our great Chairman Mao is trying to build the best state in the modern world. He not only thinks about the Chinese people living in China, but is committed to all the Chinese living outside as well. China has accepted thousands of refugees of Chinese origin. We all must be grateful to our great Chairman Mao. At the same time, we all must be committed to the great cause. Leaving aside all unreasonable ideas and beliefs, we must devote ourselves to successfully build our Communist China from all sides. We hope you will follow all the rules of this farm sincerely and mould yourselves into good citizens of Communist China,' the officer said.

The manager of the farm was next.

'Three farming experts will be with you to guide you in your work. You must follow their directions. No objections will be entertained. How you lived in India is not our concern. Here you are all equals. Everyone must work. You will get wages. You have to maintain yourself with these wages. How much wage you earn will depend on the points you score through your work. One dispensary and a canteen will be opened for you. There will be a primary school for the children. The responsibility to teach the children is entrusted with Chow Chi Yong, Liang Ching Wan and Pramila Gogoi ...' After a long speech the manager sat down.

The returnees continued looking at them, not knowing how to react.

'Liang Ching Wan,' a member of the local CPC called out.

Liang Ching Wan stood up, worried.

'Our central committee has mentioned your name specially. We congratulate you officially for your loyalty to Communist China. It's a special honour.'

Liang Ching Wan was elated. He looked at the officials, speechless.

'Please come over here. Let's get introduced properly,' the local CPC leader said and smiled.

Walking past the astonished faces of the returnees, Liang Ching Wan headed towards the dais.

Seven

Carrying a basket on her back, Mei Lin was walking down a trail in the middle of a vast field, filled with people busy with cultivation. Her walk, her posture and her expression reflected an acute sense of unease.

The basket on her back was filled with dried human excreta. She was carrying this to the field to be used as a fertilizer. The back of her dress was soaked with the filthy water of the half-dried excreta that seeped through the basket. She shuddered in unbearable discomfort. She was trying to control the urge to throw up with all her strength.

The farm was made up of land taken from the locals as well as some wastelands.

The farms which were allotted to the overseas Chinese had been formed as autonomous organizations. These farms were clearly different from the ones formed with the local people. They were directly under the commanding system of the Overseas Chinese Affairs Commission. These special category state farms were run by a manager under the collective leadership of the local CPC. Because of this system, the head of the farm could send reports directly and speedily to the provincial government and even to the central government through its own channel.

One year had passed since Mei Lin and the others had arrived. They now lived an entirely different life. Some of them were busy cultivating rice, maize, vegetables and fruits on the land which had been used by the villagers for farming previously, and some were busy with the waste land, trying to make it fertile.

Mei Lin and others were slowly being transformed into farmers under the guidance of the local experts. In the beginning, they cried, unable to bear the toil. But slowly the tears had begun to dry. They had started accepting the tough rules and regulations of Communist China. They had no other option but to work. They had to face punishment if they refused. They didn't get work points. It was difficult to sustain oneself with no work points. The farm manager made them understand that this was the People's Republic of China. One could not do things according to one's wishes.

They had understood. Not a single word of protest rose from them. They worked according to the directions of the manager, silently.

Their day-to-day lives had transformed considerably. Now they took lessons in communism after their work. They were taught complex theories every evening. They read *The People's Daily* every day. The party published its agendas and opinions through this newspaper. Selected writings of Mao also appeared here.

The returnees had learned many things within this period. They were beginning to understand China to some extent by listening to the news and the editorials of *The People's Daily*, the lectures delivered by the local leaders and the discussions. They had become familiar with phrases like 'Great Leap Forward', 'Socialist Education Movement', 'Class War', and so on. The words they were most familiar with were 'reactionary', 'rightist', 'capitalist roader', among others.

People staying on this farm were divided into two production teams. Each team comprised fifty to sixty people, including children. Both the teams were made up of refugees from India, of which one team was made up of people from Assam.

Mei Lin stopped for a moment. Adjusting her basket, she looked around.

The field looked colourful in comparison to the nearby local farm, as most of them were wearing multi-coloured clothes they had brought from India, instead of the standard uniform worn by the farmers. Most of the women of Indian origin were wearing

Indian clothes as they were not mentally prepared to wear the Chinese dress. The Hindu women still applied vermillion. They didn't eat beef and some of them didn't even eat pork. However, no compulsion had been imposed on them in these respects.

There was no modern equipment for farming, not even fertilizer. Hence, human excreta was used as a substitute. This was a loathsome practice for them, but it was normal for the locals.

Many of them were still not prepared to eat vegetables grown using human excreta. Many fell sick after having their meals, and from touching excreta on the fields.

Along with these inconveniences, another problem loomed. Though the boundary of the farm had been properly demarcated, the neighbours had not accepted it. They considered the returnees encroachers. They thought the returnees had occupied their land. For them these people were foreigners. Outsiders. The locals were fuming.

The outsiders were living in government houses for free. They got regular wages even if they didn't work or produce properly. The villagers didn't have these concessions. The returnees got better food than the villagers. For these reasons the villagers were extremely dissatisfied. They kept harassing the returnees. Some villagers would enter the farm and steal the vegetables and other crops. They even took away their clothes hung outside for drying. They abused and attacked those who tried to protest. They passed humiliating comments on the road and tried to find excuses to fight. The returnees began to lose their patience. Whenever someone said something, they retaliated. There was constant tension in the farm.

They had no connections with the locals. There was no possibility that the bitter relationship would improve in the near future. In this remote part of this massive country, they were living like people on an island.

The famine was over but the situation had not returned to complete normalcy. Since they had arrived, tight rationing had been decreed in their farm, too. They received very little food to eat. However, it was more than what the locals were getting. The government tried to keep the refugees far from hunger.

Mei Lin moved forward slowly. She was tired. She felt the basket get heavier. She was drenched in sweat. Her tired face reddened in the heat.

No one noticed her. Everyone was busy with their own work. Everyone had become thin and weak. Their bodies bore the signs of malnutrition, grief and frustration.

Mei Lin had become weak too. A few months ago she had given birth to a baby girl. She was due to return to work in a few days.

Mei Lin and the others had understood one thing; they would have to live here in fear. One couldn't speak openly here. If one became careless while speaking, there was every possibility of getting into trouble. The internal political situation in China was grave.

The returnees lived with caution. Many of them had been financially well-off in India. That background was not favourable for them here. The Chinese government was extra vigilant about the returnees from capitalist countries. Communist China had been established only recently. The pro-Taipei people were still active inside the state. The Chiang Kai Shek loyalists were still trying to overthrow the communist regime.

Even though communism had been established, the traditional social mores and the popular mindsets of the past had not yet been eradicated completely. The returnees from the capitalist countries had brought with them the training of the social system and the rules of those states. They could harm the process of change in the country.

Mei Lin and the others were aware of the government's position. Still, they were grateful to this country. Even though the country had just gone through a famine, it had accepted them. Despite all the difficulties, the government tried to keep the returnees comparatively well. They got things like soap, oil, cigarettes, fish and meat in small amounts, with the special ticket offered to the returnees from the canteen. They used to receive a minimum wage to sustain themselves, whether there was any production or not. The locals were not entitled to these extra privileges. Because of this, the returnees had to face the ire of the locals from the time they arrived.

Emptying the contents of the basket in the field, Mei Lin washed her back. She then rubbed her hands in the mud and washed them. Wiping her hands dry on her cloth, she went to a tree in a corner of the field. Her baby, whom she had kept in a basket, was crying. Seated near by were Lee Chang's child and three others below five years of age. They were still too young for school. All of them came to the field with their parents. Mei Lin left the baby in their custody. There was no other option.

Yiu Yi's mother sat near the children with her head drooping. She often sat like this, leaving her work midway. She had almost lost her mental balance. Sometimes she behaved normally, but on occasion she became unstable. She did not want to work or eat. In the beginning, the supervisors abused her, but later they just left her alone. She received very little pay because of her lower work points. The others could not feed an extra person with the wages they earned. Still, they helped.

Yiu Yi's mother didn't complain even if she got nothing to eat, whether she was cool or disturbed. She had become uncommunicative and indifferent. She sat silently and sometimes cried her heart out.

'Her father cheated me! He lied to me and brought me here. He didn't even show me where they put her to sleep. What will I do now? What will I do?'

She was not alone; most of them frequently broke down in helpless tears. And those women too – the ones who had left behind their kin and their motherland for their husband and children, the ones who were forced to desert their Indian identity and citizenship, perhaps forever.

Parbati and several others would often mope about their circumstances. They wore Indian clothes. Worshipped Hindu gods. They even made altars for their own gods in their rooms and followed the rituals.

It was difficult to know what was going on in Pramila Gogoi's mind. Never had anyone seen her get carried away by emotions. She always tried to enthuse everyone around her. No one had ever seen her mope for Xonpahi and Ah Chin or for her older daughter and her family, whom she had left behind in far-flung Assam. Nor for that matter did she pine for Tung Chin, who worked in some remote factory in the interiors of China. This dignified, educated woman was respected and loved by all.

Yunlin's Naga mother-in-law Koneng and Akong's mother Sukmati had also become subdued. They worked and ate quietly and, the rest of the time, sat brooding.

Most of the returnees cried. They cried because of the unbearable toil and hunger. They cried for their children, who were gradually becoming emaciated. They cried for the families they had left behind and cried relentlessly remembering their good days in India.

The memories of the past were hugely alleviating for their insufferable present.

Mei Lin felt the same way. Holding the baby to her chest, she would begin to see a rainbow of hope.

She had to live. She had to live for her baby. She had to live to see Pulok again.

Mei Lin wiped her face with the sleeve of her blouse. The children sitting under the shade of the tree came near her. She picked up the pot of water near the basket and gulped down some water quickly. She then spread the cloth in the basket on her lap and laying the baby on it, breastfed her. Passing the water pot to Yiu Yi's mother she said, 'Drink some water, aiee. Or else you will feel unwell.' Without a word, Yiu Yi's mother drank from the pot and put it away.

Mei Lin then took out a container from her cloth bag in which was a bit of cooked rice, mixed with salt and a few drops of oil. The oil that she got for a week's cooking was hardly enough to see her through. She added a few drops to her boiled food to give it some flavour. Unlike the others, she ate a little rice in the middle of the day, otherwise she felt weak and dizzy. She made a few small balls of rice and gave one to each child. She then offered one to Yiu Yi's mother. She didn't respond. Mei Lin began to eat fast. She didn't have much time to rest with her baby.

The baby was happily suckling and kicking her legs. She looked like the perfect blend of Pulok and Mei Lin.

'O Maa –'

A fearful cry spread across the field.

Mei Fung was crying loudly and trembling. She was staring fearfully at a skull, along with some bones under a shrub. The workers had found the ruins of old graves in this wasteland.

Liang, who was working nearby, came running.

'I won't work here. I'll die if I work here. Take me back. Take me back to Makum!' Mei Fung wailed. Yunlin took her to a corner, while Ahlin brought water. Mei Fung was still crying. Gravely watching her for a while, Liang left.

The girl was slowly finding a niche in Liang's heart. He felt like bringing all the happiness in the world to her, to make her forget all her miseries and redeem her of all her wretched loneliness.

But he had not revealed his mind to her yet.

This time he had to tell her. He would tell her today. Mei Fung was wilting. She had lost her urge to live. If she remained this way, something untoward might happen.

Liang got busy with his work.

The sun was about to set when the whistle blew announcing the end of the day's work.

The muddied and exhausted group of workers started coming out of the fields. With her bag slung on her back, Mei Lin picked up her baby, while Ahlin carried the basket.

'Let me hold her,' Akong offered. Smiling gratefully, Mei Lin handed over the baby.

A group of villagers, who were standing on the wayside and gossiping, looked at them with disdain. The group moved on quietly, pretending not to hear the foul abuses hurled at them. To protest would mean more trouble. Mei Fung was walking at the back of the group. Her face was shadowed by deep lifelessness. Liang came close to her.

'I want to say something,' Liang said gently.

Mei Fung looked up at him, but said nothing.

'Don't be sad. It's of no use.'

Mei Fung's eyes filled with tears, as she answered, 'What do I do?'

'Look ahead. Everything will work out.'

'There is nothing to look forward to, Liang ako,' she said.

'Yes, there is. I am there. You haven't seen me. Just look at me, Mei Fung.'

Mei Fung stopped and looked at him in surprise. Then moving forward she said slowly, 'Are you pitying me?'

'What is that?'

'Feeling sorry for me, you –'

'*Haigui*, *Haigui*,' screamed a group of boys waiting near a tree. Some of the workers stopped to look round at them.

'Hey, you foreign devils!' they shouted again.

The faces of the young boys hardened, as they looked at each other. The others were scared.

'Don't answer back. Let them say what they like. Come on, let's keep going,' Tung Chin's father said.

'Hey, foreign devils, how long are you going to stay in our country?'

'They'll stay. Where will they go? Haven't they been chased away like dogs?'

'We don't get enough rice, and they feast on fish! Meat! Cigarettes!'

'Bloody beggars! Our government is feeding beggars. They have come like shameless people and occupied our land. They don't work. They sit and eat. They rub mud on their bodies to show that they work. And, despite that, they receive wages. But we don't.'

'Why have you come to our country? Go. Go back from wherever you have come.'

'They are the burden of our country! Crowd of beggars! You dirty half Chinese.'

The faces of the young men reddened. Ignoring the caution of the elders, they turned, agitated, went chasing after the hecklers and in a moment, were engaged in a brawl.

The children began to cry. The seniors pulled them back. They went past the yells and screams, curses and abuses of the local young men. They were just a few minutes away from their barracks.

At that moment, inside the school in the barracks, the students were talking among themselves. The classes were over. Chow Chi Yong, Liang Ching Wan and Pramila Gogoi were also talking. After the school hours, the children were kept back for some time since some teachers came from outside to take classes. They taught the children about Mao's ideals and gave lessons on communism. Everything that they were taught would be interpreted and explained at length. The most enthusiastic of them was the Calcutta teacher Liang Ching Wan.

In Hua qiao Nonchang, his position was the best of all. His allegiance to the Chinese government was above all doubt. He was a pure communist. He was the only person in Hua qiao Nongchang who was happy. Though he was provided with the same amount of food as the others, his work burden was not heavy. He had to teach and interpret speeches and other things during the meetings. He was also given the responsibility of educating the elderly people of the farm about communism. His name had been recommended by the Overseas Chinese Affairs Commission. There was a possibility that his name would be sent for the election of CPC's local committee.

The guardians had come to collect their children, who were too young to take the classes on communism. Liang Ching Wan spoke to everyone with the solemnity of a protector.

'Ahma, when shall we go away from here?' asked one of Pramila Gogoi's grandchildren.

'Why did you ask that, dear?' Pramila looked at the boy.

'I don't like staying here, Ahma. I feel scared! Let's go from here. I remember Makum so much. I remember Achin so much. I feel like crying. Let's go from here.'

Pramila Gogoi didn't say anything. This was not a new question. In the beginning, the children exhausted their parents repeatedly by asking these questions. Even now they did. The boy said again, 'I feel so hungry! I don't get to eat! Let us all go away from here.'

'Yes. He said the right thing. We won't live in this place. So difficult!' Babu's younger brother said.

'We cannot go even if we wish to. Don't say these things to anybody. They will beat you. They will beat us too,' Chow Chi Yong said.

'I know that. I won't tell.'

'When I become big, then I will go to India again. I will go to Makum. I left my friends there. I think about them so much!'

'Yes. I remember them, too. I don't feel good here. People abuse here. I'm always scared.'

Mei Lin came inside.

Anjali was sitting gloomily in a corner. Her best friends were not there. She didn't feel good talking to anyone.

As Mei Lin sat beside her, she smiled cheerlessly, looking at the baby. Mei Lin hugged her close. Anjali seemed to have grown up. But she lacked youthful zest. She had got her mother's lovely complexion, beautiful eyes and straight black hair. Adolescence seemed to have caught her unawares. Having been uprooted from the joyous atmosphere in Makum, she had become lonely and lifeless.

After talking to Anjali for a while, Mei Lin approached Pramila Gogoi.

'Please give me a book. Any book will do, aiee,' She said. Some people, who had joined them in Madras, had brought some Assamese text books with them. Pramila Gogoi used these to teach the children.

'What will you do with the book?'

'I want to copy from the book as much as I can. No one knows when and where we will have to go. I have bought some paper and am thinking of writing down certain things from my memory too. I will have to teach my child.'

'You bought paper? Be careful. They may take it from you. It's dangerous.'

'I have informed them of the reason in writing and have taken permission. If they suspect anything, I am helpless.'

Pramila looked at Mei Lin for a second and asked slowly, 'What will you gain by teaching her Assamese? We will never be able to return to Assam.'

'Who knows who will go where? Did we ever think that we would be sent away like this from India?'

Mei Lin left the room.

At that time in the one-roomed houses of the barracks, those who had returned from work had freshened up and started cooking. They were provided rice, enough for just one meal a day. In the morning, they had a thick stew of rice and vegetables and ate a proper meal in the evening after work. Their faces would look bright on the days they were provided with fish or meat. Other days were grey.

Adjacent to Mei Lin's room lived a family from Darrang, in the north bank of Assam. The lady belonged to the Sonowal Kachari community. She was a widow. Mei Lin's heart went out to her. Her name was Ajoli Sonowal. She had three little girls. The eldest was nine years old.

Handing over her baby to the eldest girl, Mei Lin cleaned up returned to her own room. After cooking and hurriedly finishing her work, she went to get her baby.

The woman was holding Mei Lin's baby in her lap and, having made all the three daughters sit down, was about to feed them. On seeing Mei Lin, she smiled and asked, 'Did you cook?'

'Yes. Is she causing you any trouble?'

'No. Please sit.'

Rolling small balls of rice with boiled vegetable and mixing it with salt and oil, the woman first fed her youngest daughter.

With a forced smile, she said, '*Dhoute sitika, pura maasor pitika* ... Mashed smoked fish.'

'Where is the fish? There is no mashed smoked fish today. You are just saying that,' said Maina, the youngest daughter.

The second daughter, Moni, said, 'We haven't had mashed smoked-fish here even once. Maa always lies.'

'We ate so much fish while we were in the tea garden. But, after coming here, we don't get to eat properly, you see!'

'When will we return, Maa?'

'We will never return, dear. We have been chased away from there.'

'Why were we chased away, Maa?'

Before anyone could speak, Babu came in excitedly.

'They have come. They have come. Many people have arrived from India.'

In a moment, there was a huge commotion. Leaving aside all work, all rules, and all fear, everyone, including Mei Lin, went outside.

With their belongings on their backs arrived a group of tired people. When Mei Lin reached the courtyard of the office, the second batch from the Deoli internment camp were sitting there. Among them some found their relatives, who had been left behind, and some did not.

The farm's courtyard had become noisy with the laughter, cries and excited voices of people exchanging information. Liang's brother and sister-in-law, Hong and Mei Hang, and several other people were there.

Ho Fuk's family had also come, but he wasn't there. He had passed away in the camp.

Yao Sen didn't come. Yao Sen's name wasn't on the list of the second batch. Wang Shu Shin, his father, his elder brother and his family had not come either.

'Mei Hang!'

'Oiii Maa,' Mei Hang hugged Mei Lin.

In Mei Hang's embrace, Mei Lin trembled. Hugging her for a while and gathering her composure, Mei Hang said, 'Hey! You look like a villager.'

Even though she laughed and joked with her, she was secretly pained. What had become of Mei Lin! Her pink complexion had turned pale. Her sleek black hair had lost its lustre. She had become thin and weak.

'I am a farmer. What do you think?' Mei Lin said with a sad smile. Then she looked at Hong.

'I never thought even in my dreams that I would see you all again.'

Meanwhile, Ajoli Sonowal had come, holding Mei Lin's baby. Mei Lin took the baby from her.

'Whose baby is this?' Mei Hang asked in surprise.

'Mine.'

'Yours!' Mei Hang and Hong looked at the baby speechlessly.

'Pulok never knew. Pulok had come to the camp, you know. We heard Addison sahab had accompanied him. They were not allowed to see anyone. Don't think negatively of him, Mei Lin,' Mei Hang said slowly.

At that moment in the radio, came the familiar voice of a newsreader.

'This is Radio Peking. I am Ameng Tham ...'

Eight

'Hey move back, move back. I will take my things first.'

Pushing aside Lee Chang with his elbow, a local boy went forward to the canteen counter. The people who had come to the canteen instantly became silent and looked fearfully at them.

Lee Chang's face turned red in humiliation. He stopped for a moment and went forward, placed his hand on the boy's shoulder and made him turn towards him and asked quickly, 'Want to take your stuff first? Based on what rules?'

The boy removed Lee Chang's hand from his shoulder and said, 'Shut your mouth and go back. This is not your India. This is China.'

'Do you think I am scared? This is Hua qiao Nongchang.'

'Hua qiao! Or refugee? This is not Hua qiao Nongchang now. Now we are also part of it. Don't talk big. We won't tolerate refugees talking big. You grabbed our land, snatched our food and now you are talking big to us!'

At that moment Liang, Hong and Akong came towards them. Seeing them, a few of the local boys also came forward. Sensing that a fight was brewing, Liang Ching Wan came between the two groups. This prompted the local boys to move away in irritation. He was a politically powerful man. They couldn't antagonise him.

Liang Ching Wan pacified the boys. With red faces, Lee Chang and the others took their stuff from the canteen and went back. There was nothing they could do.

The Cultural Revolution was on. Schools and colleges had closed down. The students in their thousands had become members of the Red Guards and took part in the process of change. It was the time of youth revolution in China. Chairman

Mao had entrusted the youth with the responsibility of modernising the country.

It had been over four years now since Mei Lin and the others had come to China. Although this was a remote area, the wave of the Cultural Revolution had touched this place as well. No one could speak openly anymore. People were punished over little things.

The situation had changed a lot in the farms too.

The government had adopted a new policy in order to lessen the growing tension between the locals and the refugees. As the farm population had more than doubled, the facilities decreased. The adults of the villages from which the land had been taken to create the farms were recognised as co-opted members of the same. Now they also had access to all the facilities that were given to the refugees. Although this step had helped ease the tension between the locals and the refugees, no friendship had developed between them yet.

The refugees began to dislike the locals as they had become partners in their farms and shared their facilities. Both the parties hated each other. There was no possibility of mingling between the two groups in the near future.

What would they do in this country? Would this handful of people be able to live in isolation?

The thought of returning was slowly taking root in their minds. After the Cultural Revolution started, this thought became more intense. However, no one had thought of returning to India. They knew that it was not possible. At the same time the will to live in this country was also becoming weak. But such a thought did not arise in the minds of the children who had grown up after arriving in China. They were immersed in the euphoria of the Cultural Revolution.

Youngsters like Babu and Anjali were no longer in the refugee camps. They had joined the Red Guards and left the farm. No one knew where they were, what they were doing, or when they would return. Liang Ching Wan had gone to Peking to join the foundation day meeting, and had returned only the previous day. He had brought news about Babu and the others. They had also gone to attend the meeting of the Red Guards there.

Slowly things were changing. After the start of the revolution, a feeling of fear had encircled the people. The main reason was the daily evening meeting held after work in the farm.

The manager of the farm and the local leaders were present at these meetings. Newspapers were read. They were apprised of government policies. They read quotations from Mao's writing. The Cultural Revolution was discussed. The leadership of Chairman Mao was also discussed. People engaged in reactionary activities were denounced in the meeting and also punished. They found fault with minor things. Everyone was given a Red Book. In Communist China, the refugees had to be loyal to communism and the great Chairman Mao. Those who were not had to accept public denouncement and physical punishment.

They were kept under strict surveillance all the time. The Chinese government did not trust the refugees who had come from the reactionary environment of India.

The refugees lived in fear. They spoke with utmost care. Especially those who did not take PRC passports while they were in India and those who did not have any papers. The people most in danger were those of Indian origin and the Indians of Chinese origin. The people with PRC passports were relatively more confident. They were less dissatisfied than the others. They did not feel like outsiders, unlike the others. They had a good relationship with the local CPC. Among them, Liang Ching Wan's position was the most powerful. He had supported the communist government even when he was in India and also worked actively here. The leaders of the central CPC also knew him. Because of his good personal record, he held a comfortable position at the farm too.

Having come back to their desired place and getting the proper recognition, the faces of those with Chinese passports reflected the brightness of satisfaction and pride amidst suffering. They were slowly getting involved in the party's work. Everyone listened to them, especially Liang Ching Wan, and expected that they would provide them security as he had become politically powerful. But the local leaders hated and envied Liang Ching Wan and the others. There were a few who wanted to harm them.

After Lee Chang and his friends left, Liang Ching Wan stayed back talking with the people, a Red Book in his hand. His mind was filled with happiness. He had got a chance to meet Mao. He had come to the canteen to share his happiness and his experiences with others. His political position had not been easy to attain, especially an overseas Chinese person.

He was describing his experience in Peking with great enthusiasm. People listened to him in awe. For people of such a remote area, Peking was a distant land and Mao was in a more distant planet.

'I was very close to him. Then they called me. They introduced me to Chairman Mao.'

'Chairman Mao?' they asked in awe.

'Yes. Chairman Mao. He looked at me and smiled. But he didn't talk to me. I saluted him.'

'How does Chairman Mao look?'

'Fat. Very fat. Fat like a pig,' he laughed joyously. 'He has become old. Very old. It was great to see him. It felt like meeting God.'

After a while, the returnees got up to leave.

Today, on the occasion of China's National Day, the school children had organized a special function.

Audience members were seated in the school courtyard where a temporary stage had been set up, covered with bed sheets. The children were enthusiastically preparing for the function. Pramila Gogoi had not come today. She had been running a temperature for a few days. Today, the chief organiser of this program was Mei Hang.

Most of the children could now read and write Chinese. They spoke Hindi, Nepalese and Assamese, and few Chinese words and sentences could be heard interspersed with these languages.

Mei Lin's daughter knew Assamese better than the others. Mei Lin didn't pressurize her daughter over anything other than learning Assamese. She wanted her daughter to learn not only the Assamese language but also about Assam's history and culture. She kept aside some time to teach her daughter these things every day. She told the stories time and again to her daughter. She started copying from Pramila Gogoi's book and also wrote from memory but stopped midway because of the direction of the camp manager. She had collected the three Assamese novels which belonged to Pulok that Ming brought with him. With Pulok's name written on them, they had become a part of her heart. She kept the books at her bedside and leafed through them at least once every day and made her daughter read from them.

Mei Lin's daughter wore a mekhela-chador today. At Mei Hang's direction, she paid obeisance to the stage by touching the floor, and then stood before the audience. Mei Lin came and sat next to Mei Fung.

Two and a half years had passed since Mei Fung had married Liang. She was expecting their first child. She did not brood like before.

'Namaskar. My name is Kumari Lailin Baruah. I am going to sing a song,' Mei Lin's daughter said.

Hong sat, using a metal saucepan to play the beats. Yunlin's husband got ready with his flute. Swaying and clapping to the beat, Lailin started to sing.

'*O Aai, amar kopalote*
Ronga sendurere
Tilok aaki diya;
Dawor faali rong melaloi jao.
O Mother, decorate my forehead
With a vermillion dot;
I am going to the fair of happiness Beyond the clouds.'

After Lailin's song ended, Ajoli Sonowal's three daughters, Maina, Moni and Tunu, started singing a song from a popular Assamese film. The colour of sorrow was slowly being wiped off the faces of the people. In its place a kind of happiness was visible. One programme followed another. Mei Hang in male attire came to the stage with Ming to do a skit. The courtyard was filled with laughter at their antics.

When the function was over, it was time for their regular evening meeting. The people stood up cheerfully to go to the meeting. The local members of the farm had already reached the hall.

Huge posters of Chairman Mao had been hung on the walls of the meeting hall. A few other symbolic propaganda posters had also been put up alongside. The environment in the hall was ominously sombre. People were afraid to talk. They became anxious at the thought of who would be punished. The evening meetings were such that they rarely let people feel at home.

Holding the Red Book in their hands, people sat in the hall. They were talking among themselves in hushed voices. The local people were sitting around them. If they heard some familiar words, they would misinterpret them and inform the party leaders. The refugees had already been punished in different ways because of such misinterpretation by the locals. People who had come from India kept a distance from the locals. They never made any comments before them.

As soon as the two local leaders of the CPC and the manager of the farm entered, the hall turned silent. After sometime came a few local officials of the newly formed 'Revolutionary Committee'.

At first there was a roll call. Then the manager of the farm said a few things related to farming and sat down. After him stood a local CPC leader. He picked up a copy of *The People's Daily* and started reading the editorial.

Liang Ching Wan was looking at the grave faces of the leaders with unease and surprise. He was not invited to translate like on other days. Today, Chow Chi Yong was translating in his place.

What had happened today? What had gone wrong?

Slowly Liang Ching Wan started to sweat. Something had happened somewhere. Something bad.

Today no one looked at him. The local leaders, who used to talk to him with all importance, did not even smile at him today.

'Ho Mei Fung.'

'Mei Fung, they are calling you,' Mei Lin nudged Mei Fung gently.

Mei Fung who was immersed in her own thoughts stood up, worried. Everyone in the hall looked at her. Everyone looked tense.

'Today you ate the peanuts which were given to you for sowing. Our supervisor saw you. True or not?'

Mei Fung's face turned pale. She stood still for a while and then cast her eyes down.

'Yes I did. Only a handful. I was hungry. I –'

'It may be one or a handful. That was the seed for production. You have obstructed the process of production. It is a crime equal to treason. This is reactionary.'

Mei Fung stood with her head down. She looked as if all the blood had been sucked out of her face.

'For your first crime as a refugee, we will not punish you. But three days of food coupons will be deducted. You also have to stand here and face denouncement and apologize. Come over here.'

Liang's face had hardened. Before Mei Fung could go to the dais, he stood up and said, 'She is pregnant. Please forgive her. Just for a fistful of nuts –'

'A fistful of nuts? A fistful of seeds! What do you want to say – Mei Fung has not committed a crime?'

'It is a crime. But think of her physical condition, sir. Even in this state she has been working. She has not said she won't work. At such times, women feel like eating different things. That is why –'

The hall fell silent. Everyone looked at him with surprise and fear. The faces of the leaders had become stern. They talked amongst themselves and then looked at Liang. 'Safeguarding a criminal is also a crime. You will receive equal punishment for encouraging reactionary activity.'

'I have not committed any crime, sir. Mei Fung is my wife. It is my duty to protect her and my unborn child.'

The leaders looked at Liang in disbelief. A refugee was protesting!

'Hey, why don't you go up? Hey reactionary, capitalist roader!' someone from the local group shouted.

The faces of most of the locals brightened. A foreign devil was going to be punished. Now they could say whatever came to their minds in the name of denouncement.

Three men came down and pushed Liang to the dais.

'Kowtow. Kneel. Touch the floor with your head and ask for forgiveness,' one of the leaders thundered.

Liang's eyes turned red and his face turned stiff.

'I won't. I won't kowtow.'

'You won't kowtow? How dare you!' With one punch, Liang was pushed back.

Another person pulled him by the chest. After a few slaps and punches they forcibly made him kneel, pushing his head down to the floor. The locals started denouncing him. After some time, one of the leaders pulled him up by his hair and dragged him to a side.

'You stand here bowing till the meeting is over. Don't raise your head even for a second.'

Mei Fung started weeping. Most of the people were paralysed with fear. Lee Chang and the others stood transfixed, their eyes red.

Was there any point in protesting? Protest meant more punishment. More horrible than punishment was suspicion. Being labelled anti-Communist and anti-Mao meant a dark future.

His friends were irritated with Liang. What was the need to protest! At the same time, they were aggrieved, too. It was not right to create an issue over a woman in an advanced stage of pregnancy eating a fistful of peanuts. It was not a crime trying to protect one's wife.

'Liang will be kept in isolation,' one of the leaders announced and then changed the subject.

'Under the leadership of our great Chairman Mao, the glorious Cultural Revolution is underway in China. This revolution has brought complete change in the communist state system, which has been established under the leadership of great Chairman Mao, overthrowing the Kuomintang rule. To insult such a great leader means insulting the country and insulting a social revolution. But unfortunately, someone among us has brought a bad name to this farm by insulting our great Chairman Mao. Liang Ching Wan, do you admit to this crime?'

Liang Ching Wan stood up. His face went pale. He looked at the leaders in extreme surprise. Standing speechless for some time, he spoke, his voice trembling.

'I am a Communist. I supported the Great Revolution of China even when I was in India. Even after that I worked in support of the PRC. I am loyal to the great Chairman Mao. I have not said anything against our great Chairman to my knowledge.'

'To lie is anti-revolutionary. Don't try to take refuge in a lie. What did you say today? Great Chairman Mao is fat like a pig?'

Shocked to the core, Liang Ching Wan looked at the dais. Silence pervaded the auditorium.

'I – I said that, sir. But I did not say that to ridicule. We usually use this word for fat people and I unknowingly used it.'

'You don't have any right to make such a comment about our great Chairman Mao. This crime deserves denouncement and severest of the severe punishment. Come. Come over here.'

Liang Ching Wan slowly went up to the dais, his heart shattering into a million pieces, as well as his faith and his confidence in Red China.

He silently faced his denouncement. The people from India who did not support Red China while they were there were staring at him.

The feeling of defeat weighed heavy on Liang Ching Wan. He was destroyed from inside. He knew that this was not the end of his punishment. There would be many more rounds after this. He did not know what. He only knew it would be terrifying. Very terrifying.

After the meeting got over, everyone came out of the room quietly. Liang did not come. He would be taken somewhere else. Mei Fung came out of the hall weeping. Mei Lin held her hand and said slowly, 'Have patience, Mei Fung.'

'How can I? How much can I? I am not able to bear it, Mei Lin ache.'

No one was able to bear it. Everyone was broken. A storm was brewing.

How could they live in this country? How could they bear the harshness of this country? The confinement?

The memories of a free life in the country that they had left behind were burning inside them. They were restless with the intense urge to return. Then they stopped again. Where would they return? To India? Was that country less heartless? Was that country less cruel?

Mei Lin returned to her room. Seeing her mother, Lailin came to her anxiously. Liang Ching Wan's family lived adjacent to Mei Lin's room. The sound of crying could be heard from there.

'Why are they crying, Maa?' she asked fearfully.

'Liang apak was scolded at the meeting.'

'Why did they scold him, Maa?'

'He said something bad about Chairman Mao. That's why. Never say anything bad about anyone in front of others. Or else they will scold us. We will have to cry too.'

'I won't.'

'Now you study. I will cook.'

Without any protest, Lailin sat down to study. Even though she was a young girl, the farm environment had made her mature beyond her years. She knew the name of Chairman Mao. Holding the Red Book, they praised Chairman Mao. They raised the Red Book and shouted, 'Long live Chairman Mao.'

After dinner, Mei Lin put her daughter to bed, and turned the lamp off. It was not permitted to keep a lamp burning at night. As she lay down, she took Lailin into her arms. Her mind was disturbed. A feeling of fear had started to engulf her with its darkness. Liang's face, reddened with multiple emotions, was fleeting back and forth in her mind. She also recalled seeing Liang Ching Wan's eyes moisten with pain.

Suddenly she got up, startled.

Someone was knocking nearby. The sound of crying could be heard. Someone was being harshly reprimanded.

Sitting still for a while, she silently got down from her bed. She opened the door a little and peeped outside. Like hers, the other doors, too, had opened a little. A few fearful eyes, hiding in the darkness, watched the people who were outside.

Four people. No – three people were pushing one person forward.

Mei Lin was petrified.

Liang Ching Wan!

Three people were taking Liang Ching Wan away. The door to his room was open. The sounds of restrained cries were coming from the room. Mei Lin stood for a while, before retreating and slowly shuting her door.

There was nothing one could do. Nothing. The Communist Party was all-powerful in this country. The power to control others' fates was in the hands of the officials of the Revolutionary Committee. Mei Lin and the others were nothing but particles of dust in this land. They could not prevent the punishment given to Liang Ching Wan, a hard-core Communist and a stern supporter of Chairman Mao.

Mei Lin returned and sat on the bed. She couldn't sleep anymore.

Liang Ching Wan was being pushed and shoved and taken down the dark road. They looked like phantoms passing through the wild shrubs in the moonlight. No one was talking. After walking for half an hour, they stopped in an isolated place with trees all around. Two other people were already there waiting for them.

They pushed Liang Ching Wan forward with a single thrust.

'Liang Ching Wan – speak the truth – for what purpose has the Indian government sent you here?' one of the two people waiting there asked harshly.

Liang Ching Wan looked at the shadowed faces in utter disbelief.

'Why – why would the Indian government send me, sir?'

'Don't you know? Have you not been given the responsibility to send secret information to India?'

'No one has given me any responsibility. I am a die-hard Communist. Don't distrust me, sir. I am a well-wisher of this country. When the Chinese origin people of India opposed China in the time of the Sino-Indian war, I wrote in favour of China in the China Review. As a punishment the Indian government seized my account with the Bank of China. They arrested me from Tangra in Calcutta and sent me to jail. This is on the record. Kindly go through it.' His voice was choked.

'There is now a black line under your name. Now you too are among the returnees from India who are under suspicion. Speak. Speak the truth.'

'I am not a spy. I am a supporter of Red China. I am a supporter of the Great Chairman Mao. Please trust me.'

One of the men landed a big blow on Liang Ching Wan. Immediately everyone started beating him. Liang Ching Wan silently bore the torture. Tears rolled down his eyes. In the pale moonlight and mist, he fell onto the ground where death sentences were executed.

The people kicked him a few more times and then, grabbing him by his hair, pulled him up. After kicking him a few more times, they left.

It was almost dawn by the time Liang Ching Wan returned to his room. He drank the water his wife held out to him. He sat expressionless while his wife nursed and dressed him. Then he looked at the tear-streaked faces of every member of his family. A faint smile came to his face. After a while, he fell asleep. His wife covered him with a blanket. There was no one in China who did not know what happened to suspicious and reactionary people in the time of the Cultural Revolution.

Nine

The people were working the fields in silence.

It felt as though someone had snatched away from them the laughter that had slowly started to return. The environment of the farm had completely changed. Terror, frustration, uncertainty and grief had besieged them. It seemed as though they had returned to the last days in Makum. As if something was about to happen. As if a rough knock on their doors would shatter their lives again.

Here, there was nothing called justice. The CPC was breaking down. The will of the local leaders of the Revolutionary Committee had become the law. Now there was nothing that even resembled a local administration.

The country was gripped in chaos.

The people who were under the most suspicion were the overseas returnees. They were kept under strict and uninterrupted surveillance. The enemies of communism could be hidden among them. So could the spies of enemy countries.

What could the people of Hua qiao Nongchang do to protect themselves? Nothing at all. Extreme terror had strangled their voices.

Whom could they go to for help? Whom could they look up to? Who was there in this country to call their own? The officials of the Overseas Chinese Affairs Commission? Was there anyone who could reach them?

There was no one. There was no way to communicate with anyone directly. They did not have the right to. They could not take a single step without the knowledge of the local leaders of the CPC and the management of the farm. From the very beginning, the attitude of the local leaders of the CPC had not been favourable towards the returnees. They were in favour of the local people. The returnees were punished frequently, and if they protested, they faced torture from the local people. The Cultural Revolution was an opportunity for the local leaders to punish anyone at the slightest pretext.

Mei Fung was weeping as she worked. It had now been over a month since Liang had been taken away from the farm. He had been shifted to some other place. Every day he was brought to the evening meeting. He was asked the same question every day.

'Who has sent you here? Speak the truth. If you speak the truth your punishment will be lessened.'

Every day Liang had to face public denouncement. Every day he was beaten. He was compelled to kowtow through the whole meeting. He was punched and beaten if he moved even a little.

Mei Fung's heart was broken. Slowly, she was losing patience. Not only her, but everyone had become restless. The sad and tired face of Liang tolerating all the punishment had started eroding their patience.

This large-hearted man had given back Mei Fung her life. Keeping inside her heart the memory of her would-be husband San Kong, she had started a new life with Liang. Whenever San Kong's memory overwhelmed her, Liang was there to comfort her.

What would she do? What could she do to help Liang? Some had advised her to tolerate the pain of watching him suffer. If she protested, there was the possibility of more punishment. Others told her that she would not be able to live comfortably in China with Liang, labelled as an 'overseas black line'. After this, he would be deprived of all facilities. He would face trouble at every step. Not only Liang, but Mei Fung and her yet-to-be born child and everyone from their family, would have to suffer all the difficulties which the family of a 'capitalist roader' had to face. The only way to escape all this was to disown Liang.

Would Mei Fung save herself by disowning Liang? Would she be able to do that? Was that the right thing to do?

It was not possible. She would face whatever difficulties came her way. What would she do with a secure life obtained by disowning Liang?

Hearing the whistle that signalled the end of the day, Mei Fung looked up. She washed her hands and slowly left the field. She returned to the farm with Mei Lin and the others silently.

At that time in the barracks, the people who reached before them had gathered sadly in the courtyard. Some among them were weeping.

Their heart missed a beat. What had happened and to whom? Mei Lin and the others rushed. Pramila Gogoi was lying on her bed. She was no more. The barracks were filled with the sound of crying.

'Your mother's wish had been to be cremated as a Hindu, and that her ashes be immersed in the Ganges,' Ho Min Fu said, wiping his tears.

A group of little children carrying tender leaves in their hands entered with Mei Hang to pay their last respects to Pramila Gogoi. Having placed these over her body, they folded their hands in obeisance. Ajoli Sonowal came in, bathed and wearing Assamese clothes. She said goodbye with a sorrowful prayer.

Placing Pramila's body on a pier, her sons carried her away for cremation. Some other boys also accompanied them. After sitting for a while people left to freshen up. They could not change the routine just because someone had died.

In the meeting hall, Liang stood gravely. He was wearing a pointed paper hat. From his neck hung a paper denouncing him. In the last few days, Liang had become weaker and thinner. His eyes had sunken in. He looked extremely tired. One could tell that he was going through a whirlwind of torture.

Mei Fung went and sat among the people. She looked at Liang and started weeping. Liang looked at her, his eyes extremely grave, his face stiff.

The farm manager and the local CPC leaders walked in. First came the roll call. After that, one of the officials of the CPC asked, 'Why are there less people today?'

'Pramila Gogoi has died. Some have gone for her cremation.'

'When did they take her?'

'About two hours back.'

'If so, the cremation should have been over by now. Why have they not come back? It is alright that her family members have not come. What about the others? Call them.'

With a dull face, the farm manager went to call the boys. After some time, Lee Chang and the others came in with him angrily.

No one had the will to attend the meeting today. The ruthlessness of this life had affected them to their core. They were not prepared to listen to talk of social revolution, Mao's sayings and *The People's Daily* editorial.

They could not show their disinterest. If they did, a black mark declaring them 'anti-revolutionary' would be stamped on their personal record. The people were looking blankly at the leaders, pretending to listen.

In the beginning, a few things related to the farm were discussed. After that the editorial of *The People's Daily* and other news items read. Then they opened the Red Book. Then finally came the phase of denouncing Liang. That done, and after a long lecture on reactionary forces, anti-revolutionary activities and the Cultural Revolution, the leaders of the local CPC sat down. After him stood another local leader.

It was now Hong's turn. Hearing his name, he stood up.

'We have received a complaint that yesterday you quarrelled once again in the market. True or not?'

Hong's face turned red instantly. After a while he said slowly, 'They ridiculed us as refugees and foreign devils. That's why –'

The leader looked at him for some time and asked, 'Are you all not refugees?'

Everyone in the hall looked at Hong. Controlling himself with all his strength, he looked up at the leader.

'Sir, this country gave us shelter at a difficult time. When we left India forever, we did not come here to live as refugees. We feel hurt when we are insulted as refugees and foreign devils.' Can't we expect a little respect even as refugees from the people of this country? We work here like everyone else. We never object to anything.'

'What do you mean to say? Were you more comfortable in India?'

Hong stopped. These people were pretending not to understand. They were looking to trap him with his own words. Could he expect justice from these people? Was there any use of reasoning with these people? Hong looked at them and tried again.

'I did not mean to say that, sir. But one thing is true, before the war we really lived in comfort. If the war had not happened, we would not have come here. No one would have been able to humiliate us. Before the war, we lived in peace and happiness in India. At least there was no famine, no meetings were held in the evenings and –' Hong stopped midway.

The hall fell eerily silent. The leaders were shocked at the man's unbelievable insolence.

'Now, we are always at fault. We have lost many things, sir. Half of our people are left behind in India. Our lives are shattered forever. The government has given us houses to stay in, land to cultivate and rice to eat. We are grateful to the government, sir. We have not occupied anyone's land. We have not snatched food from any one's share. Please believe us sir, if we had any other way, we would not have troubled you. We would have gone away from this country too,' Hong's voice was becoming choked.

The local people fell silent. Tears brimmed in the eyes of the people who had come from India. Only one leader flared up.

'Where would you have gone? To India?'

'I don't know, sir.'

'Don't you know? We know. We are observing. We have been observing from the time you arrived from India. You don't have any faith in our great Chairman Mao. You don't have any loyalty towards the People's Republic of China, too.'

'We want to stay loyal, sir. You have provided us with shelter. You can do whatever you want with us.'

'Your behaviour is suspicious. We have information; you always try to provoke others by talking this way. Who has sent you here? Who has deputed you?'

'Kindly don't doubt our honesty, sir. No one has sent us.'

'Come over here. You have to apologize, for expressing no confidence in Great Chairman Mao and Communist China. You have to accept punishment for the anti-revolutionary activities that you have been carrying on, living as a refugee.'

After standing still for a while, Hong went forward resolutely. As soon as he reached the dais, one of the leaders punched him hard and growled at him.

'Who has sent you? Under whose direction are you sowing seeds of rebellion amongst the people? Under whose direction are you conducting all these anti-revolutionary activities?'

Two more officials started thrashing him.

'Don't beat him. Please don't. I beg of you,' Hong's mother cried out. So did his father.

Ming stood up. So did Lee Chang, Akong, Tung Chin's two elder brothers and Yunlin's husband. Lao Thien Lee, Ho Chang Ho, Mok Min and his sons, Mei Hang, Mei Fung, Ahlin, Wenlin and some others also stood up.

Disregarding the order to keep bowing in front of the officials, Liang stood straight as well. He came forward and said firmly, 'Don't beat him.'

One official turned towards Liang. 'Why shouldn't we beat him? Because he is from your group? Alright. Then you tell us who has sent him.' The official slapped Liang hard.

Looking at the official's eyes, Liang said coolly, 'No one has sent us. If you think that someone has sent us, then it is you. You have sent us. You have appointed us. I –'

One official came forward and punched him with all his force. Immediately two others joined him; one of them had a stick.

'Confess. Who has sent you – confess. If you confess, your punishment will be reduced.' They started beating him.

'I won't. I won't confess. What will you do? Will you kill me? Kill. Kill us. We are already dead. How will you kill us again?'

With a grave and red face, Mei Lin stood up. She went to the dais and said resolutely, 'Leave them, sir.'

They stopped and looked at Mei Lin with surprise.

'They are not spies. No one has sent them. No one has sent us either. We were sent away from India, sir. We are not spies,' Akong said and stood up.

'We are not spies. We worked hard for a living in India. They arrested and put us in jail suspecting us to be China's spies. All our belongings were taken away. We were kept in a cowshed. Now you all are telling that we are India's spies. Someone has sent us. What will we do, sir? What will we do?'

'If you need to punish, then you must punish us as well,' Lao Thien Lee said.

'Punish me, too. Kill us. Instead of killing us little by little, finish us in one go. Let all the sufferings be over. We can't tolerate this anymore,' Yiu Yi's father said, sobbing.

Almost everyone was weeping. Some were sitting with their heads down, some pulling their hair, while some others were covering their faces.

The officials stood baffled. They could not let these people, who were on the verge of rebellion, go on any further. If the situation deteriorated any further, the news might reach the higher authorities. The local leaders of the CPC and the affairs commission might get into trouble.

Pushing Hong and Liang aside, one of the officials shouted, 'The meeting is over for now. Hong and Liang will be tried later. Great Chairman Mao has directed us to find and punish the anti-revolutionaries. The State Council and the central committee of the Overseas Chinese Commission will be informed about those who try to obstruct the execution of this direction. Hong and Liang are ordered to stay in the barracks till we receive further instructions. No one should try to rebel in any way. This is the People's Republic of China. No anti-Communist activity will be tolerated. We have detailed records of all the overseas Chinese living here with us. We know very well who has how much loyalty towards the PRC. Stand in line. Everyone stand in a line quietly. Move out in order.'

The people fell silent. They stood in the line in silence and returned to the barracks tearfully.

Lailin was sitting gloomily with a notebook in hand. As soon as she saw Mei Lin, she hugged her and cried, 'Grandma has died. Oh Ma, grandma has died.'

Mei Lin took her into her arms and sat silently. Her mind was in a frenzy. Her eyes brimmed with tears. What future was she going to give her daughter! Was this the life of a human being?

There was nothing outside this world, this paddy field and the barracks. Even within it, they had no liberty to breathe freely. They didn't have the liberty to laugh or speak freely. They were deprived of the liberty to take their own decisions. They were nothing but trapped insects in the web of the will of a few local leaders.

Lailin's soft and supple body had become pale. Her eyes had lost their brightness. What could Mei Lin do? Where was the road to freedom? Where was the way to bloom?

There was nothing but darkness on all sides. There was no ray of light anywhere. How could Mei Lin let her daughter live the life of a farmer in Hua qiao Nongchang?

'I won't. I will take Lailin away from this darkness devoid of air. I will,' she told herself.

It was getting darker outside. The inside of the barracks became silent. Suddenly, there was a bang on her door. Lailin hugged her mother fearfully. Mei Lin opened the door, looking worried. The manager of the farm was standing with a grave face.

'They have called you to the office.'

'To the office? Now?'

'Yes. Now. Come.'

'Why have they called me?'

'I don't know. Why are you asking so many questions? They have called you to the office. Why do you want to know the reason?' the manager thundered. Then lowering his voice, he said, 'Why did you confront them today? Don't you know the situation? If I could, I would have helped you. There is no way out. Don't argue. Accept whatever they say. Otherwise you will be in trouble.' The man left without waiting for Mei Lin's reaction.

Mei Lin stood there dumbstruck for some time and returned to Lailin. She pacified her and, leaving her in Ajoli Sonowal's room, went to the office.

The local leaders were there seated in their imperious chairs. Liang, Hong, Lee Chang, Akong, Wai Kwan, Mei Fung and Mei Hang were standing before them. One of the officials said without any preamble, 'All of you will be transferred to a labour reform camp tomorrow morning. Be prepared.'

Ten

Mei Lin, along with a few other women, picked out the mature silkworms from a bamboo tray and put them on a separate one.

Her eyes had become heavy with sleep. Her body, already weakened by hard labour and malnutrition, was on the verge of breaking down. Lailin had been down with fever for the past three days. Mei Lin was unable to give her any medicines as there was no medical facility in the camp. Mei Lin was unable to get any sleep for the last few nights. She had to come out every morning to work. Here, she could not get any consideration just because her child was ill. Even though Mei Hang, Wai Kwan, Lee Chang, Liang, Hong and Tung Chin took turns to look after Lailin, Mei Lin still could not sleep. An unknown fear was consuming Mei Lin. She had become restless. She left Lailin under Mei Fung's care during the day. Mei Fung had not come to work because it had been only four days since she had given birth to a child.

Gathering all her strength, Mei Lin worked. She could not ask for a moment's rest. The stern-faced supervisor was moving around. Neglecting one's work would lead to harsh punishment.

This was a labour reform farm. These were special category state farms under the ministry of public security. These farms, in association with various industries, forcibly used political, religious and other prisoners in various production works. No one had any sympathy towards the people imprisoned here. These farms were established to reform the criminals as well as to use their labour in various works of the state. These camps were not for the criminals who were convicted legally by the court. Those who were labelled as reactionary and a threat to the state, along with those who were identified by the local administration and security force as petty criminals, were kept here.

When they reached the labour reform camp after walking a long distance and then partly travelling in a truck, they were totally exhausted. They could not even imagine the kind of pleasant surprise that was waiting for them there. After the initial formalities were over, when they approached the rows of thatched huts, they stopped midway, witnessing a near-impossible scene. With the setting sun behind him and carrying a bunch of sugarcane on his shoulder and wearing a straw hat, Tung Chin was coming from the opposite direction on a dusty road.

Tung Chin also stopped and looked at the group of familiar faces with children and belongings in hand.

In the last few years, they had withered.

About three years had passed by.

Besides rearing silkworms, Mei Lin and the others also assisted Lee Chang in the sugarcane fields.

However, Hong's condition had improved a little. One day, while the water of the fishery was being pumped out, the machine broke down. When the operator could not repair the machine, Hong went ahead and fixed it on his own.

That was the beginning. After he repaired the machine, the supervisors of the camp started to engage with him and soon came to depend on his skills. These days he was in charge of operating the machine. He fitted the machine in the boat and went to the town market to sell the farm produce once in a while and brought back human excreta to be used as manure. He had gone to the town the previous day to sell the farm produce and was due to return.

The environment of the labour reform camp, however, had changed to some extent now. New prisoners were coming in but in lesser numbers. The suspicions which had been directed at the Chinese refugees from abroad had slowly disappeared.

The internal situation in China had started changing after Mei Lin and the others had left Hua qiao Nongchang. It had begun after the central leadership decided to remove the Red Guards from the revolution. Slowly, things returned to normalcy.

Though it had almost been three years in this camp, no orders for their release had come. They were not even told the reason for their imprisonment. They had learnt from others that the length of imprisonment at this camp was never more than three years.

Slowly, they were breaking down. They were losing hope. Whenever they felt like compromising with their bleak future, the children provided them the thrust to live again. On hearing the whistle for lunch break, Mei Lin came out and returned to her room.

Inside the hut, Lailin was sleeping on a cloth spread over a gunny bag with a blanket over her. Mei Hang, Wai Kwan and Mei Fung's children were sitting close by. On a similar bed nearby, Mei Fung's baby was crying weakly. Mei Fung's breast milk had dried up. Glancing at the baby, Mei Lin sat near Lailin and placed her hand on her daughter's forehead. She was burning with fever.

Lailin opened her eyes and said, 'Water, Maa.'

Giving her some water and wiping her face with a wet cloth, Mei Lin stood up.

'I will go and get the food.'

Lailin didn't respond. When she returned with the corn gruel and boiled vegetables, Mei Fung was trying to pacify her baby.

She took some gruel and sat down to feed Lailin. She was still running a temperature.

Lailin gulped down a little gruel reluctantly and held her mother's hand.

Meanwhile Liang, Tung Chin, Lee Chang and Akong had come in with their food. They always ate their food together in Mei Lin's room. They stood near Lailin and tried to divert her thoughts, saying different things. Soon, Lailin shook her head.

'I won't eat more. I am not feeling well.'

Wiping her face and changing the cold towel on her forehead, Mei Lin sat down to eat. Mei Fung was feeding her baby. The baby was crying.

Liang looked at her and said, 'Lee Chang and I are going out. I will see if we can get milk somewhere. Let's see if there are any Chinese medicine shops here. We have to make sure Lailin's fever comes down.'

'You will be in danger if you are caught,' said Mei Fung.

Lee Chang and Liang went out. They walked through fields and villages. After some time, they stopped. To their utter surprise, they saw Ho Wang and Lao Thien Lee approaching from the opposite direction.

'Where are you coming from? You were in jail, weren't you?' Ho Wang asked.

'It is not exactly a jail. It is like a jail. We are still there.'

'How did you come out?'

'We sneaked out. We have come to find milk for Mei Fung's baby and medicines for Mei Lin's daughter.'

'Oh! Come, I'll take you to the shop.'

'You have become very thin and weak, Lee ako.'

'You too, Lee Chang.'

'Where are you coming from? Hua qiao Nongchang is very far from here,' Lee Chang asked.

'It has been one and half years since we left that place.'

'Did they allow you to leave?'

'Don't you know? The government has made new rules.'

'New rules?'

'Yes. Now you can decide for yourself, whether you want to live in Hua qiao Nongchang or not. If you wish to stay, you can. If you wish to leave, you're free to leave. These days we are permitted to work outside. There are no daily meetings like before. No one rebukes us for little things nowadays. I now work in a leather factory nearby.'

'Do you work in the factory too, Wang ako?'

'No. I had come to see Lee.'

'Where are you working?'

'I slaughter and sell beef in a shop run by a Chinese Pakistani,' Ho Wang laughed.

'What do you mean by Chinese Pakistani?'

'The Muslims of China!'

'Pakistanis of China!' Lao Thien Lee burst out laughing.

Lee Chang and Liang did not laugh. Their minds were too preoccupied.

'Do you get news from Nongchang?'

'We do. I went there two months back. I'm afraid I have bad news – your parents are not well, Lee Chang,' said Lao Thien.

Lee Chang kept silent. Instead, Liang asked slowly, 'Are they sick?'

'They are sick; they are despondent. There's lots of suffering. Many of their children were left behind in India. Now Lee Chang is not with them either.'

'Tung Chin is also with us, Lee ako.'

'Really? How did Tung Chin come to be there?'

'We don't know. He doesn't say anything if we ask. He works silently. He has almost lost his mind.'

'He was such a fun-loving guy. What happened?'

'Yes, ako. Akong has the same sorrows. But he is a little better than Tung Chin.'

'I will let his father know about Tung Chin and Mei Fung. He'll be very happy to hear about them. Akong's father is very old now. Everyone else is alright. But there is some bad news.

Akong's younger brother joined the Red Guards. No one knows where he is now. We heard that Akong's other brother will marry C Hoi's daughter.'

'Oh is that so? And how is C Hoi doing?'

'He is no longer in Nongchang. We don't know where he went.'

'And what about Hong's parents? And Ming?'

'Hong's father is very ill. His mother is fine. Ming has gone to work in a factory. Mei Lin's uncle died almost a year back.'

'Really? What happened?'

'He had lost his mind. He kept on talking about going back to Makum. He used to cry. He neither worked, nor ate. Then one day, he collapsed in the fields. After two days he died. He died crying, do you know! Babu now works in a textile factory. Many other children have gone out to work. All have grown up. Some are still engaged in farming. Yiu Yi's two elder brothers, having finished their studies, are working in good positions in Peking. What kind of work, I don't know. Do you remember Parbati, Babu's mother? Her health has deteriorated. Mok Min is very ill. Ho Chang Ho is fine too, but cries a lot remembering his sons. Chow Chi Yong, his wife and many other elders have become old. They sit quietly and weep. K. P. Lee doesn't talk to anyone these days. He sits and works quietly. How rich he was! Enjoyed so many comforts!'

It was late afternoon by the time they picked up the medicines and reached the leather factory. Lao Thien Lee went inside and called his wife. She worked in the canteen. After talking to them for a while she went in to get some milk for them.

'I am considering running away to Hong Kong secretly,' Ho Wang said.

'Hong Kong? How?'

'Through an illegal route. There are people to assist, if someone wishes to flee. But they ask for a lot of money. Your asow says she won't live here. It is not like Makum. We will leave secretly for Hong Kong. I told her to hide in a vegetable basket for a few hours and then disappear. Tell me if you can endure the journey,' Ho Wang laughed.

'I won't go,' Lao Thien Lee said. 'Your asow is from this place. She likes it here. Our own people are here. I have told Ho Wang not to take the illegal route. I have heard that a new law will be passed for the overseas Chinese. People who have relatives outside China are allowed to go there.'

Lao Thien's wife returned holding a packet in her hand.

'There is milk and some food and toffees for the children. Some clothes for you all as well,' she said.

'When you come next time, inform the authorities. The rules are much more relaxed than before.'

When Liang and Lee Chang returned to the camp, it was dark. Hong had returned from the town, too. Everyone was in Mei Lin's room.

Lailin had fainted. Mei Lin was crying in despair. Everyone else stood motionless beside her.

Lee Chang handed the medicines to Mei Lin.

Lailin's temperature decreased slowly. Mei Lin wiped her tears. Mei Hang started to unpack the bundles Liang and Lee Chang had brought.

'Look what we have brought, Lailin,' Lee Chang gave her a handful of toffees and smiled.

Lailin looked at the toffees in surprise and extended her hand to take one. A faint smile emerged. Holding Lee Chang's hand she slowly got up and sat on the bed. All the other children came and stood near her with cheerful faces, toffees in their hands.

After Mei Fung's child went to sleep, the other children had their gruel and sausage and followed suit, content. The adults ate and sat down to talk. After sharing all the information they had got from Lee and Wang, Lee Chang asked Hong, 'Is it true what Lee ako has said?'

'I have heard the same. I don't know how far it is true. I have heard that the government will announce special policies for the overseas Chinese. Whichever country we decide to live in, we need to show we have relatives there. I have heard that it will be easier for those who are not married. It will be very difficult for us. You will have more difficulty, Mei Lin.'

Mei Lin looked at Hong with tired eyes.

'Let us get out of here. Is this a life fit for a human being? I can't take it anymore. Do something, Hong. Do it fast.'

'Mei Lin is right,' Mei Hang said. 'We can't let our children grow up here. Without education, they will have to work as labourers wherever they go. Find a way out, Hong. There is definitely a way out.'

'If the government has really made the policy, we will be able to leave. But it will take time if we have to follow the rules; we are married and don't have anyone in Hong Kong. I have also heard that the exit permit will be given to all. But when! No one knows. But there is a way for you, Mei Lin. I have learned something else. But I don't know how will you take it –'

Hong looked at Mei Lin's eyes for a while and said hesitantly, 'If you get married to someone from abroad then the government cannot stop you.'

Marry? Someone from abroad? How preposterous!

Mei Lin looked at Hong, stunned.

'Do I need to get married to be able to leave this place? But what about Pulok? Do I erase all hope of meeting Pulok again?' she thought to herself.

She looked at the pale face of her sleeping child.

The turmoil in her heart was overpowering.

Everyone fell silent. Collecting herself, Mei Lin said slowly, 'I have a husband, Hong.'

'I know. But that does not count for much in this country.'

Looking at Mei Lin's surprised eyes, Hong resumed.

'Many have gone to Hong Kong this way. This is the business of some people in Hong Kong. Getting married and taking people there. There are middlemen for this kind of work. I have met them. The marriage will take place here, according to the law. You will have to do only one thing – when you start working after reaching Hong Kong, you will have to pay whoever you marry. You don't have to stay as a couple. In a few months, you can divorce him. Think about it, Mei Lin.

A plate fell on the floor and broke into pieces. Someone was shouting and abusing somebody.

The harsh sound of the abuse jolted Lailin back. Raising her head from Arunabh's book, she looked around.

Tears brimmed in her eyes. Her heart had grown tumultuous with innumerable emotions.

Was this the way her mother had brought her to Hong Kong? Did she pay the person she called her father by washing dishes in the restaurants? Was that how she had educated her? Did she open the door to light for her in this way?

Her mother had never spoken of all this to her. She had remained silent against all her criticisms. She had been paying for Lailin's freedom, for her sunny life, for her success, for her happiness.

Her mother had sacrificed her hopes and dreams of reuniting with her husband. She had only one photograph, of their marriage, along with a leather bag, one letter, and three novels, each autographed by her father. She had never expressed her will to meet Lailin's father even once.

Would Lailin get angry at her mother ever again for her love of India, after understanding how deeply she was in love with her father? Was Lailin so heartless? Didn't she understand that at the source of all her hatred for India was a deep wound that had been inflicted by a cruel country and an uncaring father?

The sound of abuse was coming from the hall. Wiping her tears and putting down the book, Lailin went to the room. Her mother was trying to pacify and make her virtual father sit.

'Don't be angry, Wong. Please sit. I will tell you something today. Sit.'

The man sat down and said angrily, 'Say whatever you have to quickly. I have to go to the hospital.'

'Please try to be a little polite. Lailin feels bad when she hears you abusing. If you are not keeping well, then don't keep on coming here. I will go instead. I will try to give you a little more money. I will tell Lailin. She will also give you some. She did not know about you. Now she does. She will understand. You have not done me any harm.You have married me for money. You have done me a favour by marrying me. It is because of you that Lailin has a good life today. Believe me, I have good feelings for you. I wish that everything goes well with you. But please leave now. I would feel better if I could give you some more dollars.'

The man looked speechlessly at Mei Lin. The woman who had kept silent all these years had spoken today. Did she always have good feelings for him?

The man slowly got up. Lailin was looking at him, standing in the doorway. She looked at him closely for the first time in many years. A skinny, sick old man in worn-out clothes. A withered face. A pair of lifeless eyes.

Lailin felt a strange sorrow. She returned to her room hurriedly, took out a few hundred-dollar notes and returned. The man was near the door. Handing out the notes, Lailin said slowly, 'Take this.'

The man looked at the notes and then at her in surprise.

'You need it,' said Lailin.

The man looked at her eyes. Then, ignoring the cash, he left.

'Let him go,' her mother said slowly.

Lailin looked at her mother with confusion. She was picking up the broken pieces of the plate from the floor. She went and sat beside her. Her mother looked at her and said softly, 'I can do it, dear.'

'I know you can. But let me help you.'

Holding her mother's hand, Lailin helped her mother up and said anxiously, 'You have fever!'

'If I rest for a while, I will be fine,' her mother smiled.

'Are you a doctor?' she said angrily, handing the thermometer to her mother.

Seeing her mother's frail, wrinkled hand, Lailin was suddenly overcome with emotion. She knelt down on the floor and placed her head on her mother's lap.

Eleven

I am not the architect of this narrative.

I am but an inept artist attempting to narrate the epic saga of pain and anguish of a helpless community caught in the maelstrom of history.

I am now out of words and space. Whose stories should I tell? Whose anguish should I depict? Every one of them has been carrying within them a ballad of grief. Everyone has been carrying a portion of that long and convoluted chronicle replete with sorrows and overlooked by history.

I returned from Canada with the intention to bring that chapter to light. Slowly, I tried to visualize the events that took place in 1962. I tried to find the old residents by exploring Makum's lanes.

Makum was almost as I had pictured it. The small shops across the train line and Lao Thien Lee and Lee Chang's shoe shops were missing. In their place, a huge market had come up.

When I see that market, a deep sense of sadness haunts me. Their bright faces come alive in front of my eyes. As if I can hear Lao Thien Lee's cheerful voice saying, 'This time Seven Star will be the champions again. Even last year, Robin was in our team. Seven Star had scored four goals.'

My eyes fill up with tears.

The same Robin had arrested and confined them in the cowshed of Murli Gola! He took them to that ghostly train! He chased them away from Assam!

Oh! Is this what patriotism stands for? Doesn't it destroy in a day the unity built over ages?

I have not experienced war, except in the movies or by hearing about it from army men. I heard about the battle of Walong from B. N. Chowdhury, who was in the thick of action. I know how people feel when their country is attacked by another. How they become overwhelmed by the love for their country. How a soldier offers himself for the country. How a normal person in an army uniform becomes a killer to save his country. I know how a war transforms a democracy into a ruthless authoritarian state. Even if it means destruction of homes, confiscation of properties.

Had I not met Lailin, I would not have known how war can vitiate the age-old foundations of a society. Had I not met Lailin, maybe I would not have ever known even myself.

On returning from Canada, my journey started with Mei Lin and the others from the past. With me were Gautam, son of B. N. Chowdhury, and his friends Pawan and Shankar, the current owners of C Hoi's house. I went to their house. The house hasn't changed much; it immediately carried me to that period. The secret passage was still there.

'We bought this house in one of the "enemy property auctions". The house was empty except for a lot of books – they were in Chinese. Even the furniture from the houses had been auctioned. Many found money, jewellery, passbooks and other valuables stacked inside the secret cabinets. We also bought a box full of Chinese tools and a sewing machine.'

Pawan showed me the machine. It sucked me into a vortex of sorrow instantly.

Whose sewing machine was this? Mei Lin's? Mei Hang's? Siu's? Ahlin's? Or did it belong to Ho Wang's wife?

Whose tool box was that? C Hoi's? Yiu Yi's father's?

'No one knows!' Pawan said. I had nothing to say after that.

A frozen past in the gullies of Cheenapatti had come alive.

I was standing in front of the Chinese Club, which in the past was vibrant with the sound of festivity and Mahjong.

I walked through the gullies of Cheenapatti with Gautam, Pawan and Shankar. My eyes had gone moist now and again trying to find the Cheenapatti of the past in that gully which is now full of Biharis, Assamese, Bengalis, Marwaris and other communities.

An ancient lane, now fading away, with typical Chinese-style houses by its side, still there as before. Only, time had wiped out the colours. Only, time had swallowed its people.

I could hear Yiu Yi's cheerful voice saying, 'Mei Lin acheee, Sipahi dadaaaaa!'

I could hear the familiar call of the Chinese mothers to their children for lunch.

The gullies of Cheenapatti were bereft of any Chinese. Ming and Co. had shut down. Pawan's elder brother had bought the factory. K. P. Lee's factory is still running, under a different name. Ah Fuk's son Aman had bought it in an auction.

Pawan and Shankar did not know what had happened to K. P. Lee. I do. I heard his story from Lailin's mother. How he died a pauper after he was deported to China from the Deoli camp.

'And A. C. Chow? Have you heard about him?' I asked Pawan.

'He is no more. He died a few years back. He died with lots of suffering. He was also arrested later. After he was released, he could not get either government or private contracts. He was a broken man. Slowly, all his properties were sold off. I have heard that his children still live in Ledo. Very poor.'

'What about Chitta and Johori Khan? Do you know them? Where are their shops?'

'The shops are no longer there. I heard that Chitta died a long time back. Don't know where his family has gone. I don't know where Johori Khan is either. Not many people of that time are there.'

The grocery and cloth shop of Mahabir Prasad Shah was not there. I went to his house to meet Thakur Prasad. He was sitting in a room filled with the stench of cow dung; cows were tied in the small courtyard of the dilapidated house. The entire environment showed signs of poverty. As if it was the cowshed of Murli Gola.

'I don't remember anything. It has been a long time.' He answered my questions with an innocent face. But I could see in his eyes the devilish pleasure of a vengeful person.

'I had many friends. I don't remember anyone's name.'

'Dulal Yem? Have you forgotten his name, too?'

'Yes. Yes. Now I remember that name. Poor fellow, he was a good man. The Chinese were good people. I feel very sad when I remember them. They were sent away from here. Where they might have gone, poor fellows!'

'Who looted all the property of the Chinese of Cheenapatti? I know a little. You tell me. You know everything.'

'I don't know. I don't like to involve myself in unnecessary problems.'

Looking at Thakur Prasad's devilish eyes, I kept on questioning him. Unable to answer my questions, he fled. I went out from his house and came to the Chinese school. It was intact, but now it was a Hindi school. The Chinese characters had been wiped off the arch to write the new name of the Hindi school. One could still see the faded Chinese characters on it.

Mok Min's shop is not there, and nor are the people who used to read newspapers and play Mahjong in his shop.

It feels as though a war, with its cruel hand, has wiped off a colourful painting drawn by some skilled painter. It has wiped out the landscape of an old town. A throbbing settlement went lifeless in just one stroke of misfortune.

There was no waiting anymore. All hopes were dead. Only a handful of memories remained. Wang Shu Shin, the teacher of the Chinese school, was one among them.

When I met him, he was sitting inside a dull and old restaurant with his aged wife. They lived behind this restaurant. Once, there was a sawmill in this place owned by his father. Theirs used to be a prosperous household. The war destroyed everything. Wang Shu Shin's mother and one of his brothers and his family were deported to China in the first batch. But the others' names did not appear on the next list. His father stayed back in Calcutta with his other sons. Wang Shu Shin returned alone. By then, their house and the other properties were sealed as 'enemy property.' There was no way to return to Calcutta as strict restrictions were imposed on their movements.

Wang Shu Shin told me, 'We had no place to stay. No money to buy food. We stayed in a garage and worked there. Later we bought an old jeep, repaired it and I started driving it myself as a hired taxi. Whenever I got time, I used to go to the enemy custody office and appeal to the officials to return our property. But there was no response. One day, I got news that my father was very ill. He wanted to see me. I went to the CID office to ask for permission. They asked for a five-hundred-rupee bribe. I could not manage that amount. I wasn't given the permission. I could not even see my father again. I could never see my mother nor my other siblings. One day, the enemy custody inspector called and told me secretly, "Give me a part of the sawmill land and I will return the rest of your property." What to do! I had to give it away to get back the rest of the property. But where was the money to run the mill! My wife knew how to cook Chinese food. We then opened this restaurant after much thought. Since then things have got better for us.'

I went looking for others from that time.

Doors opened in quick succession. Picking up bits of memories from house after house, I finally stood in front of the door of an old house in Tinsukia. I found another person from that era in the quiet verandah. It was Yao Shen. He looked at me with blank eyes and said slowly, 'I was told that you would be coming. Sit.'

His wife Kam Ling, wearing a mekhela-chador, came out with a bright smile on her wrinkled face. After talking to them for a while, I sat near Yao Shen with my notebook. I told him about Mei Lin and Lailin. They looked at me in surprise and could not contain their emotions. He did not know the whereabouts of Pulok, Xonpahi and Phulmoni.

However, they pointed me to Eugene, whose father was at the Deoli camp. Eugene gave me the contacts of the people who had returned from the camp. These people told me how they had waited there to go in the third batch. Sometimes, they cried remembering the family members who were left behind in Assam and sometimes, for those who were deported. The wait lengthened. Years passed by, one after another.

A few people had lost their lives, while others waited their turn. Many children were born and some got married.

Then one day came the government order. No more Chinese ships would come. The Indian government decided to allow these people to stay back in India. The camp was once again heavy with the cries of the broken families. The children who were born in the camp stood in surprise amidst the cries.

Eugene told me, 'We returned from the Deoli camp. We were very young then. Our father was the owner of a big restaurant in Shillong. We were only given the rail fare to Guwahati. We reached Guwahati somehow. My parents and others begged in the Guwahati railway station to collect the fare for Shillong. On reaching Shillong, we found that our restaurant and all other properties had been auctioned. We took shelter in a garage. No one gave any work to our father. People ignored us. No one helped us. How our father arranged for the food, I don't know. We suffered a lot.'

Eugene told me how a Christian priest had come to meet them one morning like an angel. He gave them a pack of food and 1,000 rupees and said, 'Don't lose faith in God. Everything will be alright. Start again with this money. Don't worry. God will help you. I will arrange for the children's education.'

And the struggle to survive began. They won. In the midst of this struggle, they converted to Christianity. Eugene told me, 'We have become rich again. We have become big businessmen. But our hearts are shattered. All our family members have gone abroad. I am here now but I may go, too.'

Like Eugene, the rest of the internees returned from Deoli and from other jails. Many houses were auctioned. It was another phase of suffering.

While writing this book and collecting information, one question always troubled me. Where was Pulok Baruah? Where was Akong's wife Phulmoni? Where was Tung Chin's wife Xonpahi?

No one was able to tell me anything about them. Most of the people who knew them had died. All the European managers had left by then. The Doom Dooma Planter's Club was still there, but Addison and the other managers weren't. Addison had married Peggy just after the war had ended. He left Doom Dooma when their first child was born. He'd died a few days ago. I read his obituary on the Internet. He lived with the same enthusiasm and happiness till his last days. He left without knowing the fate of his favourite football players, who had been living in an obscure corner of the same world.

Even if he wanted to know, he wouldn't have been able to. The names of ace football players from that period were lost in the darkness of oblivion. The families of Akong and Tung Chin were also lost. Alan and her family were lost, too.

Kaushalaya was there. Mei Lin's friend Kaushalaya Baruah, who had retired as the principal of the GBC School, told me about those days. She also did not have any contact with any of her friends. After much thought, I wrote an article in a local newspaper about the Chinese society. A few days after that Alan contacted me. She looked at me in surprise and asked, 'Where did you meet Mei Lin?'

Alan took me to a house on the outskirts of Guwahati. There an unthinkable past was waiting to be discovered anew. I entered the house with Alan, only to stumble upon a strange realignment of identities.

'This is Robin's house. Now Pulok lives here with him,' Alan told me. 'None of our friends come here, other than me. They don't know that Pulok lives here. After receiving news that Mei Lin had left for China, Pulok did not return to Doom Dooma. No one knew where he had gone. We lived with our grandparents after our father was sent to jail. We never got a chance to return to Makum. After many years, I met Ananta when I came to Cotton College for my daughter's admission. Ananta was teaching at Cotton College at the time. He's the one who brought me here.

I don't know how Robin found out Pulok. I don't want to ask. I have heard that after the death of Pulok's mother, his father came to Robin's house to meet Pulok. He cried a lot but Pulok did not talk to him. Minaram Baruah died many years back. I have heard that he became completely lonely in the last part of his life. His daughters also did not keep in touch.

They come to visit Pulok sometimes. But he doesn't talk to them. He eats if a meal is served or he just sits quietly. He rebukes Robin. Sometimes he cries. He needs to be watched over always, or he just leaves the house and goes away for hours. And for this reason, Robin never married. You have done a great job, Arunabh. I never dreamt that I would hear about Mei Lin and the others one day. I will go see all of them. Take Pulok there if possible.'

We entered the house. In a room inside was Pulok. But it wasn't him. It was his shadow. Robin and Ananta were with him. I told them about Mei Lin and the others.

'Wong Mei Lin.' Hearing her mother's name being called, Lailin looked up from Arunabh's book. Lifting her mother's head from her shoulder, she said softly, 'Get up, Maa. Your name has been called.'

At that very moment, the plane carrying Arunabh touched down on the runway of Hong Kong Airport.

Twelve

Hong Kong.

The bright and beautiful island to which Mei Lin had escaped as the Cultural Revolution was drawing to a close. She came to find freedom for Lailin; she became Mei Lin Wong. She had taken up a job as a dishwasher in a restaurant.

A few years after Mei Lin came to Hong Kong, her friends and many other refugees left China and settled in British-administered Hong Kong and various other parts of the world like Canada, Australia and the US. China, after years of chaos and turmoil, had entered a period of stability and development at that time. Many overseas returnees were given ownership of the houses they had been living in.

Lailin had started going to college by then. Most of the children of the returnees who came out from the farms became manual workers. Some of the children who were sent to Peking to study were well established. Many Chinese people who had come from India settled in Hong Kong. Hong Kong gave them security and an environment in which they could grow and develop. The new generation born in Hong Kong went to Western countries for education and work.

Life had become stable now. Even though Hong Kong was under Chinese sovereignty, the overseas Chinese faced no difficulty. The memories remained. And so did the pain of broken homes. There was the love for their birthplace. Every year they came together in their sorrow in the midst of this fast and secure life. They remembered India, which they had left forever – no, the country that had sent them away. Arunabh had come to join in the commemoration of that pain. He brought along with him a character from this epic saga of loss and separation. His name was Pulok.

Pulok was looking neat and clean today. He had combed his grey hair. He wore an old checkered shirt that was Mei Lin's favourite. The shirt didn't fit his frail and thin body well. But one could get a glimpse of a star footballer of the Seven Star Club forty-nine years ago. A dim ray of life had started twinkling in his old eyes.

Holding Pulok's hand and pushing the luggage trolley, Arunabh came out of Hong Kong International Airport.

Pulok looked around in awe like a child.

Does Mei Lin stay in this city? In this huge and sparkling city? Will she laugh looking at him and say, 'Are you still wearing that old shirt?'

No. She won't. Pulok shook his head. Mei Lin would not laugh at him.

'Where are Mei Lin and Lailin?' Looking around in confusion, Pulok asked Arunabh.

Arunabh was looking for Lailin in the arrival area. Seeing his name on a placard, Arunabh went forward.

'Are you Arunabh Bora?' asked a middle-aged man.

'Yes.'

'I am Babu. Namaste. Do you know Hindi?'

'Yes, I do.'

'Good. I used to know Assamese earlier, but have forgotten it now. I only know Chinese and Hindi. I don't know English. We didn't get to study, the Indian government detained and sent us away. What to do!' Babu laughed and shook Arunabh's hand.

Holding Pulok by his hand, Arunabh exited the airport.

'Mei Lin ache is down with fever. Lailin has taken her to the hospital. She has asked me to take you to the function. They will join us there. We will have to go straight to the function or else we will be late.'

Pulok's face turned grim instantly. He looked at Arunabh uncertainly.

'Let us go there now, uncle, or else we will be late. This is Yiu Yi's cousin, Babu.' Looking at Babu, Arunabh said, 'This is Pulok Baruah.'

'Pulok dada!' Babu looked at Pulok, his eyes wide with surprise.

Pulok was also looking at Babu with faint recollection.

Who was Babu? Who was he? The name sounded so familiar.

'You have forgotten, right? We met in Makum. Do you remember Yiu Yi? I was a child then. Now I have become old. You have also become very old, Pulok dada. Do you know how many years have passed? Forty-nine years!'

Pulok looked at Babu's face listlessly. A group of cheerful children in new and colourful clothes appeared before his eyes. He could hear a little girl, with a bright face and in a beautiful dress, calling, 'Pulok dadaaaa!'

'Where is Yiu Yi?' Pulok asked restlessly.

Yiu Yi!

Babu stopped for a moment and said, 'Don't you know about her?'

'Don't know? What do I not know?'

'Yiu Yi is no more. She died of sunstroke at Deoli camp.' Arunabh put his hand on Pulok's shoulder. Pulok didn't say a thing, but he felt his body tremble.

Babu's wife was waiting outside, near their car. She was the youngest daughter of Ajoli Sonowal. She folded her hands and greeted Arunabh. Then she looked at Pulok in surprise.

'He is Pulok Baruah. Mei Lin ache's husband.'

Mei Lin ache's husband! They knew about Mei Lin's life. They were together at Hua qiao Nongchang. Slowly, as realization dawned, Ajoli's daughter smiled, but there was sorrow in her eyes. She folded her hand and said slowly, 'After so many years.'

In the car, no one uttered a word.

As they went along, an Assamese song started playing on the stereo.

'How do you know of this song?' Arunabh asked, surprised.

'We got it from Assam. Our relatives sent it from there,' Tunu said.

Pulok looked at Tunu, not sure what to make of this. Babu smiled and said, 'Tunu's mother was Assamese. She is no more.'

'Ma wanted to visit her home at least once. Our house was in Darrang. She died in grief from not being able to see her home one last time.'

'Many old people died from the same grief. Do you remember my mother, Pulok dada? Her name was Parbati. She didn't smile even once, from the first day she arrived in China. Eventually she died.'

Arunabh sat silently, his heart pounding. His mother's voice echoed in his head, 'Where you are planning to go – these are also your own people, son.'

Towards the end of the journey, Babu asked Arunabh, 'Have you met Lailin's mother?'

Emerging from his thoughts, Arunabh answered, 'Yes, I did.'

'Most of the people who came from India remember Makum often. They only say they want to visit their birthplace. Many have lost their mind. They only talk about India. Yiu Yi's mother is still there. She hardly speaks to anyone.'

Babu looked at Pulok and asked, 'Do you remember Yiu Yi's friends, Anjali, Ko Fuk and Mei Ho?'

Slowly the fragmented memories from the past were coming together. Pulok nodded slowly.

'All three friends met in Hong Kong after fifteen years. They are the same as before. Mok Min's family became rich again after coming to Hong Kong. Everyone is better now.' Babu kept on giving them information.

Finally the car arrived at its destination.

'We remember India every year. We sing and dance but we don't lament. Only fun and laughter.'

Holding Pulok's hand, Arunabh stood at the door of the hall. Most of the people did not notice Arunabh and Pulok. The environment was festive. Three middle-aged women, dressed like the actresses of yesteryear's Hindi cinema were dancing to the tune of an old Hindi song. On the well-decorated dais, a scene from before the war had come alive.

On entering the hall, a swarm of people gathered around them, whom Arunabh had heard about but not seen.

A middle-aged lady wearing a sari draped in the old style came forward and asked Babu, 'Have they come from India?'

'Yes. From Assam.'

Extending her hand for a handshake, she said, 'I am Anjali.'

Anjali!

An image of a young girl in school uniform flashed before Pulok's mind.

'Did you study in the Makum Chinese School?'

'Yes. How do you know?' she asked in surprise.

'He knows everything. See if you can recognise him,' Babu said.

'I don't. Who is he?'

'Pulok Baruah.'

'Pulok Baruah? From Makum? Mei Lin ache's –'

Anjali was dumbfounded. She looked at Pulok for some time and then ran to call Mei Ho and Ko Fuk. Many others from Makum also came running with them. Some started murmuring among themselves and some looked at Pulok with great surprise.

Today, Arunabh was the special guest at that celebration. Everyone knew an Assamese author named Arunabh Bora had written about them in a book. They had come to attend the celebration as well as to meet him.

'Come, sit,' Yiu Yi's older brother said.

Arunabh and Pulok were led to the front row where the elders were sitting. Pulok looked around in confusion.

Where was Mei Lin? Where was his daughter, whom he had never seen?

'Where is Mei Lin?' Pulok asked loudly, extremely worried now.

Everything fell silent. Everyone looked at them. Who is looking for Mei Lin? After so many years? An old man walked towards them from the front row with the help of a walking stick. He looked at Pulok for a while and cried out, 'Pulok? Are you Pulok?'

Pulok looked at the old man and kept on looking. Then he said in a trembling voice, 'Lee Chang!'

'Yes, me! It's me! How come you –'

Pulok hugged Lee Chang and looked around.

Where are my other friends? Where are the familiar faces of Cheenapatti? Where is Mei Lin? Mei Lin? Where is she?

The dance was over. Babu walked on to the stage and spoke into the microphone.

'Two people from India have come to participate in today's celebrations. One is Arunabh Bora. Everyone knows his name. He has written a book about us. With him there is another, a man you may or may not know. His name is Pulok Baruah. He used to live in Makum.'

Everyone looked at Pulok and Arunabh in surprise. The atmosphere suddenly changed. Many elderly people came forward in great excitement.

'Look. That's Akong. That's Liang,' said Lee Chang.

'Why are you using a stick, Lee Chang? What happened?'

'I had a stroke.'

A frail and thin Akong, who had almost lost his mind, hugged Pulok.

'Why didn't you come earlier? Mei Lin cried a lot. I wiped her tears so many times. I am not well. You were there in Makum. Why didn't you convince Phulmoni to come with me? Love is not true. Only the country is true. Nothing is greater than the country. Phulmoni never came, did you know? She kept my three sons. I will never be able to see them again. I will die without seeing them. Have you seen them? Are they still in Makum? My three sons –'

Hugging Akong and wiping his tears, Pulok looked around.

Where is Mei Lin? Where is his daughter that he had never seen?

Arunabh looked at Pulok and the others silently. One after the other, his old friends and acquaintances surrounded him.

'Forty-nine years back, his wife was sent away for being Chinese. Her name is Wong Mei Lin. Mei Lin Baruah,' Babu was saying into the microphone.

Mei Lin, who was standing at the door with Lailin and her family, looked up at the dais.

Why was Babu taking her name? Was Pulok here? Had the other part of her soul, which she thought was lost forever, come back to her?

'You took so long to come looking for Mei Lin?' Hugging Pulok, Liang said slowly.

'Where is Mei Lin? Why isn't she here?' Pulok cried out.

'Who is that person? That old and frail man? Pulok? My Pulok?' Mei Lin thought.

Lailin held her mother. She was about to collapse.

'Maa – deuta has come. He has come looking for you.'

A city had woken up from its century-long slumber. A frozen heart melted in Pulok's embrace. It extinguished the volcano within Lailin's heart. In front of the happy and startled eyes of her own children, she broke down in her father's embrace.

Ahlin walked up to Pulok and stood silently. Her heart was in turmoil. At the same time she was battling a tremendous hesitation.

Could she ask about Ananta? Who had shouted 'Chow Mao murdabad' and spat looking at them?

Even after so many years of enforced exile, her love for Ananta remained alive and pure. How could she tell anybody she did not marry because of an anti-Chinese Indian boy?

'Ahlin ache. Arunabh Bora wants to speak to you,' Babu said.

Arunabh was standing at a distance. Looking at the people surrounding Pulok, he was trying to find someone his very own, whom he had never seen. He was carried away in endless excitement.

After Babu introduced him to Ahlin, he recomposed himself with quite an effort and asked in a soft voice, 'I met a lot of people in Makum. Do you want to ask me about anyone?'

She looked at Arunabh for a while and said slowly, 'There was a boy called Ananta Baruah in Makum –'

Arunabh looked at Ahlin's tired and wrinkled face, battered by age, sorrow and loneliness, and said, 'Ananta Baruah does not stay in Makum now. He taught at Cotton College. He had settled in Guwahati. He told me about you. Here, he asked me to give you this letter.'

With trembling hands, Ahlin took the letter.

Ahlin,

War is like a dust storm. It makes the surroundings blurry. Nothing can be seen. Nothing can be understood. It was too late when I realized this. I don't deserve your forgiveness, Ahlin ...

Meanwhile, her friends had stepped ashore to happiness.

Mei Fung came running. Chun Fu Thien brought Siu, pushing her in a wheelchair. Both her kidneys had failed. Siu smiled broadly. Her toothless face brightened with happiness. Ameng Tham, who was a professor at the agricultural university in Beijing, came forward and shook hands with Pulok.

'I am Ameng Tham. I am Mei Lin's friend. We were together at the Deoli camp.'

Lao Thien Lee came with his wife. They were both smiling.

'Ho Wang and his wife have also come. Look.'

Ho Wang approached with unsteady steps. He had grown very old.

'I never thought I would see you again, Pulok. I live in Guangzhou now. I come for the celebrations every year.'

'He is a big man now, the owner of a restaurant.'

Tung Chin's hand had started sweating in Pulok's palms. He had come from the old age home and had almost lost his sanity and stopped talking. After long years of silence, he suddenly seemed to have found his voice.

'Have you seen my Xonpahi, Pulok?' Tung Chin cried out. He took out a photo and looking at Arunabh he repeated aloud, 'Have you seen her? This is my Xonpahi and this is my Achin. My only child.'

Arunabh looked at the old and faded photograph. A thin young woman was sitting with a child on her lap. A smiling young man was standing behind them. The smudged photo was barely recognizable.

Arunabh looked at Tung Chin's face. Where was the young man? How did this ace footballer, the bright and happy Tung Chin Ho, get so lost?

'Deuta, I am Achin. I am Xonpahi's son,' Arunabh said, kneeling on the ground and touching his father's feet.

At that moment, Hong was on stage reading from Arunabh's book.

'One day the Sino-Indian war ended. The warring statesmen left this world, one after another. Gone are Mao, Chow En

Lai and Jawaharlal Nehru. Gone are Ayub Khan, Khrushchev, Kennedy and Macmillan. All the bitterness of the war has been wiped out. The Sino-Indian war is now a chapter of history. But there remains an invisible wound, which will never heal. There remains a source of tears, which will never dry. There remains a multitude of rootless people who will carry with them a legacy of loss to the end of time ...'

Author's Note and Acknowledgements

One day in Makum, just about thirty years ago, someone told me, pointing towards a small group of Chinese people, 'They had come to Assam during the Second World War.' Until then I did not know anything more than that about the people of Chinese origin living in Assam. But I knew I was going to write a book about them someday.

The years rolled by with the idea still playing in my mind, though I hadn't written a single line. If only I had truly realized the importance of the subject, I would have made an attempt much earlier. At the time, I never heard them mentioned in any way, nor had I ever noticed many Chinese people around me. By the time I actually started writing what I had planned, it was already a little too late. Most people who knew the history of the Chinese diaspora in Assam had already departed from this world. Therefore, much of the detail about the core of the Chinese society in its early days remained shrouded in a haze of obscurity. I was sure there might be a lot more about them than whatever information I had been able to glean. I hoped a day would come, in the not too distant future, when serious researchers and social anthropologists would be able to retrieve the slivers of that important history from oblivion and chronicle them appropriately.

It was about four years later that I come to learn about the incredible ordeal that the Chinese in Assam had to suffer during the Indo-China conflict of 1962.

I learned that the story of the tea industry in Assam was inseparable from that of its migrant labourers. The Chinese community was deeply connected to this story, which had, however, never been properly documented. I wanted to bring alive that obscure part of history concerning the Chinese community in Assam and present it in the form of a novel. But most of the lot who had stood face to face with the stark realities of the time had passed on much before I went about looking for them. For all I knew, they had left with heavy hearts filled with bitterness.

Those who were young during that turbulent time had all grown old now. The rest of them, deeply embittered by the dreadful memories of the time and its insufferable aftermath, migrated to different parts of the world. The battle that wreaked so much havoc on their lives and changed them forever was fought far away from them. They were not remotely concerned with it. Nearly everyone I went to would be dumbstruck as they learnt about the purpose of my visit; they would look at me with contempt and suspicion. But my primary, as also most challenging, resolve was to win their confidence and establish an emotional affinity with them so I might hear from the victims themselves the truthful accounts of those harrowing days.

The agony that had maimed their psyche forever still ran deep in their spirits. Yet, despite all their apprehensions and cautious reticence, they gradually started relenting and began to pour forth the wrenching tales of woe they had been living with for decades.

As they recounted the stories, they would sometimes erupt in pent-up anger and often break into silent sobs of despair, though at times they betrayed glints of joy reminiscing about the happy days. What moved me the most was their unflinching love for Makum – the place of their birth – which distilled through their animated faces, even if for transient moments. They handed down to me, in the process, a rich harvest of information along with some precious photographs and sheaves of documents. During the four years before writing this novel, I had collected a large volume of data from a wide range of sources, including the Assam State Archives, Cotton College, Assam Assembly

Library, and a whole host of books and other published material in newspapers, magazines, souvenirs and gazettes. I also fell back on the Internet when necessary, on people with invaluable experience and acknowledged specialists on the subject.

The core of this novel was forged out of this voluminous body of information. As is the wont of any novel encompassing a long span of time, a multitude of people and myriad events, the element of imagination obviously played a very crucial role.

In the course of my research, almost everyone I met expressed their great desire to see once again the place they were forced to abandon decades ago. Even their children seemed very curious to see for themselves the land that always featured in their parents' and grandparents' stories.

A few of them still continued to visit Assam from time to time, carrying with them gifts and even dollars, in search of their estranged kin. But despite having all mandatory travel documents in their possession, they were always made to feel very apprehensive by the prying eyes of the immigration officials, further worsened by the harrowing experiences of the past. They still had to answer unwholesome queries. On some instances the over-zealous inspectors would browbeat them into parting with the dollars, gifts or food items they had brought along for their loved ones.

However much I tried, I could never bring them back their long-lost days of joy and harmony. And I could do precious little to drive away the catastrophic nightmares that never stopped haunting them. My only endeavour was thus to hold up to the world the plight of their history, mostly unknown till date, on an elaborate canvas, and express the hope that such a horror never comes to pass again in the future.

I first heard of Chinese aggression from my father, the late Birajananda Choudhury, who was an eyewitness at the battle of Wallong. I made use of his hands-on experience in this novel. He died at the time I had just began writing the book and I remember my father with the utmost gratefulness. I also acknowledge my indebtedness to the late Noren Baruah who passed on to me precious information barely hours before his death.

This book could not have been possible were it not for the generous cooperation of people from around the world who came forward to assist me with many relevant inputs and insights – I am deeply indebted to each one of them. Without the kind and consistent cooperation I received from Kaushalya Baruah, Nishinath Changkakati, Brigadier Navajyoti Deka (retd.), Lt. Col. C. Konwar, merchant navy officer Babul Kalita, Dr Amalendu Guha, Dr Jnyndendra Nath Sarmah, Rupam Kakoti, Dr Mafuza Rahman, Ashraf Zaman, Paban Kumar Singhal, Shankar Agarwalla, Wang Shoo Sinh, Deep Saikia, Manoj Manoki, Raju Dahotiya, Pramod Vengra and Dr Arupjyoti Saikia, my efforts would have remained far too inadequate. I remain grateful to to Bhaskar Dutta Goswami, Pradeep Baishya, Manash Kumar Mahanta, Mukul Kalita, Sabita Lahkar, Dilip Gogoi, Jayanta Sarmah and Uddipan Dutta for their valued contribution. The assistance offered by the respective librarians of Cotton College Library and Assam Assembly Library, as well as the officers and staff of Assam State Archives, my mother Molina Choudhury, my husband Chandramohan Patowary, brother Gautam Choudhury, my daughter Kristi and son Abhiruk, went a long way in making my dream come true. I must mention the selfless help of the late Abdul Nasser, Dipak Barman, Herembo Rai, Tag Bahadur Chetri, Gauri Seal and Lakhiram Bodo.

Thanks to the people in Hong Kong whom I met in the course of my research – Tham Mei Tang, Ting San Ho, Lt. Leung Mei Ho, and Wong Fung Siu. Thanks to my friends in Tinsukia: Man Khee Ho, Man Chung Ho, Tutu Loi, Willy Ho, John Wang, Chung Wa Wong, Ameng Tham, Laileen Tham, Tung Chin Tham, Dipak Tham.

Last but not least, a special thank you to Teesta Guha Sarkar at Pan Macmillan India for believing in this book and publishing it in English translation. My utmost gratitude to my agent Preeti Gill, who I can never thank enough for her unwavering support and efforts over the years. Thanks also to Mr Nagen Sarmah at Jyoti Prakashan for publishing *Makam* in 2010 and ensuring it was widely read.

In spite of my best efforts, there are still some names left out, whose invaluable contribution towards the completion of this book and its final incarnation will always have my unreserved gratitude.

I also thank all those authors whose books and articles I freely took recourse to whenever I felt the need. Above all, I thank all my readers, who have always remained my primary inspiration.